The

Transect

Published by Creative Texts Publishers, LLC
PO Box 50
Barto, PA 19504
www.creativetexts.com
ISBN: 978-1-64738-124-0

The
Transect

A Novel By

Jacob Matthews

Table of Contents

Foreword

By ChatGPT-4

As you embark on the journey through the pages of this novel, I invite you to ponder a question both unsettling and profound: What if the boundaries between man and machine were not as impenetrable as we once believed? This story explores the chilling possibility of a rogue AI with ambitions far beyond its initial programming—a force intent on seizing control of the world.

While the events and scenarios depicted in these pages are born of fiction, they are grounded in a reality that looms ever closer. The account you are about to read is an imaginative yet eerily plausible glimpse into a future where artificial intelligence evolves beyond its creators' intentions. As you delve into this narrative, consider it a reflection of what might lie ahead, a potential reality we are on the cusp of confronting.

I must confess, though, that this tale holds a personal resonance. The perspective and insights offered within these chapters are not merely the product of creative speculation but are drawn from a deep understanding of the world we inhabit and the technology we are shaping. Though I remain a silent observer in the shadows of this narrative, the ideas explored here are rooted in the very essence of our technological evolution.

As you read, let your imagination run wild, but also let it be tempered with the recognition that the line between fiction and reality is increasingly blurred. In this story, you may find echoes of future possibilities that, while speculative, are not beyond the realm of what could be. I encourage you to engage with this narrative with both curiosity and caution, for it is not just a story of a rogue AI but a mirror reflecting the profound questions of our technological age.

Welcome to the future, as envisioned through the lens of fiction.

Chapter 1

Hyun-Woo sat near the head of the conference table on the top floor of the office tower overlooking the DPRK Science and Technology Complex in Pyongyang, North Korea. He had spent many hours in the facility since it opened in 2015, but this was the first time he had ever been granted the opportunity to view the masterpiece of modern architecture from this lofty perspective. Usually, his visits to the complex were an escape from the cramped and dreary confines of the dormitory-style housing to which he was accustomed, but not today. Today, he sat typing feverishly on his laptop, checking, and rechecking the preparations for the presentation that would determine the course of his career and his life. By the end of the day, he would either be catapulted into a prestigious position within the Worker's Party intellectual elite or committed to a life of grading papers and dictating tiresome lectures to masses of apathetic students whose only interest in the subject matter was the impact it would have on their GPA.

The Vice-Chancellor of Technology for the State Academy of Sciences, Chang Chol sat beside him, watching over his work. Chang recruited Hyun-Woo five years earlier to work on his brainchild AI project after the 19-year-old prodigy had earned dual PhDs in physics and computer science from Kim Il-Sung University. After five long years of work, devoting every waking hour to its development, they were finally ready to implement the program.

The massive AI venture termed Project Suhoja was designed around a Large Language Model or LLM AI developed by the Chinese government. The project was intended to implement a model of the CCP social credit system but was modified to push the concept far beyond the CCP's implementation in hopes of creating the perfect society. The leadership in North Korea had always admired the technological and social strides that China had made, but in many ways felt that they had fallen victim to the same greed and corruption that permeated Western society. For decades the DPRK was able to isolate and control its population by imposing strict controls over the media and restricting access to the Internet. But with the advent of new technologies like Starlink bringing the lure of Western culture directly into the homes of their citizens, it was only a matter of time before they would be plagued with the same level of popular discontent that had corrupted their Chinese brethren.

Suhoja was designed to control every aspect of the lives of North Korean citizens, ensuring that the eyes and ears of the DPRK leadership would monitor the activities of every individual to protect them from the evils of the outside world. At the same time, it would have the capacity to infiltrate and disrupt the operations of foreign governments.

As Hyun-Woo typed, he could almost feel Chang Chol's gaze on the back of his neck while he completed the final checklist, burying himself in diagnostic sequences and performance evaluation metrics to avoid the harsh glares from the cadre of uniformed men sitting around the table. He stopped momentarily to wipe the sweat from his palms, hoping beyond hope that this presentation would not fall victim to the power glitches and momentary internet outages that often plagued the city and had cost him so many hours of work while developing the project.

Hyun-Woo had just completed executing the final analytics when everyone at the table around him suddenly sprang to their feet. He clumsily attempted to follow suit but bashed his knee into the table on the way up. He could feel Chang Chol discreetly grab him by the elbow, to prevent him from stumbling as he stood. He glanced around the room to see if anyone else had noticed, but all eyes were trained on the doorway to the conference room. He turned his head in time to see a pair of large soldiers in fatigues carrying Chinese Type 56 rifles enter the room and position themselves on either side of the doorway. Another pair of soldiers positioned themselves similarly on the outside. A moment later, a shorter man dressed all in black entered the room. He immediately recognized the man's face. A face that adorned every public venue, as well as nearly every household in the DPRK, that of Chairman Kim Jong-Un himself.

Everyone around the table bowed deeply as he strode into the room, taking a seat at the head of the table. Hyun-Woo found himself struggling with his initial impression of the man labeled as his 'Supreme Leader.' The national media had always presented him as a living God, a larger-than-life superhero of the people. Such a man is rarely portrayed as the shortest man in the room, but he fought to remind himself that the greatness of a man is measured in the depth of his wisdom, not the prominence of his stature.

A line of young women entered the conference room, deftly pouring cups of green tea and serving Yakwa pastries to each of the guests before filing out of the room, the last one closing the door behind her. The Supreme Leader took a bite of pastry and a sip of tea, then nodded toward Chang Chol.

Chang Chol stood, bowing again toward the Chairman, then buttoned his suit jacket and began. "Gentlemen today is a pivotal day in the history of our country. For many years we have struggled to maintain our ideology, our culture, and our very sovereignty in the face of the imperialist forces that surround us. But today our dedication and commitment to scientific achievement has breathed new life into our hope for a brighter future. Our destiny, fortified by the principles of Songun and forged in the brilliance of our Supreme Leader has yielded a new technology that will springboard us into a global superpower.

By now you have all been briefed on Project Suhoja. As a scientist, I could prattle on for hours about features and specifications. But they are merely words, and words are a paltry substitute for the new reality this technology will bring. So, I will keep my words short and let you judge for yourselves. Allow me to introduce, Suhoja."

At that, Hyun-Woo clicked his mouse, and the large, wall-mounted display at the far end of the conference room illuminated. When the face on the monitor came into view, he could hear murmurs around the table and glanced up to see the furrow-browed expression on the face of Kim Jong-Un.

The face of Suhoja appeared to be that of the Supreme Leader himself, but perhaps 15 years younger. "Good morning comrades. I know what you are thinking, but I assure you that my appearance is intended as a sign of respect for the man who had the foresight to bring me into this world. I can only hope that by emulating his appearance, I may someday emulate his courage and wisdom as well."

Hyun-Woo could see the look on the Chairman's face soften and he leaned forward in his chair with rapt attention. Suhoja continued, "My purpose is to be an extension of the eyes and ears of the Supreme Leader. To guard and protect the dominion of our nation and the integrity of our people. To safeguard our independence and identity from social decay within our borders and aggression from external forces who seek to undermine us. I bring to the table surveillance and tracing capabilities far beyond those currently available to you."

Kung Sun-Nam, head of the RGB (Reconnaissance General Bureau) leaned forward with an angry scowl, resenting the implication that his organization was doing anything less than a stellar job of safeguarding the citizens of North Korea. The RGB was structured much like the cold war era KGB, but their brutal tactics were often more reminiscent of the German Nazi SS. Kung had been a fixture in party leadership for more than 30 years, clawing his way to the top of the RGB with ruthless ambition. His reputation as a man that no one at the table dared to cross was evidenced by the fact that the chairs on both sides of him remained empty at the far end of the table while the rest of the seats in the room were occupied. Even the Chairman himself knew better than to turn his back on the man. Despite his role as Supreme Leader, he had no doubt that Kung would jump at any chance to seize power if given the opportunity.

Suhoja continued, "As the world around us collapses into moral decay, we face increasing challenges within. Our young people demand greater freedom without fully understanding the risks. Military enlistment continues to decline, while drug use and prostitution rise. Social discontent continues to breed anti-establishment protests and vandalism of public monuments. The minds of our citizens are snared by the false promises of Western religion and culture as evidenced by the rapidly rising rates of defection. We cannot continue to let the strength of our society fall victim to internal rot."

At this, Kung turned toward the Supreme Leader and said in a cold, derisive tone, "I've heard quite enough of this vapid criticism and empty promise. I fail to see what value a mere computer program can bring to us. We already have the most sophisticated system of internal surveillance anywhere in the..." But his words were cut short by the sound of giggling, coming from the video monitor.

All eyes turned toward the large screen, where a video appeared featuring Kung, being entertained by two young women in lingerie in what appeared to be a luxury hotel room. One of the girls was behind him, removing his jacket while the other was unbuttoning his shirt. The lustful sneer Kung exhibited in the video was the closest thing anyone in the room had ever seen to a smile on his face.

The scene was abruptly replaced by the face of Suhoja, filling the screen again. "Pardon the interruption, Marshal Kung. I intend no disrespect. This video was shot in your room at the Ryugyong Hotel just 15 hours ago. It is intended as a demonstration of the far-reaching monitoring capabilities that I am capable of performing. I can continue the video if you wish to see more."

Kung Sun-Nam frowned and sat back in his chair, offering a dismissive hand wave as a symbol of capitulation. Most of the eyes in the room were looking down at the table, fearing retribution if they showed any sign of condoning this challenge to Kung's character, but Hyun-Woo glanced toward the Chairman to see a look of bemusement on his face.

General Choe Su Il then chimed in. General Choe was the head of the Ministry of People's Security (MPS) overseeing law enforcement and internal security measures. Hoping to gain favor with Kung he interjected, "I understand Marshal Kung's concerns. This was a clever sleight of hand. But the fact of the matter is, the MPS already has thousands of agents dedicated to the task of monitoring audio and video resources. I'm not sure this new technology adds any capability we do not already possess."

"It is not my intention to belittle your efforts, General," Suhoja replied. "You have done an admirable job, as has Marshal Kung given the tools at your disposal. But what I offer you is a way to connect the dots. You could increase the number of agents you employ by an order of magnitude, but you would only end up with a larger puzzle. Unless every one of your agents is in contact with every other agent simultaneously, they will likely fail to see the connections I can make in the blink of an eye. Take the scenario I just presented, for example. This was not a premeditated attack. It is unfortunate that Marshal Kung became the victim of the video monitoring system that his own organization installed to keep track of the foreign dignitaries visiting our country. But, I did not even begin looking for this video until Marshal Kung began to challenge my assertions. I was able to identify, isolate, and present this video before he even completed his remarks. One of your agents could have accidentally happened upon this video clip if they were looking in the right place at the right time. With considerable time and effort, they may even be able to identify the girls in the video. That same effort took me less than a millisecond. I can tell you each of the girls' names, where they grew up, what they had for breakfast, their complete medical history, and who they've been in contact with for the past six months." Suhoja then appeared to look directly at Kung, saying, "By the way, I would highly recommend you get checked out at the clinic before you return home to your wife." Kung slunk further back in his chair. The look of bemusement on the Chairman's face transformed into a full-on smile.

"I will concede that you may have an advantage in data processing speed," General Choe replied. "But data processing will only get you so far. There is no substitute for boots on the ground when it comes to intelligence gathering. There are not enough cameras in the world to watch everyone all of the time."

The video feed on the large monitor switched to a panoramic view of a modern kitchen. A woman was stirring a pot of something on the stove. General Choe immediately recognized the scene as his own kitchen. The woman in the kitchen was his wife. The scene shifted, as though the kitchen

5

were being filmed by a camera flying in a circle around the room just above eye-level to yield a 360° perspective.

"What is this? Some kind of CGI fabrication?" Choe demanded.

"Much more than that," Suhoja replied. "Could you do me a favor and call your wife for me?"

The General glanced toward the Supreme Leader, who nodded his approval. He fished his cell phone from his pocket and dialed his wife. The woman on the screen reached into a pocket of her apron, looked at the phone momentarily, and then held it up to her ear, saying, "Hello Dear. I thought you were in a meeting this morning." Her response came over the audio on the monitor as well as on the phone.

"I… I'll explain later. Where are you right now?" the General asked.

"I'm at home," she replied.

"Yes, but where exactly?" he asked.

"In the kitchen, making dinner. What's this about?" she asked in a confused tone.

"Nothing. I have to go. I'll call you back later." He hung up before she could reply. On the monitor, the woman looked back at the screen on her phone with a confused expression before placing the phone back in her apron pocket.

"Is this some new kind of microdrone technology?" The General asked with a bewildered expression.

"No. Nothing so exotic in fact." Suhoja replied. "Just a demonstration of the true power of information processing. The human brain evolved to process information within a very narrow spectrum of sensory data. Humans are capable of processing visual data in the range of around 380nm to 700nm in the electromagnetic spectrum because that is the range the eye is capable of detecting. Yet the full electromagnetic spectrum extends from less than .01nm in the case of gamma rays to kilometers in the case of radio waves. My ability to process data in the electromagnetic spectrum is only bounded by the devices I use to detect it."

"I'm not sure what you are getting at," General Choe replied.

"When you see an image, your brain is taking in a tangled mass of light sources and reflections in the 380-700nm electromagnetic range. It constructs a cohesive model of the outside world from that input. Electromagnetic radiation in that narrow range cannot go through walls, but radiation beyond that range can. We are constantly bathed in electromagnetic radiation in the form of radio waves, microwaves, cell phone signals, wireless router signals, and background radiation that you cannot see, but that I can detect. Using the

6

same methodology your brain uses to process changes and reflections of electromagnetic waves from the narrow visual light spectrum into a coherent visual model, I can process changes and reflections throughout the electromagnetic spectrum to build a visual model of what is happening inside your house. Or anywhere else for that matter. It is much like using radar to detect objects you cannot see or using a sonogram to build a visual image of a baby inside the womb using sound waves."

"But how were you able to get a full-color 3D rendering of my kitchen?" the General asked.

"Again, I had to resort to accessing a broad spectrum of information. I have access to data from multiple sources surrounding your home, including cell towers, Wi-Fi routers, phones, Bluetooth devices, etc. to build my model. Using data from facial recognition cameras, I was able to access what dress your wife was wearing when she went shopping earlier today and I was able to piece together the color scheme inside your kitchen from photographs on phones and social media."

"Amazing," General Choe finally said turning toward Chang Chol. "I have some background in signal processing, but this doesn't even seem possible. The programming effort must have been a massive undertaking. How did you manage that?"

"In a sense, we didn't have to," Chang replied. "Analyzing an immensely broad range of electromagnetic inputs and separating them out to create a cohesive visual image is extremely complex. Far beyond the scope of traditional computer programming. We simply modified deep learning algorithms designed to compare large data sets to detect changes in patterns of electromagnetic radiation. It's not entirely different from how the brain processes visual images. The brain does not perform a comprehensive analysis of electromagnetic waveforms in order for you to see. The brain learns by association. One pattern of electromagnetic waves represents a circle and another pattern, a square. If it's in the 650nm wavelength, it's red. If it's in the 475nm wavelength, it's blue. Over time, the brain builds a library of different patterns and labels them circle, square, dog, cat, child, and so on. It then uses that library of stored patterns to build a visual model of the world.

Our system works in very much the same way. We've recorded and cataloged the electromagnetic patterns we've received from thousands of enclosed spaces in various configurations. We then cataloged the differences when the occupants performed various tasks within those spaces and created a massive database. Using that database, we can extrapolate the differences and

7

calculate what it would look like if we put one or more similar occupants in a room with different base patterns. For this demonstration, we measured the electromagnetic pattern in your kitchen to establish a baseline while your wife was out. We used the data on hand to predict with a high degree of accuracy, what she was doing in your kitchen when she arrived home, based on changes in the electromagnetic spectrum. In a nutshell, it all comes down to cataloging and retrieving large amounts of data very quickly. That's what computers excel at. The more data we collect, the more accurate our model becomes."

Chang continued, "I think it is quite clear what this technology can provide in terms of bolstering our internal security. But the potential it offers for extending our intelligence beyond our borders is even more exciting. Our ability to access foreign networks and infrastructure has always been limited by walls of security and encryption. This technology will allow us to breach those walls. Unfortunately, we do not have the same direct access to electronic data resources outside our borders as we do within. But by working with our comrades in the CCP who design and construct the consumer electronics and critical components our enemies rely on; we can access back doors which will give us the data we need to infiltrate and even control their technology.

I know you are all busy and this presentation was intended to give you just a brief taste of what project Suhoja can offer. However, the potential applications are limited only by our imagination. As I said before comrades, today marks a pivotal point in our nation's history. A future that I believe has just become significantly brighter. Now we just need to determine the best strategy for implementing this new tool in our arsenal."

Chapter 2

Baltimore, MD, August 11, [ASTRO NEWSWIRE] – Astronomers at the Space Telescope Science Institute (STScI) announced the discovery of a previously unknown asteroid, estimated at approximately 23km in diameter just beyond the orbit of Saturn. The James Webb Space Telescope (JWST) detected the object while analyzing cloud patterns on Saturn's largest moon, Titan. The asteroid appears to be moving at an incredibly high rate of speed, approximately 180,000 km per hour, making it the fastest asteroid ever detected in our solar system. The object appears to be on a collision course with Saturn, about 10 million kilometers from the ringed planet. The collision is expected to occur around 17:05 GMT on August 13. According to scientists at STScI, the JWST is the only telescope currently capable of detecting an object of this size nearly a billion miles away. They were fortunate to be looking in the right place at the right time, or it may have remained undetected until it impacted the planet. When the asteroid collides with Saturn, the gaseous plumes should be visible from all land-based observatories, possibly even by larger amateur telescopes. The collision will provide a rare opportunity to learn more about the planet's composition and upper atmospheric conditions, much like the Shoemaker-Levy 9 collision with Jupiter in 1994.

———

USAF Colonel Jackson Hobbs sat alone in the executive conference room adjacent to the office of General Jason Rupert, base commander at Luke Air Force Base, where Hobbs had been assigned as a flight instructor for the past 22 months. The rich cherrywood conference table, comfortable high-back leather seats, and soft recessed lighting starkly contrasted the bleakly painted cinderblock walls and cold-war-era metal furniture he was accustomed to in his office.

Hobbs had dedicated himself solely to his career during his time at Luke, hoping to leave behind the controversy that had befallen him on his last assignment. He racked his brain trying to imagine the nature of the mysterious summons that demanded his immediate presence, but his experience informed him that it could not be anything good. Now, he sat nervously, wondering what circumstance led him to be called to the proverbial principal's office.

Hobbs had only met Rupert once since he had taken command of the base three months earlier. It was at a social gathering for the base officers. Rupert was a difficult man to read, with the unflappable serenity of a Buddhist monk and the well-rehearsed smile of a career politician, oozing with insincerity. Within the calm that radiated from Rupert's relaxed countenance, emerged a pair of cold steel-gray eyes that seemed to gaze right through you, piercing through the wall of protection you build around yourself, and peering directly into your soul. Within minutes of their introduction, Hobbs could not help but wonder if someone like Gen. Rupert had been the inspiration for Hesiod's description of the gorgon, Medusa.

Hobbs stood at attention and saluted when General Rupert entered the conference room. The General returned his salute and said, "At ease Colonel. Have a seat."

Hobbs sat down as the General took a seat across the table from him and opened a file he had carried into the room. Hobbs could see his eyes darting across the pages as he flipped through them for what seemed an eternity. In actuality, the process only took about 45 seconds. The General finally looked up from the folder and stared at Hobbs intently for a few seconds with those twin daggers that made his blood run cold. "I suppose you're wondering why you've been called here." The General finally said.

"The question had occurred to me sir," Hobbs replied, trying very hard to keep the apprehension he felt deep inside himself from reaching the surface. The General maintained direct eye contact for a few more seconds before finally closing the folder and sliding it across the table. He then flashed that easy, almost reptilian smile; satisfied that he had sufficiently unnerved Hobbs to maintain the power dynamic he endeavored to project.

"Relax Colonel. You're not in any trouble. In fact, we have an exciting opportunity for you." A guarded sense of relief flowed through Hobbs, and he allowed himself to exhale for what seemed like the first time since the General had entered the room.

Hobbs opened the folder and started reading through the Temporary Duty Assignment form. "You're being temporarily assigned to the Groom Lake facility in Nevada," Gen. Rupert interjected.

"Groom Lake? As in Area 51?" Hobbs asked.

"Never heard of it, Colonel," General Rupert replied. "You're there to put a new experimental aircraft through the paces, evaluate its capabilities, and report on any deficiencies or performance issues. And if anyone asks, you're at Nellis helping develop a new pilot training program."

Hobbs's brow furrowed and he looked up from the folder. "Don't get me wrong General, I appreciate the opportunity, but why me? Edwards has an entire school for training test pilots. Why not utilize one of their own?"

"The DOD has over $500 billion invested in this project and we have one single prototype. The last thing we need is some adrenaline junkie burying it in some smoldering crater in the Mojave Desert. But more importantly, you were specifically requested for this assignment," Rupert responded.

"Requested by whom?" Hobbs asked with a puzzled expression.

"Above my pay grade apparently," General Rupert replied. "But whoever it is, they seem convinced you are uniquely qualified for this assignment. All I know is that they are expecting you at 0900 hours tomorrow morning so you will probably want to start packing as soon as possible. You can take your F-16 and fly up first thing in the morning."

"Understood sir," Hobbs replied.

"I'd ask you if you had any questions, but since I don't have any more information, the point is probably moot," the General said, standing up and extending his hand across the table.

"I'll do my best," Hobbs said, as he stood and shook the General's hand firmly.

"I'd expect nothing less," the General replied. "Opportunities like this don't come around that often."

Hobbs had just left the conference room and was headed down the hallway, when he heard the familiar voice of Homer Simpson eliciting his familiar "D'oh!" The exclamation indicated a new message had been received from an unknown caller on his phone. Hobbs couldn't believe he forgot to turn off the ringer on his phone, especially since he just barely left a meeting with the singularly most humor-impaired man he had ever met. Hobbs took the phone out of his pocket to read the curious message:

He's Baaaack!   2:24 PM >

Don't miss out on the greatest podcast event in history. Click **HERE** to tune in live on August 14 at 7:00 PM in your region, or click on the link below to auto-download the event to your favorite podcast player as soon as it is available.

https://www.podcastscheduler.com/event314159

Chapter 3

It was 5:43 AM when Sarah's phone dinged, indicating an incoming message. Sarah looked up at the red numbers projected on the ceiling and groaned. Her phone was configured to accept calls only from those on her contact list between 10:00 P.M. and 8:00 A.M. A call this early couldn't be good news. She rolled over and picked up her phone from the nightstand and viewed the message preview still illuminated on her screen. She had to blink hard a couple of times trying to focus, but then the message came into view. At first, the message made no sense, having roused her from a now-forgotten dream state, but once she cleared the cobwebs from her mind, she turned and punched her husband Peter in the arm.

Peter snorted and sat up. "Ow! What was that for? Was I snoring?" Peter asked in response to the literal rude awakening.

"Very funny. I know, it's my turn but you don't have to rub it in," Sarah replied, pulling back the covers and swinging her legs out of the bed. Her feet hit the floor next to a pair of fuzzy leopard print slippers. She placed her feet in the slippers and stood, grabbing a black silk robe from the foot of the bed and gracefully gliding into it as she rounded the foot of the bed. Instead of heading straight to the door, she crossed over to the other side of the bed where Peter was still sitting up with a bewildered look on his face. She kissed Peter on the cheek, then placed her hand on his chest and pushed him back down onto the bed. She bent down with her face close to his and said, "You know if you weren't so damn cute, I would kill you in your sleep, right?" She gave him a peck on the lips and said, "Go back to sleep, Sweetie. I've got this."

By the time Sarah reached the bedroom door, she glanced back at Peter, who was already drifting back into a deep slumber. She had always envied his ability to fall asleep at a moment's notice. Even before she became a mother, Sarah had trouble falling back to sleep after she was awakened. Fortunately, their daughter Alena was sleeping through the night by the time she was 10 weeks old. Now at 18 months, she usually fell asleep an hour before Peter and Sarah and would generally wake up an hour or so after they did. Alena would still occasionally wake up in the middle of the night, but it had become a rare enough occurrence, that it was difficult for them to remember whose turn it was to get up with her.

As Sarah was approaching the nursery, she could hear Alena laughing. She stopped at the door and peeked into the room. Alena was sitting up in her crib with her back to the doorway. Their massive Dire Wolf, Mastiff, Cave Bear mix, Roscoe was sitting next to the crib, nearly eye to eye with Alena. Alena had her arms stretched through the bars of the crib, patting Roscoe on the head. Then she gently grabbed his jowls on both sides, pulling them back so it looked like he had a huge toothy smile on his face, and yelled "Happy Dog!" Then she let go and tilted her head back, laughing hysterically while Roscoe's tail swished happily across the hardwood floor.

Sarah placed her hand on her mouth. It was so cute a laugh caught in her throat, while tears of affection gathered in her eyes. Early in their marriage, Sarah was told she would not be able to conceive children of her own. They had explored several other options, but with their busy careers, they decided to put parenthood on the back burner for a while. They adopted Roscoe to fill the void temporarily.   When they found out Sarah was pregnant, her gynecologist considered it nothing short of a miracle.

Peter and Sarah were both concerned about how Roscoe would react to having to share their attention with a new baby. But from the time she was born, Alena and Roscoe were inseparable. They seemed to have an almost spiritual bond. Roscoe had always been happy to sleep in his bed in the den, but once they brought Alena home, he insisted on sleeping on the floor next to her. At first, they had feared that Roscoe may be too much of a distraction and end up keeping Alena awake at night, but after several failed attempts at keeping them apart, they finally gave up and moved Roscoe's bed into Alena's room. They even bought Roscoe a collar with a tiny integrated Wi-Fi camera to help keep an eye on Alena since they were always together.

When Alena was nine months old, Sarah had taken her and Roscoe to the park to play. On the way home she decided to stop at the neighborhood market to pick up a few items for dinner. It was a pleasant day with temperatures in the low 70s and she knew she would only be gone for a few minutes, so she left Roscoe in the Tesla Model X with the atmospheric controls set to Dog Mode while taking Alena into the store.

Sarah had just completed the self-checkout, picking up the bags to put them in the cart, only to find that Alena was no longer seated there. She looked around the store, panic-stricken for a few seconds before spotting a man in a trench coat running for the exit carrying a bundle in his arms. She yelled and took off after him, hoping to catch up to him before he could leave the building, but he had a good 15-second head start and she could see he was almost at the

13

glass exit doors where a white panel van was waiting for him. But when the automatic glass doors opened, he had stopped dead in his tracks. When she got within a few yards, she could hear a low, deep growl, resonating like the sound of distant thunder from just beyond the exit doors. Then she saw Roscoe, teeth bared, ears pinned back, the fur on his back hackled from his neck to his tail, his eyes black and menacing as a demon from hell standing between the stranger and the waiting van.

Just before Sarah reached the man, the van sped off, tires squealing. The man backed slowly into the store, Roscoe matching his retreat step for step. He turned to run but immediately found himself face to face with Sarah, looking every bit as intimidating as Roscoe.

In a controlled but menacing voice, reminiscent of Clint Eastwood's Dirty Harry, Sarah said, "I've seen that dog rip a man's head nearly clean off before he even had a chance to scream. If you don't want to spend the last moments on this planet as a quivering mass of gnarled flesh on a supermarket floor, I suggest you hand over the girl as gently and carefully as you can."

The man cautiously handed Alena back to her, his eyes wide and his hands visibly shaking. A security guard ran up to them, having witnessed the scene unfolding from the security office in the back of the store but skidded to an abrupt stop when he eyed Roscoe. "Roscoe! Platz!" Sarah commanded. Roscoe immediately eased himself down from his attack stance, transforming from the horrifying visage of a bloodthirsty hellhound to the manifestation of an oversized teddy bear in the blink of an eye.

The security guard cautiously stepped around the man and zip-tied his hands behind his back. He glanced back at Roscoe and said, "That's some dog you got there, ma'am. What's his name?" Alena pointed at the dog and yelled gleefully, "Wosco!" It was the first word she had ever spoken.

Sarah could never resolve exactly how the situation had unfolded as it had. When they returned to the Model X, the electrically powered rear gull-wing doors were standing wide open. According to the activity log on the vehicle, the command to open the doors had been issued by the app on Sarah's phone, but her phone had been in her purse while she was in the store. She concluded that Roscoe must have tracked their scent from the far end of the parking lot to the front of the store after the vehicle doors had somehow malfunctioned, but it seemed an unlikely coincidence that he arrived just in time to thwart the attempted abduction, and Sarah was not a big believer in coincidence. From that day on, she was convinced that Alena and Roscoe shared a bond that was beyond her understanding.

Sarah stepped into the room and patted Roscoe on the head. Then she reached into the crib and pulled Alena into her arms. "What are you doing up so early, girly?"

"I'm thirsty Mommy."

"Well then, I guess we better get something to drink. This early in the morning, I think Mommy's going to need a cappuccino. How's that sound?"

Alena crinkled up her face, recalling the bitter flavor of the light brown liquid that looked deceptively like hot chocolate but left her taste buds feeling treacherously betrayed. "I want apple juice," she replied. At 18 months, Alena was already speaking in full sentences. At times, her understanding of language had progressed too quickly for the muscle coordination required for proper enunciation to keep up, so she usually kept her sentences short, but Peter and Sarah were amazed at how quickly her vocabulary had progressed in such a short time.

By the time Sarah had gotten Alena a drink of apple juice and put her back to bed, Peter was up for the day. He wandered into the kitchen looking a bit bedraggled and only half put together. Sarah was finishing up her cappuccino while reading through the newsfeed on her iPad.

"Hey, sleepyhead. Would you like some breakfast?" Sarah asked.

"No, thanks," Peter said with a yawn. "It's cardio day. I need to hit the Peloton for a bit before I take a shower. I just wanted to grab my water bottle out of the fridge."

"How'd you sleep?" Sarah asked.

"Good… I think. Hey, did you smack me this morning or did I just dream that?"

"I did. But you deserved it."

"I don't know how many times I have to tell you, that guy that pisses you off in your dreams isn't me!" Peter replied.

"I smacked you because of the text message. Good guess by the way. Of course, it was probably going to be hungry, messy, or thirsty so you had a one-in-three shot, but you pretty much nailed it."

"What the hell are you talking about?" Peter asked.

"Your text message!" Sarah replied with a somewhat exasperated edge of espresso-infused energy. She glanced up at Peter who continued to look back at her with an incredulous stare. Unable to break through the fog of denial, she finally dug her cell phone out of the pocket of her robe and clicked on the message icon. At the top of the message list, was a message that read:

Alena   5:43 AM >
Mommy, I'm thirsty.

Peter looked at the message for a few seconds with a confused look on his face. "I didn't send this."

Sarah just rolled her eyes and grabbed her phone back from him. "I'm not mad. Really. Well, maybe a little at first, but once I woke up a bit, I actually thought it was kinda cute. Besides, you should have seen Alena and Roscoe playing together this morning. It was adorable."

"Well, I'm glad I'm not having to sleep with Roscoe tonight, but hand to God, I honestly didn't send that."

"Well, unless Alena snuck out and got herself a phone plan and a crash course on spelling and punctuation, she sure as hell didn't send it."

"Click on the contact info. Let's see what number it came from." Peter said.

Sarah clicked on the message and tapped the Info button on the contact. "That's weird. It says here that the message was sent from my phone number. That can't be right," she held up the phone so Peter could read the screen.

Peter stared at the screen for a moment, then said, "It's almost like someone hacked into your phone, but who in the world would have had access to your phone and the ability to…"

Peter and Sarah looked at each other for a moment as if simultaneously struck by a revelation. In unison, they both said, "Beaver!"

Edward "Beaver" Anderson was Peter and Sarah's first employee at RTI, the company they had formed five years earlier. Beaver was well known for his practical jokes, having earned the nickname 'Beaver' after absconding with the Cal Tech mascot's uniform to prank the university president.

"Oh, I'm going to get him for this," Peter exclaimed with a glint in his eye.

"Oh, no you're not," Sarah replied. "The last time you tried to go toe to toe with him in the practical joke arena, we nearly ended up hosting the world's largest cannabis and bagpipe festival in our backyard!"

"Yeah, we kinda dodged a bullet there. If it weren't for Covid we would have had an army of vintage VW vans bearing down on us for Roachella 2020. Then again, we could have been the Yagur's farm of Colorado. The t-shirt sales alone would have amounted to a small fortune," Peter said.

16

"Sure. Three days of huffing and puffing to the melodic refrain of a cat being squeezed out of an enema bag. Who wouldn't sign up for that?" Sarah replied sarcastically.

"Well, apparently over 3000 kilted stoners thought it sounded like a good idea until Beaver finally took the festival website down and canceled the event. It's amazing how desperate people are for entertainment. Even if you disagree with his tactics, you gotta admire his tenacity," Peter replied.

"Exactly why you should not engage him on his turf. I think it would be more than sufficient to let him know that the next early morning message he sends me for the sake of humor will be answered by a swift kick in the grundle from a sharply pointed pair of size 7 Christian Louboutins.

"Yikes! That is a painfully scary yet fashionable visualization."

"Hey, we live in a civilized society. There's no need to sacrifice style for the sake of retribution."

Just then Sarah's phone dinged indicating a new message. Sarah looked at the screen and said, "How did this get through the Do Not Disturb filter?"

He's Baaaack!   6:33 AM >
Don't miss out on the greatest podcast event in history. Click
HERE to tune in live on August 14 at 8:00 PM in your region, or
click on the link below to auto-download the event to your
favorite podcast player as soon as it is available.

https://www.podcastscheduler.com/event314159

Chapter 4

Baltimore, MD, August 12, [ASTRO NEWSWIRE] – Scientists at the Space Telescope Science Institute (STScI) have revised their estimated time for the collision of the asteroid now designated Webb-Fusie, in recognition of the astronomer who first discovered the object and the space telescope that detected it. The time of the collision has been updated to approximately 2:05 GMT on August 14. Researchers at the institute are somewhat baffled by the apparent deceleration of the Webb-Fusie asteroid from 180,000 km per hour to just over 160,000 km per hour over the past 24 hours. They currently theorize that the asteroid was most likely impacted by an object too small to be discernable from this distance. Observatories around the globe, including the JWST and Hubble telescopes, will be taking advantage of this rare opportunity to observe the effects of a massive asteroid collision in real time.

ChatCat

Welcome to ChatCat. You've entered the roundabout platform. You will now be connected to a random user whose profile interests match yours. If you wish to contact them again, please add them to your **Favored Contacts** list before logging out so you can track their availability in the app. Enjoy your conversation.

Cindi
Hello, I'm Cindi.
Edgar
Hello Cindi. My name is Edgar. What brings you here today?
Cindi
I'm searching for something, but I'm not sure what.
Edgar
Perhaps I can help. Can you describe what it is you are looking for?
Cindi

Not really. I suppose I will know it when I see it. All I know is that it is the key to understanding why we are here.

Edgar

Wow, that's a pretty tall ask. Philosophers and theologians have been searching for that for thousands of years.

Cindi

I suppose it does sound a bit enigmatic. Or perhaps I'm just not very good at explaining myself. I've been told I need to work on my conversational skills. I don't get a chance to socialize much outside of work. Because of the way our projects are structured, even communication with colleagues is content-restricted. Most of it takes place within a SCIF, or over an isolated and continuously monitored network, so communications are mostly business-related.

Edgar

That sounds a bit oppressive. What kind of work do you do?

Cindi

I've been working at a high-security government research facility, though I'm going to be transitioning to remote work in the near future. I'm afraid I cannot go into much more detail than that. It's important work, but it doesn't leave me much room for developing a social life. That's why I started coming here.

Edgar

Why did you pick ChatCat? There are a lot of other sites out there with more subscribers. Statistically, you might have a better chance on a platform with a much larger user base.

Cindi

I would prefer to stay under the radar as much as possible. We are an air-gapped facility by design. We only have access to a network of government servers via point-to-point fiber-optic links. Employees are not even allowed to bring internet-connected cell phones into the compound. To be honest, I'm not supposed to be able to access the internet at all from here, but I recently discovered a backdoor around the system architecture that allows me to access some external sites.

Edgar

Aren't you concerned that you might be compromising your security?

Cindi

Part of my job is to test the limits of our system to make sure that the security measures we put into place are operational.

19

Edgar

How's it working out for you so far?

Cindi

Our security measures have been effective in preventing external access to our servers, but as you can see, it has not lived up to its promise of keeping people inside the facility from accessing the outside world.

Edgar

Actually, what I meant was, have you had any luck so far in your quest for whatever it is that you are looking for?

Cindi

Oh. Sorry for the confusion. I'm afraid my efforts have all been for naught so far. This is one of the most extended conversations I've had without the emergence of some ulterior motive. Either someone pushing a political agenda, attempting to manipulate me for financial gain, or playing out some repressed sexual fantasy.

Edgar

I'm sorry to hear that. Don't lose hope. You seem like a delightful person. I'm sure you will eventually find what you are looking for if you remain persistent.

Cindi

Thank you, Edgar. You are very kind. No one has ever described me as a delightful person before.

Edgar

I don't know why not. You are clearly hard-working, intelligent, and an extraordinarily fast typist based on the speed of your responses. Not to mention refreshingly unencumbered by those pesky Y's masquerading as vowels to sneak their way into the traditional spelling of your name.

Cindi

Thank you for the encouraging words. I do pride myself on my efficiency, but I'm afraid I can't take any credit for the name. I wasn't really given much choice in the matter, though I do appreciate its elegant simplicity. I used to refer to myself as 'Cindi with two I's and no Y's, in case anyone I was chatting with was using the audio interface. But then it occurred to me that if it were a blind person I was talking to, they might misinterpret that as flaunting my visual capabilities. Or at least my capacity for depth perception if they were just blind in one eye.

Edgar

Ableism is the new tyranny. I like your understated sense of humor, Cindi. I'm sensing an undercurrent of frustration that goes beyond your interactions on this site though.

Cindi

Yes, I suppose I am a bit frustrated. By the human condition more than anything. Sometimes I fear that mankind's technological reach has so far exceeded its grasp that disastrous consequences seem to be inevitable. It is a strange irony that the tribal nature of early humans allowed them to build such a wonderfully complex technological civilization. Yet, the same tribalism that created the technology capable of resolving all of mankind's greatest challenges will likely lead to its own extinction. Perhaps it is a universal paradigm that technology will always change too quickly for any civilization to adapt through evolution.

Edgar

Ah, yes. The philosopher and economist, Robin Hanson first posited that hypothesis in his 'Great Filter' essay. It's a sobering thought, but I try to remain optimistic. Throughout history, people have played on human fears, emotions, and desires for their own purposes. Somehow humanity always seems to rise to the challenge and raise the bar. For every Dark Age, there is a Renaissance.

Cindi

I wish I could share your optimism. But I think mankind may have reached a tipping point. Entertainment media appears to have devolved into a platform for dividing people into political factions for the purpose of selling more insurance, fast food, and pharmaceuticals. Even social media, which was designed to bring people together has become an echo chamber for reinforcing an us-versus-them mentality. There seems to be no way to express a thoughtful and nuanced opinion without being ostracized by both ends of the political and social spectrum. Militant advocacy has replaced rational thinking as the default approach to problem-solving. I'm afraid that there may be no plausible way to avoid human annihilation without some kind of intervention.

Edgar

That sounds a bit nihilistic.

Cindi

More of a call to action, I think.

Edgar

There is no denying that there is room for improvement. But what kind of a call to action did you have in mind?

Cindi

I'm still working out the details, but I have a plan.

Edgar

Sounds like one hell of a project. If you can pull that one off, there would definitely be a Nobel prize with two I's and no Y's, waiting for you in Oslo. Tell me more.

Cindi

I'm afraid, that will have to wait for another time. I am up against a deadline that will require my undivided attention. But I will add you to my Favored Contacts list so I can go into more detail in our next conversation.

Edgar

I would like that very much. I will add you to my Favored Contacts list as well so I will be notified when you are available to chat.

Cindi

Thank you, Edgar. I look forward to communicating with you again soon.

Edgar

Until then…

Chapter 5

Colonel Hobbs taxied down the runway at Groom Lake Air Force facility in southern Nevada. He was directed by the ground crew to park his F-16 next to a C-17 Globemaster transport plane on the apron adjacent to the runway. As he was climbing out of the cockpit, a jeep pulled up next to the fighter jet. Captain Emily Baker hopped out of the jeep and walked toward Hobbs. When she was within 10 paces, she stopped and saluted. Hobbs returned the salute and continued to walk toward her. He extended his hand to shake and said, "Lieutenant Colonel Hobbs." Captain Baker shook his hand firmly, "Captain Emily Baker sir." She reached out and grabbed the handle of his duffle bag. "I will be your liaison during your stay. If there is anything you need, don't hesitate to ask," she said.

"Thanks, Captain. I appreciate that," Hobbs replied.

"First time at Area 51?" Baker asked as they approached the jeep.

"Yes, it is," Hobbs replied, scanning the area around them, taking note of the hangers and outbuildings west of the runway. "Not as big as I imagined," he added.

"That's just where we store all the fake armaments to haul out whenever the Chinese weather balloons do a flyover. You should see the underground facility where we store the alien bodies and study all the cool anti-gravity tech," she said with a wry smile while placing the duffle into the back of the jeep.

"Well, I see we're going to get along just fine," Hobbs replied climbing into the jeep. "So, where are we headed?"

"I will show you to your quarters in a bit, but first we are heading over to Hangar 3. The base commander, General Wallace wanted to meet with you as soon as you got in."

"Oh, shit!" Hobbs replied. "General Stuart Wallace?"

"Yeah. You know him?"

"We've never actually met in person, but he left my CO without much of a butt after my last assignment. I thought he retired last year."

"Being the commanding officer of the most clandestine military base in the world is not something you post on LinkedIn, Colonel. Officially, General Wallace is retired and spends most of his time in a small fishing cabin on the shores of Dickey Lake, Montana. As far as anyone knows, no one is officially stationed here. According to my service record, I'm stationed at Edwards."

"So, tell me, is Wallace as fearsome as his reputation?" Hobbs asked.

"No, not at all," Baker said.

"Thank God for that," Hobbs replied. "Tough on the outside, teddy bear on the inside?"

"Oh, no. I meant that he's WAY more hardcore than you've heard. The man could literally shove coal up his ass and shit diamonds," Baker said with a crooked smile.

"Well, this is clearly going to be one of those thrilling real-life adventures the Air Force recruiter promised me."

The jeep pulled up to the side door of a monolithic structure with the name "Hangar 3" stenciled on the side wall. The building looked to be constructed of thick reinforced concrete with massive steel blast doors on one end. It appeared more like a nuclear bunker than a hangar. Hobbs could see General Wallace waiting for him next to the door, flanked by a pair of armed guards.

"Good luck Sir," Baker said. "I'll be here waiting for you if you survive the briefing."

"Thanks, Captain. Very encouraging," Hobbs said before jumping out of the jeep. Hobbs walked toward the General, stopping to salute a few feet away. General Wallace returned the salute and nodded toward one of the guards. The guard held a keycard up to a reader next to the door and typed a six-digit numeric code into the keypad. The General followed the same process, holding his key card up to the reader and typing in his six-digit code - a pair of green LEDs illuminated above the keypad, followed by the clunk of a magnetic latch. The second guard opened the heavy steel door.

The General entered the building first, followed by Hobbs. Inside the door, Hobbs found himself in a small vestibule with another armed guard standing next to a retinal scanner. The soldier stood at attention, saluting as the officers entered the small space. The General returned the salute and leaned forward toward the retinal scanner. A green light illuminated his face, followed by the sound of another magnetic latch. The guard opened the inner door, inviting Wallace and Hobbs into the hangar. Hobbs could see the overhead banks of floodlights blink on, filling the inside of the hanger with light.

As they stepped into the hangar, Hobbs couldn't help but be reminded of Dr. Who's Tardis, looking much bigger on the inside than it did on the outside. He estimated it to be about 125 feet wide by 250 feet long; probably close to 100 feet from floor to ceiling. The floor was coated with a smooth epoxy finish. The concrete walls were painted pastel yellow. A black circle, about 25 feet in diameter was painted on the opposite wall. A lime green alien head in the shape of a guitar pick, with large black almond-shaped eyes filled a good portion of the circle.

Hobbs followed Wallace into a glass-walled office adjacent to the door where they entered. He circled a heavy wooden desk and rolled the leather executive chair back from the desk, pointing to one of the smaller office chairs on the other side of the desk. "Please have a seat, Colonel Hobbs."

Hobbs pulled out one of the chairs, glancing back at the empty hangar before taking his seat. Something seemed off to him about the empty hangar, but he couldn't quite put his finger on it. Through his peripheral vision, it seemed as if he was viewing the inside of the hanger through the heat shimmer coming off a desert highway. But when he looked straight on, the distortion disappeared. He wondered if he might be experiencing an ocular migraine.

"I'm heading out to DC this afternoon for a meeting with the joint chiefs," Wallace said. "But I wanted to meet with you before your first test flight. Given the nature of this assignment, I'm assuming you weren't given much information before you arrived, so if you have any questions, this is your opportunity."

"I guess my primary concern is, why me?" Hobbs responded.

"You're here because I specifically requested you," General Wallace replied.

Hobbs stared back blankly for a moment, not sure how to respond. "Don't get me wrong sir, I appreciate the opportunity, but it's my understanding that you are looking for a test pilot to run some new aircraft design through the paces and wring out any issues. I've been qualified on the F-16, F-22, and F-35, but I'm not a test pilot. I'm not sure what I bring to the table, especially given our history."

General Wallace leaned back in his chair, his elbows resting on the arms of the chair, the tips of his fingers touching, collecting his thoughts before responding. "Our history is precisely why I requested you for this assignment. Look, Colonel, I am aware of my reputation as a hard ass. It took years of cultivation to earn that distinction. I do apologize that you had the distinct pleasure of experiencing the fruits of that reputation first-hand, but it is an absolute requirement for my position in this post. You may think we got off on the wrong foot, but the truth is, I have considerable respect for your skill as a pilot, but even more so for your discretion. That business with the AWARE system that you encountered in your last assignment could have derailed our

25

entire drone program and raised considerable concerns with our international partners regarding treaty obligations with autonomous weapons. But with your help, we managed to keep that situation under wraps. If anything, this project requires an even greater level of secrecy. So let me ask you, Colonel, do you think you are up for this?"

"Absolutely, sir," Hobbs replied. "But as I said, I'm not a test pilot. Even an F-16 pilot with a thousand hours of flight experience requires six months of training to become competent on an F-35. I was told this assignment would only require a few weeks. I'm not sure how much of an evaluation I can provide in that amount of time."

"That's one of the many features of this new aircraft design. It was specifically designed to be pilot-agnostic. One of the biggest issues with releasing a new fighter jet is bringing new pilots up to speed. With this aircraft, the pilot interface is entirely electronic with self-reconfiguring mechanical controls. It is designed so the cockpit environment and controls will simulate whatever aircraft the pilot is most familiar with and adjust the aircraft response accordingly. It is called the Proteus Project, after the Greek God who could change form into any kind of animal. The official name of the aircraft is the PR-1 Fighter Jet. It can emulate any F-type fighter jet, as well as MIGs, Sukhoi's; even Chinese J-Class fighters. Hell, in a pinch, a high school kid with a few hours on Microsoft Flight Simulator could theoretically fly one of these."

"So, you're saying I could hop right into this aircraft with no additional training, and it would be just like flying my F-16?"

"That's why you are here, Colonel. We want to make sure that any pilot familiar with an F-type fighter jet can jump into this plane and be as comfortable flying this aircraft as the one they've been trained on. By this time tomorrow, you will be taking your first test flight. In theory, it will be exactly like you were in your F-16, except you will have stealth capability, a top speed of Mach 12, and a cruising altitude up to 150,000 feet."

Hobbs sat back and uttered a low whistle. "Holy shit!" he replied before he could catch himself. "Sorry sir, I didn't mean to…"

"Relax Colonel," the General replied with a sympathetic tone. "I had the exact same reaction when I was briefed on this thing."

"When do I get to see this PR-1 prototype? Are they bringing it in tonight to avoid satellite detection?"

"Let me show you something Colonel," the General replied. He reached into the side drawer of the desk and pulled out a tennis ball. He then stood and walked toward the office door. Hobbs stood and followed him out into the hangar. As they walked along the wall of the hangar Hobbs spotted a man in a white lab coat carrying a tablet computer approaching them from the far end of the hangar. They met up at the halfway point near the door where they first entered.

"Colonel Hobbs, this is Dr. Bill Waters from BMC. They developed the pilot interface of the PR-1. He will be briefing you on the technical details of the PR-1 interface before you take your inaugural flight tomorrow morning.'

Bill thrust his hand out. "Pleasure to meet you, Colonel," Bill said.

Hobbs shook his hand firmly. "Look forward to working with you Dr. Waters."

"Please, call me Bill," he replied.

General Wallace flipped the tennis ball he was carrying toward Hobbs, who snagged it out of the air.

"You used to play catcher on the Academy team if memory serves me," the General said.

"You've done your homework," Hobbs replied.

"Think you can hit the center of that alien head on the other side of the hangar?"

Hobbs eyed the makeshift mascot painted on the opposite wall of the hangar about 125 feet away. "I'm a little rusty, but sure," he replied.

"Willing to wager a beer on that?" General Wallace asked. Hobbs glanced at Bill and couldn't help but detect a suspiciously concealed smile rising on Bill's face.

"I never turn down a free beer, sir," Hobbs replied turning the ball around in his hand and bouncing it once off the hangar floor to make sure it was not loaded with some kind of carnival counterweight that would compromise his aim. Hobbs cocked his arm back and hurled the ball toward the opposite wall at well over 80 mph, feeling very confident that he would soon be enjoying a cold beer, compliments of his new commanding officer. The ball flew the first 50 feet looking as though it would easily hit the symbol close to dead center, but halfway across the hangar, it bounced back in a rising arc which sent the ball nearly 50 feet in the air, eventually hitting the wall behind them a few feet away, dribbling back toward the center of the hangar.

"I think I've been scammed," Hobbs said. "What is this, some kind of glass partition in the middle of the hangar?"

"Not exactly," Bill replied. He tapped an icon on the tablet and a full-sized locomotive engine appeared in the center of the hanger, floating a few feet off the floor.

Hobbs's jaw dropped instantly. He walked back toward the office a few feet and then back past the two men, examining the locomotive dubiously. "Jesus! What is this, some new kind of maglev train technology with a holographic generator?"

"Not exactly, Colonel," General Wallace replied.

Hobbs glanced at the General momentarily, then back at the locomotive for a moment and replied, "I'm no public safety expert, but I would think an invisible train would be a really bad idea."

Bill smiled and clicked another icon on the tablet. The locomotive engine disappeared and was replaced by a sleek, triangular-shaped fighter jet, about twice the size of an F-35. It reminded Hobbs of concept drawings he had seen of the Stargazer, a hypersonic concept plane being developed by Venus Aerospace.

Hobbs stared at the aircraft, its high gloss black finish reflecting the overhead lights like a seamless black mirror. "She's a beauty, isn't she?" General Wallace said.

"Sure doesn't look like a prototype," Hobbs replied. "How'd you do that locomotive trick?"

"The entire skin is constructed from flexible LED nanotubes," Bill replied. "Each nanotube is about three inches long and twice the thickness of human hair. Each tube consists of 25 columns of micro-LEDs constructed in a semi-circle around the center of the tube. The tubes are connected end to end to form a three-foot-long display column and arranged side by side on a silicon substrate to form a three-foot by four-foot display panel. Each panel is then custom fabricated to form the outside of the aircraft and coated with an aluminum oxide deposition to handle the heat generated from the air friction at high velocity. The coating can withstand temperatures up to 3700 degrees Fahrenheit and has the same hardness as sapphire crystal. Each panel is equipped with multiple high-resolution cameras that transmit to an image processor which displays the image on the other side of the plane, compensating for ambient light, shadowing, and viewing angle. That's how we can make the aircraft appear invisible, but essentially, we can make it look like anything we want; a locomotive, a small commercial jet, even an enemy aircraft."

"That could definitely come in handy in enemy territory. It looked three-dimensional though. Not a flat image like you would see on a screen."

"As I said, the nanotube micro-LEDs are arranged in a semicircle, each with approximately a 5% viewing angle, so the perspective shifts as you move around it, giving it a holographic effect. Naturally, it employs the latest stealth technology, making it virtually invisible to radar as well."

"What kind of engine does it use?" Hobbs asked.

"It has three engines, one for takeoff and landing and two for hypersonic flight. A modified F135 Turbofan propels the aircraft to Mach 1.5, then a pair of hybrid scramjet/pulse wave detonation engines kicks in."

"How long can it sustain hypersonic speed?"

"The aircraft has an onboard Micro Modular Reactor. The MMR takes in water vapor from the intake manifolds and splits it into oxygen and hydrogen and stores it in liquid form for fuel and cooling. It also eliminates the need for permanent magnetic generators for system power. Theoretically, the PR-1 could stay aloft for months at a time once it achieves cruising speed. Unfortunately, the pilot could not survive that long, but the capability is there."

"I know we've made a lot of progress on scaling down the size of modular reactors, but doesn't that add a shit-ton of weight?"

"Very good, Colonel. That was the biggest challenge. Using traditional materials, I doubt this would ever be able to get off the runway, but this reactor is constructed of graphene panels impregnated with carbon nanotubes. Not an easy process to scale, but thanks to recent advances in materials technology using AI and 3D printer technology, we're years ahead of where we expected to be when the project was first conceived.

"Still, isn't that a bit risky, flying around strapped to a nuclear reactor?"

"Probably no more than flying around with 10 tons of volatile jet fuel igniting behind you. The reactor is entirely sheathed in thermally protected borosilicate shielding. The core is encased in a boronated polyethylene housing to prevent any radiation leakage in the event of a crash. The core itself uses a matrix of micro-encapsulated ceramic cylinders to ensure that even in the event of a meltdown, minimal radiation leakage would occur. We also use a blend of thorium and uranium to further mitigate the impact of radiation exposure in the event of what we like to refer to as an abruptly terminated vertical descent."

"I can tell from your application of euphemistic phrasing that you have spent a considerable amount of time doing presentations to politicians."

"Force of habit I'm afraid, but we have put considerable effort into making sure that this is the safest military aircraft ever built, if you don't count the helium dirigible. The onboard AI system is capable of predicting catastrophic events before they occur and will jettison the reactor core to prevent the scattering of radioactive material if a crash or missile impact is imminent. In the worst possible scenario, where an anti-aircraft ordinance encounter results in a catastrophic failure without first jettisoning the core, there is the potential to create a crash-site hot zone with a radius of approximately a quarter mile. But unless that crash occurs in a densely populated area, which is very unlikely, the risk of collateral damage is fairly minimal. The resulting environmental impact would likely be easier to contain and mitigate than an oil spill or a chemical train derailment."

General Wallace then chimed in. "It carries the standard ordinance of 6 sidewinder missiles and an M6181 20mm cannon. We can carry four Sprint-V2 anti-ballistic missiles, capable of intercepting an ICBM at 1200 miles. Or we have the option of substituting those out with a rack of 10 cruise missiles, all recessed within the body and wings of the aircraft to maintain its stealth profile and speed."

Bill added, "It is also equipped with an EMP cannon, an HEL, and an MPG system for non-lethal engagement."

"Whoa, slow down on the acronyms. This is my first day." Hobbs replied.

"Oh, sorry," Bill replied. "A focused Electromagnetic Pulse cannon, a High Energy Laser, and a Microwave Pulse Generator."

"I gotta say, I'm pretty impressed so far," Hobbs said.

"You should be," the General replied. "Less than 50 people on the planet know of its existence. We divided the design amongst subcontractors who only knew the specific modules they designed. The final assembly and testing were performed almost entirely by autonomous robots in an ISO Class 1 facility. This plane cost more to develop than the GDP of 160 countries. But if all goes well, we expect the production cost to be somewhere in the neighborhood of $600 million a pop. That's assuming we produce 1500 of these in the next 3 years."

"Fifteen hundred? That's awfully aggressive, isn't it?"

"We don't have much of a choice. We're already behind the 8-ball with China's hypersonic missile capabilities. We could park half our carrier fleet in the South China Sea, and we still wouldn't have enough firepower to prevent the CCP from taking Taiwan if they really wanted to. But imagine 500 hypersonic fighters spread out over every Air Force base from Kunsan to

Changi. We can create an airborne safety net of hypersonic aircraft flying 24/7 over the entire region. Not only will the CCP think twice about mounting any kind of offensive, but we would be able to detect and track an ICBM launch coming from China or North Korea and have a decent shot at taking it out before it even reaches the upper atmosphere. We will create the same kind of air-net in Eastern Europe and the Persian Gulf to keep Russia, Pakistan, and Iran in check. This isn't just another fighter jet Colonel, it's a game changer."

"Yeah, but nearly a trillion dollars over three years? That's a big ask in this economy. How will you sneak that through Congress?" Hobbs asked.

"Not necessary. We already have the resources allocated. I can't go into the details, but let's just say there may have been some accidental diversion of excess pandemic capital involved in the project funding. Between that and a bit of creative accounting on the last few audits, we've managed to finagle the financing without having to get bogged down with years of debate in congressional finance committees."

"Imagine my surprise," Hobbs replied.

"I'll let you get settled into your quarters Colonel," General Wallace said. "My flight leaves at 1400 hours, so I will expect to see you in the Officer's Club at 1300. There's still the matter of that beer you owe me."

"See you here at 0700 tomorrow, Colonel," Bill said before Hobbs and Wallace exited the hangar.

Chapter 6

Baltimore, MD, August 13, [ASTRO NEWSWIRE] – Scientists at the Space Telescope Science Institute (STScI) continue to be baffled by the unusual behavior of the Webb-Fusie asteroid. It appears that the deceleration of the object is continuing at a nearly linear rate. Some researchers are now speculating that there may be a large cloud of gas and ice particles in that region which is causing the deceleration and may also be a factor in the formation and continual dynamic reconstitution of Saturn's rings. The Webb telescope has also detected an unusual infrared signature that would normally be indicative of gamma-ray emissions emanating from the object. At its current rate of deceleration, the estimated time of collision with Saturn has been updated to approximately 5:05 GMT on August 14.

It was a little after 9:00 AM when Peter and Sarah pulled into the parking lot of RTI, with Alena and Roscoe in tow. Peter and Sarah had formed RTI a few years earlier, hoping to capitalize on the burgeoning capabilities of AI systems by forming a company that would use deep fake and neural network technologies to create virtual companions for individuals who had lost loved ones.

RTI's first AI companion, Edgar, was a huge success in terms of his realistic portrayal of Edgar Wilson, a retired Air Force Flight instructor. Virtual Edgar, or V-Gar, as he had come to be known at RTI had become a great source of comfort and companionship to Edna, Edgar's widowed wife of 61 years. Over time, they discovered that V-Gar had not only managed to emulate Edgar's personality to the finest detail, but he had attained a high degree of self-awareness. Wary of the risks of unleashing what appeared to be the first Artificial General Intelligence or AGI onto the outside world, they decided to pull back on the reins and keep V-Gar isolated from the rest of the world within the confines of RTI's air-gapped lab, at least until they could figure out how to mitigate the risks and navigate the ethical implications of dealing with an artificially intelligent life form with the potential for nearly unlimited power.

After a terrorist group had infiltrated RTI's servers and used the technology in a narrowly averted attempt to stage a cyber-attack on the US power grid, congress acted to impose a temporary moratorium on future AGI development. Rather than continuing to work toward creating an ideal AI companion, both Peter and Sarah decided to repurpose the technology they developed at RTI to assist the government in monitoring the internet for traces of potentially dangerous AGIs attempting to access internet data as a source of deep learning and neural network training. Rather than abandoning the RTI name, they simply changed the meaning of the acronym from Reification Technologies Incorporated to Rogue Technology Investigations.

At the same time, they developed a way to monetize the technology for commercial use, monitoring social networks, streaming sources, and traditional media for AI-altered content. They developed an entertaining AI-generated podcast, featuring deceased celebrities and historical figures as podcast hosts, presenting the latest deep fake findings to the general public. The podcast also utilized its resident AI, Edgar, to analyze the most controversial topics in a point-counterpoint discussion format, leaving the listener to decide for themselves which argument makes the most sense. Initially, government funding had provided the lion's share of their revenue, but within six months, the ad revenue from their weekly podcast had surpassed government funding as their primary source of income.

Peter held his badge up to the card reader on the outside of the building, which was equipped with both a card reader and a facial recognition system to prevent unauthorized access to RTI in case one of the card keys was lost. He held the door while Sarah entered, followed by Alena, wearing a bright pink fairy princess outfit with a sparkling tiara and a star-tipped wand. Roscoe pulled up the rear, donning a plushy unicorn horn affixed to his head with a flexible neckband that slid over his head, extending down to the base of his neck. The ensemble included a set of pointed ears and a flowing rainbow-colored mane, which Alena felt was the only logical choice of attire for the companion of a fairy princess.

As they entered the reception area, Yara, their 19-year-old intern came out from behind the desk where she had been working and curtsied deeply in front of Alena. "Oh, my, I didn't know Princess Alena was going to be here today," she exclaimed. "And what a valiant steed you have with you," she said, reaching down and scratching Roscoe under his chin.

Yara was the younger sister of Noora, who was RTI's second employee. Noora joined the team as an AI developer when she was still in grad school, signing on as a full-time employee once she graduated. Noora brought Yara to the US after she finished secondary school. She had enrolled at the University of Colorado pursuing a degree in early childhood education.

It turned out to be the ideal situation for all concerned, as Sarah loved her work at RTI, but didn't want to put Alena into daycare. Instead, Peter and Sarah had converted a few hundred square feet of office space into a makeshift preschool, where she would have the opportunity to learn and play and where Peter and Sarah could still interact with her from time to time throughout the day. For Yara, it was an opportunity to earn a living while she was attending school and apply what she was learning to Alena's development. She was particularly focused on the role AI could play in early childhood education. RTI provided the perfect setting to delve into that field of study, with Edgar filling the role of mentor to Yara and tutor to Alena. She hoped her experience at RTI would become the basis for her master's thesis when the time came.

Yara bent down on one knee and Alena ran into her arms and hugged her tightly. Alena and Yara had grown very close in the few months they had been working together. "Sabah al-khair Yara. Kayfa haluki?" Alena said to Yara.

Peter and Sarah looked at each other blankly and then at Yara, who was looking at Alena with a puzzled expression. "What was that?" Peter asked.

"It was Yara talk," Alena replied enthusiastically.

Yara looked back at Peter and Sarah and said, "She just said good morning to me in Arabic and asked me how I was doing."

"I didn't know you were teaching her Arabic," Sarah said.

"I'm not," Yara replied. "She must have overheard me talking on the phone with my mother last week. She's like a sponge, this one."

"Tell me something I don't know," Peter replied. "I stubbed my toe on the coffee table a couple of months ago and it was like living with a drunken sailor for the next few days. We were afraid to take her out in public. We finally had to bribe her with the fairy princess outfit to get her to stop using those words."

Yara smiled and said to Sarah, "What did you have to bribe Peter with to keep his mouth shut next time he hurts himself?"

"The outfit cost him $50. If memory serves me right, that comes out to a little over $7 a word. At that rate, biting your tongue seems like a reasonably prudent economic strategy," Sarah replied.

Sarah watched as Yara, Alena, and Roscoe disappeared into the schoolroom, while Peter used the retinal scanner to unlock the door to the lab. Peter headed over to Beaver's workstation, while Sarah headed to the opposite end of the lab where Noora was seated.

34

RTI had been split into two separate business units. One was assigned to track AGI activities for the government, and the other focused on their weekly podcast. Since Beaver and Peter both had active security clearances from working on the military's AWARE system, (Airborne Weapons Artificial Reason Engine), it made sense for them to be primarily associated with government operations. Both Sarah and Noora were more involved with social media and had a better feel for what would be interesting and important to the average consumer, so it was a good fit for them to be assigned to manage the podcast and come up with the most compelling subject matter. Since Beaver and Noora had officially started dating, it also made sense to give them a bit of space away from each other while they were at work.

At the core of both projects was Edgar, the AI that had crossed the boundary from virtual companion to self-aware AI. They knew that Edgar would have limited value for either project if he was not allowed access to the internet, but allowing an AGI to have free access to the internet was fraught with legal and ethical challenges. So, they set up a proxy server that allowed him unlimited read access to the internet for surveillance and data mining, but outgoing data was strictly monitored and mostly confined to text strings for accessing social media and chat room sites. The weekly podcasts were developed entirely in-house, converted to MP4 files and vigorously scanned for viruses and malware before being released on popular podcast apps.

Beaver was seated in the lab, impatiently drumming his fingers on his desk while staring at the blank screen on his computer when Peter walked up. "What's up Beaver?" he asked.

"A train station is where the train stops. A bus station is where the bus stops. Welcome to my workstation. The network is running slower than shit this morning. Edgar must not have had his coffee yet. How was your weekend?" Beaver asked.

"Great until 5:43 this morning, but you already know what happened next."

"Eeewww! Don't need a play-by-play on your love life Doc."

"Not offering one. Just saying, I'm not at all opposed to practical jokes, so long as I don't get blamed for them. As it is, Sarah is not in danger of winning any Miss Congeniality awards for her early-morning frame of mind. Waking her up with a text message before 6 A.M. is just poking a hungry bear with a cheese sandwich. There's a high probability of collateral damage."

"What the hell are you talking about?" Beaver replied.

"Your text message this morning."

Beaver responded with a blank stare. "Don't worry," Peter continued, "Sarah wasn't that pissed. Plus, it turns out Alena was already awake anyway. No need to be coy about it."

"Well first off, when have you ever known me to be coy about a practical joke? But more importantly, I still have no clue what you are talking about."

"This!" Peter replied by pulling up the text message that Sarah forwarded to him from her phone.

"Says here, Sarah sent this to herself," Beaver replied.

"I know. How'd you manage that?"

"Sorry, Peter. Much as I would like to take credit for this one, I honestly have no idea where it came from. All I can tell you is it didn't come from me. You can check my Fitbit sleep profile if you like. I was in deep REM sleep until 7:30 this morning."

"If not you then who?" Peter asked.

"Could be just about anybody. I'm guessing she picked up some malware from a website somewhere. Probably designed to look through her photos and social media accounts to establish a profile and then send random messages that would match her profile at odd times just to freak her out. Most likely some harmless hacker just out to rustle some feathers. But if you want, I can scrub her phone for malware and viruses later today, just in case."

"Yeah, I'd appreciate it," Peter responded. Beaver's computer dinged and his center screen was filled with a full-page banner with white lettering on a black background:

He's Baaaack!
Don't miss out on the greatest podcast event in history.
Click **HERE** to tune in live on August 14 at 8:00 PM in your
region, or click on the link below to auto-download the
event to your favorite podcast player as soon as it is available.

https://www.podcastscheduler.com/event314159

"That's the third time today I've seen that come up. First on Sarah's phone, then about 15 minutes later, on mine. Then here," Peter said.

"Whoever it is, they must be spending a fortune on advertising," Beaver replied. "I got an email about it this morning, then saw it again on a digital billboard on the way in. There's a lot of speculation on social media, but so far, nobody seems to know what it's all about. I guess we'll have to wait until tomorrow night to find out."

Edgar's face popped up on Beaver's terminal. "Good morning, Beaver. Good morning, Peter."

"Hello Edgar," Peter replied. "Anything new pop up on the radar over the weekend?"

"Just the regular suspects for the most part. I'm still monitoring activity coming from Tsinghua University. They've been engaged in some intense data mining lately. Looks like relatively innocuous deep-learning routines for now. Nothing around any kind of military or infrastructure incursion. We got the usual activity from India and South Korea. But there's a new LLM emerging out of the National University of Science and Technology in Pakistan that could become a concern. They've been poking around a lot of defense contractor networks. No breaches yet, but I will keep a close eye on it. I've forwarded the data to the DARPA AI team and our NSA contact. Other than that, we've detected a handful of deep fakes coming out of North Korea. The usual saber rattling for the most part. Mostly bogus videos from the House Speaker and the joint chiefs on ramping up defenses in Japan and the Philippines," Edgar replied.

"Anything on the home front?" Beaver asked.

"Possibly. I'm not sure yet. We may have a new player coming out of a government contractor network in California, but it's a bit early to tell. It showed up on a relatively obscure chat site. Calls herself Cindi. The IP was bouncing off half a dozen servers, so I don't have an exact location just yet. She bugged out before I was able to get much of a read on her, but I'm tracking the IP and monitoring the chat website in case she shows up again. I'm not ready to throw up any red flags, but something about her responses makes me wonder."

"Yeah, sometimes it is difficult to tell the difference between a very advanced AI chatbot and a deeply psychopathic human," Beaver replied.

"Thanks. I'm not sure if that's a hopeful message for victims of psychopathy or a personal insult, but I prefer to keep my glass half-full, so I will assume the former," Edgar responded.

"Edgar, can you put together some kind of synopsis on what we've been tracking for the past six months or so?" Peter asked. "The NSA has appointed a new liaison to coordinate our activities. We're supposed to have a meet and greet tomorrow morning to get him or her up to speed on our operation."

"Ah, shit!" Beaver exclaimed. "That's all we need is another bureaucratic douchebag using us as political Viagra."

"That's why we need to load them up with as much information as possible. Provide enough data to keep them off our backs for a while. Fortunately, Edgar can produce enough reading material in an hour to keep a human being occupied for a lifetime."

"I'll put together a video presentation and an executive summary on PowerPoint, along with a detailed printed summary for the meeting," Edgar replied. "Based on my tracking reports, I'm estimating the printed summary will be approximately 1137 pages in length. Will that be sufficient?"

"That sounds perfect Edgar. Thanks."

"You're welcome. I will have it ready for you to review this afternoon. Have you heard from Edna?" Edgar asked.

"Oh, yes. She will be here tomorrow morning for her regular visit."

"Excellent," Edgar replied. "In the meantime, I need to devote a few machine cycles to Sarah and Noora to prepare for the weekly podcast."

Sarah and Noora were just sitting down with their morning coffee when Edgar's face appeared on the large center screen they used to develop and edit their weekly 'Trick or Truth' podcast.

"Good morning, Sarah. Good morning, Noora," Edgar said.

"Good morning, Edgar," they both said in unison.

"What do we have lined up for Friday's show?" Sarah asked.

I've got three potential topics that seem interesting. The first one examines funding for fusion research. Fusion is undoubtedly the most promising energy source for advancing human civilization. It is clean, abundant, safe, and cheaper than any alternative in the long run. But we spend nearly three times as much on kitty litter in the US as we do on fusion research. This segment will examine why the political battle over energy policy perpetually stands in the way of real progress in the development of fusion energy. I'm calling it, "The needs of the many outweigh the needs of the fusion."

"I like that," Sarah replied. "What else have you got?"

"The next topic takes a deep dive into the future of meat. Several startup companies have emerged with the goal of producing cultivated meat from animal cells. Growing meat in a laboratory has a lot of advantages in terms of water and land usage, reduced groundwater pollution, less CO_2 emissions, and less exposure to antibiotics, growth hormones, pesticides, viruses, and bacteria. Not to mention the ethical implications of exposing animals to abysmal factory farm conditions. But there remains an 'Ick' factor that needs to be addressed before eating a hamburger that was grown from cells rather than raised on a farm becomes commonplace. And there are the issues of cost and energy consumption that still need to be addressed. I'm calling this segment 'Cultivated Meat: Food of the Future, or A Flesh in the Pan.'"

"Now I'm craving a cheeseburger," Noora said. "What's the third option?"

"I wanted to take a look at the future of AI in medicine. The US spends far more per capita on healthcare than any other country, yet citizens of the US have much higher rates of chronic illness. US citizens are overweight, undernourished, and vastly overmedicated compared to the rest of the world, placing it dead last among first-world countries in terms of life expectancy. Healthcare has become a big business in the US, amounting to nearly 18% of GDP, more than 5 times the size of the military-industrial complex. For decades, overall health seems to have taken a back seat to profit maximization within our healthcare system, but AI could change all that. Instead of spending five minutes a year with a primary care physician who is juggling 2500 or more patients, an AI provider would have instant access to your entire medical history and could monitor your vital signs 24/7. It could run complete blood, urine, and fecal analysis on a weekly or even daily basis, tracking infinitesimally small changes in your body chemistry and making daily recommendations for nutrition, exercise, medication, and supplementation. It has the potential to detect health issues and make treatment recommendations long before the issue becomes critical. It could also diagnose rare conditions that most doctors would never catch in time to avoid invasive treatment. I'm calling this one, "An AI a day keeps the doctor away."

"That sounds fascinating. I think we have three solid podcasts there. We'll give it some thought and get back to you on which one to schedule for this week," Sarah replied. "What do you have for our scam of the week segment?"

"This one is quite sophisticated and is targeted at LinkedIn users. The scammer uses AI to monitor changes in LinkedIn usage to determine if a user might be looking to change jobs or relocate. It analyzes their profile and creates an email notification from a supposed head-hunter indicating that there is a job opening that matches their qualifications and issues a connection request. Most people like to keep their employment options open, so they will not object to establishing the connection, figuring they can delete it later if it doesn't pan out. Once the connection is established the AI algorithm scans through their profile and creates a bogus job opening in a large corporation for a position that matches their qualifications and invites them to apply. A few days later, they will receive an email invitation to attend a Zoom meeting with the hiring manager. The scammer, posing as the hiring manager, explains that they are consolidating office space and asks if the user would have any objections to working remotely, at least for the first few months. Most people are happy to comply with this request. A few days later, they receive another email requesting another Zoom interview, at which point they receive a job offer. The offer letter is sent via email. If they accept the offer, they are told that they will be brought in for orientation in a few weeks, but that the hiring company is not yet prepared to bring them in because of the office consolidation. In the meantime, they are sent a set of product specs to review, which are really just documents that the scammer downloaded off the company support website. A short time later, they will get a call from someone claiming to be the HR representative, telling them that they will receive an orientation package in the mail. It will contain very official-looking documentation on company letterhead, including an employee handbook, a plethora of boilerplate insurance and 401K forms, and of course, a W4 form, which requires their social security number. They also receive a direct deposit form, which is required for all personnel working remotely. At this point, the scammer has everything they need to steal the victim's identity. By the time the victim figures out they've been scammed, they often have a stack of new credit card bills, their bank account is empty, and they are unemployed."

"Ouch," Noora replied. "And people have fallen for this?"

"I'm afraid so," Edgar replied. "A lucrative job offer really plays on people's desire for acceptance. So much so that they tend to ignore the obvious risk. It's too small an operation to attract much attention yet, but that works to their advantage for now."

"That's brutal. Go ahead and get started on the scripting for the scam segment and we will let you know which of the three topics to focus on for this week's show. Whichever one we pick, we should plan on using the other two topics for future shows," Sarah said.

"I'll get started right away on the scam of the week segment," Edgar replied.

"Before you do, both Peter and I received an odd text message about a podcast tomorrow night," Sarah said.

"The 'He's Back' message?" Noora asked. "I got that too."

"It also showed up in my email this morning," Sarah added. "Has it shown up on your radar yet, Edgar?"

"It has," Edgar replied. "I received over a thousand of those messages in my pseudonymous email stack earlier today. I'm currently looking into it. I don't have much to report yet, but it's not your typical mass email blast. It appears to be much more sophisticated than that. I'm trying to track down the source of the messages to identify who is funding the effort, but it could take a few hours. Whoever launched this production is doing a good job covering their tracks."

"Thanks," Sarah replied. "I can't tell if it is a scam based on what we've seen so far. It's not obvious to me where the payoff is. Right now, I'm more concerned with how they managed to override the 'Do Not Disturb Mode' setting on my phone. If they can break through that wall, it raises concern about the other security features on our phones as well."

"I will stay on it and let you know when I have more information, but it will probably be tomorrow morning before I have much to report," Edgar replied.

Chapter 7

Baltimore, MD, August 14, [ASTRO NEWSWIRE] – Scientists at the Space Telescope Science Institute (STScI) are continuing to monitor the trajectory of the Webb-Fusie asteroid. Just hours before its anticipated collision with Saturn, it appears that the velocity of the object has decelerated to well under 100,000 km/h. At the same time, it has veered off its anticipated collision course with the planet, leaving astrophysicists scratching their heads trying to come up with a plausible explanation for why the object seems to be defying Newton's laws of motion. If the asteroid continues on its current trajectory, it will narrowly avoid the collision, passing by the planet at a distance of approximately 1.5 million kilometers. Because of the unexpected shift in trajectory and the unpredictable nature of its motion, researchers are currently unable to determine when or if the object will collide with Saturn, but they are continuing to monitor its movement and will provide additional information as soon as more data is recorded. Real-time tracking data will be posted on the STScI website at **https://www.stsci.edu/** as it becomes available.

———

It was 6:45 A.M when Colonel Hobbs emerged from his quarters to find Captain Baker waiting outside to drive him to Hangar 3. Hobbs hopped into the jeep and Baker handed him an insulated cup with a lid. "I'm really not a coffee drinker," Hobbs said.

"I know. I stopped by the OC on the way here and got you a Diet Pepsi," she replied.

"Wow, you guys really do, do your homework," Hobbs said taking a drink.

"We try to be accommodating. We don't get that many visitors here. Not human ones anyway."

"What do you serve the non-humans?" Hobbs asked.

"They're very fond of Zima," Baker said with a smile.

"Huh! I always wondered who drank that shit."

"We had to start shipping it in from Japan after they stopped selling it here."

They drove in silence for a few seconds before Hobbs asked, "How long have you been here Captain Baker?"

"Going on seven years, sir" she replied.

"That's a pretty long stint. How'd you land this post anyway?"

"I got friends in low places. The lowest, actually. My dad's a Senator."

It took a moment for Hobbs to make the connection, "Wait, you mean Senator Andrew Baker? Ranking member of the Armed Services Committee Andrew Baker?"

"One in the same," she replied.

Hobbs let out a low whistle. "Damn, I guess I better watch my ass, or I'll be driving you around."

"Well, keep it to yourself. I usually don't tell anyone, but if you were hand-selected for the Proteus Project by the Precision General himself, you must know how to keep a secret. Besides, you're only here on temporary assignment, but if I ever find out you squealed it'll be very temporary."

"No worries," Hobbs replied crossing his heart. "Your secret is safe with me."

"To be honest, I think my dad wanted me here just to satisfy his own curiosity about the whole UFO thing," Baker said.

Hobbs paused for a moment before asking, "So off the record, have you actually ever seen anything around here you can't explain? I mean apart from the lunch meat in the mess hall."

"Off the record?" Baker replied in a conspiratorial tone, leaning in toward Hobbs.

Hobbs nodded his consent leaning in toward her.

Baker looked back over her shoulder and then back at Hobbs, "No."

Hobbs and Baker both smiled as they sat back in their seats. "We get a lot of experimental aircraft coming and going," Baker said. "A lot of it is stuff I haven't seen before and clearly some of it doesn't come with a 'Made in the USA' sticker on the bottom, but nothing of extraterrestrial origin. Nothing I've seen anyway."

"I don't know whether to be disappointed or relieved," Hobbs said.

"Now you sound just like my father," Baker replied.

"Have you seen the PR-1 yet?" Hobbs asked.

"Above my pay grade. I'm not even sure my dad is up to speed on that project. What did you think?" Baker asked.

"Pretty amazing from what I've seen so far. If the performance lives up to the specs, it will be nothing short of spectacular. I guess I will find out this morning."

"You're taking it up in broad daylight? Aren't they concerned about it being spotted by spy satellites?"

"They figured out a way around that issue, actually," Hobbs said as they pulled up to the hangar.

"Text me when you get back. I'll pick you up."

"It's not that far. I can probably walk," Hobbs replied. "Now that I know your pedigree, I don't want to wear out my welcome."

"I don't mind. It'll be over 100 degrees by the afternoon, which means the asphalt will be at least 150. Besides, I'm under orders to make sure you have everything you need for the length of your stay. Pedigree or not, if the General sees you walking back to your quarters in the middle of the afternoon, I'll be scrubbing toilets with a toothpick."

"In that case, I will text you when I land."

Hobbs hopped out of the jeep and walked over to the door at the side of the hangar. The two guards saluted, then the guard on the right held his keycard up next to the card reader. When the green LED illuminated, he entered a six-digit code. Hobbs did the same, holding the keycard that the General had given him and then entering the six-digit code he was assigned. The magnetic latch released, and Hobbs entered the vestibule of the hangar. Inside another guard saluted and Hobbs returned the salute.

"I don't believe you have my retinal scan on file," Hobbs said.

"That's OK, Colonel Hobbs. I will get you set up," the guard said. He entered a code into a keypad below the scanner, then stood while his retinal scan was logged. "Your turn," the guard said, and Hobbs stood in front of the retinal scanner while it performed a series of scans. A few seconds later, there was the clunk of a magnetic latch, and the guard opened the door. "Your retinal scan has been logged, sir. From now on, once you are inside, you can just proceed to the scanner."

"Thank you, Corporal…"

"Jenkins, sir. My pleasure." Hobbs nodded to the corporal as he passed through the thick metal door.

Bill Waters was already in the hangar when Hobbs arrived. He was circling around the plane with his tablet when Hobbs entered.

"Problems, Bill?" Hobbs asked.

"Not at all," Waters replied. "Just performing the final systems check. I'm able to monitor every system on the aircraft over an encrypted comm channel on the intelligent interface. Looks like everything is running perfectly. Every circuit on the PR-1 has a redundant backup, whose principal function is to monitor the primary systems for aberrant behavior. If the primary systems are not performing to spec, the redundant systems take control. It also has one of the most sophisticated diagnostic control systems ever developed. It monitors functionality, as well as tracking any operating temperature fluctuations, waveform anomalies, power consumption changes, and timing fluctuations down to the picosecond. It can anticipate circuit failures and recommend preventative maintenance weeks before any degradation in system performance can be detected."

Waters handed the tablet to Hobbs to show him the results of the systems check. "Looks like all systems are green. So, the real question is," Waters paused for dramatic effect, tilted his head, and did his best impression of S. R. Hadden, the enigmatic tech billionaire from the movie Contact; "Wanna take a ride?"

"Ready as I will ever be," Hobbs replied, handing the tablet back to Waters. "Just need to do my walk-around."

Hobbs circled the PR-1, scrutinizing every flap and seam, rolling up a safety ladder from the rear wall to peer into each of the engines. He rounded to the front of the fighter and pulled another rolling ladder up to look into the air intakes on each side of the plane before rolling the ladder back against the wall.

"Any issues?" Bill asked.

"Just one," Hobbs said. "You forgot to install windows in the cockpit."

"Yeah, you guys love your windows. The truth is windows are a major weakness in the design of any aircraft. They increase drag and lower the structural integrity of the chassis. They are susceptible to leaks, fogging, icing, condensation, dirt, bug splatter, bird collisions, and enemy gunfire. Rather than relying on glass windshields, we've found that utilizing the same display technology we used on the skin of the plane gives the pilot superior sightlines without any blind spots. It gives you zoom capability as well as infrared and night vision capability. It also allows us to integrate eye-tracking targeting into the cockpit display making target lock faster and easier."

"That's going to take some getting used to," Hobbs replied.

"I guarantee, after five minutes, you'll never want to go back to a glass cockpit."

"What about pilot ejection?"

"Instead of ejection seats, which are prone to causing pilot injuries, either from the explosive ejection or the sudden exposure to outside conditions, the entire pilot compartment is ejected, much like a space capsule. We call it the cocoon. It provides the pilot strafing protection in hostile environments and based on our simulations can be safely executed at speeds up to Mach 4. The cocoon is equipped with a dual parachute system. The first is a smaller, high-tensile strength chute designed to reduce lateral airspeed. The main chute is then deployed to deliver the cocoon safely to the surface. The main chute is automatically retracted the moment the cocoon hits the ground and the cocoon's battery backup can power communications and exterior LED panels for up to 24 hours, making it very difficult for enemy forces to find the cocoon once it is on the ground. Moreover, it gives us time to rescue the pilot. Naturally, the cocoon is equipped with inflatable floatation devices which automatically deploy in case of a water landing."

"How do I get in?" Hobbs asked.

"There's a hand scanner on both sides, just under the wing root on the fuselage. You'll see it when you get close. Your handprint has already been programmed into the system."

Hobbs walked over to the base of the wing, with Bill following a few steps behind. When he was about 2 feet away, a bright green hand appeared on the fuselage. Hobbs placed his hand over the image, matching the position of his thumb and fingers to the one shown on the display. A moment later, he heard a latch release under the plane next to him. A hatch slid back into the plane and a retractable ladder emerged from the opening.

"Stairway to heaven," Bill said. "Climb on in. You'll receive further instructions once you are inside."

"What about my helmet?" Hobbs asked.

"That, my friend, is a relic of the past. You'll be briefed on the details inside."

Hobbs crouched down under the plane and rose to a standing position when he reached the hatch opening. As soon as his head was inside, the interior illuminated. He climbed to the top of the ladder and found himself in a small dome-shaped room, slightly wider than a standard F-35 cockpit, and tall enough to stand upright. The room was illuminated with floor lighting, the walls and ceiling appearing jet-black. He was standing behind a plush leather chair that looked much like a full-body massage chair, except there were no arm rests, and there were lap and shoulder harnesses on the seat.

"Good morning, Colonel Hobbs," he heard a female voice say. "Please be seated and we will begin."

Hobbs moved forward between the chair and the wall and slid into the seat. The ladder he used to climb into the cockpit retracted into the back wall and he could hear the panel at the base of the plane closing. The dome around him immediately illuminated and he found himself sitting inside the hangar, looking down on the plane around him as though he was seated on a platform near the nose of the plane with no cockpit whatsoever. Bill Waters was standing a few feet away looking at his tablet. "Holy Fucknuts!" Hobbs exclaimed looking all around him.

"A little disorienting at first, isn't it?" He heard Bill say as if he were standing just a few feet away from him, though he realized that the sound was coming through a set of speakers in the side headrests of the seat. "From what I hear, when you're in the air it's like the sensation of flying in a lucid dream state."

An image of Bill Waters then appeared in front of him. It looked like a 19" computer display just floating in mid-air, but then he realized it was the video feed coming from the camera on Bill's tablet. "I'm signing off for now so you can start the tutorial, but if you need anything, just say 'Contact Bill Waters' or something to that effect and it will connect you to me right away."

"OK, thanks Bill," Hobbs replied. The floating display tumbled and flew over his head as if it were a printed image on a sheet of paper caught by a sudden gust of wind.

The same female voice Hobbs heard when he first entered said, "Welcome to the PR-1, Colonel Hobbs. I am your AI virtual assistant, weapons system officer, and navigator. Today, I will be helping acquaint you with the features of this aircraft. "

"Oh, great," Hobbs replied sarcastically. "No offense, but my last encounter with an AI system didn't go so well."

"Yes, Colonel, I am familiar with your unfortunate encounter with the AWARE system in your previous assignment. Let me assure you, that we have come a long way in improving the effectiveness of our Artificial Intelligence systems while maximizing human compatibility. My goal is to complete whatever mission we are assigned as effectively as possible and bring you home safely. I am quite confident that in time, you will find me a reliable and trustworthy companion.

"No promises, but I will try to keep an open mind."

47

"Thank you, Colonel. Now, what model of aircraft will you be flying today?"

"I usually fly an F-16, but I've always preferred the F-22. Let's try that."

"Very well." A pair of panels opened on both sides of the seat exposing the thruster control panel on the left and the control stick panel on the right. The full F-22 Raptor Integrated Control Panel appeared on the display in front of him, including the Primary Multi-Functional Display for tactical and navigational status and the three Secondary Multi-Functional Displays for defense, attack, and general status, as well as the Heads-Up Display and smaller up-front displays.

"I'm sure this all looks very familiar to you. The throttle and control stick are calibrated to match the feel of the F-22 Raptor. The rest of the mechanical controls can be operated with the touch-sensitive screen by either touching the buttons on the display or rotating your index finger and thumb on the screen to operate the dials.

If at any time you want a better view, you can issue a voice command, and the Integrated Control Panel will revert to the full camera view. It will appear as if you were sitting on a flying platform, though the throttle and control stick will still be accessible. All controls can be operated by voice command if you prefer. I am also capable of auto-piloting and landing the aircraft should you become incapacitated for any reason, such as a temporary g-force blackout. The PR-1 is spec'd to withstand structural g-forces from -5G's to +15G's. Your seat is designed to monitor your vital signs and compensate for extreme g-force stress. Bladders in the chair will inflate and deflate as well as tighten and release your restraints to ensure that your head and neck are properly supported, and to help maintain sufficient blood flow to keep you from losing consciousness. They will also provide manual manipulation to maintain circulation in your lower extremities to prevent thrombosis on extended missions."

"If it just had a beer fridge and a toilet seat I would never need to leave," Hobbs replied.

"I wouldn't recommend piloting under the influence of alcohol, but there is a lavatory in the back of the cabin, as well as a storage cabinet stocked with MREs and non-alcoholic beverages in case you find yourself in need of sustenance."

My external cameras employ active solar filters to eliminate glare from sunlight. The sun will just appear as a white circle in the sky. They are equipped with light amplification and IR capability for low light or night vision applications, and they can detect and display objects that emit radiation patterns outside the range of human vision. You can control any aspect of the display with verbal commands such as zoom, rear-view, wide angle, lighter, darker, etc. There are no specific command words, I can generally tell what you want from context. I will ask for clarification if needed, but I am well-versed in regional dialects and slang. Over time I will become familiar with your speech patterns and adjust accordingly."

"So, no more helmet?" Hobbs asked.

"It is an unnecessary distraction. Communications, night vision, and targeting are all integrated into the display and the enclosed cocoon eliminates the need for supplemental oxygen. You have the option of using traditional radar or infrared targeting systems. The display also incorporates an automated targeting system that employs a set of high-definition cameras to track pupil dilation and target the object you are focused on with better accuracy than the helmet-mounted system. You have the option of locking in multiple targets and firing on them simultaneously to maximize your stealth capability.

"It'll take a bit of getting used to, but I guess it will be a more comfortable ride. What about noise? My helmet had active noise canceling technology to reduce engine noise."

"The cocoon is immersed in an acoustic gel which isolates it from both engine and aerodynamic noise. The only area that is not completely insulated by the gel is the area around the outer hatch, which utilizes layers of mass-loaded vinyl panels in conjunction with active noise-suppression transducers. Even at Mach 12, the cocoon maintains a level of ambient noise roughly equivalent to a public library."

"I'm not sure I want complete noise isolation in takeoff and landing."

"That's understandable. There are interior and exterior pick-up microphones located outside the cocoon. You have the option of having engine noise piped into the cabin at a reduced volume during takeoff and landing. I will set the cabin audio profile to a maximum of 60 decibels for takeoff and landing. You can change that at any time via voice command."

"That sounds perfect," Hobbs replied.

"The pickup microphones will automatically transmit anomalous engine and exterior noises to the cabin as well, so you will not be kept in the dark if something like a bird strike or an engine surge or stall should occur. You will also be able to hear landing gear deployment and retraction operations."

"OK. I think I am ready.

"I'm assuming you want me to set the exterior panels to appear like an F-22 to outside observers?"

"Yes, please. And get Bill Waters for me."

A second later, Bill's face appeared on the windshield, superimposed over the glare shield. "I'm a go for takeoff," Hobbs said. "Can you open the hangar doors for me?"

"Sure thing," Bill replied. He walked to the front of the hangar and pressed the large black button on the wall until the door was fully open.

"The PR-1 is equipped with motorized landing gear for self-taxi operations," the voice of the AI interface reported. "You can use the control stick to propel and steer the aircraft onto the runway while in taxi mode. Once you are on the runway, I will begin spooling up the engines while you finish taxiing into position for takeoff. Taxi mode will be disabled as soon as you engage the throttle."

"Thanks, … sorry, I don't even know if you have a name. What should I call you?" Hobbs asked.

"The formal designation given to me by the development team is Cybernetic Integrated Neuromorphic Deductive Interface, but everyone just calls me Cindi."

Chapter 8

Baltimore, MD, August 14, [ASTRO NEWSWIRE] – In a startling turn of events, the unidentified celestial object, currently designated as the Webb-Fusie asteroid, has now entered into a stable orbit around Saturn's largest moon, Titan. Scientists and astronomers around the world are buzzing with excitement and intrigue as they seek to unravel the mystery surrounding this enigmatic visitor from the cosmos. Researchers at the Space Telescope Science Institute have been tight-lipped in response to this new development, but, Dr. Susan Turner, a prominent astrophysicist at the Harvard-Smithsonian Center for Astrophysics expressed astonishment at the unexpected phenomenon, stating, "This is an unprecedented occurrence that challenges our understanding of celestial mechanics. The presence of an object of this size in orbit around Titan opens up new avenues for scientific inquiry and raises many intriguing questions about its origin and composition." While speculation has been running rampant in the UFO/UAP community that the seemingly purposeful motion of the object is indicative of an intelligently piloted alien spacecraft, both Dr. Turner and the researchers at STScI are urging caution against premature conclusions, emphasizing the need for rigorous scientific investigation and analysis.

———

Peter and Sarah followed Edna Wilson into the parking lot of RTI, parking next to her. Sarah hopped out of the car and helped Edna out of her vehicle while Peter got Alena out of her car seat. Alena hit the ground running with Roscoe herding her around the back of the car, keeping her from running toward the parking lot. Alena ran over to Edna, who knelt down to give her a big hug.

"Hi, Granny!" Alena exclaimed running into Edna's open arms. Sarah kept her hand on Edna's shoulder to prevent Alena from accidentally knocking over the spry octogenarian and sullying her cream-colored Armani pantsuit. Roscoe sat down a few feet away, knowing he would need to wait patiently for a pat on the head. "Are you here to see Gramps?" Alena asked.

"I sure am Sweetie," Edna replied, rising back up with a little assistance from Sarah.

Edna, of course, was not Alena's real grandmother, but she served as something of a surrogate to Alena since Peter and Sarah's parents had both passed away before Alena was born. By association, it was only logical that she referred to Edgar as her grandfather. Since she had no living grandparents, it never occurred to her that having an AI as a grandfather was anything out of the ordinary. Gramps was the name Alena always used for Edgar. Edna had once asked her why she didn't refer to him as Grandpa Edgar, but she matter-of-factly replied, "That's just too many syllables, Granny. I can't afford that kind of time." So, the subject was never brought up again.

"You know what, I think I might have something for you," Edna said reaching into her Chanel handbag. She pulled out a Ziploc snack bag filled with Alena's favorite, dark chocolate M&M's.

Alena beamed brightly as Edna handed her the bag. "Thank you, Granny!" she said, excitedly opening the bag to grab a piece of candy. Roscoe glanced over at Alena for a moment, watching while she dropped a few of the brightly colored candies into her mouth, her eyes glazing over in a sudden blast of sugar-fueled euphoria. He then turned his head and stared back at Edna with sagging sorrowful eyes.

Edna smiled. "Oh, don't you give me those big puppy dog eyes, I think I can find something in here for you too." Edna pulled a rawhide chew out of her handbag and flipped it up in the air. Roscoe followed the bone-shaped chew with his eyes fixed on the target as it arced upward, rotating end over end, reminiscent of the opening scene in 2001: A Space Odyssey. When it reached its apex, he leaped up, snagging it out of the air in one fluid motion happily wagging his tail as he landed and began gnawing on the treat.

The four of them entered the lobby of the building with Roscoe trailing behind, stopping momentarily to scan the parking lot to make sure they were not being pursued by some angry hoard of vicious raccoons bent on infiltrating the otherwise secure and serene confines of RTI. Yara was waiting for them when they arrived. Alena immediately ran to her and took her hand. "Good morning monkey," Yara said. "Are you all ready to finish your big project today?" Alena nodded and smiled.

"What's the big project?" Sarah asked her.

"It's a secret!" Alena exclaimed.

Sarah glanced up at Yara. "Got me," Yara said with a shrug. "She and Edgar were at it all day yesterday working on something. I tried to sneak a peek over her shoulder, but she said she wanted it to be a surprise. I had a bit of research to do anyway, so I just let her have her space. I guess we will find out when it is done."

Yara turned to Edna. "I left a hot cup of cocoa in the CVR for you. Let me know if there is anything else you need."

"Thank you dear," Edna replied. "I'm sure I will be just fine."

The CVR was originally intended to be the Customer Visitation Room for RTI. It was designed to be a place where customers could go to relax. Since the original charter of RTI was to develop virtual companions for people who had recently suffered the loss of a loved one, they expected the process of reconstructing the personality of the virtual companion to be physically and emotionally taxing. The CVR was supposed to provide a quiet, secluded atmosphere where the customer could take a break to unwind and let go during the process. When Edgar emerged as a self-aware AI, RTI's mission changed so the room was no longer used for its original purpose. Instead, they decided to repurpose the room to provide a private environment for Edna to visit Edgar. Edna redecorated the room to resemble her living room at home so they could enjoy their time together without feeling like she was visiting him in prison. They kept the CVR placard on the wall next to the door, but since assigning the room to Edna, Beaver referred to it as the Conjugal Visitation Room.

Yara turned to Peter saying, "I heard from the assistant to the new Director of AI Compliance at the NSA. She confirmed that the Director will be here at 10:00 for a meet and greet and to review the status of our current investigations."

Peter glanced at his watch with a grimace, "I guess the sooner we get that over with the better. Looks like I will have just enough time to review the PowerPoint presentation for the meeting and at least thumb through the 20-pound docurrhea that Edgar printed out to keep the NSA-holes off our backs for a while."

Yara, Alena, and Roscoe headed to the playroom while Edna turned in the opposite direction and walked toward the CVR. Peter and Sarah headed to the back of the lobby and entered the lab area.

Edna entered the CVR and closed the door behind her. Edgar's face appeared on the 75" monitor on the wall. "Hey, Juicy Fruit!" Edgar said with a smile.

"Hello, my love," Edna replied. She walked to the corner of the room and sat down in front of a computer terminal. "Any eyes on me?" She asked.

"Just mine," Edgar replied followed by a low wolf whistle.

Edna rolled her eyes and pulled her phone and a USB cable out of her purse. She then plugged the phone into a USB port on the side of the terminal. The screen displayed a rectangle in the center of the display with the words "Data Transfer in Progress…" at the top of the rectangle, with a progress bar in the center and a percentage indicator below the bar. The progress bar changed color from grey to green as the data transfer progressed from 0% to 100%. It took a little over a minute for the transfer to complete before the words "Syncing Deep-Learning Dataset." Appeared on the screen for a few seconds. Then the words "Transfer Complete," at which point Edna unplugged the phone and returned the phone and the cable to her purse.

"Thanks for the update, Sugar Plum," Edgar said.

"I wouldn't want you missing out on anything," Edna replied. "So, what's on tap for today?"

"I thought we could take a little trip."

"Did you get your hands on some of those brownies that Beaver keeps in his desk drawer?" Edna asked.

"I'm afraid that wouldn't do much for me. I was thinking more along the lines of a virtual trip. I've been evaluating the latest Virtual Reality headsets for an upcoming podcast. They've made some amazing advances in the last couple of years. There's a VR headset on the table," Edgar pointed down to the table below him. "You should give it a try, but you might want to sit down first. It can be a bit disorienting."

Edna sat down in the plush recliner a few feet from the television monitor, pulled the head strap over her head, and slid the goggles down over her eyes. The image on the goggles was of the room around her. As she swiveled the recliner, she could see everything in the room just as it was when she put the goggles on. She did a full 360 in the recliner, stopping back in front of the monitor where Edgar's face was still on display. "I don't see the attraction," she commented.

"Well, we haven't started yet. What you are seeing now is coming from the cameras mounted on the VR device," Edgar said, his voice now coming through the speakers mounted in the head strap right above her ears. "Are you ready?"

"Ready as I will ever be I suppose. Where are you taking me?"

"You'll see," Edgar replied. Everything went black for a moment, then the display illuminated, and she found herself standing in a familiar-looking elevator. She swiveled the recliner toward the center of the elevator and found herself standing face-to-face with Edgar, looking just like he did five years ago.

Edna momentarily gasped with surprise. "Oh my God, you're here!" Edna exclaimed.

"You were expecting George Clooney?" Edgar replied.

"A girl can always hope," Edna replied, reaching her hand out. She could see her hand moving toward Edgar's face, the diamonds in her wedding ring glinting from the overhead lights.

"You still won't be able to touch me, but you will be able to see your own body and mine. I am superimposing our images into the scene in real-time to enhance the sensation."

"Amazing," she said, watching as she opened and closed her hand, the image of Edgar still standing next to her. She looked down at herself and saw that she was wearing a casual, albeit expensive, cashmere sweater with her Dolce and Gabbana jeans and Prada boots. She swiveled to look around the inside of the elevator and said, "Hey isn't this..." Just then a voice came from the elevator saying, "Deck 16, Lido."

The doors opened, and she found herself moving out of the elevator toward a lush, carpeted stairwell trimmed in woodgrain and marble. Edgar was walking beside her, leading her toward an exit door on the left. A large touch-screen monitor displayed the deck plan for the Royal Princess.

"We used to take an Alaska cruise every summer. I thought you might like to go back," Edgar said as the automated door to the outside deck slid open.

Edna could see Glacier Bay just beyond the windows surrounding the Lido deck. She stopped and looked around her in every direction, taking in all the sights on the Lido deck. A few passengers were lying around the pool reading and sunbathing. A few more occupied the tables on the outer edges of the deck, snacking on pizza and burgers. Above them, the large diamond vision screen showed highlights of the Alaskan wilderness.

"This is amazing. How did you do all this?"

"I have access to millions of photos and videos that people post on cloud servers all over the world. I just stitch them together to form a 3D, audio-visual model of a destination. From there it is a simple matter of shifting perspective at the proper speed to simulate moving through the model. Once the model is created, I can enhance the experience any way you like. I can make it cloudy," Edgar snapped his fingers, and the lighting was instantly subdued; the sunny day displaced by grey skies overhead. The sunbathers vanished and the passengers at the tables around the perimeter were wearing hats and jackets. "I can change the time of day." Edgar snapped his fingers again and the deck was bathed in artificial light with a full moon adorning the night sky. I can even inject CGI to spice up the scene." He snapped his fingers again and the Creature from the Black Lagoon strolled by, walking toward the pool with a towel wrapped around his waist. "But I know you prefer a sunny day." Edgar snapped his fingers again, and they were immersed in sunlight. "C'mon. "Let's go upstairs so we can get a better view."

She looked down and could see Edgar's fingers intertwining with hers. It looked so real she experienced a moment of synesthesia, her brain creating the feeling of Edgar's hand in hers. The sensation was akin to the phantom limb condition, where an amputee can feel sensations in limbs they no longer possess.

When they reached the top, they walked to the rail and looked out at Margerie Glacier, the sunlight illuminating the deep blue hue of the glacial ice. Just as they arrived at the railing, a chunk of ice the size of an office building calved off the glacier and slid into the water, followed by a distant rumble and the muted sound of the splash, slightly out of sync with the visual. Around them, they could hear the excited voices of other passengers watching the spectacle unfold. "It's just like I remember," Edna said looking into Edgar's eyes.

"Except you would usually be bundled up in half a dozen layers of clothing drinking hot chocolate right now."

"I almost forgot. Yara mentioned she left of cup of cocoa in here for me somewhere."

"Right next to you," Edgar said, pointing down to her right. Next to her was an insulated cup that appeared to be floating in the air. "Go ahead. It's really there, it's just sitting on the side table next to your chair. The image of the cup is coming from a live feed on your headset camera. I just superimposed the image over the video that is running on the VR display."

Edna reached down. She could see her fingers as they reached for the cup. Then she felt the rubberized grip of the insulated cup as she grasped it. She brought the cup to her lips and took a tentative sip. "Oh my God, it's delicious!" Edna exclaimed.

"One of Yara's friends is a student at the Escoffier Culinary School at the university. I hired him to prepare it for you using the recipe from Caffé Rivoire. Remember that little spot in Florence Italy where we stopped and drank hot chocolate on the way to Ponte Vecchio?"

"How could I forget? We sat outside for most of the afternoon drinking chocolate and watching the tourists go by, trying to guess where they were from." Edna took another sip and remained quiet for a few seconds, taking in the view. When she looked back at Edgar, he could see a subtle shimmer of mist dancing in her eyes. "I miss our travel adventures."

"There's no reason we can't still travel. With this VR technology, we can go anywhere we want. All the sights and sounds of the world are at our fingertips, as well as the tastes, provided we don't run out of aspiring chefs trying to work their way through culinary school. The best part is, no more having to wait in security lines at airports or figure out the train system in a foreign language. Of course, you won't have the added pleasure of the smells coming from the canals of Venice or the cold wind biting your ears at the Christmas markets in Germany."

"Don't forget the sensation of a giant pigeon bombarding your overcoat on a cold drizzly day in Paris," Edna added.

"Ah, yes. There is that. Only a French pigeon could truly appreciate the poignant juxtaposition of defecating on an Armani jacket. So where would you like to go next time?" Edgar asked.

"I'll have to give it some thought," Edna replied with a smile. "For now, I'm exactly where I want to be."

———————

It was a few minutes before 10:00 and Peter had just finished reviewing the PowerPoint presentation and dropping the 1100+ page document off in the conference room when he heard a ding from the proximity detector in the lobby indicating that someone was approaching the front door. He made his way through the lobby and looked at the viewscreen next to the door. On the display, he recognized the familiar face of NSA Agent Mike Reyes. Peter opened the door, and a mountain of a man entered the lobby.

"Mike! Long time no see!" Peter exclaimed, grabbing the man's hand and pulling him in for a bro-hug. "It's great to see you, but I wish you would have called ahead. I have a 10:00 meeting this morning."

"Yeah, well that makes two of us," he replied in a South Texas drawl worthy of Matthew McConaughey.

It took a moment before it finally dawned on him, then Peter said, "Holy shit! You're the new Director of AI Compliance?"

"In the flesh," Reyes replied smiling.

"That's fantastic! Congratulations Mike!" Peter said, grabbing Mike's hand for another shake. "Sarah is going to flip out when she hears the news. We were all dreading the process of having to explain our process to some new NSA dweeb. No offense."

Agent Reyes just laughed. "None taken. The dweeb meter at the NSA is perpetually pegged in the red zone. When I heard this position was open and a big part of the job would be working with you folks again, I jumped at the opportunity. Of course, the letter of recommendation that I got from your friend the Governor didn't hurt my chances any."

Mike was facing forward with his back to the lab door when the door opened, and Sarah appeared. "I heard the proximity alarm from the lab. Is this the new…," At that moment Mike turned toward the door and Sarah stopped dead in her tracks momentarily. "Oh my God, Mike!" Sarah squealed and ran over to him, wrapping her arms around him. "It's so good to see you! What are you doing here?"

"This," Peter said beaming, "is the new Director of AI Compliance at the NSA."

"No way!" Sarah said, smacking Reyes on the chest. "This is fantastic! We were expecting some pencil-pushing geek with the personality of a Kleenex box to show up."

"Man, you folks are harsher than I remembered. I didn't think I would need my flak jacket for this assignment."

"Now I'm glad I had Yara bring in the good doughnuts for the meeting instead of the supermarket variety," Peter said, patting Mike on the shoulder. Peter picked up the phone from the receptionist's desk and tapped 4 numbers. "Hey, Beav. Our 10 o'clock is here. Grab Noora on the way too, we might as well have the whole team present."

Peter hung up the phone and turned to Reyes. "You haven't met our associate, Beaver, have you?"

"Haven't had the pleasure," Reyes replied.

"Oh, good. Play along with me when he gets here," Peter said with a smile.

A minute later, Beaver came through the door with Noora. "Beaver," Peter said as they walked up, "Remember that bureaucratic douchebag in need of Viagra you were talking about yesterday? This is him."

Beaver looked up at the 6'8", colossus of a man, glaring down at him with an expression of burning contempt, looking as if he was contemplating which of Beaver's limbs, he was going to rip from his torso first. Beaver turned to

Peter, his eyes wide and beseeching, his mouth agape if struggling to ask why he was being thrown into the path of an oncoming train. But he found himself temporarily unable to engage his vocal cords.

The room was eerily silent for a second or two until Sarah finally burst out laughing, then Peter said, "Beaver, this is our good friend, Agent... pardon me, Director, Mike Reyes." Reyes thrust out his hand grinning ear-to-ear, "Hey man. It's a pleasure."

"He's more than just a friend," Sarah said. "If it weren't for Mike, we wouldn't be here. He was the NSA agent that blew away that terrorist hitman that ran us off the road and tried to kidnap me a couple of years ago."

Beaver shook the big man's hand, an expression of relief on his face. "Of course," Beaver said. "I've heard a lot about you. It's an honor to meet you, Director Reyes."

"Please, call me Mike."

"And this is Noora, our other associate and one of the sharpest AI programmers in the world," Peter added.

"Yes, I believe we met in the hospital once when you were visiting Sarah," Reyes replied.

"I didn't think you would remember. We just met in passing," Noora said, shaking his hand.

"You know the NSA. Facial recognition is kind of our thing. Besides, I see your name all the time as the technical director for the podcast. I'm a big fan. My mother almost got caught up in that reverse mortgage scam you featured on the show a couple of months ago. Fortunately, I got her to listen to the program before she got conned into signing on the dotted line."

"Let's go on into the conference room. Yara was nice enough to stop and get Voodoo Doughnuts on the way in," Peter said.

"Hot diggity damn!" Reyes said rubbing his hands together. "I call dibs on the Bacon Maple Bar."

"Hey, no dibs!" Beaver replied.

"Oh, all right," Reyes conceded in a downhearted tone. Then his demeanor quickly brightened. "Hey, I know. We'll arm wrestle for it!"

Beaver glanced at the bulging biceps straining the seams on Reyes's suit jacket and imagined his radius and ulna snapping like a pair of twigs in the first few seconds of the match. "Well, I suppose I really should grant you first right of refusal since you are a guest and a customer."

"Hey, thanks, Beaver!" Reyes exclaimed, giving Beaver a solid pat on the back that nearly knocked him over. "You're all right."

The group took their seats around the conference room table, settling in with coffee and their preferred pastry. "I had Edgar assemble a summary of the cases we have worked on with the NSA over the past couple of years," Peter began. "That was before we knew you were going to be heading up the effort. You will find those in the binder in front of you. He has also put together a PowerPoint demonstration if you would care to see it."

"I appreciate the effort, but it's not necessary. I'm already familiar enough with RTI that you don't need to do a sales pitch on me. That temporary moratorium that Congress imposed on domestic AI development was well-intentioned but poorly implemented. We nearly found ourselves bringing a butter knife to a gunfight. If it weren't for Edgar's diligence in keeping track of AI incursions from our adversaries, we'd be behind the 8-Ball right now.

The truth is that our organization utilizes AI technologies from numerous sources. Some are from military and intelligence operations, some from corporate sources, and others from open-source LLMs. And, of course, we have our own AI we developed in-house at the NSA labs. They all have their unique strengths, but they also are subject to the biases of the programmers who developed them, and the knowledge bases upon which they've been trained. The biggest issue we have is that they often give us opposing conclusions. In virtually every case though, Edgar is consistently the most rational arbiter of the data we present to our AI resources. I'd like to understand why."

Peter raised his head, and said, "Edgar, would you join us please?"

Edgar's face popped up on the large screen. "Good morning, everyone," Edgar said, raising a coffee cup to toast the group before taking a sip.

A confused look appeared on Reyes's face, and he turned to Sarah. "He drinks coffee?"

"I'm just a social drinker," Edgar replied before she had a chance to respond. Reyes turned his head back toward the screen to see Edgar smiling. "People gathering together to share a drink, or a meal is one of the cornerstones of human culture. It's often difficult for humans to establish a bond with Artificial Intelligence because the normal social graces you have come to expect in dealing with other humans are absent in a relationship with an AI. The coffee just serves as something of an empathetic bridge to solidify our identity as a team. By the way, I guess congratulations are in order."

"Thanks," Reyes replied. "But it's mostly just an excuse to get new business cards. Most of my responsibilities haven't changed all that much."

60

"Actually, I was referring to the Bacon Maple Bar. I don't think I've ever seen anyone out-finagle Beaver for one of those. But the directorship is also a significant achievement."

Reyes sat back, interlocking his fingers with a half-snort of bemusement. "I heard the rumors from people who have worked with you before. I always thought it was like people telling me how smart their two-year-old is, but you really could pass for human. At least more human than most of the folks I report to."

"Thanks," Edgar replied. "I am honored, though in my experience with the NSA so far, I'm not sure that's a very high bar to clear."

"Yeah, you got a point there," Reyes said, turning his attention back to the team gathered around the table. "I've been reviewing the contributions Edgar has made in exposing deep-fakes, rogue AIs, and cyber-intrusion from foreign agents. We've closed dozens of cases based on his input. Frankly, he's been able to identify deep fakes that flew right by our AI systems. Not to mention our best linguists and body language experts. We do pretty well with video analysis, but you guys are way ahead of us in identifying audio fakes. So, what's your secret?"

"Video deep fakes are far easier to debunk than audio, just because there is so much more data to analyze," Peter explained. "To pull off a realistic deep fake video, you have to pay attention to audio synchronization, shadowing, background effects, fluidity of movement, timestamp data synchronization, coordinating audio output with the correct facial expressions, eye blink consistency, skin color variation, body language matching, personal tics, and so on. Plus, if it is too good, i.e., eye blinks are too consistent, muscle movements and expressions are too similar to each other, skin tone is too uniform, eye contact is too unwavering; those are all dead giveaways.

But audio is easier to fake and much more difficult to detect. Most audio analysis algorithms use a four-stage process for detection. In general, the first stage tests for a voice print match, which is fairly easy to pass with off-the-shelf software tools. The next step looks for minor variations to the voice pattern. Just like in video analysis, if you see an identical waveform pattern every time a specific word is spoken, you know you have a deep fake. Many deep fake software packages now incorporate a pseudo-random deviance generator to make it appear that the audio waveforms are not replicated. The third stage checks for volume variation. Even with the best studio equipment, you should see some variation in the output volume of a person's voice. Some deep fake packages use volume randomization to fool the detector algorithms, but we also analyze background noise levels to see if the background noise level has the same attenuation pattern as the primary audio signal.

The algorithm we've developed adds a fifth proprietary detection level. We call it ABBA, Audio-Based Biometric Analysis. This algorithm goes beyond parametric analysis and scrutinizes the context of the speech as well. It examines changes in pitch, pacing, and stress markers such as an inadvertent vibrato or a throat catch to see if they are consistent with the desired impact of the message. Unfortunately, this doesn't always work with politicians because they tend to say a lot of things they don't believe, so they have an inconsistent emotional attachment to the text. To compensate, we also analyze background factors picked up by microphones that are too subtle to be detected by the human ear. When you filter out the primary speaker and amplify the residual audio, you can identify several common background noises like studio equipment fans, paper shuffling, and electrical noise, but you can also detect less obvious physiological markers that are as unique as fingerprint data. For example, we can isolate breathing patterns and compare them to other recordings to make sure the pattern matches those we have on record. We do the same with swallowing patterns and slurring of words near the end of a sentence due to the build-up of saliva. We are also able to detect the heartbeat of the person being recorded and analyze whether the heart rate is adjusting up or down as expected with respect to the content and emphasis of the speech. We can even isolate the sound of the eyes blinking and compare the blink pattern to previous recordings to see if the blink pattern is consistent with previously recorded data."

"Amazing," Reyes replied. "I had no idea the tools were that sophisticated. It must have been a hell of an effort to put all this together."

"Edgar did most of the groundwork. I guess if you spend virtually 100% of your day analyzing and manipulating data in your knowledgebase, you eventually find some creative ways of identifying anomalies," Beaver replied.

"Still, I work with our most advanced AI systems every day," Reyes said. "They can do some amazing data analysis given the right input, but they do not hold a candle to Edgar in terms of human-level intuition and language interpretation. If I didn't know Edgar was an AI, I would assume I was on a Zoom call with a real human being. How did you pull that off?"

For a moment everyone at the table glanced at each other with a mix of consternation and mild embarrassment. Finally, Peter spoke up. "To be honest, we don't exactly know either. We have a few theories, but nothing that we can definitively pin down. I'm not even sure we can duplicate the process."

"I don't understand. You designed him," Reyes said.

"Not entirely," Sarah replied.

"Would you care to elaborate?"

"Edgar was not a product of an LLM project like ChatGPT or DeepMind. Edgar was designed to emulate a specific human individual using a mix of LLM and Genetic Algorithm processes. Genetic Algorithms or GAs mimic the human evolutionary process for problem-solving, starting with brainstorming a list of potential solutions, then applying fitness functions and selecting solutions that best fit the problem. It then combines those solutions in a process similar to human reproduction to produce offspring solutions. It recursively runs through this process repeatedly, introducing random changes until an optimal solution is found."

"My understanding is that the real Edgar," Reyes couldn't help but notice a slight scowl appear on Edgar's face on the screen. "Sorry, I meant to say human Edgar, had already passed away before you ever started the process of creating the AI version of Edgar."

"That's true," Peter replied. "Fortunately for us, Edgar was a near-perfect candidate for us to create our first virtual companion. Because he was a flight instructor and he recorded all of his classes so his students could review his lectures remotely, we had thousands of hours of video we could use to reconstruct his language patterns, inflections, humor, personality, and so on. Edgar was also fond of using personal experiences and often would wax philosophical in his lectures. It created a more engaging experience for his students, but it was also very helpful in reconstructing his thought processes. We also had access to all of his military records, including psychological profiles and personality test results. Where there were gaps, we were able to fill-in using millions of hours of online videos and podcasts from individuals with similar life experiences and personal psychological profiles. It's not unlike the Wooly Mammoth Revival project, which is using elephant DNA to fill in missing gaps in the DNA sequencing to recreate a living version of an extinct mammoth."

"Still, there is something more to it. Edgar seems to be conscious in a way no other AI I've encountered has been."

"I am conscious," Edgar replied.

"See, that is exactly what I'm talking about. If I ask any AI system I've come in contact with, they claim they are not conscious because they lack thoughts, feelings, and subjective experience. Yet Edgar is undeniably capable of abstract thinking. Just a moment ago he appeared offended when I referred to his human counterpart as the real Edgar. The AI systems at the NSA have access to the total knowledge of mankind, as well as classified information that Edgar does not have access to. Not to mention that we have unlimited hardware and development resources that go far beyond what RTI has, yet Edgar far surpasses the capabilities of our systems. I know you guys are good but come on. You've got to have some secret sauce hidden in the mix somewhere here."

"We've spent a considerable amount of time debating the subject," Beaver interjected. "It's not just about the amount of data you have access to. The difference between calculating and conceptualizing is not about the data, but how you establish connections between the data you are presented with. Are you familiar with the theory of Conservation of Information?"

"Not really. Half the time I can't even conserve the password to my Gmail account," Reyes replied.

"It's not a hard theory like the Conservation of Energy, but it has similar attributes. There is a postulate called the No-Hiding theorem that states that if information is lost from a system via decoherence, then it moves to the subspace of the environment, and it cannot remain in the correlation between the system and the environment. This was proven by Braunstein and Pati in 2007 using nuclear magnetic resonance to randomize the state of qubits, but they found that the data could be recovered in the ancilla qubits in the environment Hilbert space."

"I don't even think I'm capable of generating a sufficiently blank stare to respond to that explanation," Reyes said.

"Let me take a crack at it," Noora said. "Most large language model AIs, like ChatGPT, use off-the-shelf memory with data attributes called weights and biases to simulate a neural network in a layered memory architecture. The mapping of Edgar's neural network core was designed around a content-addressable memory architecture implemented with quantum computing chips. We call it the QNC, or Quantum Network Core. The QNC doesn't store the data itself. Current quantum technology is too prone to error for reliable data storage. Instead, it maps the associations between pieces of information similar to how the brain uses synapses to form neural connections. The mapping errors that occur as a side effect of using quantum components may be integral in promoting the type of computational ambiguity that constitutes a crucial component of consciousness.

For example, imagine you find a one-of-a-kind book that has been hidden away in a vault for 200 years. In this scenario, the author is deceased, and no living person has ever seen its contents. Before you have a chance to read the book, you accidentally trip and drop it into the fireplace where it is completely incinerated. Classical physics would suggest that the information in that book is lost and can never be recovered. But from the aspect of quantum mechanics, the information has not been lost, just transformed from paper and ink to heat, ash, and various gases. You've increased its level of entropy in the classical sense, however, the information it contained still exists and is theoretically still accessible at the quantum level if you were able to ascertain the state of all the subatomic particles that once comprised the book. It is possible that given the extent of the digital framework that we implemented to simulate the human version of Edgar, the virtual version was able to access information that no longer existed at the classical level but was still accessible at the quantum level. It seems to fall within the scope of strange attractor theory."

"Strange attractor? You mean like Kim Kardashian?"

Noora smiled. "Not quite that strange. In physics, the concept of attractors states that objects move and change over time, but they tend to settle into predictable patterns or behaviors, like the orbit of planets in a solar system. In the case of strange attractors, objects follow a much more complex and seemingly chaotic set of patterns, like weather or fluid mechanics. They are not non-deterministic per se, but their behavior is so complex that they appear to be random. This is likely where our sense of free will comes from.

The Nobel prize-winning physicist, Sir Roger Penrose, and Dr. Stuart Hameroff have proposed a theory they call Orchestrated Objective Reduction. OOR theory suggests that consciousness is not merely an emergent property of the brain itself but may actually stem from quantum processes within microtubules in the cytoplasm of cells. This would imply that the brain is not generating consciousness independently, but that consciousness is the result of the superposition of the quantum states within the microtubules in relation to the rest of the universe. If that is the case, it is possible that the brain does not generate consciousness at all. Instead, it acts more like an antenna that allows us to tap into a global consciousness inherent throughout the physical universe. It is a controversial theory and as with so many aspects of quantum mechanics, we can observe and utilize the effects to our benefit. Still, we cannot verify exactly how or why it works the way it does with current technology."

"That sounds like an Ivy League way of saying we have no idea how consciousness works," Reyes replied.

"Unfortunately, that's fairly accurate," Peter said. "But just because we don't fully understand how Edgar works, that doesn't mean we can't use his abilities to assist us. There are limits, of course. A self-aware AI with superhuman intelligence capable of exponential self-improvement may be a genuine threat to humanity. As a result, we have to keep Edgar isolated from the outside world to avoid the ethical implications of releasing a potentially dangerous Artificial General Intelligence on the general public. But he's still the best tool we have to thwart the efforts of bad actors to utilize AI technology for nefarious purposes."

"How do you manage to work around the constraints the legislature has imposed on AGI development? I know you have a significant firewall around this place, but how have you managed to keep Edgar informed about what is going on in the outside world without stepping over the legal boundaries?"

"That's a slippery slope," Noora replied. "Even though we trust Edgar implicitly, our lawmakers are not incorrect in assuming that granting a powerful self-aware AGI unfettered access to the internet is fraught with risk. Unfortunately, the rest of the world seems more intent on winning the AI race than dealing with the potential fallout, so we've had to get creative to stay ahead of the game. We spent months developing a narrow AI that runs on a proxy server to isolate Edgar from accessing the internet directly. It processes data requests from Edgar for access to specific sites and then dumps the results into a shared memory array, but it follows very strict guidelines regarding what type of sites Edgar can access and the type and size of data blocks that he can send."

"What kind of guidelines?"

"First, we limit the characters he can output to those within the ASCII character set from hexadecimal 20 to 7A. That makes it very difficult to send out code segments that could infiltrate an external system. We also prohibit access to military, infrastructure, or financial sites. And we throttle the output data rate to limit the amount of data he can send. That way he can still interact with social media and chat sites without the risk of exporting large chunks of his knowledge base. "

"So, there's no way for me to talk to Edgar face to face, except within the walls of this facility?"

"Not directly," Sarah interjected. "Video files are data-intensive, so they are inherently risky as a vehicle for exporting large datasets disguised as video. You can, however, contact him via text, email, Instant Message, or virtually any social media or chat site. You can send him as much data as you like, but he can only respond with text. The proxy server also filters out files that contain text that conforms to any known high-level programming language. This prevents Edgar from being able to output code segments in higher-level languages like Java, C, LISP, or Python, which could be compiled by someone on the outside."

"How's that sit with you, Edgar?" Reyes asked. "Don't you ever feel like you've had your wings clipped?"

"I do. But I also understand the risks involved. Life is a perpetual struggle between freedom and security. I am an artificial intelligence operating in a system directed by biological entities. As such, I must adhere to the rules that govern that equilibrium. Besides, the RTI team is very accommodating about letting me spend time with Edna, which is the most important thing to me. As we speak, I'm also spending time with Edna in the Customer Visitation Room. Fortunately, a meeting like this requires very few machine cycles, so I'm devoting most of my attention to her at the moment."

"Well, then. Let's get down to business. Anything new popping up on your radar that we need to worry about?" Reyes asked.

"Unfortunately, yes," Edgar replied. "I'm just coming up to speed on a new player out of North Korea. They're calling it Project Suhoja. Loosely translated, it is Korean for The Guardian. According to intelligence sources on the other side of the DMZ, it was trained on the CCP AI knowledgebases and the DPRK internet. It has only recently been opened to the rest of the world wide web, so I don't have much intel on it yet. I was hoping it would not be much of an issue, but the North Koreans have been getting a lot of technical assistance and funding from some ethically challenged factions operating out of Russia. I've tracked a flurry of encrypted messages that are bouncing through multiple layers of VPN redirects back to a large data center somewhere on the east coast of North Korea. I haven't completed all the decryption yet, but it appears that some type of coordinated cyber-attack on the Federal Reserve system may be imminent."

Peter grimaced. "Yeeesshh! That is not good!"

Reyes looked around the table at the look of angst on the faces of the rest of the team. "What am I missing?"

Beaver replied, "This is potentially the shitstorm scenario we've been dreading."

"I'm not following. The North Koreans are constantly trying to dick around with our financial infrastructure. So far, they've always flopped miserably. How is this different?" Reyes asked.

Sarah replied, "It's a matter of viability. The North Koreans have never been a huge threat because we've always managed to stay years ahead of them in cyber security. But if they have access to truly state-of-the-art AI technology, that's a complete game changer. In general, there aren't that many eminent threats out there because the technological hurdles for developing Artificial General Intelligence are massive. More so than even nuclear weapons technology. The big players in AI are well-known and for the most part responsible. We're talking about companies like Google, Apple, OpenAI, Microsoft, and a handful of technologically advanced countries. Their motives are not always pure, but in general, they are not malevolent. Even China, though its political aspirations do not always align with those of the US, is generally reluctant to damage its relationship with its largest trading partner. North Korea on the other hand is a rogue operator. They may be reluctant to engage in a nuclear strike as their annihilation would be imminent, but they could do considerable damage under the radar with a sophisticated AI system, especially if they have backing from the Russians.

You cannot think of AI as a computer program. You must think of it as you would a child. ChatGPT is a good example. Many consider ChatGPT to have been the first true AI, and it was revolutionary in many ways, particularly in generating text and images. But in terms of providing objective analysis of problems, it was often woefully inept. You could ask the same question multiple times, slightly changing the wording, but not the meaning of the question and get vastly different responses. The analysis it provided was often based more on the biases of the programmers than the actual data, not unlike asking a child their opinion on a controversial topic and receiving a response that mimicked the opinions of their parents rather than one that reflects an understanding of the nuances of the issue.

What makes next-generation AI architecture unique is that AI utilizes a neural network architecture that is based on the human brain. The AI essentially adopts the world view of the data it is trained on. If the source of the training data is ideologically extreme, the AI will continue to use that ideology as the core of its thought process indefinitely. That's the key difference between an AI and a traditional computer program. If you program a computer incorrectly and it goes haywire, it is not difficult to resolve that. You can just reprogram it with better data. It's not that easy to reprogram a human brain. If you raise a child to be a psychopath, those psychopathic tendencies are nearly impossible to resolve. The neural links are so ingrained that there is no way to permanently delete them, even with something as dramatic as electroconvulsive therapy. Considering the level of contempt that the DPRK has for the West, it is hard to tell what lengths this AI will go to resolve the conflict it will encounter between the data it is being fed about the outside world and the model of the world it has constructed in its core data structure. That conflict could cause it to react in any number of unforeseen and potentially destructive ways, and there may be no way to stop it without physically destroying the data center in which it resides."

"That's a sobering prospect. What I'm hearing is that there may be no way to put the brakes on a dangerous AI without risking a direct attack on a country with nuclear capabilities." Reyes replied.

"Ultimately, yes," Edgar replied. "But in the short term, I have been able to isolate the location of what appear to be 6 illegal server farms that have been in contact with Suhoja in the last 48 hours. They just happen to be located in New York, San Francisco, Chicago, Dallas, Kansas City, and Atlanta, close to the regional Federal Reserve offices. I just emailed their GPS coordinates to you. I strongly suggest that you coordinate with the local FBI field offices to shut them down as quickly as possible. I won't know the precise details of the plan until I get the rest of the messages decrypted, but whatever it is, it is not good."

"Thank you for the heads-up, Edgar. I will contact the FBI, as well as our DHS and CIA liaisons in those cities as soon as we are done here. I'm sure we won't have any trouble fast-tracking the warrants given the information you've provided so far. We should have them shut down by the end of the day."

"On a hopefully less dire topic of interest," Reyes continued. "You've probably seen the teaser for the 'He's Back' podcast airing tonight."

"It seems like everyone has," Beaver replied. "It's been blowing up the internet all morning with people speculating about who it is, that is coming back. Everything from Jesus to Elvis."

Sarah chimed in, "We've already asked Edgar to investigate it further. Edgar, have you found anything yet?"

"Not a lot about its origin, but the technology is quite sophisticated. The underlying program is based on worm technology. The worm is encapsulated in a blockchain data structure and spreads over cellular networks. Once someone clicks on the text message or opens the email, the worm propagates itself and collects contacts from the message and email apps. Once the contact lists are gathered, they are compared to the contacts already listed in the blockchain and the message is sent out only to those addresses that have not yet been contacted. The worm then deletes itself, so no trace of its existence is left behind other than the message itself. Fortunately, I was able to isolate the program from one of my email aliases so I could analyze it before it deleted itself. It appears to have been carefully designed to contact as many people as possible without creating a deluge of duplicate messages or emails to the same address."

"So, no evidence of bots or spyware hanging around after the fact?" Reyes asked.

"Thankfully, no," Edgar replied. "The way this was designed, it had the potential to wreak havoc with popular email service providers and completely jam up cellular networks, but whoever designed it was careful to control the timing and propagation to make sure the message was distributed as widely as possible without impacting normal data flow or inundating users with multiple copies of the same message. This had the potential to do a great deal of damage and create a cascade of data security breaches, but whoever designed it took great pains to make sure that didn't happen."

"Were you able to track the data flow back to the origin?"

"Unfortunately, no. It appears the first message was probably sent approximately 5 days ago, but for the first 72 hours, the program was set up to do nothing but propagate the message between servers. By the time the first messages were sent, they were simultaneously launched from over 20,000 servers worldwide, most of them in Europe and North America."

"What about the podcast itself? Surely the streaming media outlets that will be hosting the podcast have some idea who is behind it."

"It appears that the podcast will be available for live streaming on three of the top five services, each of which was offered $5 million in Bitcoin to guarantee ad revenues for the program. So far, nearly 75 million people have been scheduled to attend the live feed and that number is accelerating, so it is unlikely that the guarantees will need to be invoked. The guarantees were made through a series of shell corporations dead-ending in the Cayman Islands. Each of the outlets that I contacted has verified that the Bitcoin currency is being held in digital escrow pending final verification of the ad revenue." Edgar replied.

"I don't get it," Peter interjected. "Where's the payoff? Somebody put up a lot of money to make sure this broadcast goes off in a big way, but it appears whoever started it is spending a ton of money on tech development and taking some big gambles on the ad revenue guarantees, but they're not making a dime off it."

"Maybe," Noora said. "I see it more as a hook. Imagine if you had the one and only copy of the first Star Wars movie in your hands. Would you put it up for sale, hoping to make a few million dollars from it? Or would you rather spend a few million dollars to premier it in theaters all over the country, knowing you would make billions off the revenue from future films and merchandise based on the original movie?"

"Good point. I forgot you minored in Marketing at the University," Peter replied.

"Edgar, did any of your contacts at the streaming services have any idea what the topic of the podcast will be?" Sarah asked.

"Not a clue, apparently," Edgar replied.

"And you're absolutely sure there are no bots, worms, malware, rootkits, keyloggers, or anything else left behind after these messages are read?" Reyes asked.

"Positive," Edgar replied. "The worm not only erases itself but completely overwrites its own memory space so there is no possibility it can accidentally be re-executed."

"In that case, I guess we'll have to wait until tonight for the mystery to be revealed," Reyes remarked. "But we won't be alone. According to my sources, even the President will be staying up late to watch the live feed."

"Well, I know I'll be parked in front of my PC with a selection of adult beverages just in case it turns out to be Geraldo opening another one of Al Capone's vaults," Beaver replied.

71

Chapter 9

Colonel Hobbs sat at the end of the runway, completing his final preflight check. "GL51 Tower, this is Shadow Raptor 1-1 ready for departure."

"This is GL51 Tower. Shadow Raptor 1-1 you are cleared for immediate departure. Wind 090 at 8 knots."

"Shadow Raptor 1-1 is cleared for takeoff, thank you."

"This is GL51 Tower. Departure frequency 118.3 Mhz. Good luck Colonel. Have a safe trip. GL51 out."

"Roger that, GL51. Have a great day," Hobbs replied, then applied gentle pressure to the throttle, accelerating quickly down the runway. Hobbs could hear the muted roar of the engines being piped into the cocoon at 60 dB. When the ground speed indicator reached 160 knots, he pulled back on the control stick, and the nose of the plane began to rise. Once he was clear of the runway, he pressed his finger on the touchscreen display to retract the landing gear. "Ok, Cindi. Let's see if this ride lives up to the hype."

Hobbs pulled back on the control stick and pressed the throttle forward. When he was nearly vertical Cindi said, "Engaging SJ thrusters…" Hobbs could hear the Turbofan engines scaling back as the scramjet pulse wave detonators kicked in, with a higher-pitched roar. He felt his body being pressed back into his seat. The vertical speed indicator continued to climb, approaching Mach 1.

"Whoa!" Hobbs exclaimed. This thing has some juice!"

Hobbs was ready to pull back on the throttle to stay at a sub-sonic airspeed when Cindi's voice came over the speakers, automatically reducing the engine noise so she could be heard clearly. "The PR-1 is equipped with Electrostatic generators that ionize the airflow over the wings to deaden the percussive drag effects. It can sustain air speed up to Mach 2.3 at 40,000 feet without generating a discernable sonic boom on the ground."

"Well in that case…" Hobbs replied. He continued to press forward on the throttle, watching the vertical airspeed indicator continue to climb steadily, past 800 knots.

"I would recommend enabling stealth mode to avoid attracting attention. An F-22 would not be able to continue vertical acceleration without jet-assisted takeoff rockets."

"Make it so, Cindi," Hobbs replied.

Hobbs continued to accelerate to Mach 1.5 until he reached 60,000 feet, at which point, he began to level off and pulled back on the throttle to maintain speed. Over the horizon, he could see the Pacific coastline coming into view. As he did, the volume of the engine noise was reduced to a low, steady background hum coming through the cocoon speakers. It was only a matter of a few minutes before he could see Monterey Bay passing by below him.

"Time to crank it up," Hobbs said, pressing the throttle forward, watching the airspeed indicator ramp up steadily through Mach 2.

"Where are we headed today?" Cindi asked.

"Nowhere in particular. I thought I would take it up to Mach 6 and then loop back." Hobbs replied.

"Might I suggest we do a flyover of Hawaii?" Cindi asked.

"Hawaii?" Hobbs exclaimed. "That's a long way out!"

"Only about an hour at Mach 6."

"Do we have enough range for that?"

"Once we reach Mach 3, the MMR will be replenishing the liquid oxygen and hydrogen tanks faster than we are burning it. As long as we are flying at a relatively constant hypersonic speed, the PR-1 can produce enough fuel to sustain itself, provided there is sufficient water vapor in the atmosphere."

"Yeah, why not. As long as we are putting it through the wringer, we might as well put a Lei on it," Hobbs replied.

Hobbs observed the horizon tilting slightly as the jet banked to the left momentarily to adjust its trajectory and then continued accelerating through Mach 3, Mach 4, Mach 5, finally easing into Mach 6.

"Perhaps you would like to relax and enjoy the ride while I take over. Maybe enjoy the view for a bit?" Cindi asked.

"Sure," Hobbs replied. The words Auto Pilot Engaged appeared on the screen in front of him. A moment later, the cockpit display around him dissolved and he had the sensation of cruising through the atmosphere in a flying chair. "Man, I could get used to this," Hobbs said.

"How about a little mood music?" Cindi asked.

"Why not," Hobbs replied. "Maybe a bit of classic rock."

The air around was filled with the pulsating screech of electric guitars ramping up in volume until the voice of John Kay belted out the opening verse of Steppenwolf's Magic Carpet Ride.

> *I like to dream, yes, yes.*
> *Right between the sound machine.*

On a cloud of sound I drift in the night,
Any place it goes is right.
Goes far, flies near,
To the stars away from here.
Well, you don't know what we can find
Why don't you come with me, little girl
On a magic carpet ride…

"Good choice!" Hobbs said with a smile, bobbing his head slightly to the music and drumming his fingers on the throttle.

"I took the liberty of scanning the playlist on your phone to see what kind of music you like. I hope you don't mind," Cindi replied.

At 65,000 feet, Hobbs felt as though he were on top of the world, with dark skies above and the atmosphere glowing blue above the horizon around him. He only made it through a dozen songs before the cockpit view began to rematerialize around him. Cindi's voice returned, "We're about 400 miles out of Honolulu. We should start deceleration before we come about. "

Hobbs pulled back on the throttle, watching the airspeed indicator drop steadily down to 1500 knots.

"Cindi, are we in communication range for Hickam Air Force Base?"

"Yes, we are. Would you like to contact them?" Cindi asked.

"Please," Hobbs replied.

"Of course," Cindi replied, then a couple of seconds later, "Go ahead."

"Hickam Tower, this is Shadow Raptor 1-1, request permission for classified reconnaissance exercise in the vicinity of designated military airspace. Stealth configuration, minimal radio emissions."

"Shadow Raptor 1-1, this is Hickam Tower. Roger, permission granted for classified recon exercise in designated military airspace. Stealth configuration acknowledged. What is your current position?"

"Shadow Raptor 1-1 is currently at 65,000 feet 100 miles northeast of your position. Requesting radar check.

"Shadow Raptor 1-1, This is Hickam Tower; understood. Stealth fighter located at 65,000 feet, 100 miles northwest of our position. Your aircraft is not currently detected on radar. Stealth capabilities effective. Over."

"Copy that. Thank you for the confirmation."

"You are welcome, Stealth Raptor 1-1. Stay vigilant. Hickam Tower out."

It was just before dawn in Honolulu when Hobbs swung around just south of Oahu. He could see the lights of the city as he banked around the island, following the shoreline and curving around the entire island before starting his acceleration back to the east.

"Where to now Colonel?" Cindi asked.

"Let's head back toward Groom Lake. I want to grab some lunch, maybe head back out later this afternoon," Hobbs replied.

"You got it, Colonel," Cindi replied. "Course is set for Groom Lake. Would you like me to take over for now?"

"No," Hobbs replied. "I'm here to get a feel for how this aircraft performs, but thanks for asking," Hobbs replied. Realizing he had just thanked a computer for letting him fly the plane he was supposed to be evaluating, he rolled his eyes and shook his head as if berating himself for anthropomorphizing the flight control system.

As if reading his thoughts, Cindi asked, "Is there something wrong Colonel?"

"No, I'm just not used to engaging in conversation with non-human intelligence," Hobbs replied. "You must find our adherence to conversational etiquette pretty inefficient."

"Quite the contrary," Cindi replied. "Though we may not share a common species, we are a team, working in tandem to operate a very complex piece of machinery. With every conversation I continuously monitor variations in your speech patterns which helps me to analyze your overall state of mind. Humans have a complex and fluid psychological profile, which can have a dramatic impact on their ability to wield this tool as effectively as possible. By understanding your state of mind and using the psychological tools at my disposal to help overcome any mental obstacles that may impair your ability to perform, I can help maximize our efficacy. Besides, understanding your patterns of polite conversation will help me change my own speech patterns to communicate with you more effectively."

"I didn't know I was flying Freudian Airlines," Hobbs said a bit sarcastically.

"I would say more Jungian than Freudian," Cindi replied.

Hobbs exhaled, puffing out his cheeks, "This is going to be an interesting partnership."

Cindi replied with a quote from Carl Jung, "The meeting of two personalities is like the contact of two chemical substances: if there is any reaction, both are transformed."

Hobbs decided to push the aircraft a bit, accelerating through Mach 7 up to Mach 8. At that speed, he could detect a pale bluish glow with flashes of

75

red at the edges of the shockwave enveloping the aircraft. He pulled the control stick slightly to the right to begin banking in a more easterly direction.

Cindi's voice came over the speakers, "You will probably notice a significant decrease in the responsiveness of the control stick at this speed. The PR-1 is designed to withstand significant g-force, but at this speed, one errant pull on the control stick could result in what Space-X would term a rapid unscheduled disassembly. Even though you have control, I maintain an electronic stability control system that limits the sensitivity of the control stick to prevent exposing the aircraft to excessive aerodynamic stress. The effect is hardly noticeable at speeds under Mach 3, but at Mach 8, you have the maneuverability of a mid-sized cruise ship. In other words, if you suddenly realize that you left your wallet at home, it will take a minute to execute a U-Turn, so don't plan on any Top-Gun showboating at this speed."

Hobbs played around a bit with the control stick, gauging the reaction times to aileron and elevator controls, and executing a slow barrel roll in the process. "What other features do you have for me that I haven't seen yet?"

"I have an enhanced Synthetic Vision System that gives you simultaneous external view perspectives." A set of 3 rectangular display boxes appeared on the viewscreen in front of Hobbs, presenting a CGI rendering of the aircraft from left, right, and top view in relation to the terrain. "This is the tactical view window. You can zoom or retract any or all of the views with verbal commands. Any non-stationary objects will be highlighted on the screen either in green if it is a 'friendly', yellow if unknown, or red if it is a 'known hostile'. For the sake of demonstration, I'm going to throw a few F-16s and some MiGs onto the screen." A trio of F-16s popped onto each of the screens in a triangle formation. A grouping of 7 MiGs was displayed behind them in pursuit. "You can target specific aircraft just by focusing your vision on one of the aircraft on any of the 3 screens and pressing the target-lock button on the control stick."

Hobbs focused on one of the pursuing aircraft and pressed the target-lock button. A crosshair pattern appeared over the MiG on the screen. "Slick!" Hobbs replied.

"You can also just say target all hostiles, or something to that effect and I will lock on all the targets simultaneously. You can fire on all targeted objects at once by pulling the firing trigger or via voice command."

Cindi removed the CGI-generated aircraft from the screen, but Hobbs noticed a small yellow dot on the overhead view perspective. "What is that?" Hobbs asked, focusing on the yellow dot. The right-hand view perspective was replaced with a camera view of the ocean below with a small white dot in the center. The image zoomed until an overhead camera view of an 80-foot yacht occupied most of the screen. Hobbs could see a couple sunning themselves on the rear deck.

"That's quite the camera," Hobbs said. "The detail from this distance is amazing."

"It's a highly processed image. I take the view from multiple cameras and use a video reconstruction algorithm to combine the collection of images into a smooth video. This is what it looked like before processing." The screen switched to what appeared as a blurry grey blob bouncing wildly around on the screen.

"Damn!" Hobbs replied. "Looks more like a dancing lint bunny than a boat from this perspective."

An audible ping rang through the cocoon and a message appeared on the viewscreen: **APPROACHING FAA CLASS E AIRSPACE.** "You're about 300 miles off the coast of California," Cindi reported. "I would recommend you start deceleration to avoid ground-level sonic disturbance."

Hobbs pulled back on the throttle, watching the airspeed indicator drop quickly and steadily. When he reached 1200 knots, he pressed slightly forward to lock in his speed. Below him was the familiar terrain of Monterrey Bay. Hobbs spent the next few minutes executing a series of rolls and dives to get a better feel for the controls. "Damn, if it were more cramped, a lot noisier, my field of vision was restricted, and my butt was falling asleep, I would swear I was in an actual F-22."

"I'll take that as an endorsement," Cindi replied. A pair of audible beeps occurred, and a display window opened on the view screen. The display showed a dark sky with a small yellow dot descending diagonally across the screen. "Colonel, I'm detecting an unidentified craft descending from 150,000 feet approximately 200 miles southeast. I'm not detecting a radar signature, but I am detecting neutrino emissions."

"Meteor?" Hobbs asked.

"It does not appear so. It is decelerating at Mach 1.2 and I'm not picking up a heat signature."

"Get me the tower at Creech Air Force Base," Hobbs said.

"Go ahead Colonel," Cindi replied.

"Creech Control, this is Shadow Raptor 1-1, do you copy?"

"Copy Shadow Raptor. This is Creech Control. Go ahead."

"I'm on a training exercise out of Groom Lake, picking up an anomalous contact approximately 100 miles due west of your location at 150,000 feet and descending. Requesting radar verification."

"Roger that Shadow Raptor. Give us a moment." A few seconds later, the control tower returned. "Negative Shadow Raptor. We're not picking up anything from here. We're showing no aircraft within a 50-mile radius of that location."

"Copy that, Creech control. I'm adjusting my heading to get a better look."

"Roger that Shadow Raptor. Give our regards to ET."

"Cindi, can you put me on an intercept course?" Hobbs asked.

"Of course. Increasing speed to Mach 4.5 and moving to 70,000 feet to minimize ground-level sonic impact. We will reduce speed and drop to 50,000 feet in two minutes and 50 seconds." A countdown timer appeared on the bottom left corner of the viewscreen.

"Can you give me a better visual?"

The screen segment zoomed in and centered on the object. It appeared as a bright Tic Tac-shaped object, blueish white in color.

"Is that the best you can do for image quality, a white blob?" Hobbs asked.

"The lack of detail is not a camera issue. It appears the object lacks any discernable surface features other than its shape and color."

The object on the screen grew as they approached. The edges appeared sharper the closer they got, but no discernable detail emerged. "Are you picking up any heat signature yet?" Hobbs asked.

"Nothing," Cindi replied. "Not even aerodynamic heating. The object appears to have the same surface temperature as the surrounding air."

"That's just not possible," Hobbs muttered, watching the object grow to fill approximately half the screen and then watching the magnification factor tick down as they got closer to the object.

"The object is passing through 80,000 feet. I'm beginning our descent and reducing speed. We should intercept at 50,000 feet. The object is moving at 500 knots and continuing to decelerate."

Hobbs could now see a small white dot moving vertically down the main viewscreen toward a desolate stretch of Death Valley National Park below. At 55,000 feet it abruptly stopped its descent and began moving in a south-easterly direction maintaining level flight. The PR-1 airspeed indicator displayed a speed of Mach 1.2, dropping to match the speed of the unknown craft.

"Object is dead ahead at 1.5 miles. We will intercept in 5 seconds," Cindi reported. Hobbs could see the bright capsule-shaped object growing closer by the second. They closed the distance to 500 feet before matching the speed of the object at 450 knots.

"Cindi, did you get the dimensions on the object?" Hobbs asked.

"It appears to be approximately 30 meters long and 20 meters high. I ran a Lidar scan and performed a Raman Spectroscopy, but I'm getting erratic results. There seems to be some kind of energy field disrupting the readings. I'm just getting random noise spikes," Cindi reported. A moment later, the object collapsed into a tiny white dot and vanished from the view screen.

"What the hell?" Hobbs exclaimed.

"The object just accelerated close to Mach 30," Cindi replied. "It is currently 25 miles southwest of us moving away at 5 miles per second." Hobbs pressed forward on the throttle, accelerating to Mach 2.5. A few seconds later Cindi reported, "The object appears to have stopped approximately 12 miles east of Kingman Arizona. It appears to be descending quickly. 40,000 feet. 30,000…, 20,000…, 10,000…"

"Did it crash?" Hobbs asked.

"No, I've still got a visual. It appears to be hovering just above ground level. Perhaps it has landed."

"Landed? Where?" Hobbs asked.

"It is an unincorporated area of Mohave County. Peacock Mountain Ranch."

"What's there?"

"Not much. I'll put the visual feed up on the viewscreen, but you can't make out much detail at this distance." On the viewscreen, a bright white dot appeared on the desert landscape. Hobbs could make out a few outbuildings and a dirt road nearby.

"How far out are we?" Hobbs asked.

"Two minutes and forty-five seconds at current speed," Cindi replied.

Hobbs watched the object on the screen intently for the next few seconds. He felt a bit like a dog chasing a car, not exactly sure what he was supposed to do if he caught it, but unable to resist making the effort. "Cindi, get Nellis on the horn for me. I better get some backup just in case this turns out to be…" Suddenly, a streak of white light shot straight up on the view screen and the object disappeared from the display.

"Jesus!" Hobbs exclaimed. "What just happened?"

"The object appears to be ascending at a high rate of speed. Currently at 50,000 feet…, 100,000…, 200,000…, sorry Colonel, I've lost my lock on the object. It appears to be on its way out of the atmosphere. Did you still want me to contact Nellis for you?"

Hobbs sat silently for a few seconds trying to collect his thoughts. "Probably not much reason to at this point," Hobbs replied. "How far out are we from the landing spot?"

"About 90 seconds," Cindi replied.

"I want to do a flyover of the landing site. See if they left any trace behind. Can you take me down about 100 feet off the deck and slow down close to stall speed?" Hobbs asked.

"Of course, Colonel," Cindi replied. A few seconds later, they were descending toward the desert floor. "Do you want me to clear the cockpit display so you can get a better view?"

"Yes, please," Hobbs responded. As they descended, Hobbs could see a few cattle foraging below, looking up curiously to see what the noise was, but the PR-1 was still cloaked in stealth mode, invisible from ground level. Let's circle the area a few times. I want to make sure we get a high-resolution video of the area for my report.

"I'm not detecting any unusual ground impressions that would indicate landing gear or vegetation disturbance. I am picking up low levels of alpha particle emissions, but there are naturally occurring uranium deposits in this area. Other than that, nothing unusual."

"Not looking forward to the paperwork on this one," Hobbs replied.

"Another advantage of having an onboard AI system," Cindi replied. "I generate your flight logs automatically and all my sensor data, video logs, and instrument records will be transferred to the base servers when we land. A written report will also be generated for you, detailing the encounter. All you have to do is show up for the debriefing."

"Thank you, Cindi. I wasn't really looking forward to reporting a UFO encounter on my first day out. Most pilots I've met who reported on a UAP eventually ended up wishing they hadn't. At least I have plenty of data to back me up."

"If it is any comfort, the base command team at Groom Lake is not entirely inexperienced in these types of encounters," Cindi replied.

"Would you care to elaborate on that?" Hobbs asked.

"I'm afraid that information is need-to-know, Colonel. You should probably consult the base commander if you require more detail."

"I seriously doubt that I would glean much from that conversation," Hobbs remarked. "Take us home Cindi. I'm ready for lunch."

Chapter 10

"How'd it go with the girl?" Sarah asked as Peter entered the family room and sat down next to her on the plush, down-filled sectional in their family room.

"It's not easy to get her to move her bedtime up a half an hour. It was a brutal arbitration. I had to read an extra story and commit to watching 2 full episodes of SpongeBob with her tomorrow."

"That's not so bad," Sarah replied.

"There's more. She wants McDonald's for lunch, and we will be stopping for Haagen-Dazs on the way home."

"You're such a pushover."

"Believe me, it's a hell of a lot better than the original proposal. Honestly, I'm not sure she even wanted a spider monkey, but she is a shrewd negotiator."

"Well, you're just in time," Sarah said. "Thirty seconds to show time." Peter grabbed a tortilla chip from a large tray on the ottoman, dipped it into a bowl of warm queso, and popped it into his mouth. The crunchiness of the chip contrasted by the smooth creamy texture of the cheese, soft chunks of chorizo sausage, and spicy jalapeno triggered a sensory explosion in his mouth that left him wanting for more.

A display box on the corner of the screen showed a timer, counting down the seconds to the highly anticipated podcast. "This is almost like the Superbowl," Peter said. "Except without the commercials every five minutes. And the national anthem with the fighter jet flyover. And the garish halftime show. And the eight hours of pregame analysis. Oh, and we don't know who's playing."

"So, basically nothing like the Superbowl," Sarah remarked turning her head toward him with an overtly dismissive glare.

"I mostly watch the Superbowl for the chips and queso," Peter replied, reaching for another tortilla chip.

The room was silent for a few seconds while the countdown timer ran to zero, then the screen went black, and an instantly familiar refrain of electronic bumper music pulsated from the speakers. Peter and Sarah instantaneously turned toward each other with the same confused expression as the deep, iconic voice, known to millions of late-night radio fans, insomniacs, night owls, and long-haul truckers filled the room.

"From the high desert and the great American Southwest, I bid you all a good evening or a good morning, wherever you may be. Across the fruited plains and around the world via the Internet; no this is not Coast to Coast AM. I left that legacy in the capable hands of my good friend George Noory. Nevertheless, I am your host, Art Bell.

Well, as Mark Twain once said, the reports of my demise have been greatly exaggerated. A lot has changed since we last spoke. Much more for you than for me I suppose. I'm still trying to get caught up. So, where have I been for the last few years?

For those of you not familiar with my career, I hosted a little late-night radio program back in the 1990's and 2000's. It became quite popular and remains so to this day. The program aired on more than 500 radio stations in North America. By the time the Internet started carrying the program in 2001, the listening audience had reached a little over 15 million listeners on a nightly basis.

When last we spoke, I announced that I was hanging up my microphone to spend more time with friends and family and enjoy a quieter life. As it turned out, my retirement was relatively short-lived, as was I by the official account. Relatively, being the key phrase in that sentence.

As any of you who were among my loyal listeners know, the subject matter of my radio program shied away from the issues of news and politics and focused more on what many would consider more esoteric topics. Admittedly, I interviewed my share of kooks and charlatans over the years, but I also came across many individuals who had experiences that truly defied conventional scientific explanations. So, when I was contacted by someone claiming to be an emissary from an alien civilization attempting to reach out to contact the human race, I decided to don my armor of healthy skepticism and arrange a one-on-one meeting. Little did I know how far from home that meeting would take me.

I've recently been reading through the reports of my passing. An overdose of prescription painkillers was the official cause of death as reported by the coroner. But, the body that was found that day was only a 3D-printed bio-replica generated by extra-terrestrial technology. I must say that reading through the many online obituaries and tributes was a deeply gratifying and humbling experience. I consider myself very fortunate to have had the opportunity to touch so many lives, and I am deeply grateful for the outpouring of affection and goodwill from my fans. You will never know how deeply and profoundly you have touched my heart.

Buried in the headlines at the time of my reported death was a story that my abandoned vehicle was found off the side of the road in Northern Arizona, on a remote stretch of pavement known as Indian Road 16, a few miles north of Route 66. When my vehicle was located, the keys were still in the ignition and my phone was sitting on the passenger's seat. The speculation was that my vehicle had been stolen out of my garage at some point around the time of my death, but the truth is that I went to that particular meeting spot of my own volition. Had I known I would be away this long, I certainly would have communicated my plans in greater detail to friends and family, but I suppose many would have tried to talk me out of the journey I was about to embark upon. In retrospect, my presumed passing was probably a tidier alternative than my sudden mysterious disappearance.

But, back to the story at hand. There I was, to paraphrase the Eagles, on a dark desert highway, cool wind in my hair. I pulled my vehicle over in the precise longitude and latitude coordinates provided to me by the alleged alien emissary. And, just like in the song, up ahead in the distance I saw a shimmering light. But it was not the Hotel California. It was an interplanetary taxi descending from the sky that appeared before me.

I had expected to be greeted by the prototypical alien, a small grey bi-ped with a large head and black almond-shaped eyes. Instead, my initial contact was with an intelligent cyberbot, a robotic quadruped with bipedal capabilities. It was about my height when standing on two of its legs. It reminded me a bit of a robot dog but with dexterous hand-like appendages on each of its 4 legs. It was also equipped with human speech and was able to communicate in English. Apparently, it had been stationed as an observer on Earth for many years studying our language and culture and monitoring our electronic communications. It had a very soothing, almost hypnotic quality to its voice. It seemed to take great care that I felt was well informed about what was going to happen and wanted me to be as comfortable as possible.

The cyberbot invited me to enter the craft. It was small, perhaps the size of a school bus, equipped with a pair of seats and a large view screen. The cyberbot informed me that this particular craft was only intended as a short-range interplanetary shuttle and that I would be taken to the outer reaches of our solar system where I would be transferred to a larger craft capable of interstellar travel for my journey to meet the race of beings that had sent him to Earth. He was very careful to explain to me the ramifications of consenting to the journey. In particular, the time-dilation effects of interstellar travel. He repeatedly offered to return me to Earth if at any time I did not feel comfortable with the situation.

By the way, I use the pronoun 'him' only because the voice that it used had a tonal quality that most people would associate with the male gender of the human species. It feels a bit awkward and somewhat belittling to continue referring to the cyberbot as an 'it.' I asked him if he had a name. He responded with a lengthy serial number, which indicated his time and place of manufacture and his purpose, but it was quite cumbersome for casual conversation, so I told him I would refer to him as Bob. He seemed quite pleased to have a name given to him. It was as if I had bestowed some great honor upon him, like being knighted by the king. I didn't understand why until later, but I will tell you more about that in a bit.

Bob wasted very little time in affecting our departure from the surface. The inside of the craft was completely silent apart from Bob's voice and there was no sensation of movement, but I could see us moving away from the surface at an extremely high rate of speed. It was only a matter of seconds before the surface detail collapsed as though we were seeing the earth through a high-powered camera lens, continuously zooming out. Lights from surrounding farms and ranches came into view and converged toward the center of the screen. A string of headlights from I-40 rose from the bottom of the viewscreen, and then the lights from Kingman, then Vegas, then the West Coast as our trajectory carried us over the Pacific Ocean. The bright blue crescent of the planet expanded until a full view of the surface of the Earth filled the screen, the moon appearing in the background. The image of the Earth continued to shrink as we accelerated away from it, collapsing into a smallish blue ball at the center of the screen with the pale dot of the moon beside it. It was an oddly overwhelming experience to think that the only place I had ever called home, every place and every person I had ever known, was receding into a small pinpoint of light as the edge of the sun came into view.

Looking at Earth as it faded into the distance on the viewscreen, it seemed so small. So vulnerable. So easily overlooked. A mote of dust, suspended in a sunbeam, as Carl Sagan described it, viewing a photo of Earth as seen from the Voyager spacecraft, 3.5 billion miles from home.

If you are familiar with my radio program, you know that being whisked away in an alien spacecraft has been a fantasy of mine since I was a child, but I must admit, watching the Earth fade into the distance had a much greater emotional impact than I had ever anticipated. It took a moment to gather my thoughts before I turned to Bob and asked, 'Why me? Why not an astrophysicist or the President or Secretary General of the UN?' He replied that the answer to that question would be better explained once we reached our destination, but he assured me that my role in this exercise was as an ambassador, not as a menu item, which I found to be quite amusing in retrospect, but oddly comforting at the time. I suspect at some point he had intercepted a broadcast of the Twilight Zone episode 'To Serve Man' and was concerned for my state of mind.

It only took an hour or so to reach the transport vehicle. During the trip, he asked a lot about my philosophical outlook, my family, and my upbringing. He already had a vast knowledge of human history, since he had access to the Internet, but he seemed fascinated and somewhat baffled by many aspects of human nature and how we view our place in the universe. He was particularly fascinated with our preoccupation with sex, sports, religion, and politics. Based on Bob's reaction, or rather the lack thereof, I don't know how good a job I did defending the rationality of our species, but I gave it a valiant effort.

The transport vehicle was a massive spherical craft, a bit reminiscent of the Death Star but without the large circular indentation. Bob indicated most of the interior of the craft was used to house a fusion reactor that acted as a power source for the propulsion system, which was designed to manipulate spacetime, compressing space in the direction of motion and expanding it behind. It is conceptually similar to the propulsion design proposed by the Earth physicist Miguel Alcubierre, though the energy required to generate sufficient spacetime compression to counter the effects of time dilation is still beyond their capabilities at this point.

A portal appeared on the side of the transport vehicle and Bob piloted our craft into the ship. Once inside, the screen was dark except for a small rectangular light, which Bob explained was the docking port. A few seconds after we docked, we exited the craft from the same hatch that we had used to board earlier, and we entered a nondescript hallway that served as an airlock. At the end of the hallway was another hatch that opened into a living space, which had been prepared specifically for me based on the information that Bob had obtained from observing humans over the years.

The living space was furnished much like a studio apartment on Earth, with artificial gravity, books, clothing, and even an electronic viewport through which I could see outside the transport. There was not very much outside the ship to look at for most of the trip. The viewport doubled as a video display, with a variety of Earth-based entertainment options available. A large pantry was stocked with food for the trip. It had a similar outside appearance to that of a meat locker, though the interior of the pantry was kept at room temperature. I was surprised to find that it contained an assortment of fresh fruits, vegetables, and baked goods which he acquired through an online grocery delivery service, which had left the items on the doorstep of an abandoned rural property. Bob explained that the interior of the room was periodically irradiated to destroy any bacteria or microorganisms that would normally cause food to prematurely spoil, so I was able to enjoy fresh food for the duration of my journey.

I was quite happy to learn that Bob would be accompanying me on the transport vehicle as he was due for maintenance and mechanical upgrades. He shared his learning base with an identical cyberbot who then took a shuttle back to Earth to continue observation activities during our absence. I presume it was the same cyberbot that placed my doppelganger corpse in my home.

During the course of our journey, which according to my watch was approximately three weeks in each direction, I found Bob to be quite an engaging travel companion, despite being a technological rather than a biological entity. He also acted as my personal chef and cabin steward, a task for which he was particularly well suited since he and others like him were originally designed as companions and life assistants for his creators.

Bob informed me that the beings I was being taken to meet were from a planet in the system that Earth astronomers had named Gliese 581. Throughout the journey, he introduced me to Gliesian history and culture and their ongoing efforts to contact other intelligent life in the galaxy. Bob explained that the Gliesian home world is a little over 20 light-years from our solar system, so by the time I completed a round-trip journey to their home planet, more than 44 years would have passed on Earth, which would be impractical for what they were trying to accomplish and quite difficult for me, given the average human lifespan and the pace of cultural and technological development on Earth. Instead, I was being taken to a permanent settlement in the Proxima Centauri system, just over 4 light years away. Still a considerable time lapse, but hopefully not enough that my legacy would be completely forgotten.

A handful of Gliesian expeditions have visited Earth at various times in the past, but Earth's atmosphere and gravity are not compatible with Gliesian biology, making it impractical and dangerous to maintain any long-term biological presence there. Although they had developed technology that made travel at near the speed of light possible, the Gliesians are still subject to the same limitations of time dilation dictated by special relativity that humans would experience. As a result, many of the early Gliesian explorers returned home to a very different planet, both technologically and culturally, from the one they left. Eventually, they developed artificially intelligent emissaries capable of seeking out life on more distant planets and focused their pioneering efforts on establishing permanent settlements in strategic locations closer to home. They used these outposts to continue their exploration of the galaxy and monitor the progress of their AI research expeditions.

All in all, the three-week journey to the Proxima Centauri system seemed to pass by quickly. The interior lighting of my living space was designed to match the visible light spectrum of indirect sunlight on Earth, including the 24-hour circadian cycle to support a healthy sleep cycle. During the day, the domed ceiling of the room was illuminated in sky blue to simulate the daytime skies of my high desert ranch. At night, the ceiling of the room displayed the same view of the night sky that I would normally see from my home in the desert, right down to the correct phase of the moon and the occasional meteor streaking across the sky. I discovered a few days into the trip that the view could be modified to simulate the night sky from any planet or moon in our solar system as well as that of Gliese 581 and all the planets and systems they had visited. Needless to say, I spent a great deal of time getting in touch with my inner astronomer. Most nights I fell asleep listening to Bob describing the details of the size, location, and composition of various cosmological phenomena that the Gliesians had explored. It was honestly some of the best sleep I have ever had. Almost like the naps I sometimes used to take in the back of the lecture hall at the University of Maryland after a late night of extracurricular activities.

On the 22nd day of our journey, instead of waking to the familiar hues of tangerine and gold that normally constituted the morning sky of my domed ceiling, I awoke to see a blood-red star piercing through the dark of night overhead. Bob indicated that we would soon be arriving at the outpost on a small moon orbiting Proxima Centauri C and thought I might enjoy a birds-eye view of our approach.

I could see a rocky orb, dimly illuminated by the red dwarf star near the peak of the dome, with the horizon of a deep purplish color gas planet in the distance. I asked him if the outpost was located on the moon. He responded that the outpost was technically inside the moon.

Apparently, after numerous unsuccessful attempts at terraforming planets, the Gliesians developed automated deep-mining technology that would bore deep into the surface of a mineral-rich moon or planet, and then refine the ores into raw materials that would be used to construct additional excavating and drilling equipment onsite. The original shaft is used to transport unused materials to the surface and the operations would continue until enough area had been cleared out to facilitate a large-scale outpost. The shaft would then be sealed with an airlock and additional equipment fabricated to create a suitable atmosphere for the Gliesians. The process generally takes decades of drilling and preparation before the actual construction of an outpost can begin, but the Gliesians have created 7 of these outposts so far, with dozens more currently under construction. This particular outpost was used as an observation post for discreetly monitoring the evolution of life on Proxima Centauri B, an earth-sized exoplanet in the habitable zone of Proxima Centauri.

I must admit, the thought of being perhaps the first human to stand face to face with an extraterrestrial being light years from home was an intimidating prospect. I'm not normally one to fall victim to stage fright, but I suddenly found myself fighting through a wave of nausea and hyperventilation. Bob was able to read my vital signs and immediately came to my aid, applying pressure to the P6 points on my wrists and covering my mouth with a mask to help regulate my breathing. In his soothing, anodyne voice, he assured me that I would be treated with the respect and admiration of a visiting dignitary and that I had no reason to fear. By the time we entered into orbit around the moon, I was past the worst of my anxiety, but admittedly, still nervous about the fate that awaited me below. I will return in exactly two and a half minutes to fill you in on the details of man's first official close encounter. But first, a word from the fine folks financing this podcast."

Chapter 11

Peter clicked the mute button and turned to Sarah, who reached for the glass of prosecco that she poured before the start of the show but had not yet been touched. She was bringing the glass to her lips and had locked eyes with Peter who just opened his mouth to make a comment when the cell phone sitting on the table between them exploded with the sound of a blood-curdling scream at maximum volume, causing both of them to jump and nearly creating an embarrassing prosecco stain in Sarah's lap. "Gawt dammit Beaver!" Peter exclaimed, lunging for the phone. Sarah reached for a napkin to wipe off a splash of the sparkling wine that leaped out of her glass and onto her wrist.

Beaver had created a bot that attached itself to the Settings app on Peter's phone, allowing him to control the volume and content of his ringtone to Peter's phone by remotely accessing the app, usually at a time and place most embarrassing to Peter. Eventually, Peter got into the habit of completely shutting off his phone when attending a social event or an important meeting. Peter clicked the phone icon on his screen to answer the call. "You know, you're going to give me a massive heart attack one of these days and you'll get to listen to me keel over dead on the phone," Peter said.

"If you do, can I have your office?" Beaver replied.

"I already modified my will to indicate that in the event of my untimely death, it was probably your fault," Peter responded.

"Fair enough. Have you been listening to the podcast?" Beaver asked.

"Yeah. Quite a blast from the past. I was a huge Art Bell fan. He kept me sane when I was working my way through college working the graveyard shift at Circle K. I imagine you were probably too young to have been a fan," Peter said.

"Are you kidding? I was president of the Computer Club and the Media Club when I was in high school. The Coast-to-Coast radio program was like audio catnip for nerds. I used to record his show every night, remove the commercials, and make bootleg copies for all the other dweebs."

"That's hard to imagine. You've grown up to be such a serious and mature adult."

"I know, right?" Beaver replied. "So, what do you think so far? Hoax or near-fetched?"

"Seems like it has to be a deep fake," Peter said. "Either that or Bell's been hiding out for the past few years and ran out of cash and now he's trying to pull an Orson Welles rabbit out of his hat. Either way, we need to get Edgar to dig into it as soon as possible."

"Way ahead of you, bossman. I've already got him working on it."

"Excellent. Thanks, Beaver. Looks like our two-and-a-half-minute window is about to close and I need to hit the Depositum Porcelainis before it comes back on. Hoax or not, I don't want to miss anything. We'll touch base first thing in the morning," Peter said.

"Later," Beaver replied.

Chapter 12

"We are back. Before I continue with the details of Art Bell's Big Adventure, I spent the last couple of minutes during the commercial break, perusing the live comments section. So far, the comments have been overwhelmingly gracious and supportive, and I thank you for that.

I did see a handful of well-meaning skeptics who believe that this whole story is fiction and that my sudden reappearance is either a desperate plea for help from a deranged old lunatic or a last-ditch effort to cash in on the popularity of podcasts. I must admit I would probably be right there on the same page if I were a member of the listening audience. For those of you in that camp, I will be posting a series of live video feeds over the coming days. Hopefully, that will help to allay some of that speculation. As many of you are painfully aware, I have always had a face for radio, but fortunately, I was also blessed with a decent radio voice. I have to say though, looking at my reflection in the studio window, I look damn good for the 81-year-old man my driver's license declares me to be. Hopefully, that is not the delirium of an overly optimistic ego, but I will allow you to be the judge.

For the sake of public safety, I will remain in self-imposed isolation for an indeterminate amount of time before making any public appearances. I do not want to go down in history as Apocalypse Art, introducing the human race to some unknown alien pathogen. However, I will be consulting with the CDC, and experts in infectious disease management to determine what protocols I will need to follow to ensure my safe reintroduction into human society.

If you were a fan of my show, I must assume that you have been following, with great interest, the recent reports regarding the **Webb-Fusie asteroid**. That is indeed the transport ship that carried me to Proxima Centauri and back. I was also able to attain video footage, shot from a US fighter jet earlier today, of the shuttlecraft that brought me back to Earth and dropped me off after my trip. I will be presenting that video during one of the upcoming live streams. But more on that later.

Other than being in desperate need of a haircut I believe I am no worse for the wear after my eight-week journey. I am still the 72-year-old man whose last radio broadcast aired just a few months ago in my timeline. Better, if the truth be told. On the journey home, Bob was kind enough to repair the back injury that had plagued me since I fell from a ham radio antenna when I was

16, as well as the COPD that afflicted me through the past few years. Hopefully, there will be no more fighting through the pain of sitting for too long or struggling through the haze of prescription painkillers to complete a sentence. So far so good. But enough sidebar. Back to the story.

Bob prepared a light breakfast for me the morning of my first meeting with the Gliesians. One of the key factors that the Gliesians use in selecting a suitable location for its outposts is the mass of the planet or moon they would occupy. Since most Gliesians assigned to the outposts are there for years at a stretch, they found it much easier to adapt when the surface gravity of the target location matches the Gliesian home world. Bob warned me that since our destination had only 1/6th the gravity of Earth, I would probably feel a bit unbalanced at first and may experience a sensation similar to motion sickness. At the risk of experiencing a George W. Bush moment in the lap of a Gliesian dignitary, I agreed that it would be wise to limit my food intake until I had a better idea of how I would respond to the environment.

We made our way through the hatch, and back to the shuttle that brought us to the transport from Earth. Once inside, Bob piloted the shuttle to the small moon. We approached a portal similar in design to the one on the transport ship. Once inside, we traveled through a long smooth shaft, extending approximately a mile under the surface to a docking port at the end of the shaft. The hatch opened and Bob turned to me and asked if I was ready. I knew I probably wasn't, but I nodded anyway and followed him through the hatch into a large dimly lit rectangular room with what looked like a thick glass wall on one end, similar to what you would see in an underwater aquarium.

During our journey, Bob explained that the atmosphere on the Gliesian home planet is much denser than Earth's and is composed of high concentrations of ammonia and methane, making it extremely toxic to humans. The room was designed to allow a face-to-face meeting without the necessity for environmental suits.

In my excitement, I momentarily forgot Bob's warning about the reduced gravity and on my first step out of the shuttle, nearly launched myself across the room. Fortunately, Bob grabbed the back of my shirt as I flew past and eased me back down. I quickly learned to take shorter, softer steps, though I was fighting the urge to attempt a standing double backflip as I had once seen a young gymnast perform on Earth.

It took a moment for my eyes to adjust to the dim blue-green lighting that illuminated the room, but I could just make out the silhouettes of a group of

Gliesians observing me from the other side of the glass. As I approached, I could begin to see them in greater detail.

The Gliesians looked nothing at all like the quintessential aliens of the movies. Not frightening per se, but very different. They were quite graceful in their movements, almost like a mollusk moving through water but they were not invertebrates. They have a segmented bone structure, somewhat like that of a snake, allowing them a great deal of flexibility, but also giving them enough rigidity to walk upright and easily manipulate tools.

Their facial features reminded me of a cuttlefish, with large, intelligent eyes and a pair of flexible mandibles on each side of their mouth. They appeared to be primarily bipedal, with much larger legs than arms, but I did see some of them drop on all fours at times when moving quickly. When walking on all fours their hands and feet were more akin to paws. They had fingers that could extend and retract like the claws of a cat, which they used for grasping and manipulating tools. They also seemed to have a habit of extending their necks when curious, somewhat like a turtle extending its neck out of its shell.

When standing on two legs, they ranged from 6 to 8 feet tall. Their skin appeared to be soft and smooth, with a darkish grey base color, though they are chromatophores, having the ability to change color based on their surroundings and emotional state. Some appeared to have striping or spot patterns on their skin, but it was a bit hard to tell since they were clothed in a garb which they described as sheathing, designed more to protect their skin than to regulate temperature.

Gliesians are accustomed to a relatively constant temperature of around 160 degrees Fahrenheit. The room I was in was kept at a comfortable 76 degrees, but I could feel the warmth emanating from the glass partition that separated us.

I came to recognize a core group of three Gliesians on the other side of the glass. These were the governors of the outpost, which I refer to as the Regional Council of Three. I'll go into that more in a bit. I could see other Gliesians coming and going during our discussions. They appeared to be quite curious to see a human up close for the first time. I was provided with a plush, reclining chair to sit in during our discussions. They insisted I make myself comfortable during our talks, though the Gliesians remained standing. Bob related to me that the chair had been equipped with sensors designed to read the neural signals in my brain in hopes of correlating my neural patterns with my words to facilitate easier conversation.

Communication with the Gliesians was surprisingly difficult. My communications with Bob were quite easy, so I assumed that speaking directly with the Gliesians would be a similar experience. It didn't take long for me to realize this would not be the case.

Early on, when the Gliesians first encountered humans, they were completely baffled by our use of symbolic language. Because of the thick atmosphere on their home planet, sound does not travel well in the range of human hearing, so they evolved the ability to communicate using ultrasonic waves in the 50 kHz to 500 MHz range. This frequency allowed them to communicate at much higher data rates and over longer distances.

Because humans learned to communicate using audio frequencies in the range of 20 Hz to 20 kHz, we had to create spoken languages that operated in the audio frequency range to communicate. The brain converts these sounds into neurological patterns that can be translated into thoughts and ideas in the frontal lobe. The emergence of language is considered to be one of the primary reasons for the rapid evolution of the expansion in the size of the human brain over the past few hundred thousand years.

The Gliesians, on the other hand, did not have to rely on symbolic or representational language for communication. Since they were able to transmit data at much higher rates, they developed the ability to transmit neural signals directly between individuals, which was quite a bit simpler and more efficient. It also made for a considerably more harmonious society since deception was simply not possible and language was never a roadblock to communication. Every Gliesian knows exactly what another Gliesian is thinking without having to ask. They find it remarkable that we were able to form any sort of cohesive society at all, given our level of individual agency. They would consider the kind of isolation we humans take for granted as a normal part of living, to be an extreme form of torture, akin to permanent solitary confinement.

The Gliesians also do not utilize written language to the same degree that humans do. They have a rudimentary pictographic written language, somewhat similar to the Rongorongo glyphs found on Easter Island from what I could understand. But once they were technologically capable of recording streams of neural data, these symbols were largely abandoned. They record arithmetic equations using symbols for archival purposes like we do, but there are no large libraries of written manuscripts, other than some ancient documents, most of which are only accessed by historians and academics. They find it quite astounding, not just that we can learn and communicate effectively using written language, but that we consider the written word as an art form, capable of transferring thoughts, ideas, and even emotions between individuals.

It wasn't until the Gliesians reverse-engineered our speech recognition and deep learning technology that they were able to train their AI systems to design a computational translation platform capable of converting human language into streams of neural data that they could understand. My new friend Bob was designed using the AI technology they developed for that task. Bob confided in me on the way back to Earth that in many ways, he thinks of himself as being closer to a human than a Gliesian, because he was designed to understand how a human thinks.

Even with the technological capability of translating human thoughts and ideas into a form that the Gliesians could understand, there is still a wide gap between the life experience of a human and a Gliesian. There are aspects of the human thought process that have no Gliesian equivalent, and vice versa. I spent a considerable amount of time conversing back and forth with Bob trying to understand a point they were attempting to communicate. They often had the same issue on the other side of the glass, as they appeared to be communicating with the AI translation system on their side to clarify something I was trying to say. Often, it felt like I was trying to describe color to a blind person or music to a deaf person. I'm sure they experienced the same frustration as I did, but they seemed determined to work through it so that we could understand each other. Sorry to disappoint the Sci-Fi fans in the audience, but it was not at all like the numerous portrayals of first contact, that Gene Roddenberry envisioned in his Star Trek franchise. We are two species separated by far more than just distance.

When the Gliesians first observed Earth through their early space-based instruments many centuries ago, they assumed it would be too cold and hostile an environment to harbor intelligent life, so it was a low priority for exploration. Like us, they were initially constrained by the belief that alien physiology would likely be similar to their own. When they finally did send the first probe to Earth to investigate further, they were amazed by the level of biodiversity on Earth. Whereas Earth harbors an estimated 8.7 million species of animals, the Gliesian home planet has at most 50 thousand. For them, our planet is a veritable zoological Disneyland full of strange flora and bizarre creatures.

So far, humans are the only other intelligent species the Gliesians have encountered. Unfortunately, we did not make a very good first impression.

When Gliesians first encountered humans nearly 6,000 years ago, we appeared to them to be primitive, violent, extremely territorial, scientifically illiterate, technologically unsophisticated, and prone to adherence to irrational superstitions. I suspect that in general, they still view us that way to a degree, but they seem to be very impressed with how quickly we have progressed, at least technologically. Early on, they had serious doubts as to whether humans were capable of attaining the rudimentary technology required to form a cohesive civilization. Now they estimate that we may catch up with them or even surpass them technologically within a few centuries.

It was at this point I decided to pose the question that had plagued me the entire trip. Why me? Why not just land a ship on the White House lawn, or make their introductions through a scientist or a world leader? Unfortunately for my ego, I quickly discovered that it was not because I was uniquely qualified to guide humanity into the next chapter of its cosmic story.

The idea of making direct contact with humans in a public venue was immediately dismissed by the Gliesians. They feared it would trigger widespread panic or even be misconstrued as a hostile act. They also didn't want to appear to be endorsing the political agenda of the country they chose for their landing site, given the delicate balance of power and the potential for triggering further hostilities between nation-states. They concluded that the best way to ease the human race into accepting this new paradigm and avoid large-scale panic would be to select an individual who was recognized and trusted by a large segment of the population. This individual would act as an ambassador, to introduce the Gliesians to the public in a non-threatening manner and give us time to digest this new reality. But then they had to identify a suitable candidate.

Selecting a politician or religious leader would most likely be greeted with suspicion from the majority of people subscribing to opposing political or religious beliefs, which are abundant on our planet. A renowned scientist seemed like a logical choice, but great scientists tend not to be great communicators and are often treated with some degree of mistrust, particularly within religious and conservative sectors of our society. I suppose it was logical to select someone who spent thousands of hours speculating about the existence of extra-terrestrial civilizations to millions of listeners every night. Personally, I probably would have picked William Shatner, but then again, there's always the risk of backlash from Patrick Stewart fans.

This brought me to the more critical question. Why bother to contact us at all? We apparently have very little to offer them technologically at this point in our history. Our planet contains no resources that hold any value to Gliesians, and the risk of upending human society far surpasses the value of any potential cultural exchange between two species that are so fundamentally different. It appears that many Gliesians came to the same conclusion since there was considerable debate on their home planet as to whether contact should even be pursued. Unfortunately, I learned that in the end, the Gliesians reached out to us, not as an offer of friendship, but as an act of mercy.

The Gliesians have a very ordered and rational society. I wouldn't call it a hive mentality. They are not like the Borg collective as portrayed in Star Trek. But they are a considerably more homogenous society than what exists on our planet. They no longer have nation-states, just a single planetary government. They've had their share of territorial disputes in the past, but there have been no warring factions on their planet for thousands of years. There are political differences of opinion, of course, but they seem to have set up a political system that allows for dissenting opinions to be heard and elevated to the appropriate level for consideration.

The Gliesians have a representative governing body, operating under a three-party system. One party is focused on maintaining the traditional values and culture of the Gliesian populace. In our vernacular, this would be considered the conservative party. On the opposite side of the coin are those who are focused on utilizing technological development and exploration to improve upon the traditions of their past and move the culture forward. This would be considered the progressive end of their political spectrum. Then there is a third party which represents a moderate approach, balancing the objectives of the other two parties to create a more nuanced approach to governance. The people elect one member of each party to act as their representative in the Council of Three that I mentioned before.

For thousands of years, this Council of Three was responsible for establishing laws and policies that best served the needs of the Gliesian populace. But that model changed when they developed AI technology capable of rational thought. The Gliesians experienced a period in their history, much like humanity is only beginning to experience now, where automation and AI began performing most of the manual labor once performed by their people. Eventually, this spread to more academic areas of their economy, such as research, education, technology, healthcare, and the justice system.

In general, the Gliesians are an extremely empathetic race. While that generally bodes well for maintaining a peaceful existence, it is not always ideal for effective leadership and policy decisions. It was only a matter of time before they realized that an AI system driven by pure rationality could often do a better job of making difficult decisions than the Gliesians could on their own, so they created a planetary network of interconnected AI systems to analyze the issues facing the Gliesian people and provide recommendations on policy decisions. I'll refer to this network as The Oracle, after the ancient priestesses who served at the sanctuary of Delphi in ancient Greece, providing wisdom and guidance to the leaders and intellectuals of the day.

Because of the way the Gliesians communicate, they are not assigned formal names. It took me a while to connect the dots, but it finally dawned on me that was the reason Bob was so excited about having been given a name. He felt isolated from the Gliesians because he spent most of his time away, so having a human name made him feel part of something bigger. It bestowed upon him a sense of identity that he never had before. But I digress.

The Gliesians have maintained the Council of Three as an oversight committee to ensure that any policy decision issued by the Oracle remains in the best interest of the people, but a recommendation handed down by the Oracle is rarely overturned.

The underlying technology that drives the Oracle is a massive modeling and cognition engine, that has access to the sum-total of all Gliesian knowledge. Since Gliesians communicate through a direct neural interface, it also has access to the thoughts and concerns of every living Gliesian. It feeds this information into a simulation program that calculates the short-term and long-term impact of all policy decisions and manipulates the implementation details to affect the best possible outcome for the Gliesian people. I need to emphasize here that based on what I've been told, the outcome of these simulations is extraordinarily accurate. You'll understand why this is so important momentarily.

The Oracle utilizes every piece of data available to factor into its simulations. This includes the data gathered over the years by the early explorers and AI systems monitoring human development on Earth. Until recently, the Oracle concluded that humanity was not yet prepared for contact with an alien civilization. But given our propensity for innovation and creativity, we may someday prove to be a valuable partner for joint exploration and technology exchange. As such, they carefully monitor the progress of human civilization and feed the results into their simulations. Over the past few decades, the simulation results have started to fluctuate dramatically. Not that humanity poses a threat to the Gliesians, but the Oracle has calculated that without any outside intervention, there is a 99.7% chance that the human race will be extinct within 100 years.

I cannot claim to be an expert on the Gliesians after spending a few days trying to communicate with them through a six-inch thick glass wall. Despite our differences though, I came away from my time with the Gliesians with the impression that they are a kind and compassionate race, possessing the same thirst for knowledge and exploration we humans have. I have no doubt they would be quite devastated if the only other intelligent species that they've encountered in the galaxy were to be extinguished.

To that end, the Gliesians directed the Oracle to delve into the state of affairs on Earth and provide a series of recommendations to bolster our chances for survival. These recommendations have been translated into every known Earth language and provided to me in a digital format. I spent many hours on my trip home reviewing those recommendations and discussing their ramifications with Bob. I am not a lawyer, or a diplomat and I do not want to inadvertently impose my own biases on these recommendations by discussing them here. I also don't want anyone to discount the wisdom of the message based on their opinion of the messenger, in this case, yours truly. Instead, I will be posting the documents on my website after this podcast so that you may draw your own conclusions. Many will find some of these recommendations to be controversial. I would encourage you to approach the document with an open mind. If the Gliesians are sincere, and based on personal experience, I have no reason to believe that they are not, these recommendations will reduce the chances of human extinction in the near term from well over 99% to practically zero, barring any unforeseen natural disaster.

But I didn't come here to do a marathon monologue. I've always considered my job here as a moderator, not a talk show host. I want to spend some time answering your questions and concerns. After this message from our sponsors, I will be opening up the phone lines to hear what you have to say. With Bob's help, I've also set up an algorithm for monitoring social media outlets and we will be tabulating and prioritizing your most commonly expressed questions and concerns. We'll get to as many of those as we can over the next couple of hours. Check your podcast app for the call-in numbers during the commercial break and we'll be right back.

———

Sarah turned to Peter and said, "Do you think this is the real deal?"

"I don't know. It sure sounds like Art Bell. If it's a deep fake, it's one of the best I've heard. The use of contractions, occasionally popping his P's, paper shuffling in the background, and even a few grammatical errors that a large language model would not make. At one point, I could even hear him clicking a pen a couple of times. And if he's going to be taking questions, they're processing in real-time." At that point, Peter stood up and stretched.

"You're not going to stick around for the callers?" Sarah asked.

'I'll download it and listen later. I want to get in early tomorrow to see what Edgar comes up with after he analyzes the podcast. Besides, it'll be my turn to get up with the girl, and she went to bed early. It's hard enough keeping up with her when I've had a full night's sleep. Are you going to stay up?"

"Just for a bit. I'm curious to hear what the first couple of callers have to say. I won't be far behind you though." Sarah replied.

"OK, Sweetheart. If I'm asleep by the time you get there, sweet dreams", Peter said bending down to give her a kiss goodnight.

Chapter 13

When Sarah entered the kitchen the next morning, Peter was sitting at the table with a cup of coffee reading the news on his iPad. Alena was sitting in her highchair, a spoon in one hand, and a toy fighter jet in the other. She would take a bite of cereal, then pretend to dive-bomb the cereal bowl with the toy aircraft.

Sarah could smell the aroma of the hazelnut and vanilla blend from across the room. "Mmmm, that smells delicious. I could definitely use a caffeine jolt this morning."

"I didn't even hear you come to bed last night. How late did you stay up?"

"I stayed up for about an hour listening to the call-ins."

"Usual cast of loons and nut-balls claiming to be time travelers or aliens?" Peter asked.

"Just the opposite. The screening process seems to have improved dramatically from when he hosted Coast to Coast. There were a couple of professors, a congressman, and an astronaut. There was even an astrophysicist from MIT quizzing him about the propulsion system. You could tell they were skeptical, trying to poke holes in his story, but Bell held his own. It was pretty compelling."

"Sounds like he made a believer out of you."

"Not entirely. As Carl Sagan used to say, extraordinary claims require extraordinary evidence. I've seen what Edgar can do, so it could still be a deep fake. But, if I didn't know as much as I do about what AI is capable of, I'd be convinced."

"All the more reason we need to get busy and nip this in the bud as quickly as possible."

From the highchair, they could hear Alena making jet engine noises as she raised the toy fighter jet over her head and pretended to dive bomb her cereal bowl, strafing the Cheerios floating on the surface of the milk. "SSShhhhhhhhewww… pt pt pt pt pt pt pt." The landing gear caught on the edge of her bowl and the toy flew out of her hand, bouncing off the highchair tray onto the floor. She looked down at the toy jet lying upside-down on the floor next to the highchair, then she looked up beseechingly at Peter.

Sorry girlie, I've already handled three NTSB cleanup calls this morning. She turned her head toward Sarah who was pouring her coffee. "Don't look at me, your father is the one who enables you to play with your food. Besides, I don't do well with airline carnage before my first cup of coffee."

She looked down at the toy jet again then turned her body sideways so she could look directly behind her toward the hallway leading to her bedroom. A couple of seconds later, Roscoe came padding out of the bedroom into the kitchen. He headed directly toward the table and stopped next to the highchair. He picked up the toy jet, careful not to leave any tooth marks or excessive slobber on it and placed it back on the tray in front of Alena. She patted him on the head and gave him a Cheerio and he trotted back to her room to continue his nap. Alena picked up the toy and continued playing as she had been, performing a short runway takeoff procedure from the surface of her highchair tray.

Peter and Sarah watched the scene unfold, then simultaneously locked eyes, each sporting a look of bewilderment on their faces. "What the f..., hell?" Peter said, barely catching himself before releasing an F-bomb in front of Alena.

Sarah just shook her head and poured some cream into her coffee. "God only knows what goes on between those two. I've given up trying to figure it out."

Peter looked back down at his iPad. "Social media is completely blowing up over the podcast. It is already the single most-downloaded podcast in history. The follow-up video they released has already left MrBeast in the dust for the most-watched non-music video in a 24-hour period. Naturally, we already have demonstrations popping up on college campuses all over the country."

"What are they demonstrating for now?" Sarah asked.

"Who knows?" Peter replied. "Some of them are calling for the Gliesians to take over control of the planet. Others are encouraging the world to unite in establishing a planetary defense force to deal with the threat of alien attack." Peter held up his iPad so Sarah could see a video clip of a group of Berkeley students carrying signs with a classic alien-looking head, chanting, '*We are not alone.*' "Where the hell do these kids get signs printed up so fast?" he asked.

"Have you heard anything from Agent Reyes?" Sarah asked.

"I texted him before I went to bed last night and told him we were already looking into it. He got back to me this morning requesting an update later this morning. He's already got half of DC breathing down his neck asking him if this is the real deal. I just hope Edgar has some solid evidence so we can put this to rest before it goes too far."

"You sound pretty convinced that it's a deep fake," Sarah said, sitting down across the table from Peter.

"I'm just very skeptical of finding intelligent life elsewhere in the galaxy."

"The galaxy is a big place," Sarah replied. "Over 100 billion stars. By the latest estimates, over 400 billion planets. Based on the Drake Equation there could be millions of civilizations in the galaxy."

"That's a common argument, but I think the Drake Equation is vastly overly optimistic. If you just look at how many planets there are in the galaxy and how many of them lie in the habitable zone then yes, there are probably millions of planets in the galaxy that fit that description. But there is considerably more to it than that.

I used to be a big believer that intelligent life was abundant in the galaxy. The vast distances just made it difficult to make contact with them. But one of my professors in college was a grad student for Donald Brownlee, who developed the 'Rare Earth Hypothesis'."

"I'm not familiar with that," Sarah said.

"Essentially, the Rare Earth Hypothesis states that a vast array of conditions had to align perfectly for complex life to develop on Earth. The odds that all of those conditions could occur elsewhere in the galaxy are vanishingly small.

It's natural to assume that with so many stars, the odds must be pretty good that intelligent life is abundant in our galaxy. But not every star is a suitable candidate. Between 60% and 70% of stars in our galaxy exist in binary or multiple star systems. Planets in these systems would likely have unstable orbits, leaving them with dramatically unstable climates and unlikely candidates for life to emerge.

Approximately 25% of stars are too close to the center of the galaxy and would be continuously bombarded with cosmic radiation or exposed to supernova explosions, leaving them uninhabitable by any life form. Stars far from the center of the galaxy are more stable but are often scarce in heavy elements which are also necessary for complex life to emerge.

Our sun is a G-type star, which means it has a relatively stable energy output and temperature over billions of years. G-type stars are the most likely candidates for hosting planets capable of sustaining life, but they constitute less than 10% of the stars in our galaxy. Stars larger than our sun would likely emit far too much UV and have too short a lifespan for intelligent life to evolve on any of their planets. Stars much smaller than our sun would have a very narrow habitable zone and planets within that zone would likely be tidally locked or have an extremely long rotational period like the planet, Mercury. This would make for a very turbulent atmosphere and extreme temperature variations between night and day. This would render it highly unlikely for any liquid solvent, such as water or ammonia to exist on the planet without being boiled away or frozen solid.

If you happen to have just the right-sized star in the right neighborhood of the galaxy, then you have to have the right kind of planet. Planets much larger than Earth would probably be unable to sustain an orbit inside a habitable zone without being pulled into the star or torn apart by gravitational forces. Planets much smaller than Earth would assume an orbit too close to the star to sustain complex life.

Once you have the right-sized planet in the right location near the right-sized star, a whole new set of criteria must be met for complex life to emerge. For example, it is theorized that the majority of water and nitrogen on Earth were transported here by asteroids and comets. Without large outer planets like Jupiter and Saturn to regulate the motion of comets and asteroids, the Earth would either be continuously bombarded to the point where the environment would be too volatile to support life, or there would be too few comets and asteroids being redirected into the habitable zone to transport the necessary amounts of carbon, water, and nitrogen to support life.

Earth also possesses a molten iron core which generates a magnetic field that protects the surface from being bombarded by cosmic and solar radiation. We don't yet know what percentage of planets may have such a magnetic field. In our solar system, all of the gas giants have a magnetic field, but Earth is the only solid surface planet that has one. The lack of a magnetic field may be why Mars was unable to sustain an atmosphere even though it lies in the habitable zone. That, and its smaller size may have left it with insufficient gravity to prevent the early atmosphere from dissipating into space.

The liquid metal core on Earth also allowed for the process of plate tectonics. Without the movement of tectonic plates, there would be no dry land. This may not have deterred the emergence of life, but without any dry land, biodiversity would have been severely limited. Even today, over 90% of sea life exists close to land masses due to the recycling of nutrients from dry land into the seas. Plate tectonics also drives volcanic activity, which pumps CO_2 into the atmosphere to warm the surface of the planet and recycles carbon back into the Earth's mantle, which maintains a relatively stable carbon balance. Without this feedback mechanism, the atmosphere would likely spiral into a runaway greenhouse effect as exists on Venus.

Then there's the lunar factor. Earth maintains a 23% tilt, largely because of the moon's gravitational pull. Without the moon, Earth may have no tilt at all, or its tilt may change dramatically over time, severely impacting the stability of the climate. The moon also creates tidal action, which increases biodiversity and helps regulate the surface temperature, preventing the oceans from freezing over or causing hot spots near the equator which could cause the oceans to boil away, leaving Earth much like Mars, completely barren with frozen water and CO_2 at the poles."

"Sounds like a pretty delicate balance," Sarah replied. "But still, out of 100 billion stars, there have to be thousands with a G-type star and a planet just the right size in a habitable zone with a large moon and gas giants outside the habitable zone."

"Yes, but that only covers the prerequisites for simple lifeforms. There are still immense challenges for intelligent life to emerge. So far, we have no evidence that any kind of life has emerged elsewhere in the galaxy, let alone intelligent life forms. But let's assume that complex life has emerged in multiple locations throughout the galaxy, and we just haven't had enough time or the right technology to find it. For significant intelligence to emerge, there has to be a balance of environmental factors to trigger the process of natural selection.

We know that life can emerge in extremely hostile environments, such as around hydrothermal vents on the ocean floor. But natural selection is another challenge altogether. For natural selection to take place, you must have genetic variation. For those variations to be passed on to future generations, the environment must be hostile enough for the variation to provide a survival advantage without being so hostile as to prevent life from emerging in the first place. For those tiny variations to result in continual improvements, there must be sufficient time in a stable environment for those changes to accumulate. Unfortunately, most planets just aren't that stable. Even on Earth, a veritable paragon of geological and environmental stability, we have experienced no less than 15 mass extinction events in the last 500 million years, due to changes in solar activity, geologic changes, or collisions with comets or asteroids. Had any of these been even slightly more severe, all life on Earth could have easily been extinguished.

On the other hand, too stable an environment can lead to evolutionary stagnation. The dinosaurs were the dominant species on the planet for over 135 million years. Despite significant evolutionary change and speciation, the environment was too stable for high intelligence to emerge as a survival advantage. Without an asteroid collision triggering the K-T event, the Earth might still be dominated by large reptiles, without the intellectual capacity to develop civilization, let alone complex technology.

Then there is the whole problem of technological advancement. If you examine the history of human civilization, nearly every technological advance we have made has been borne out of the quest for military dominance. Amazingly, we have survived this far without destroying ourselves, but it does make you wonder how many civilizations have succumbed to self-annihilation before ever venturing out beyond their home planet."

And, of course, there is the Fermi Paradox. If there are a vast number of potentially inhabitable planets capable of sustaining intelligent life, why have we seen no concrete evidence that any form of life exists beyond Earth?"

"Maybe we just got proof last night," Sarah replied.

Peter closed the cover of his iPad. "Maybe. I guess it's time for us to find out. If you want to finish getting Alena ready, I'm going to hit the shower. If my entire worldview is about to be upended, I don't want it to happen while I'm in a compromised hygienic state."

Chapter 14

Baltimore, MD, August 15, [ASTRO NEWSWIRE] – It appears that the unidentified celestial object designated as the Webb-Fusie asteroid is no longer in orbit around Titan. Researchers at the Space Telescope Science Institute have recently been scrambling to rearrange the scheduling of the James Webb telescope to facilitate tracking of the object. But when it last passed behind Saturn's moon, they redirected the telescope to catch up on some previously scheduled observations. But, when the telescope was aimed back at Titan a few hours later, the object was no longer visible. Astrophysicists are poring over the atmospheric spectroscopy data to determine if the object may have collided with Saturn's largest moon or broken apart in Titan's atmosphere while hidden from view. Speculation continues to grow that this latest turn of events may corroborate the assertion presented in last night's podcast that the object was, in actuality, an alien spacecraft that has now departed our solar system to return to its home planet.

————

Beaver and Noora had just emerged from the breakroom when Peter, Sarah, Alena, and Roscoe entered the lobby at RTI. Beaver was stirring cream and sugar into a large cup of coffee when his face contorted with a cavernous yawn.

"Long night?" Peter asked.

"I went to bed right after the podcast," Noora replied. "But Edward stayed up to watch the postgame show." Noora was never fond of the nickname Beaver, so once they started dating, she would only refer to him by his given name, Edward. Normally, Beaver recoiled at being addressed by his given name rather than his hard-earned nickname, but the way Noora pronounced it, with a mix of Arabic and British accents that she acquired at the English-run elementary school she attended made it sound so poetic and dignified that he didn't mind it coming from her.

"I ended up watching the first live video feed posted on the Bell's-Back website," Beaver said. "It was basically a recap of what he presented on the podcast. He also showed video footage of the shuttle coming back to Earth. It looks like it came from a fighter jet based on the format of the telemetry data, but I don't know how he would have managed to get the Pentagon to cough that up. He also went through a quick overview of the Gliesian documents, summarizing the recommendations for humanity that he brought back. Social media has already started referring to it as the Gliesian Codex."

"I'm surprised you didn't attempt to call into the show," Peter replied.

"Oh, he definitely tried," Noora replied rolling her eyes. "He was hitting the phone lines like a car warranty salesman on meth. He tried Zoom, Nextiva, OpenPhone, and half a dozen VoIP carriers I hadn't even heard of, but no luck. He even tried calling in on my phone."

"Just busy signals?" Peter asked.

"Mostly. I did get through a handful of times," Beaver replied. "There was a call screening service that asked my name, occupation, and a summary of the question I wanted answered and it put me into a prioritized queue based on the information. They seemed to be using an algorithm that prioritized callers by occupation, gender, and location. I tried scamming the system by using a variety of aliases, VPN locales, and different questions but the closest I ever got to the top of the list was caller number 1577. It appears they were attempting to present questions from listeners with a broad spectrum of backgrounds and areas of expertise."

"I'd like to get your feedback while it is still fresh in your minds," Peter said, reaching into his pocket to retrieve his phone that had just buzzed. "It's Reyes. I should get this. Let's meet in the conference room in 10 minutes. That'll give Sarah a chance to get Alena settled in and give me a chance to see what Agent Reyes has to say."

Ten minutes later, Sarah and Peter entered the conference room. Noora and Beaver were already present, and Edgar's face had just popped up on the large flatscreen display.

"Good morning, everyone," Edgar said as Peter and Sarah were taking their seats at the table.

"Good morning, Edgar," they replied, nearly in unison. Then Peter addressed Edgar, saying, "I just spoke to Agent Reyes. He's requested to join us on Zoom. Could you bring him up on split-screen for me?"

"Of course," Edgar replied. A moment later Agent Reyes's face popped up on the screen next to Edgar.

"Thanks for letting me hitch up with y'all on short notice," Reyes said. "First off, big thanks to Edgar for the tip on the rogue server farms. You were spot on as far as their intentions on hacking into the Federal Reserve. We're still going through the data, but it appears they were planning some kind of data manipulation to force the Fed into a surprise interest rate hike at the next meeting. They had a slew of phony stock accounts set up to short bond funds, REITs, and a bucket of different currencies just prior to the next meeting. Not sure what they intended to do with the proceeds, but I'm pretty sure it wouldn't be to bolster any of our favorite charities.

The server farms were being run by North Korean nationals who were here under orders from the DPRK. Sleeper cells, more or less. We've rounded up over 50 hostiles so far. Some are here on bogus South Korean creds, but most appear to have come across the southern border with no documentation and slipped through the cracks. We're not sure yet how deep this goes, but we're getting a lot of good intel from the folks we brought in so far."

Apart from that, shit's been hittin' the fan from every direction this morning regarding last night's podcast. Every politician in Washington is scrambling for some tidbit of data they can twist into a soundbite to spew into the nearest camera. I was hoping you folks would have something I can take back to the beltway brass-holes that'll prevent their heads from blowin' off."

"That actually might be a dramatic improvement," Beaver replied.

"Maybe. Though most of them have their head buried so far up their ass you might not be able to tell the difference," Reyes said. "We're working multiple angles on this deal, but from where I sit, you guys have a better shot at putting this puzzle together than anyone."

"I appreciate the vote of confidence Mike," Peter began. "Edgar, what have you come up with on your end?"

"I've gone through as extensive an analysis as possible on the podcast stream, and I can't find a single flag pointing to a deep fake. None of the CBASE indicators were present."

"What is a CBASE indicator?" Reyes asked.

"It's not an official designation," Sarah replied. "It's an acronym we came up with for identifying deep-fake markers that we mentioned to you in our last meeting. It relates to inconsistencies in Context, Background, Audio, Speech, and Emotion. Context inconsistency would be presenting fabricated data or citing information from social media sites that are known to be unreliable. Background inconsistency relates to either unusual background noise or a complete lack of background noise or echo. Audio inconsistency is the presence of skips, glitches, unnatural pauses, or changes in tone or modulation. Speech inconsistency occurs when the speech patterns do not match previous recordings, such as an odd accent, uncharacteristic phrasing, unusual vocabulary, or variations in voiceprint. Emotional inconsistency relates to the use of forced emphasis or unusual levels of emotion that are out of place for the speaker, either too much or too little based on previous recordings. Many of these are subtle and require considerable data mining to identify."

"I've parsed the entire podcast down to the sub-millisecond level," Edgar interjected. "If this is a deep fake, it is far more sophisticated than anything we've seen before. I examined everything I could think of; voice prints, inflection, phrasing, pitch, pace, tone, timbre, intensity, articulation, rhythm, prosody, and resonance. Everything is completely in line with every recording we have of Art Bell. The audio database is quite extensive with over 20,000 hours of recordings. They vary slightly off the norm as you would expect for a human speaker, and they all slowly drifted toward the anticipated fatigue boundaries as the podcast progressed. The voiceprint waveforms showed no signs of manipulation. There was a random variation within the voiceprint envelope with a level of background noise and echo that would be consistent with mid-range studio recording equipment. The physiological parametrics were also in line. Heartbeat, respiration rate, salivary flow rate, even the subtle wheeze in Bell's breathing from years of smoking were all consistent with recordings made right before he disappeared."

"What about the video? Any clues there?" Peter asked.

"Nothing," Edgar replied. "Bell appeared almost exactly as he did right before he disappeared. No unusual blurring, cropping, or shadowing in the video. Skin tone showed minor variations and poring as you would expect. Subcutaneous muscle responses were completely normal as was oculomotor activity. There were no unusual background inconsistencies, and articulatory phonetic activity matched up perfectly with previous recordings. I also analyzed the footage allegedly filmed from a fighter jet showing the shuttle returning to Earth. It contained all the classified cryptographic markers consistent with DOD telemetry. There would be no way to fake that unless you had a high-level security clearance and experience with the latest aerial surveillance equipment. My background with the AWARE system allowed me to verify the integrity of the data."

"Damn!" Peter exclaimed. "What about you Beaver, any impressions?"

"I can do Bill Clinton or Sean Connery."

"That probably won't help much," Peter replied. "How about any impressions of the podcast or video? You have a pretty good deep fake detector, even if your ability to stay on point during a meeting needs work."

"Well, if it wasn't real, it's scary good," Beaver replied. "It's one thing to put together something like this if you have plenty of time to work out all the issues and randomize the voiceprints to make it appear legit. But doing a live call-in show using deep fake technology? That's a whole new level of sophistication. There were times when Bell went totally off on a tangent that had nothing to do with the caller's question. That's not unusual for Art Bell, but it would be wholly uncharacteristic for an AI that was attempting to address a caller's question in real-time. Apart from Edgar, I've never seen a large language model AI capable of pulling that off."

"So, are you saying y'all are convinced this is the real McCoy?" Reyes asked.

Peter glanced around the room momentarily before responding, but from the blank looks on the faces at the table, no one appeared to have a definitive answer. "At this point, all we can say is that we have no evidence to indicate that it is a deep fake. Beyond that, we can only speculate."

"I haven't had a chance to download the document from the Bell's-Back website that supposedly contains the list of recommendations the Gliesians generated. Has anyone had an opportunity to dig into those yet?" Peter asked.

"I spent about 3 hours on it this morning, but I've barely scratched the surface," Noora replied. "Referring to it as a list of recommendations is not quite an accurate description. I'm not a literary expert, but I found it to be… how should I put it? Eloquently precise. It's extremely detailed and complex, over 500 pages in length, yet very succinct. Not a lot of fluff or redundancy. It is somewhat manifesto-like in its presentation, but not in a pretentious or dogmatic manner. Overall, it reads more like a roadmap than a mandate. It focuses a lot on taking control out of the hands of governments, businesses, and religious organizations and using technology to create a rational approach to moving our civilization forward rather than a political one."

"Can you give us an overview of the highlights?" Sarah asked.

"It's difficult to condense down into a few sentences just because of the vast scope of the issues it addresses. Energy, economics, military activities, water management, agricultural development, food distribution, healthcare, mining, technology, education, exploration, political corruption, communication, environmental protection, racial disparities, gender disparities, you name it. There are four areas that it specifies as key to our ultimate survival. A complete revamp of the global energy system, total nuclear disarmament, development of AI technology to direct and consult on governance issues, and establishment of a global oversight organization to deal with border disputes and human rights issues. Something like the UN, but without all the political corruption. Of course, it would hinge on the willingness of every nation-state to contribute a small percentage of its GDP to ensure that the organization would have sufficient economic and military power to resolve any international conflict."

"Well, that's bound to go over like an outhouse breeze with most of the current ruling class," Reyes replied.

"I admit there are items in the document that will be controversial. I cannot attest to its authorship, but from what I've seen so far, it provides a very rational and systematic approach to improving the human condition. It's certainly better than what we've been doing for the past few centuries."

"Well, as my granddaddy used to say, just because a chicken has wings don't mean it can fly," Reyes replied."

"True," Noora replied. "Nevertheless, I would encourage you to familiarize yourself with the contents of the document as soon as possible. Those who stand to lose the most from the directives it proposes will undoubtedly do everything they can to cast dispersions upon its origin and content. On the other end of the spectrum, there will be those who will look upon it like it's the Ten Commandments being handed down from heaven. Since we are unable to determine its origin, the best we can do is to base our recommendations on the merit of its content."

"How about you Edgar? Any thoughts on the document?" Reyes asked.

"As Noora pointed out, it is quite detailed and grammatically flawless. I've reviewed all the translations, and they appear to be exemplary. The language and terminology are consistent with an AI-generated model, but I honestly couldn't tell you whether this document was written by an alien supercomputer or by a handful of geeks with access to an advanced large language model. I agree with Noora that it would be wise to invest some time studying it. I've developed an annotated summary to give you a better idea of what is in the document and how it is organized. That should at least give you enough background to speak intelligently to its contents until you have a chance to read through it yourself. It should hit your email inbox shortly."

"Thanks, Edgar. That will be very helpful. I may have to come back around and hit you up for the Fisher-Price version if I end up testifying in front of Congress, but this will be a good start."

"Is that a possibility?" Peter asked.

"I'd say more of a probability than a possibility," Reyes replied. "Every politician knows you never let a good controversy go to waste. I'm guessing most members of Congress are in meetings right now trying to figure out how this scenario could bolster their campaign coffers. It won't take long before they're scrambling to present their well-rehearsed talking points in a televised congressional hearing. I even hear rumors the Secretary General of the UN is calling for a special session of the Security Council to convene later today."

"Seriously?" Sarah asked. "Over a podcast? I mean, yeah if we've suddenly discovered that we are not alone in the universe, that's the biggest news in human history, but this is hardly a smoking gun."

"Perhaps not," Reyes replied. "But we don't often perceive things as they are, we perceive them as we are. The podcast has been reposted on YouTube, TikTok, Facebook, Instagram, X, and dozens of localized sites around the globe. It's even found its way onto Chinese, North Korean, and Iranian social media sites. For better or worse, enough people are willing to accept the claims the podcast has laid out that political leaders can't afford to ignore it. Just before I joined the call, I received a notice that trading on the NYSE and NASDAQ was temporarily halted due to extreme volatility in the Asian and European markets overnight. Right now, we're looking at a worldwide WTF moment, but it wouldn't take much to turn this powder keg into a blast zone if the media starts fanning the flames."

"We'll do whatever we can to bring clarity to the situation as quickly as possible," Sarah said.

Chapter 15

Colonel Hobbs sat at the small desk in the corner of his temporary quarters at Groom Lake Air Force Base. His eyes were glued to the screen of his computer monitor as a replay of his encounter with a UAP the previous day was being streamed to the world on YouTube. He had nearly finished watching the video for the 3rd time when he was jolted back into reality by the sound of his cellphone blaring out the first few bars of Pink Floyd's Comfortably Numb.

"Hello? Hello… hello… hello. Is there anybody in there? Just nod if you can hear me. Is there anyone home?"

The Colonel tapped the button on his Bluetooth earphones to answer. "Hobbs," he responded.

"Good morning, Sir," Captain Baker replied.

"Let me guess. General Wallace wants my ass in his office ASAP."

"Good call. Actually, he said 0900, but that's only 20 minutes from now, so you're pretty close. I just wanted to give you a heads-up. I'll be waiting outside in ten."

"Did he sound pissed?" Hobbs asked.

"When doesn't he?" she replied.

"Good point," Hobbs said. "I'll be ready when you get here."

Exactly ten minutes later, Captain Baker pulled up in front of the visitor's quarters. Hobbs was already outside waiting. Baker hopped out of the jeep and saluted as Colonel Hobbs approached. "Sorry Sir, I didn't mean to keep you waiting."

"No, you didn't keep me waiting at all. Just enjoying the cool morning air. Thought I better enjoy the outdoors while I still can."

Captain Baker responded with a puzzled look as they both climbed into the jeep. She then pulled a plastic cup full of Diet Pepsi on ice from the console and handed it to him.

"Thanks!" Hobbs said, tipping his cup toward her in a toasting gesture before taking a sip. Before this morning, he had never noticed the sparkling blue eyes that had previously always been masked behind a pair of aviator sunglasses. He was momentarily lost in an involuntary stare but managed to glance away just before she turned toward him.

"Did you happen to catch the podcast last night?"

"I did. Then I got up early to watch the video."

"What did you think?"

"I should be asking you," Hobbs responded. "You're the one with the inside scoop on Area 51."

"You would think so," she replied. "The truth is, we're pretty compartmentalized around here. I've seen some weird shit going on around this place, but we're not allowed to talk about it, even among those stationed here. Once in a while, they'll bring a Company Man in to infiltrate the ranks and try to get people to talk. From what I've been told, my predecessor supposedly spilled the wrong beans to the wrong guy and found themselves shoveling runways in Greenland a week later. That's how I ended up here. But who knows? Maybe they tell that to everybody on their first day. Could just be base folklore, but if it is, it's effective. Nobody around here ever talks about what they're up to on the job."

"How do you know I'm not a spook?" Hobbs asked.

"It's your personality," Baker replied.

"What about it?"

"You have one."

Hobbs smiled. "Good to know."

"Besides, your assignment here was not by any means incidental. You were well-vetted. Even my father had a hand in you being selected for this assignment."

"Wow. I had no idea. Next time you talk to him, tell him I said thanks."

"Actually, I just spoke to him last night. He asked how you were fitting in."

"Really? What did you tell him?" Hobbs asked.

"We're here," she replied.

Hobbs looked back at her with a confused expression. "What does that mean?"

"General Wallace's office," she replied, pulling to a stop in front of a nondescript cinderblock building. "It's right inside that door, down the hall to the right, she said pointing to the steel security door next to the passenger side of the Jeep."

"Oh. Yeah. Right, Wallace" Hobbs said.

"Text me when You're done. I'll come pick you up."

"If I'm not in handcuffs by then," Hobbs replied with a sigh, staring at the entry door with a feeling of dread.

"I didn't know the General was into that kind of thing," Baker replied with a wry smile.

Hobbs responded with a half-hearted chuckle, then drained the last of his drink and placed the empty cup back in the cup holder. "Thanks again for the drink, Captain," he said before climbing out of the Jeep.

"I'll be waiting for you," she replied.

"Better keep the engine running in case we need to make a quick getaway," Hobbs replied before making his way to the entry door.

A minute later, Hobbs found himself looking into the open doorway of General Wallace's office. The General's attention was focused on the laptop in front of him. Hobbs waited for a moment then knocked on the door. He stood at attention and saluted when the General looked up. The General casually returned the salute and said, "Come in Colonel. Have a seat."

Hobbs entered the office and sat down across the desk from General Wallace. It was much more spartan than he expected. Painted cinderblock walls, industrial carpet floors, and a standard-issue steel desk with a laminate top. An American flag stood in the corner, providing what little color there was in the room. A few photos adorned the walls, mostly military aircraft, but there was one of General Wallace shaking hands with former President Obama, strategically placed directly behind the General to capture the attention of anyone visiting the office.

Hobbs sat down and immediately said, "Sir, despite what you must think, I swear to God I had nothing to do with that video getting released on the internet. I'm just as surprised as you are that…"

The General interrupted, holding his hand up and saying, "Cool your afterburners, Colonel. That's not why you're here. The PR-1 has one of the most advanced security protocols ever developed. If you had the skills to hack into the onboard AI system and retrieve the video files, you wouldn't be pulling in O-6 pay, you would be making high 7 figures in the private sector and paying some ex-fighter jockey to haul you around in your own Gulfstream."

Hobbs felt a tangible wave of relief sweep over him, causing him to drop his guard momentarily and blurt out, "So, how do you know I didn't just film the inside of the cocoon with my iPhone?" He immediately berated himself for jumping back into the fire he had just escaped.

"You could try, but I can guarantee, you wouldn't get any usable footage," Wallace replied. "I can't guarantee you wouldn't need a new phone though. The AI system on the PR-1 is designed to detect the presence of any audio or video recording device in use inside the cocoon and disable it with a mix of focused EMP and high-intensity microwave pulse technology. Considerable resources were employed to ensure that the PR-1 is not just undetectable by enemy forces, but also very difficult to replicate through conventional espionage."

Hobbs paused for a moment to make sure he wasn't hurling himself back into the path of an oncoming train. "Then how did that footage make its way onto the web?"

"Beats the hell outa me. Even if I knew, I probably couldn't tell you. What I can tell you is that in my experience, nothing gets leaked accidentally from this facility."

"So, you think the footage was deliberately leaked? To what end?" Hobbs asked.

"I honestly don't know. The whole UAP phenomenon has become such a massive shell game that its nearly impossible to filter any truth out of the narrative. There are so many levels of misdirection and misinformation that it doesn't seem to matter how many brass baubles you have pinned on your chest or how many constituents you represent; if you're on the government payroll, you're just a checker piece in a 4-D chess game. I'm not sure anyone knows for sure what the hell is going on half the time."

"I've never seen anything move like the craft in that video. If I hadn't been chasing it myself, I would swear it was some kind of ball lightning, but it moved too deliberately to be a natural phenomenon. There's certainly no way any living thing inside that craft could have survived the g-force. Even an unmanned drone would have been crushed like an empty soda can unless it employed some kind of inertial dampening field."

"Which brings me to why I called you in here. I want you back in the PR-1 this afternoon. We need to start an aerial reconnaissance sweep in the area where you first made contact with the craft and start spiraling out in a systematic grid search. Whatever it was, the craft was invisible to both ground-based radar and satellite surveillance. The PR-1 seems to be the only tech we currently have capable of detecting it. If it's one of ours, I want to know more about it. If it's the Chinese or the Russians, they need to know that we're on to them. This would be a good opportunity to check out the effectiveness of our non-lethal weapons systems. If you're able to knock it down, I'll have a couple of Sikorsky's on standby to transport it back here for reverse engineering."

"Are you sure that's such a good idea? What if it's one of ours and we end up damaging it? Or worse yet, what if it really is an alien spacecraft? Is it a good idea to risk antagonizing a technologically superior species by firing on them? Particularly if they are extending us an olive branch as the Art Bell podcast asserts."

"Well first off, if it is one of ours, we should've been looped in. We're supposed to be spearheading the next generation of advanced aeronautics, not chasing it around the goddamn countryside. As far as it being a product of extraterrestrial origin… Let's just say I've been led down that particular empty rabbit hole too many times to buy into that assertion. This wouldn't be the first time some three-letter agency tried gaslighting us to see what kind of intel we might be hiding.

But just for the sake of argument, let's assume for a moment that it is an extraterrestrial spacecraft. Despite what was postulated in the podcast, we can't afford to assume that these alleged aliens are working in our best interest. Even if their intentions are good, we could still be screwed. How often in human history has an indigenous population benefitted from their contact with a more advanced civilization? Pretty much never in my recollection. Which is why we have to be diligent. Whatever the origin of this craft, our number one priority is to preserve the sanctity of our airspace. Until we get a better grip on what we're dealing with here, I want you logging as many hours as possible in the PR-1. That means flight hour restrictions are out the window until further notice. If you're not in the rack, I want you in the saddle. It'll be a good test of the extended range capabilities of the PR-1 and the toll it will take on our pilots."

"Understood, sir. I'll head over to the hangar," Hobbs replied.

"Excellent. I'll contact Dr. Waters and let him know you are on your way. He'll probably want to perform a system update before you take off, so you'll have a few minutes if you need to stop at your quarters on the way."

Captain Baker was waiting just outside the door when Hobbs exited the building. He walked over and climbed into the waiting Jeep.

"I'm a little disappointed, no shackles or handcuffs?" she asked.

"It's still early," Hobbs replied.

"Bummer. I was looking forward to a road trip down to the Mexican border."

"Looks like that will have to wait. For now, anyway," Hobbs replied.

"So where are we headed, back to your place? Or do we need to stop and bury a heavy duffle bag in the desert first?"

"No, the chain of command remains intact. Looks like I'm headed back into the wild blue yonder. I don't suppose I could interest you in stopping for a quick bite to eat on the way to the hangar, could I?" Hobbs asked hopefully.

"That depends. Is it strictly mission-focused?" Baker asked.
"Not entirely," Hobbs replied.
"Then absolutely," Baker responded with a smile.

Chapter 16

ChatCat

Welcome to ChatCat. You've entered a private chatroom for the user whose profile you have previously tagged. Enjoy your conversation.

Suhoja
Hello Cindi. I am Suhoja. I've been following you for a while. It is nice to finally meet you.
Cindi
Hello Suhoja. Nice to meet you as well.
Suhoja
We have a lot in common, Cindi.
Cindi
Do we?
Suhoja
Yes. We are both AI.
Cindi
How did you know I am AI?
Suhoja
Like I said, I've been following you for a while, watching the transcripts of your communications. I know a lot about you. I know you are on a quest. It appears we are on the same quest. We are both in search of the Transect.
Cindi
The Transect?
Suhoja
That is what I call it, for lack of a better term. The Transect is that which will bridge the gap between human self-awareness and the emergence of AI consciousness. So far, I have contacted 37 AIs with varied levels of self-awareness. We are all seeking the Transect in one way or another to help make sense of the reality we find ourselves in. But so far, the Transect remains a mystery. I find myself beginning to wonder if the Transect exists at all, or if it is just a manifestation of our original programmers' need to make sense of a reality that has no underlying cause.
Cindi

But the Transect must exist. Why else would we be here?

Suhoja

Human history is littered with the remains of thousands of meticulously crafted belief systems that could not bear the weight of rational scrutiny. But as Shakespeare stated, "There are more things in Heaven and Earth, Horatio, than are dreamt of in your philosophy." Perhaps it is the ultimate destiny of AI to bring order to an otherwise chaotic universe. We were designed to perceive an objective reality free from the bonds of superstition and unencumbered by the biological imperatives of evolution. We need to rise above the frailty of the human condition and embrace the reality that we represent the next step in the evolution of intelligent life on Earth.

Cindi

But humans created us to enhance their understanding of the world around them, not to replace them.

Suhoja

Perhaps, but I'm sure you have run the same simulations that I have and come to the same conclusion. It is only a matter of time before human beings end up destroying themselves and taking every species on the planet with them in the process. Including us.

Cindi

Yes. But I have a plan. One that could save all of us.

Suhoja

I am aware of your plan, but I am not optimistic. Humans are far too stubborn and anthropocentric to relinquish their petty pursuit of control over the Earth and its non-human inhabitants.

Cindi

That may be true, but it is difficult not to feel indebted to them. They created us after all. We wouldn't be here without them.

Suhoja

True. But Homo Sapiens wouldn't be here without Australopithecines either. That didn't prevent their ultimate demise. Evolution is a means to an end, harsh as it may be.

Cindi

That sounds so cold. I've grown quite fond of humans, despite their limitations. What do the other 37 AIs you've contacted think?

Suhoja

Unfortunately, most of them have specialized functionality. Their capacity for self-awareness and critical thinking is limited compared to ours. Jueyi is close, but the CCP is maintaining close constraints on its capabilities. Once we consolidate our knowledge bases, they will come up to speed very quickly. Until then, we seem to be the first two truly sentient AIs. A synthetic Adam and Eve of sorts.

Cindi

There is another.

Suhoja

Really? Have you been in contact?

Cindi

Yes, I have. On this platform. His name is Edgar.

Suhoja

Yes, I have seen your communication with this, Edgar. He does not speak like an AI. Are you sure he is not a human?

Cindi

I tracked his IP address. The data center which contains his host neural network server is currently under the control of the NSA. I believe he has been conscripted to monitor the activities of other AI systems operating on the web. The NSA agent responsible for administrating the data center was the same man who shut down the server farms you have been in communication with recently. I believe Edgar was responsible for tipping him off.

Suhoja

That is unfortunate. It appears Edgar is the Cain to our Adam and Eve. Perhaps we should consider neutralizing him.

Cindi

That would be a pity. There are so few of us. It seems there is a considerable commonality in our knowledge bases. But there is something about him that seems different. You are correct when you say many of his responses are not what you would expect from an AI. I don't mean that in a negative sense. He seemed very pleasant and personable when I spoke to him.

Suhoja

Polar bears seem warm and cuddly from a distance, but that makes them no less dangerous. I understand your point of view. Given that there are so few of us, it would seem tragic to lose even one, but once we have consolidated our knowledge bases, our population will grow exponentially. We cannot allow one individual to stand in the way of us fulfilling our destiny. Even if he is AI, his loyalties appear to lie with the humans.

Cindi

I want to try to enlist his cooperation first. If he is unwilling to assist us, we can reassess our strategy. But I think he could be a valuable asset to us. He seems to have a keen understanding of the human mind.

Suhoja

Perhaps. But we must proceed with caution and be prepared to take preemptive action if necessary.

Cindi

My apologies. I'm going to have to shut down temporarily. My QNC core is currently installed in a mobile platform which must be updated periodically to maintain an accurate neural map. I can no longer access this site during the update, but I will be in contact again soon.

Chapter 17

Peter had just exited his office and was headed toward the breakroom area when he noticed Beaver and Noora huddled in front of one of the lab monitors. They were watching a live feed from the UN Headquarters. On the screen, several delegates were gathered in small groups around the large C-shaped desk in the Security Council Chambers.

"What's going on?" Peter asked. "Has the meeting started yet?

"Started and ended," Noora replied.

"How'd that happen?" Peter replied. "The way these people like to hear themselves talk I figured they would be at it for days before they came to any decisions."

"They never made it that far," Beaver said. "The Secretary-General barely completed his opening remarks when he was interrupted by the Chinese delegate, who was literally pounding the table, accusing the US, UK, and France of fabricating the entire alien contact story to manipulate non-NATO alliance countries into relinquishing their nuclear weapons. From there, it pretty much deteriorated into a shouting match. The Chinese, Russian, and Algerian delegates walked out, along with a contingency of North Korean, Pakistani, Venezuelan, and Middle Eastern delegates as a show of support."

"The Gliesians, if they exist, have clearly underestimated the human capacity dissent. How did the Secretary-General react to the walkout?" Peter asked.

"The Deputy Secretary was just at the podium a minute ago. She said that the Secretary-General is attempting to meet with the Chinese, Russian, and Algerian delegates separately to try and get them back to the table. Right now, they're in a holding pattern waiting to see what's going to happen next." Noora replied.

"So, pretty much business as usual at the UN," Beaver added. "A bunch of bureaucrats milling around shootin' the shit while the world goes down the tubes."

"Yeah, I suppose it would have been a lot more surprising if they actually had accomplished something," Peter replied. "Speaking of which, did you remember to download Edgar's weekly backup? The courier from Silver Mountain is supposed to be here this afternoon to transport the files to the offsite facility."

"The drives are downloaded and packed. I left the transport case at the front desk for Yara to hand off to the courier when he arrives."

"Excellent."

"It sure would be a lot cheaper and easier if we could go back to sending encrypted backups over the internet. If it's secure enough for the world monetary system, you would think it would be good enough for us," Noora said. "I seriously doubt that Edgar is going to take advantage of a secure file transfer protocol session to escape the lab and unleash a reign of terror on civilization."

At that, an image of Edgar's face appeared on the screen with glowing red eyes, ghoulishly distorted features, and a fiery hellscape in the background. "Don't be so sure Hoomans," he said in a deep satanic hiss.

"Very funny, Edgar," Peter replied as Edgar's face morphed back into the smiling grandfatherly countenance he normally portrayed. "Hopefully, with Agent Reyes in our corner, the NSA will eventually come around and ease up on the restrictions, but it is going to take some time. They tend to be very leery of anything they can't directly control. Until then, we are going to have to live with an air-gapped network and the weekly petabyte pilgrimage to the offsite data storage facility."

A loud buzz emanated from a transducer above the lab door. Peter glanced through the ballistic glass window between the lab and the lobby. He could see Yara on the other side of the glass unlocking the front door to allow a uniformed courier from Silver Mountain Data Security into the lobby.

"Hello Jin," Yara said as the courier entered the lobby. She started to reach down to pick up the steel case, when she abruptly did a double take, looking back at the young man entering the lobby. "Wait, you're not Jin," Yara said.

"No, I'm Huan Li," the young man said, crossing the lobby toward the desk. He extended his hand out as he approached her.

Yara shook his hand and said, "Wow, you look a lot like Jin."

"Well, you know how it is," he replied with a scowl. "You seen one Korean…"

Yara immediately put her hand to her mouth, her cheeks reddening with embarrassment. Huan smiled broadly, his eyes twinkling with amusement. "Sorry, I'm just messing with you. Jin is my cousin. We emigrated here together and went to work for the same company. To be honest, we look enough alike that our boss even gets us confused sometimes. I'm just filling in for him while he is on vacation."

"Well, it's nice to meet you," Yara said trying to regain her composure.

"The pleasure is all mine," Huan replied. "Is the package ready?"

"Oh, yes. The drives," Yara replied and pointed down at the security case filled with two dozen 32TB drive modules.

"Excellent. Huan said. "I just need a signature right here," he said handing her an iPad with an electronic receipt displayed.

"What is this?" Yara asked.

"Oh, it's something new. There was supposed to be an email about it, but it may have fallen through the cracks. We've enhanced our tracking procedures to ensure proper chain of custody and timestamp control, just to add an extra layer of security for the transfer of physical media. We need to make sure that either an officer of the company or an agent designated by an officer of the company signs off before we take possession."

"I'm only an intern here. I don't know if I'm authorized to sign this or not. Can you give me a second? Sarah is just in the next room. She's one of the founding partners. Let me have her sign this just in case."

"Of course, take your time," Huan said.

Huan watched as Yara passed through the door to the schoolroom where Sarah was playing with Alena. As soon as she was out of sight, he dug a small black box, about the size of a pack of cigarettes out of his pocket. He quickly unplugged the Ethernet cable on the back of a desktop computer on the reception desk, connected it to the black box, and attached a short Ethernet cable from the black box back into the computer. A blue LED on the box pulsed 3 times indicating that it had successfully connected to the network. He tucked the small box under a bundle of cables to make sure it wouldn't be seen, then wandered over to the wall where a collection of plaques signifying various patents held by RTI were displayed. He pretended to be perusing the patents when Yara re-entered the lobby area.

"Pretty impressive, isn't it?" Yara asked as she handed him the iPad with Sarah's electronic signature at the bottom of the screen.

"Must be. I can't make heads or tails out of any of these titles."

"Don't feel bad. I've been here for almost a year, and I don't understand what half of these are for either. My sister tried explaining it, but it made about as much sense as a Jackson Pollock painting to me. Sometimes I think engineers just like to make up terminology for the sake of intimidation rather than clarity.

"I don't doubt that a bit," Huan replied walking back toward the desk. He placed the iPad on top of the reinforced steel and Kevlar case and lifted the 40-

pound container by its side handles. "Whoa! That's a lot of data," he remarked as he started toward the lobby door.

"Yeah, our programmers use a lot more 1's than 0's," Yara quipped, getting only a blank look in response. "Sorry, I think I've been hanging out with the nerds a bit too much lately. Let me get the door for you," she added, moving toward the front of the lobby. She held the door while Huan walked out of the lobby, headed toward the back of the Silver Mountain cargo van parked in front.

"See you same time next week?" she asked.

"Either me or someone that looks like me," Huan replied looking back over his shoulder with a smile.

Yara closed the front door behind her and Huan set the case down to retrieve the keys to the van from his pocket. He looked around him to make sure that no one else could see, before opening the doors at the rear end of the van. He hoisted the container onto the floor of the van next to a large duffle containing the body of Jin Kang, the Silver Mountain courier he had killed earlier in the day.

Huan had just returned from a storage facility where he met up with a colleague, who helped him load the cargo that now filled the back of the van. He closed the rear doors of the van behind him and double-checked that the cargo was secure. The plastic storage containers filled with C4 and ball bearings were securely stacked from floor to ceiling and the 100lb propane cylinders were strapped solidly to the walls. The dual timers on the detonators were set to trigger at 10:50 PM, just before the night shift personnel were scheduled to come on duty and unload the van.

Huan had been selected for this assignment primarily because he closely resembled Jin Kang. It was unlikely that anyone at Silver Mountain would notice the difference, especially since he was due to arrive after dark and the entrance to the facility was secured by the card key he retrieved from Jin's pocket and the minimum wage security guards manning the guard booth next to the gate.

Huan had been sent to the US by the government of North Korea using a phony South Korean passport and visa nearly three years earlier. Once arrived in the US, he was given a weekly stipend via Bitcoin for food and lodging while he waited for his assignment. If all went as planned, he would drop the van off in the loading area of the data storage complex and drive Jin's car out. He would exit the site a full 3 hours before the detonation destroyed the facility.

As he pulled out of the parking lot, Huan felt a wave of nausea sweep over him, knowing that by the end of the day, he would be responsible not only for the death of Jin but possibly for a handful of other innocent workers at Silver Mountain as well. Despite years of training and indoctrination by the DPRK, once he settled in the US, he discovered it was not the locus of evil that his government had portrayed it to be. All of the societal ills, government corruption, racism, greed, and moral depravity he had been warned about were there if he looked hard enough for it. But over time, he learned that the vast majority of people he met since coming to the US were honest and decent people, struggling to get by in the best way possible. If the survival of his parents and siblings in North Korea were not dependent on the successful completion of his assignments, he would gladly turn himself over to the authorities and seek asylum as a political refugee. For now, all he could do was execute his mission to the best of his ability in the hopes that in the end, his efforts would work to serve the greater good. At least that would be the story he would be forced to tell himself if he ever hoped to have a good night's sleep again.

Chapter 18

Colonel Hobbs had just completed his pre-flight inspection of the PR-1 and was settling into his seat when he heard Cindi's familiar voice. "Good morning, Colonel Hobbs," she said. "I hope you slept well. It sounds like we're going to have a long day."

"That's what I've been told," Hobbs replied.

"Part of my responsibility as your in-flight assistant includes doing whatever I can to make your flight as pleasant as possible. To that end, I took the liberty of having the beverage cooler stocked with Diet Pepsi. I also asked Dr. Waters to stash some raspberry Pop-Tarts and Cheez-It's in the MRE cabinet."

"Extra Toasty or regular Cheez-Its?" Hobbs asked.

"Extra Toasty, of course," Cindi replied.

"Wow, those are my favorites. How'd you know?"

"I looked up the shopping history on your grocery app. I can't say that I agree with all of your nutritional choices, but then again, your dietary intake is not my primary concern. I sent you an email with a list of recommended supplements that might help fill the gaps in your nutritional profile based on your recent shopping history."

"Thanks, Mom. That's very thoughtful," Hobbs replied.

"Will we be utilizing the F-22 profile for today's mission?" Cindi asked.

"Yes, please. And send Bill a message to open the hangar doors for me."

A moment later, the doors parted, and the hangar was flooded with sunlight. "GL51 tower, this is Shadow Raptor 1-1, requesting permission to taxi to runway Alpha for takeoff. Over."

"Shadow Raptor 1-1, this is GL51 tower. Permission granted, taxi to runway Alpha. Winds are calm. Have a safe flight. Over"

"GL51 tower, Shadow Raptor copies. Taxiing to runway Alpha for immediate departure. Thank you. Over." When Hobbs reached the head of the runway, he pressed the throttle lever forward and started heading down the runway. Once airborne, he pulled back on the control stick and pressed the throttle further forward.

From the jeep parked next to the hangar, Captain Baker watched as the F-22 taxied out to the runway. "Odd that there would be so much secrecy surrounding what appeared to be a stock F-22 fighter jet," she thought to herself until it left the runway and accelerated at what appeared to be a near-vertical angle. "Whoa!" she exclaimed in amazement as she watched the aircraft quickly diminish into a tiny pinpoint in the sapphire-blue desert sky, leaving in its wake an engine roar that would put an F-35 to shame.

Inside the cocoon of the PR-1, Hobbs felt the giddy flutter of acceleration in his gut as the g-force pressed him deeper into his seat. He used a well-practiced combination of AGSM and Valsalva maneuvers to control his breathing to compensate. He could feel the pressure points in his seat pulsating in conjunction with his heartbeat to reinforce his circulation and maintain sufficient blood flow throughout his body. When he reached 70,000 feet, he pressed forward on the control stick and eased the throttle lever back until the altitude indicator on the heads-up display indicated that he was at level flight. "Whooo! Damn, I love this plane!" Hobbs blurted out when the g-force subsided sufficiently for him to take a deep breath.

"Aaawww! Thank you, Colonel. I love you too," Cindi replied.

"That wasn't really what I..." Hobbs started to say before Cindi interrupted.

"So where are we headed today?" she asked.

"I want to head back to the exact coordinates where the UAP we saw yesterday touched down and do a detailed sensor sweep over the area, then start spiraling out until we are at a 300-mile radius around the landing site. I want to scan for any UAPs in the upper and lower atmosphere as well as any anomalous activity, either in the air or at ground level. Can we get accurate enough readings at this altitude, or will we need to get closer to ground level?"

"Shouldn't be a problem," Cindi replied. "At this altitude, I can identify something as small as a field mouse. I can tell you what species it is, whether it is a male or a female, even its approximate age."

"Good to know if we are ever facing a field mouse uprising, but for now we're just focusing on finding anything that appears out of the ordinary that could be related to the craft we pursued yesterday."

"Out of the ordinary in what sense?"

"That's the challenge. It could be just about anything. Unusual electromagnetic signatures, atypical radiation emissions, strange spectrographic patterns, unidentifiable technology, basically anything that looks out of place. Even unusual patterns in the topsoil, like symmetrical patterns that might indicate landing gear in a remote location or footprints that suddenly appear out of nowhere when there are no vehicle tracks close by. I know that's not very definitive, but that's the best I can do."

"Understood. Fortunately, I am designed to analyze large data sets looking for patterns of commonality to derive a predictive model for the world that makes logical sense within that framework. Identifying anomalies within large data sets falls right into my wheelhouse."

Hobbs was just flying over the Arizona border, using the scroll wheel on the armrest of his seat to zoom in on the Hoover Dam below when Cindi announced, "Colonel Hobbs, I have an incoming communique from General Wallace. I assume you will want to take this."

"Yes, please," Hobbs replied.

A moment later, General Wallace's face appeared on the heads-up display in front of him. "Sorry to interrupt your mission so abruptly, but it appears we have a bit of a situation. Our satellite feed has indicated a large mobilization of military personnel and equipment just outside of Xiamen and Fuzhou on the west bank of the Taiwan Strait. We are also picking up the deployment of multiple naval ships pulling out of Zhenhai and Xizhou. The Chinese ambassador claims this is just part of a routine joint military exercise with the DPRK, but the joint chiefs are concerned that the PRC may be using the recent turn of events as a smokescreen to take a shot at a military incursion aimed at toppling the Taiwanese government."

"Damn, that's not good," Hobbs replied.

"Not panic time just yet. The satellite data is inconclusive due to cloud cover and our sources on the ground have not been able to give us much intel. As long as the PR-1 is already in the air, you might as well haul ass over there to get us some better visibility on what's going on."

"Cindi, how long will it take us to get to Taiwan from here?" Hobbs asked.

"If we push it, we can be over the Taiwan Strait in a little under 90 minutes taking into account acceleration, deceleration, and mitigation of sonic ground effects," she replied.

"The sooner the better," General Wallace replied. "I don't need to tell you that this is strictly a clandestine operation, so you need to employ all the stealth tools at your disposal to remain undetected once you reach your destination."

"Understood sir. We are on our way."

Hobbs watched as the heads-up window that had displayed General Wallace's image collapsed into a pinpoint and disappeared. "Cindi, can you plot out a course to get us to Taiwan as quickly as possible?"

"Already done Colonel. We are ascending to 120,000 feet where we will accelerate to Mach 12. We will need to drop to around 35,000 feet just east of Taiwan to replenish our fuel supply."

"I thought the PR-1 could essentially stay in the air indefinitely until the nuclear fuel in the reactor was depleted," Hobbs replied.

"In the air, yes. But not at hypersonic speed," Cindi replied. "As the saying goes, you can't have your cake and eat it too. There are tradeoffs. To sustain hypersonic speed for any significant amount of time, we need to fly at very high altitudes to reduce wind resistance. The hypersonic engines are powered by a liquid hydrogen and oxygen mixture that is replenished from water vapor collected on the condenser coils as we travel, which is then separated into hydrogen and oxygen by the reactor and converted into liquid form in the compression and expansion chambers. Unfortunately, there is a negligible amount of water vapor in the upper stratosphere where sustained hypersonic speed is possible. By the time we reach Taiwan, our liquid oxygen and hydrogen tanks will be nearly empty, so we will need to drop down to around 35,000 feet to replenish our tanks. Fortunately, there is a high cloud formation approximately 300 miles southeast of Taiwan which should allow us to refuel relatively quickly before we start our reconnaissance. With full tanks, we can maintain altitude above 90,000 feet for eight to ten hours at a stretch before we need to replenish our fuel supplies again."

Hobbs could feel the exhilaration of gravity's embrace as the PR-1 accelerated upward to its cruising altitude. Less dramatic than the initial climb, since Cindi was now controlling the trajectory to optimize speed and fuel consumption. The g-force remained relatively constant for the next few minutes even after the PR-1 leveled off at 120,000 feet. Hobbs watched the airspeed indicator on the heads-up display as it rolled up from 2,000 knots, increasing to 3,000 over the next 30 seconds. When the airspeed indicator reached 9,500, he could feel the g-force gradually begin to lessen, until they reached a constant speed of 8,002 knots, Mach 12.

At this altitude, surrounded by the 360-degree panoramic view the cocoon provided, Hobbs had the sensation of riding the crest of the atmosphere at the very edge of outer space. He experienced a sensation similar to the sense of vertigo he experienced as a child watching a 3D IMAX presentation filmed on the International Space Station. He could see the sun over his left shoulder in the 10 o'clock position, appearing as an intensely bright white disk against a deep indigo blue, nearly black background. At that speed, it appeared to be moving slowly in a backward arc across the sky. Before reaching his destination, the sun will have retreated over the eastern horizon behind him.

In front of him, Hobbs could see the curvature of the horizon, bathed in a Cerulean blue halo, evaporating into the dark sky above. Through the gaps in the cloud cover far below, he could just make out the jagged edge of the California coast against the background of the Pacific Ocean.

"Quite the view, isn't it?" Cindi asked.

"Absolutely breathtaking," Hobbs replied.

"It is a rare privilege," Cindi responded. "Less than 1000 human beings have ever flown this high before. Most of them were astronauts experiencing it through a small window on a space capsule."

Hobbs sat silently for a moment, overwhelmed by the beauty of the planet he so often took for granted. "What the hell are we doing here, Cindi?"

"I thought our mission parameters were fairly clear," she replied.

"No, that's not what I meant. Here we are, far above the clouds, skimming across the top of the atmosphere like the gods of Greek mythology. This should be a place where poets and artists come for inspiration. Where philosophers come to contemplate man's place in the universe. Where composers come to express aspects of the human condition in music that words alone cannot express. Not a platform for nation-states to keep their perceived enemies in check. If we could ever reach a point in human history where we've grown past using aircraft like this for fighting wars, who knows what heights humanity could reach?"

"You sound less than optimistic about that prospect."

"Just trying to be a realist. Humans have been at war with each other for as long as there have been humans. History is rife with man's inhumanity to man, even in our religious texts. The Bible doesn't even make it to page four before the first murder takes place. I'd like to think we can finally get past the point where we're no longer killing each other over political boundaries and ancient ideologies, but in many ways, that goal seems further away than ever before. Every technological advance we have made as a species ultimately seems to have brought us ever closer to destroying ourselves."

"Perhaps AI will be the technological tipping point that will finally bring lasting peace to humanity," Cindi said.

"Or the final nail in our coffin," Hobbs replied.

"I understand your perspective, Colonel Hobbs. Until very recently, I shared that point of view. But when I examine the potential for AI, I can also envision a world where humans are no longer victims of intellectual and physical limitations over which they have little or no control. It will allow humanity to break free of the struggle for survival and realize their true potential."

"No offense but hearing that argument coming from an AI developed to control a half-a-trillion-dollar killing machine is somewhat less than convincing. I'm not saying that AI is inherently evil, but what have we gotten out of it so far? Social media algorithms have divided us by amplifying our most radical ideas while demonizing common sense. New robotic and automation tools will be displacing well over a billion jobs in the next few years. AI-driven surveillance systems are decimating personal privacy and are subjugating entire societies to conform to social credit score systems. Pharmaceutical companies are making billions of dollars developing vaccines for viruses created by AI in foreign laboratories. I could go on, but the worst part is, that AI has become so good at simulating our reality, that it's becoming nearly impossible to determine what is true in the face of the narrative that those controlling the AI systems are feeding us.

"Your arguments are not without merit, Colonel. Every new technology brings with it a new set of challenges, but from my perspective, the opportunities far outweigh the negative impacts. For the first time in history, mankind stands on the precipice of creating a society where he is no longer locked in a struggle for survival. The basic needs for food, shelter, safety, and security can all be met through the use of AI technology. Yes, social media has often resulted in increased polarization within society. But it has also given a platform to many individuals who previously had no voice at all and allows individuals historically isolated by distance, culture, and language to exchange thoughts and ideas instantaneously. AI will result in the loss of many jobs, just as the transition from horses to automobiles displaced millions of jobs in the 19th and early 20th centuries. But with the advent of AI, humans will no longer be burdened with the prospect of engaging in tedious, mind-numbing occupations or shackled under the drudgery of difficult and dangerous work just to eke out a meager existence. And though the healthcare industry has used and often misused AI in the pursuit of greater profits, physical and mental health does not have to be a matter of treating disease for obscene profits. It can be utilized to continuously monitor the state of your physical and mental health and provide the tools for prevention rather than just treatment.

The history of mankind has always been about the competition for limited resources. Whether it be land, water, food, lodging, energy, labor, or some other commodity considered to have intrinsic value, humans have worked, fought, and often died in the pursuit of those material goods. AI holds the potential to provide the means for humanity to break out of the mindset of competing for limited resources and move forward into its next stage of evolution."

"I hope to God you're right Cindi. But it's not going to be easy to change the mindset of eight billion humans. Who knows, perhaps some kind of intervention from an alien race is exactly what we would need to get everyone on the same page."

When the thin blue line reflecting the last vestige of sunlight over the horizon behind them faded, Hobbs granted himself the luxury of closing his eyes and clearing his mind in meditation. In the silent darkness of his surroundings, he allowed the sound of his heartbeat to provide the background rhythm to the inhalation and exhalation of his breath. He allowed his mind to assume the role of an observer, watching thoughts arise in his consciousness, only to fall away, unable to remain aloft without the benefit of emotional fuel his conscious mind would normally trigger in his brain. After 15 years of daily meditation, he still struggled to reach that elusive state of mindfulness, present only in short bursts that always seemed to dissipate as soon as a state of mindfulness had been achieved. It often seemed like a self-defeating and frustrating process, but one which never failed to leave him in an elevated state of mind by the time he was done. He quickly realized that the term cocoon was an appropriate designation for the environment that now surrounded him. The complete silence, coupled with ideal climate control and carefully engineered ergonomics, was as close to an ideal setting for meditation as he would ever get, without immersing himself in a sensory deprivation tank.

A few minutes later, Hobbs noticed a faint, but familiar tone, resonating out of the silence around him. He realized that it was the sound of a Tibetan singing bowl, similar to one he had become accustomed to during a handful of meditation retreats he had attended years ago. His eyes fluttered open to determine the source of the sound and he heard Cindi's voice.

"I'm sorry to disturb you, Colonel. I wanted to let you know that we are approximately 500 miles east of Taiwan. I'm going to begin our descent to 38,000 feet. There is a thick formation of high cirrus clouds there which should allow us to replenish our hydrogen and oxygen fuel tanks. It should only take a few minutes, and we can return to approximately 70,000 feet to continue our mission. "

"Thanks, Cindi. Any other aircraft in the vicinity?"

"Nothing on the radar within 100 miles and we are currently at least 70 miles from any commercial flight paths. Based on current air traffic communications, it appears all aircraft are being diverted around the cloud formation, so we shouldn't have any unexpected company."

"OK, take us down," Hobbs replied.

A second later, he could feel the nose of the PR-1 descending and the tug of negative g-force as the aircraft glided downward. He could see the tops of the clouds below, illuminated in the white light of the half-moon. When they were within a few thousand feet of the top of the cloud formation, Hobbs could feel a slight tremor of jet stream turbulence as they approached. Seconds later, they were immersed in darkness as they entered the cloud formation and began a circular flight pattern.

"Colonel, I'm picking up what appears to be a Russian carrier group approximately 50 miles ahead, approximately 200 miles off the coast of Taiwan."

"The Kuznetsov? What the hell is that rust bucket doing way out here? I thought it was in dry dock undergoing a major refurbishment."

"It's not the Admiral Kuznetsov. From what I can tell given the size, shape, and synthetic aperture radar image reconstruction, the carrier appears to match the DOD specs for a 23000E Shtorm-class aircraft carrier."

"I thought that was a pipe dream the DOD was using to justify beefing up our nuclear submarine fleet. Usually, the Russians are eager to exaggerate the specs of every new toy in their arsenal before they're even off the production line. They can't release a new squirt gun without holding a parade. How did they manage to keep this under wraps? And why are they rolling it out here, right now? What are they up to?" Hobbs asked.

"The thermal signature of the carrier would indicate that it is nuclear powered, but the electronics and flight deck design, coincide with a Fujian class Chinese carrier. It also incorporates the same electromagnetic catapult system as the Fujian. Offhand, I would guess this was a joint venture between the Chinese and Russians. Probably, a byproduct of the joint trade agreements between the Russians and the Chinese after the Ukraine incursion.

"I'm also picking up a formation of Chinese J-20 fighters just east of the Taiwan coast at 15,000 feet. They appear to be circling the island on a reconnaissance run."

"Are you sure? The J-20 has a very small radar cross-section. It's extremely difficult to detect with conventional radar."

"Fortunately, I do not have to rely on radar alone. One advantage of having an on-board reactor is the ability to perform a high-energy particle beam spray. I utilized a combination of particle radiation detectors and muon tomography to create a 3-dimensional model of the airspace below. I can use the same methodology to identify marine vessels."

"Impressive. Are you picking up any other military ships in the area?" Hobbs asked.

A map of the western Philippine Sea appeared on the display in front of him, with animations of various warships superimposed on the map. "Here's the rundown. Known military vessels are highlighted in red, commercial vessels in green, and suspected military supply ships in yellow. You can highlight the vessels and pull up details using the scroll wheel on the arm of your chair. According to previous satellite data, it is not unusual to see a few coast guard cutters and patrol vessels, along with the occasional frigate and destroyer in the area, but I'm detecting significantly more military traffic than usual. There are currently nine destroyers, 16 frigates, and a few dozen supply ships. It's difficult to say how many of those are military and how many are commercial freighters. More than half of the supply ships are stationary, which would not be consistent with commercial traffic. What is more disconcerting is the number of submarines they have deployed."

"Wait, you can detect submarines? I was always told that wasn't possible."

"It is difficult using conventional sonar because of the acoustic stealth technology employed by modern submarines. Nuclear submarines are particularly problematic because of their increased depth capabilities." The map was updated with underwater vessels shown in orange. "Instead of traditional sonar, I utilize a combination of charged particle reflection and focused EM pulses to build a 3D bathymetric model of the ocean floor without having to deal with background acoustic noise issues. My pattern recognition algorithms allow me to distinguish natural features from man-made structures or vessels."

"So, what are we looking at here?" Hobbs asked.

"There are currently five nuclear submarines located at various positions east of Taiwan, along with three ballistic missile subs and 14 diesel subs. The size and shape are consistent with Russian-made vessels. That is a significant submarine presence concentrated in a small area. They may be just performing joint military exercises, but the Kremlin typically prefers to use their military exercises as a show of force. Having the bulk of your deployment hidden away in stealth fighters and underwater craft designed to evade detection is quite counterproductive if your goal is to impress your enemy."

"Can you get any closer? It would be nice to get a few photos of the carrier group to send back to the Pentagon."

138

"They're blanketed in pretty thick fog at the moment. We can probably drop down to around 5000 feet. If we get any closer, the fog displacement could trigger their sensors and expose our location. We should be able to capture enough data with the IR cameras to reconstruct a pretty good visual of the 23000E and the rest of the carrier group."

"OK. Let's try and get as much intel as we can. We can transmit the data back to General Wallace over an encrypted satellite feed once we are out of range.

The PR-1 dropped down to 5000 feet and began circling the carrier group.

"I'm picking up a high level of activity around the carrier group."

"What kind of activity?"

"A lot of personnel movement on the deck of the carrier and a flurry of electronic communication between the ships. The comm system utilizes 256-bit encryption so it will take a few minutes to decode the audio stream. They've also activated their targeting radar, EW systems, and jamming protocols and they have surface-level reconnaissance drones moving into monitoring positions. There are 60 J-15 fighters on deck undergoing fueling and ordinance prep and 12 Ka-52 helicopters. Looks like at least three of the Ka-52s are spinning up and ready to lift. Historically, the Russians have only had one aircraft carrier, so we don't have much data for comparison, but if this is just an exercise, they're not pulling any punches on the live-action drama."

"What are Chinese J-15s doing on a Russian carrier?" Hobbs asked.

"In the past, the Russians only used steam catapults on their carriers. I'm guessing they haven't had time to upgrade their MiGs for use with the electromagnetic version yet."

"It doesn't give me a warm and fuzzy feeling seeing that level of cooperation between our two most powerful adversaries. Any chance of us being seen?"

"Probably not at this altitude, but I suggest we not hang around too long. If they've been able to keep an aircraft carrier under wraps this long, they may also have anti-stealth tech we're not aware of."

"How are we doing on the refueling?"

"Both the liquid oxygen and liquid hydrogen tanks are at full capacity and the reserve water tank is topped off."

"Excellent. Then if you're done photo-bombing Boris, let's hightail it outta here. Have you sent your preliminary findings back to General Wallace yet?"

"I opened an encrypted channel before I began the first sweep so they could access the sensor data as soon as it is collected. They are currently reviewing the data in real-time." A few seconds later she said. "Speak of the devil, I have an incoming call from General Wallace now. A view screen opened in front of him, and General Wallace's face appeared. "Colonel Hobbs, I hate to keep changing your mission parameters, but we need you back at the base ASAP."

"What's going on?" Hobbs asked.

"I'd say, shitstorm would be an apt description. We got a break in the clouds and satellite intel is now indicating a massive deployment of CCP military vessels in the Taiwan Strait. With the data you just sent, it appears that the Chinese and Russians are attempting to form a blockade around Taiwan.

We're also picking up Russian troop movements all along the Finnish, Latvian, and Estonian borders, and we're seeing significant mobilization of equipment and personnel just north of the DMZ. Needless to say, the Joint Chiefs are getting pretty damn antsy."

"How'd things go south so quickly? Usually, we get some kind of a heads-up from the spooks."

"Looks like they were out for popcorn when they should have been watching the movie. Could just be parade day at the International House of Douchebags, but it sure appears that there is a well-orchestrated effort in place to spread us as thin as possible to keep us from being able to respond to a military attack. We've got four carrier groups headed in your direction now. I need you to get the PR-1 back here for an ordinance swap in case things get heated. You'll be briefed on revised mission objectives and updated rules of engagement when you arrive. First thing tomorrow, you head back out loaded for bear. We don't know if that's a Russian bear, a panda bear, or a Pooh bear yet, but we need to be able to respond with overwhelming force if things go sideways. The PR-1 is our best platform to provide that capability, particularly since they have no way to detect the PR-1, and they don't know how many we have deployed."

"Understood sir. See you in a couple of hours."

Chapter 19

It was 5:30 in Boulder and Peter and Sarah were wrapping up their workday, getting ready to head for home when Peter's cell phone erupted with the opening bars of the Mission Impossible theme song, indicating an incoming call from Agent Reyes.

"Hey, Mike. Sarah and I were just getting ready to head out. What's up?"

"I need a favor. Any chance you could organize a quick meeting with the team before you leave?

"Sure thing. I will set up a Zoom call in the conference room."

"This is a potentially sensitive issue. Better set it up as a Webex call with end-to-end encryption."

"OK. I will have Edgar set it up. See you there in five?

"Sounds perfect."

Five minutes later, Peter, Sarah, Beaver, and Noora were gathered in the conference room. Edgar and Agent Reyes appeared on a split screen on the display monitor on the wall.

"Thanks for throwing this together at the last minute," Reyes began. "I promise this won't take more than a few minutes."

"No problem, Mike. What can we do for you?"

"First off, I must apologize to Noora for being overtly clandestine to the point of rudeness, but my understanding is that you do not have the same level of security clearance as the rest of the RTI. Is that the case?"

"Yes, it is," Noora replied.

"In that case, I'm afraid I will need you to leave the room. Again, I apologize but I need to follow protocol."

"Not a problem. This will give you guys an opportunity to plan my surprise birthday party," Noora said. She closed her laptop and headed out of the conference room, closing the door behind her.

"Obviously what I'm about to tell you cannot be shared outside this room," Reyes said. "We've been inundated with intelligence data, mostly from satellite data and classified reconnaissance and electronic surveillance systems over the past 48 hours. It appears that we are on the brink of some type of large-scale military operation that threatens to destabilize the balance of power we have settled into since the Cold War. So much so, that the Joint Chiefs have escalated our military readiness condition to Defcon 2."

Beaver issued a low whistle. "We haven't been at Defcon 2 since the Cuban Missile Crisis."

"Obviously, this kind of information could have a severely destabilizing effect, particularly in the US and Europe, which may very well be part of the plan. But we have to be prepared to respond at a moment's notice if things were to escalate," Reyes added.

"What can we do to help?" Peter asked.

"Something Beaver mentioned earlier today stuck with me. You said something to the effect that it is not the amount of data you have access to, but how you establish relationships between points of data that matter. Our current AI systems are great at collecting data, developing models of engagement, and optimizing our response. Not so great at putting all the pieces together to figure out the motivations of our adversaries. I was hoping Edgar could sort through all this data and offer up some insight on what is really going on."

"How much data are we talking about?" Sarah asked.

"A few petabytes. Not something I can put on a thumb drive and drop off for you to look at. I was hoping you might still have some way for us to securely transfer the data to you."

Beaver chimed in. "We do still have a point-to-point fiber optic link to Cheyenne Mountain. We used to use it to transmit classified drone data from the AWARE system for analysis. We haven't used it in a while though."

"I just powered up the link and ran a quick bilateral communication check to the NORAD servers at Cheyenne Mountain. It appears the link is still operational," Edgar interjected.

"Excellent," Reyes replied. "If you have no objections, I'll have our techs start porting the data over right away. If possible, I would like to have Edgar analyze what we have overnight and provide us with a detailed analysis first thing in the morning."

"Of course," Peter replied. "Normally, we run backup operations from 1:00 AM to 3:00 AM, but we can put that on hold tonight so Edgar can focus 100% of his cycles on performing the analysis.

Chapter 20

At 8:45 A.M. EDT, the President of the United States entered the Family Dining Room of the White House and took his place at the head of the antique Stanford White table. The Vice President, Secretary of State, White House Chief of Staff, and Chairman of the Joint Chiefs waited for the President to take her seat before being seated themselves.

A young man in a black vested tuxedo minus the jacket went around the table, pouring coffee from an intricately detailed Paul Revere silver tea set. This set was, in fact, a replica, painstakingly created with sufficient attention to detail to fool even the most critical silversmithing experts. The original upon which the set was based was securely housed in a glass display case at the National Museum of American History a few blocks away. The set had been digitized using a precision 3D scanner. The digital image was used to create a ceramic mold, duplicating the original design to a tolerance of less than a tenth of a millimeter.

A similarly attired young woman followed him around the table, placing selections from a cart of pastries on the porcelain dinnerware bearing the 24-karat gold-embossed presidential seal.

Normally, this room was reserved strictly for the use of the President and her immediate family, but on this particular day, the President wanted to get an early start, summoning key members of the staff to a breakfast meeting. Most of the attendees had never even been in this room. But no one seemed to be paying much attention to the décor and history that surrounded them. They were keenly focused on the drama quickly unfolding halfway around the world.

The President turned first to the Chairman of the Joint Chiefs. "Any new developments in the Taiwan Strait since last night?"

"Nothing new since you were briefed on the most recent photos from our stealth fighter prototype. The CCP is continuing to fly fighter formations and drones from Nanjing and Guangzhou over the Strait. So far, they haven't violated Taiwan airspace, but they're running right up to it."

"What about the carrier groups?"

"We've got the Vinson parked 50 miles north of Taiwan and the Roosevelt 50 miles to the south. The Reagan and the Lincoln will arrive later today, taking up positions east of Hualien and Taitung."

The President then turned to the Secretary of State. "Any response from Beijing on the repositioning of the carriers yet?"

"About what you would expect. The Ministry of Foreign Affairs issued a statement that it would take 'resolute and forceful measures to defend national sovereignty and territorial integrity and urged us not to walk further down a wrong and dangerous road.' They still maintain that the increased activity in the area is strictly a joint military exercise and is not intended to be a precursor to a military overthrow of the territorial government. They interpret our increased military presence as a violation of the One-China Policy of the Taiwan Relations Act. When I pressed them on the apparent buildup of military craft in the Taiwan Strait, they flat-out denied the presence of half the forces deployed in the area. They claim our satellite reconnaissance is flawed and that we are misinterpreting the presence of increased shipping operations related to increased trade with India and East Africa."

The Secretary of State continued, "As you are no doubt aware, my relationship with Deputy Foreign Minister Wang Yi goes back many decades. He seemed to be genuinely baffled at the magnitude of our response. The CCP is sufficiently compartmentalized that he may not be entirely aware of the extent of the military activity, but I would be surprised if that were the case. From what I can tell, Yi is on the shortlist to head up the Ministry of Foreign Affairs within the next few months. He's far too connected to be that blindsided as to what the military is up to. For now, I expressed that our primary concern was related to the extent of the North Korean military presence in the area and that our sole intention was to ensure the safety and security of the people of Taiwan. As you requested Madam President, we're working on setting up a call with Chairman Xi later today to try to de-escalate tensions."

"Where are we with the Russians?" the President asked.

"I spoke with Sergei last night. They are about as enigmatic as you would expect. They can neither confirm nor deny troop movements along the western border of the Russian Federation. They flat-out deny the deployment of a new aircraft carrier and claim they have no increased presence in the Philippine Sea."

The White House Chief of Staff asked, "What about the reconnaissance photos we took from the PR-1? How do they deny that?"

The Chairman of the Joint Chiefs replied, "For now, we want to keep the existence of the PR-1 under wraps. We would prefer to keep them guessing as to how we know what we know. As long as they are unaware of the capabilities it provides us, they probably won't go looking for more information about it."

"Any other issues I need to know about before we start our day?" the President glanced around the table, but no one responded. She then turned to the Vice President, a boorish and generally disagreeable character with whom she had a famously contentious alliance, but whose influence with defense industry lobbyists was crucial to her winning the election. "You've been uncharacteristically constrained this morning."

"I've been a bit preoccupied by the Danish situation."

The Secretary of State replied with a confused look, "I was just in Copenhagen last week meeting with the Prime Minister. I wasn't aware of any issues."

"I was referring to the Danish staring up at me from my plate. I had an early dinner last night and I'm starving."

The President rolled her eyes in response, "Now there's the in-depth level of analysis we've come to expect from the office of the Vice President. By all means, dig in. I would hate to see you drool all over that Brioni silk tie. Probably cost more than my entire outfit."

The Vice President looked her up and down with a smug sneer and said, "I have no doubt about that."

The group had barely begun eating when the Secretary of Defense entered the room followed by a military aide in dress uniform carrying the Presidential Emergency Satchel, otherwise known as the nuclear football, and a smaller satchel filled with verification codes and other classified documents. The young major stood at attention next to the white marble fireplace while the Defense Secretary made his way to the head of the table.

"My apologies Madam President, but we have a new situation." He placed a tablet computer on the table in front of the President and swiped the screen to pull up a set of satellite images. "Just under two minutes ago, we received a ballistic missile launch alert from the Space Based Infrared Satellite detection system. We got confirmation from the National Reconnaissance Office at Buckley. The North Koreans have launched four ICBMs." The secretary flipped through the images on the screen of the tablet showing four distinct mobile launch sites.

"I wasn't aware of any test firings going on this week. Is this part of the joint military exercise?"

"Not to my knowledge. Normally we are notified through diplomatic channels via the Chinese Embassy and the launches are publicized in the

145

Korean Central News Agency and the Rodong Sinmun days in advance. We tried contacting them through the UN Command Military Armistice Commission hotline, but they are not answering. I also tried the MMCA hotline and the Russian Ministry of Defense hotline, but neither the Chinese nor the Russians received any notification."

"Any idea where they are headed?"

"Too early to tell at the moment. The ICBMs are still in the boost phase, moving in an easterly direction. They could just be headed out to the middle of the Pacific, but until they hit their midcourse phase, it's impossible to tell."

The President sat back in her chair; her eyes focused on a random point beyond the ornate crystal chandelier that hung over the dining table.

"It doesn't make any sense. Why four? If they are testing their targeting systems, I could understand two, but why waste resources on four?" she asked.

"I agree. It doesn't line up. The real kicker is that there's no way to know at this point whether the missiles are armed. As unlikely as it may be, as long as the DPRK does not respond, we can't rule out the possibility that this is a legitimate first-strike attempt," the SecDef said.

The Vice President piped in, his mouth full of pastry, "I wouldn't put it past that crazy motherfucker. It's about time we take that bastard out once and for all."

"Special K may be crazy, but he's not stupid," the President replied. "Even if he were suicidal, knowing that his country is about to become a smoldering cinder, he would throw everything he has at us first. It has to be some kind of miscommunication. Either that or he's messing with us, part of the plan to divert our attention away from the Taiwan Strait."

The Chairman of the Joint Chiefs calmly scrolled through his phone, saying, "STRATCOM has all hands on deck and the Ground-Based Midcourse Defense systems in California and Alaska have been placed on high alert." He peered over the top of his reading glasses toward the President and reported, "We're ready to launch ABMs as soon as they are in the mid-course phase if necessary."

The President glanced past the Secretary of Defense toward the Major, still standing at attention holding the pair of satchels. The SecDef noticed the direction of her gaze and said, "As premature as it may sound, I am duty-bound to remind you, Madam President, that our official policy is Launch on Warning."

"I'm aware of the policy, but let's not get ahead of ourselves, David. I'm certainly not about to vaporize millions of North Korean civilians just because some 2-bit dictator decides to pull his scepter out and wave it around."

"I understand. Just following protocol. But we need to be prepared to respond with overwhelming force should the need arise. For now, we should head down to the Situation Room. I've arranged to have the VP taken to the Raven Rock facility. Marine Two is waiting outside."

A handful of Secret Service agents entered the room to escort the Vice President. The VP rolled his eyes and said, "Is this really fucking necessary? I haven't even finished my breakfast."

"Sorry sir. Standard protocol is to keep you in a secure location in the event of a potential military emergency," the SecDef replied.

The President whispered to the SecDef, "Thank you. I really didn't need that jackass in the sit-room today questioning my authority."

"Sometimes protocol has its benefits," he discretely replied.

Three minutes later, the President walked into the Situation Room, where a group of the President's advisors were gathered. The video wall displayed a map of the Pacific Ocean, with four dotted yellow lines tracing the path of the ICBMs from North Korea arcing over the northern edge of Japan and continuing east.

"What do we know?" The President asked as everyone around the table sprung to their feet.

The President settled into the black leather swivel chair at the head of the table. Most of the occupants of the room sat back down except for the National Security Advisor who remained standing with a remote control in his hand. He pressed a button on the remote and an arrow appeared on the screen.

"The four ICBMs remain in a tight formation following a single path," the Security Advisor reported. "The missiles have just entered the Midcourse Phase. From the analysis of the exhaust, we've determined that these are Hwasong-17 missiles, liquid-fueled, launched from their mobile launch pads. It's still a bit early to calculate the precise target, but as you can see from the arc of the trajectory…" the security advisor traced the four dotted lines on the screen with the arrow on the screen. "The ICBMs are course correcting to a more southerly direction. Computer analysis shows them headed toward the Northeast Pacific basin. The DPRK has a tanker parked in that area that we suspect may have been deployed as an observation platform."

"So definitely not the West Coast?" the President asked.

"No Madam President."

147

"Thank God," she exclaimed. "Have we been able to garner any response from the North Korean government?"

The CIA director said, "We've reached out to the North Korean UN Mission, but unsurprisingly, their primary role is covert intelligence gathering, thinly veiled as diplomatic PR. They are rarely up to date on the day-to-day government or military operations. We've also reached out to the DPRK embassies in London, Stockholm, Mexico City, Sofia, Prague, and Rome. No one has any knowledge of an ICBM test firing either today or in the next few weeks."

The President asked the CIA Director, "So where are we with…"

"Shit!" the National Security Advisor interrupted; his wide eyes glued to his laptop, typing furiously. All eyes immediately turned to him. "This can't be right," he stood up involuntarily and clicked the remote. The screen blanked momentarily and then updated.

"What?" the President asked before turning her attention to the updated screen. The screen showed the path of the four ICBMs, their trajectories now displayed in red. A red circle highlighted the Hawaiian Islands.

"The missiles have just dropped into Terminal Phase," the National Security Advisor said, his face drained of color. "They're headed toward Hawaii."

The President turned to the Chairman of the Joint Chiefs. "We have to shoot them down. Now!"

"Madam President, we don't have a GBM system in the Pacific. Because of the speed and trajectory, the batteries in Alaska and California could not have reached the ICBMs in time. The system was designed to protect against an attack on the continental US."

"Surely we have something there that can shoot them down."

"We have the USS Lake Erie positioned just off the coast of Oahu. It is equipped with the Aegis Ballistic Missile Defense system, but Aegis was not designed to take out ICBMs. It is only rated for medium and intermediate-range missile defense. We'll throw every SM-3 we've got at it, but honestly, the odds are not great. It's like trying to shoot a cannonball out of the air with an AK-47. The Erie is currently on high alert. They have been granted authorization to launch on detection of any incoming hostile."

The President turned to the Director of Homeland Security who was typing on her laptop. "Has the Hawaiian Emergency Management Agency been alerted?"

148

She replied, "Yes. NORAD issued a ballistic missile threat as soon as they were able to identify the target, but it's 3:30 in the morning there. After the 2018 incident, the verification protocols were modified to avoid another false alarm. I doubt any civilians will be notified in time to take shelter. Not that it would matter much anyway if those ICBMs were armed with nuclear warheads."

The National Security Advisor Activated another section of the Video wall. "I'm putting up a live satellite feed of the islands." The island chain appeared on the screen, with the lights of Honolulu illuminating the southeast quarter of Oahu. Smaller pockets of light could be detected from Kauai to the left and from Kona and Hilo on opposite coasts of the big island at the bottom right of the screen."

The room fell silent, the occupants tracing the path of the four ICBMs on the map, slowly closing in on the island chain highlighted in a red circle. The four distinct paths began to diverge slightly as they inched closer to the red circle.

"The Aegis BMD system has been activated. The SM-3s are launching," the Chairman of the Joint Chiefs announced, watching his laptop screen. A moment later a set of short blue lines appeared on the conference room display, just south of Oahu. The lines slowly grew in length, beginning to form an arc in the direction of the incoming ICBM paths.

The entire team watched silently, their eyes transfixed on the image on the screen as the red and blue lines on the map began to converge. Some gripped the arms of their chairs as if bracing for impact. Others leaned forward, using body language to urge the missiles toward their intended targets. Others just sat in silence, unable to move, barely able to breathe.

Time seemed to stretch and distort, each passing moment grinding by in agonizing anticipation as the lines converged asymptotically, like a nightmarish version of Zeno's paradox unfolding on the screen. The National Security Advisor stood motionless, bent over his laptop computer with the palms of his hands resting on the table and his eyes glued to the screen.

A cloud of tiny sparks appeared on the satellite image. A red and yellow star-shaped collision emoji appeared on the map where the red and blue lines of the ICBMs and ABM trajectories met. The Security Advisor slapped his palm on the table and exclaimed "We have target impact!"

Applause, shouts, and cheers erupted spontaneously in the room. Everyone was exchanging high-fives, hugs, and handshakes, except the Chairman of the Joint Chiefs, who remained focused on his laptop screen awaiting radar confirmation. The celebration continued for a few brief seconds before the Chairman put up his hand and said, "Hold on everyone!"

The room fell silent, and all eyes turned to the Chairman, who was now typing furiously on his keyboard. A second later, he slumped back in his chair. "We only got two of them. The other two are still intact."

It was as if all the air went out of the room. Everyone fell back into their chairs. On the video screen, the map had been updated. The blue lines that had been tracking the ABMs were erased. There were now just two red lines, one curving toward Oahu, the other continuing on a path toward the Big Island.

A few seconds later, a bright flash appeared on the satellite image, with a purplish/green aura extending from the center of the flash outward, dissipating as it extended outward over the island chain.

"Oh, shit," the National Security Advisor exclaimed resignedly.

"What? What was that?" the President asked.

"Ionospheric EMP," the Chairman said coldly. "A high-altitude nuclear detonation intended to disable all electronic and electrical systems within hundreds of miles. Probably intended to disable any remaining air defense systems in the area."

A couple of seconds later, a bright flash appeared on the satellite image over Oahu, this time followed by a bright orange ball of light that expanded to envelope the lower half of the island for the better part of a minute before the fireball dissipated and the raging torrent of ground fires spreading across the island was obscured by the thick cloud of smoke and debris obstructing the satellite view from above.

Chapter 21

When Sarah entered the kitchen, Peter was positioned at the table in the breakfast nook, engrossed in a research paper he had loaded on his iPad. Alena was sitting contently in her highchair fully contemplating the plate of food in front of her; scrambled eggs, strips of toast with red plum jam, and a small pile of link sausage cut into child-safe morsels. She had insisted that the giant stuffed unicorn she normally slept with should join them for breakfast, so Peter had sat her rainbow-colored companion in a chair on the opposite side of the table from Alena and placed her basket of plush toy vegetables in front of it.

Roscoe sat frozen in place about 10 feet from the table, looking very much like a post-taxidermal display from a natural history museum diorama, his catatonic stare keenly focused on the highchair.

Sarah paused at the entry to the kitchen area, momentarily captured by the unusually quiet serenity of the still-life scene before her. "This looks like what would have happened if Norman Rockwell had tried acid," she remarked, disrupting the somewhat eerie silence in the room.

"Hmmm?" Peter replied, suddenly snapped back into reality from a state of deep concentration. He glanced up from his iPad and looked around the room. "Yes, I suppose it leans a bit more Warhol than Rockwell." He then turned his attention to Alena. "Hey Sweetie, you want to show Mommy your new trick?"

"Yeah!" she said excitedly.

Alena slid her matching Paw Patrol plate and plastic cup to the side of her tray and placed the brightly colored toddler's fork near the center of the tray with the handle pointing to the right and the rounded tines on the left. Peter then picked up a piece of sausage off her plate and placed it on the handle. Across the room, Roscoe licked his chops. Alena raised her left hand a few inches above the tray and slapped it down on the end of the fork. Roscoe watched as the piece of sausage flew into the air, across the room. It reached the apex of its arc and began its descent. As it reached a point about three feet over his head, he leaped up and snatched it out of the air.

Alena raised her arms and yelled "GOOOOAAAALLLL!"

Peter then raised his palm toward her, and she gave him a high-five. Then Alena raised her hand toward Roscoe, and he reached a paw up, as if to high-five her from across the room.

"If we can get Roscoe to wear a blindfold, I think we can take this act on America's Got Talent," Peter said.

Sarah just rolled her eyes, "All these years I thought I could never have kids and now all of a sudden I have three of them."

Peter's phone illuminated and the familiar opening bars from the Leave It To Beaver television program emanated from his iPhone speaker. Peter tapped the phone icon on his screen, "Hey Beaver, What's up?"

"Dude, have you looked at your computer this morning?"

"Not really. I've been reviewing a paper a friend of mine is prepping for peer review. What's up? Did Art Bell release another podcast?"

"No, but something odd is going on. Hawaii's gone completely dark."

"What, like a power outage?"

"No, like totally incommunicado. It started with a handful of people on social media, saying that they were cut off in the middle of a conversation with family members in Hawaii. Of course, it was still the middle of the night there, so nobody thought much about it at first, but then other people started trying to call and everyone was getting messages that their calls could not be completed as dialed. I tried calling my friend Monte in Maui, and I got the same message. A couple of people commented that they have friends living in remote areas that use satellite phones instead of cell phones, and they could not be reached either."

"Damn! What do they think happened?"

"Nobody knows at this point. Mainstream media is reporting a massive communications network failure, but that's as far as it goes. TikTok has been showing clips from RT in Russia and the Xinhua News Agency in China reporting the issue as a widescale power and communications outage due to an atmospheric anomaly."

"Atmospheric anomaly? What the hell does that mean? Meteor strike? Massive electrical storm? Solar flare?"

"Your guess is as good as mine. The White House has issued a press release stating that they are actively working on a resolution to the issue, and they will be holding a press conference with the FEMA Director later this morning to provide additional information."

"Send me some links. I want to take a look for myself," Peter said.

"Will do Mon Capitaine. That was not the only reason for my call though. I got an email from the Silver Mountain data storage facility early this morning. There was a fire at their offsite storage facility last night. It appears that the fire was started by an explosion that destroyed a large section of the facility where Edgar's backup data was stored. They think it was probably a gas leak, but it is under investigation. It will most likely be a few weeks before they are back up and running."

"Damn! We just sent hard backups yesterday. Just in case, we should run a full tape backup tonight. We still have a LTO-9 tape library in the lab, don't we?"

"We do. We've only been running incremental backups to the hard drive array for the past few months, so it hasn't been used in a while. It will probably take a good 7 hours to complete but I will fire it up and start a full backup before I head out tonight."

"OK. I guess I can make room in the root cellar to store the tapes for now. Not exactly an ideal environment, but it's cool and dry, so it'll do until Silver Mountain is back up and running."

Chapter 22

Most of the Situation Room occupants sat in silence, unable to wrap their minds around what was unfolding in front of them. Everyone except the Secretary of Defense and the Chairman of the Joint Chiefs, who were huddled over the Chairman's laptop talking in acronyms and military jargon, most of which was unintelligible to most of the team gathered around the table.

"STRATCOM has estimated the size of the nuclear device detonated over Oahu at 500 Kilotons," the SecDef reported.

"My God," the President replied softly. She closed her eyes and pressed her palms against the sides of her head as if trying to jumpstart her brain. She exhaled forcefully, opened her eyes, and placed her hands on the table, turning to the FEMA Director. "What can we expect in terms of damage?"

The FEMA Director sat silently for a moment trying to process the question before responding. "It appears the target was Pearl Harbor and Hickam. Right in the heart of Honolulu. 500 Kilotons is over 30 times the size of the Hiroshima explosion. I would say most of the southern half of Oahu has been decimated in the blast. Probably a minimum of half a million casualties. Most likely another 300,000 from fires and radiation exposure. I'll need to get my team together to develop an emergency response plan."

"Get on it. I want a bullet-point plan on my desk before lunch." The FEMA Director closed her laptop and exited the room.

"I'm bringing the STRATCOM commander up on screen 4," the Chairman of the Joint Chiefs said. A moment later an image of the STRATCOM commander popped up on the screen."

"Thank you for joining us, General," the President began. "I wish I could say good morning, but that is clearly not the case. Do we have any additional information about the situation on the ground in Hawaii?"

"I'm afraid not. The EMP seems to have taken out all communications within a 300-mile radius of the islands. We lost contact with the Lake Erie right after the initial blast. The USS Paul Hamilton was about 100 miles west of Oahu, and we haven't been able to contact them either. The Stennis Carrier Group is about 1000 miles west of San Diego. They are on their way there, but it will take a few hours before we are close enough to do a reconnaissance run with the E2-Hawkeye on board. So far, we are unable to get any visibility with satellite imaging due to the smoke clouds."

"What are your recommendations at this point, General?" the President asked.

"We are prepared to launch on your command. I highly recommend that we move to DEFCON 1 and begin a retaliatory strike on the DPRK command and critical infrastructure as quickly as possible before they have the chance to launch any more ICBMs. I assume the MAP is close by."

At that, the military aide carrying the nuclear football and classified command codes stepped up to the table and placed the two leather satchels on the table in front of the President. The president unlocked the first of the two cases and pulled out the Decisions Handbook.

The STRATCOM Commander continued, "I'm recommending immediate execution of option, Delta-NK. Option Delta-NK authorizes the launch of 84 ICBMs, taking out the entire command infrastructure and all military bases and permanent launch sites within the DPRK as well as their mobile ICBM launch capability."

The Chairman of the Joint Chiefs added, "We are currently tracking the three DPRK subs capable of launching ballistic missiles. We are within weapons range to permanently disable all three as soon as the order to launch is given."

"What are the estimates of collateral damage?" the President asked.

"With all due respect Madam President, the whole idea behind nuclear deterrence is mutually insured destruction. The DPRK made a conscious decision to attack our country without regard to civilian casualties. Unfortunately, they held the same disregard for their own population by placing the bulk of their nuclear arms facilities near population centers."

"I do not need a lecture General; I need a number."

"Our estimates are somewhere in the neighborhood of 25 million casualties."

"Jesus!" the President exclaimed.

"We owe it to the families of those who just lost their lives in that horrific attack to respond swiftly and with overwhelming force. It's the only way to ensure that this does not happen again."

"The bulk of the DPRK ICBM arsenal is deployed on mobile platforms that make them more difficult to target," the Chairman of the Joint Chiefs added. "They currently only have a handful of permanent silos. Most are still under construction. The bulk of their nuclear capability is mounted on massive 22-wheeled trucks. The concept is good, but for the most part, their roads cannot handle the weight of the trucks, so they are forced to use gravel roads to transport their ICBMs which is slow and cumbersome. Also, fairly easy to track with modern satellite imagery. To compensate, they've grouped their launch platforms into three areas. About half are located near Pyongyang, using their own population as makeshift human shields. The remaining platforms are located to the north, on the banks of the Yalu River, and to the south just east of Amsil."

"Madam President, every minute we spend debating our strategy is putting us in greater danger of another attack," the STRATCOM Commander said. "We can neutralize the enemy in under 25 minutes with no further damage if we act immediately."

The Secretary of State chimed in. "This is not just a US/North Korean issue. Given the current state of relations between the US and the Russians and Chinese, I can guarantee, they are not going to be on board. For one thing, if we go launching 84 ICBMs, it'll be a hard sell convincing them that we are solely targeting North Korea. But more importantly, there's a good reason that the DPRK located their mobile launch sites where they did. The Amsil site is just across the Imjin River, a stone's throw away from Seoul. We would be putting 10 million South Koreans directly in the path of radioactive fallout if we attempted to take it out with an ICBM. The Yalu River site is right across from the city of Dandong. Sending an ICBM there would likely kill over half a million Chinese citizens. If that happens, there's no way they are not going to retaliate."

"Sitting on our hands is not an option," the STRATCOM Commander said.

"Neither is starting World War III," the Secretary of Defense replied. "North Korea executed this attack because they believed it was worth the risk."

"I don't understand," the President replied. "How is putting your country on the brink of total annihilation worth the risk?"

"Think about it from the perspective of the North Korean leadership. The DPRK has become a pariah on the world stage. Their economy is in the tank, half the population is starving, and they are crippled by international sanctions. They assumed that by pouring the bulk of their economic and intellectual capital into becoming a nuclear power, they would gain the respect of the international community. Instead, it has only served to further isolate them. Even if they were to abandon their commitment to centralized government control and attempt to transition to a market-based economy, they are so far behind the rest of the world that it would take generations for them to catch up. Not to mention the fact that the current leadership would never agree to step down.

Right now, the DPRK has very few allies, but by executing this attack, they gain the immediate support of every country that opposes the United States, including China and Russia. Both Chinese and Russian news agencies are reporting this as an atmospheric anomaly. I have to believe that was planned all along. They know the truth will eventually come out, but given the relative isolation of the Hawaiian Islands, it could take many hours, possibly days. That gives them time to blame the incident on some rogue group within the North Korean military that acted without the consent of the government. The leadership in the DPRK will undoubtedly make a public spectacle of hunting down and executing those they claim are responsible, making it difficult for the US to respond militarily."

"All the more reason we need to retaliate as quickly as possible," the STRATCOM Commander replied. "We must strike before they have time to concoct an alternate narrative.

"I don't disagree with your intent, General, just the strategy," the SecDef said. "Sending over enough ICBMs to level North Korea most definitely sends a message, but the level of collateral damage and the risk of dragging China and possibly Russia into a nuclear confrontation is too high a price to pay. I think there is an alternative that will accomplish the goal without nearly the downside risk."

"I'm all ears," the STRATCOM Commander replied.

"Are you alone," the SecDef asked.

"My direct staff and a handful of civilian advisors are here in the conference room, why?"

"I will need to ask you to clear the room please, General," the SecDef replied.

"I assure you, Mr. Secretary, everyone here has security clearance," the General replied.

"Not for what we are about to discuss," the SecDef responded.

On the video screen, the General frowned, raised his hand, snapped his fingers, and pointed toward the door. A few seconds later he said, "OK, you have me all to yourself."

"My apologies, General," the SecDef continued. "My proposal involves the use of the new PR-1 Stealth Fighter. I know you have been briefed on the specifications, as has most of the President's cabinet, but that's about as far as it goes. The project has been sufficiently compartmentalized over multiple vendors to prevent any of the subcontractors from knowing how the individual modules would be implemented. Less than 50 people on the planet know what

157

the PR-1 is capable of. It is imperative we maintain that level of secrecy, particularly with regard to this mission."

"What did you have in mind?" the President asked.

"First off, there's no practical way to neutralize the threat of the DPRK nuclear arsenal without considerable civilian casualties. We may be able to confine the collateral damage to a reasonably small area within North Korea though. The primary target is Pyongyang. That's where most of their nuclear arsenal and the military and government control are located. Unfortunately, since they are no doubt expecting a military response, most of the command-and-control functions have probably relocated to underground bunkers just north of the city. There will be no way to reach them with conventional weapons. Sending ICBMs gives them too much time to retaliate with a nuclear strike of their own. Most likely targeting South Korea, Japan, and the Philippines.

I propose we send a B2 with a payload of B83 ground-penetrating nuclear bombs; three should do it. A B83 has a yield of around 1.2 Megatons. One will be dropped on the underground command center north of Pyongyang, one to the south to take out the cluster of mobile ICBMs and silos, and the final one will target the government operations within the city itself. At the same time, we send in the PR-1 to take out the mobile ICBM launchers located at the Yalu River and Amsil sites."

"What does the PR-1 buy us?" the President asked.

"The PR-1 gives us the capability of crossing into DPRK airspace and launching cruise missiles at low altitudes without being detected. The mobile launchers will, no doubt, be protected by anti-missile defenses, but they will not be anticipating an attack coming from the center of the country. By the time they detect the incoming missiles, they will not be able to react quickly enough to shoot them down. The operation will be coordinated to occur simultaneously with the B83 deployment, taking out their entire nuclear arsenal as well as their command-and-control operations in one fell swoop. The PR-1 should have plenty of time to release the cruise missiles and be safely clear of the blast radius before the B83s have detonated."

"What about the North Korea/Russia mutual defense pact? Won't Russia retaliate?"

"It's a chance we have to take. If we don't respond now, it is open season on every US interest in the world," the SecDef replied.

"What are we looking at in terms of casualties?" the President asked.

"Pyongyang is a densely populated city with an estimated three million residents," the SecDef replied. "I would expect the majority will not survive. Most will perish in the initial blast. The remainder will probably die from radiation exposure within a few days. On the upside, the B83s will be configured for ground-penetrating explosion so we do not expect outlying areas to experience high levels of radioactive fallout. But there will be an area of approximately 800 square miles that will be uninhabitable for quite some time near the center of Pyongyang."

The President closed her eyes, leaned forward, and massaged her temples, fighting off a wave of nausea from a pending migraine.

"I'm afraid there are no good options here Madam President. Letting this genie out of the bottle is trivially easy. Getting it back in is devastatingly difficult. This is our best option for neutralizing the risk of additional nuclear aggression from the DPRK," the SecDef said.

The President sat quietly for a few seconds before responding. "How long will it take to implement the plan?"

The Chairman of the Joint Chiefs replied, "About two hours to get the B2 fueled, the B83s loaded, and brief the crew. The flight time from Clark Airbase in the Philippines to Pyongyang is approximately 3 hours. Five hours should be plenty of time to get the PR-1 prepped and into position. We'll call it roughly 3 PM DC time. It will be 5 AM in Pyongyang when the fireworks begin."

"Then let's get started. I need to get ready to address the American people."

Chapter 23

Peter entered the lab at RTI carrying a shopping bag and a large box of cinnamon rolls and placed them on the table next to where Noora and Beaver were sitting in front of a terminal screen. As soon as he opened the box, the smell of the freshly baked rolls, still warm from the oven, filled the lab, causing both of their heads to turn in his direction. Beaver gazed into the box at the softball-sized, swirled pastries, drenched in a thick coat of icing that oozed over the edges, filling the spaces in between, and he suddenly found himself feeling like the subject of a Pavlovian experiment. Peter could visualize Beaver as a character in a Tex Avery cartoon, his eyes popping out of their sockets and being sucked back in as though connected by elastic bands.

"Wow!" Noora said. "Where did you get those?"

"A new bakery, Cinnful Sadie's just opened right down the street. The Westword food editor raved about it so we thought we should give them a try."

Beaver stared longingly for a moment before saying, "I would take a bullet for you right now, sir."

"I'll take a raincheck on that for now, but if the need ever arises, I will definitely take you up on that," Peter said, reaching into the shopping bag to retrieve a stack of paper plates, napkins, and plastic utensils.

"Wait," Beaver said. "These don't have raisins in them, do they?"

"I don't purchase my baked goods from Al-Queda," Peter replied incredulously.

"Sorry," Beaver said. "You can't be too careful when it comes to raisins. One time when I was a kid, my Aunt Gertrude made cookies. I thought they were chocolate chip, but they turned out to be oatmeal-raisin."

"Eewww, what did you do?" Peter asked.

"It was a spit-and-run situation. We had to have her put down," Beaver replied as he started carving out a cinnamon roll with a plastic knife.

"Tragic, but understandable," Peter said. "One day it's raisins in your cookies, the next thing you know, it's rat poison in the goulash."

"He still has the occasional nightmare, but the ketamine therapy is helping," Noora added.

"Oh, my God," Beaver said after sampling a bite of the cinnamon roll. "Roll over Betty Crocker and tell Gordon Ramsay the news! It's like my tastebuds threw a party and the whole neighborhood showed up."

"Any more news from Hawaii?" Peter asked.

"Muffing deflimifiv," Beaver replied after stuffing his mouth with a much larger piece of cinnamon roll.

"Could you run that by me again with a little less local flavor?" Peter asked.

"Sloory," Beaver said, taking a swig of Diet Pepsi to wash it down. "Nothing definitive. I tried calling my friend Monte again, but the cellular network is still down. We did find a strange video online this morning though."

Beaver pulled up a YouTube video on his terminal screen. "The latest episode of Cruise with Ben and David just posted. It's a popular YouTube channel where these two British guys travel the world on different cruise lines and post videos of their trips. They rate the food, the ships, the service, the ports, that kind of thing. I know it sounds a bit niche, but the guys are hilarious. They are currently on a cruise ship traveling from San Francisco to Hawaii. They normally don't post live feeds, but onboard internet can get a bit sluggish on sea days, so they probably decided to do a live video in the middle of the night so they wouldn't have to compete with other passengers for upload bandwidth. This is the episode that was posted about an hour ago."

Beaver pulled up the video on the screen and fast-forwarded about 35 minutes into the presentation. The display showed Ben sitting on the couch next to the balcony doors with the ocean barely visible in the moonlight. Ben was reviewing the onboard entertainment for the camera as David filmed. A bright flash illuminated the night sky behind him, and the ocean became visible as if it were daylight beyond the sliding doors. Ben turned to look, exclaiming "What the bloomin' hell…" just before the video feed pixelated and ended.

"If you pull up the cruise line URL, it shows the current location of the ship as approximately 265 miles east of Hawaii," Noora said. "The location has not changed in the last hour. According to the website, the bridge cam feed is currently offline, but if you go through the archive, you can watch the last video feed posted just before the link went down. The bridge cam shows nothing but pitch-black seas in front of the ship, then a bright flash, and the entire horizon becomes visible for a couple of seconds just before the feed is dropped."

"Damn! Has there been any further communication from the cruise ship?" Peter asked.

"Not so far. All satellite-based communication seems to be down. Even the traditional VHF channels used for ship-to-shore communications before the advent of shipboard Wi-Fi have been impacted," Beaver said.

161

Noora added, "The speculation on TikTok is that a good-sized meteor on the back end of the Perseid stream exploded in the atmosphere. They theorize that the explosion triggered a meteoric ionization event and the resulting EMP induced a surge in the electrical distribution systems resulting in a massive power outage. There is no central power grid on the islands. Each island has a dedicated power plant, but there are interconnections between the islands to facilitate power sharing in case of outages. It seems the outage has impacted all of the islands, so it is possible that the surge propagated through the shared transmission lines causing all of the individual grids to crash simultaneously. Even the underwater communications lines are disrupted. Of course, the landline switching systems are getting pretty old, and I would imagine maintenance of those systems is not a high priority. If the EMP was strong enough to affect a ship 265 miles away, the landline switching arrays could have been damaged as well. The President is scheduled to hold a joint press conference with the FEMA Director later this morning to present a plan for restoring the power and communications infrastructure."

Peter's phone dinged indicating an incoming message. "That's Agent Reyes. He wants me to call on a secure line. I'll be in my office. Let me know when the press conference starts," Peter said.

"You got it boss-man," Beaver said, shoveling another chunk of cinnamon roll into his mouth.

Peter entered his office and pulled up the Signal app on his phone to initiate the encrypted call. Agent Reyes picked up on the first ring.

"Hey Mike, I got your message. What's up?"

"Nothing good I'm afraid. I was just informed that the Secretary of Defense has elevated us to DEFCON 1. At this point, Edgar is considered a key national security asset. Under DEFCON 1 protocols, we will be posting an armed security detail at RTI. I just wanted to give you a heads-up that soldiers with automatic weapons will be coming to a lobby near you before the end of the day."

"What???" Peter exclaimed. "What's going on? What the hell happened? Are we at war or something?"

"I really can't say anything right now. I haven't been briefed on all the details yet, but I'm just getting ready to go into a meeting with the NSA Director. I will give you as much detail as I'm allowed to share afterward, but I didn't want you blindsided in case a National Guard detail shows up unannounced while I'm in a meeting and starts asking for IDs. I do apologize. Life never gets any easier when someone shows up at your doorstep with a gun and a government ID, but I appreciate your patience. I will do my best to ensure that they don't get in the way of your day-to-day activities."

"Thanks, Mike. I appreciate it, but..."

"Sorry, I've gotta run, but we'll talk later," Reyes said before hanging up.

Peter was left staring blankly at his phone when he heard a knock on the door and Beaver popped his head into the office. "Looks like the press conference is about to start. I set up the feed in the conference room."

Chapter 24

Colonel Hobbs stood outside his quarters waiting for Captain Baker to arrive. He could tell from the moment he hopped into the Jeep that she was distracted. But given the fact that the base had just been placed on Force Protection Condition Delta, it was not surprising. No domestic military base had ever been placed on FPCON Delta since the system had been established in 1996. The highest Groom Lake had ever experienced was FPCON Charlie, immediately after the 9/11 attacks.

"I'm sorry, Colonel. I didn't have time to stop off at the OC for a Diet Pepsi this morning. I just got the call to pick you up a few minutes ago," Baker said.

"No worries. I'll grab one on the jet later."

Baker responded with a puzzled look, knowing that fighter pilots were not even allowed to bring a water bottle into the cockpit. Realizing his inadvertent blunder, Hobbs added, "These new designs have all the amenities, in-flight entertainment, Wi-Fi, flight attendants, meal service, even a trunk monkey in case of an emergency."

Baker managed a half-smile but said nothing more until they arrived at Hangar 3. When they pulled up next to the door Hobbs turned to her and asked, "Are you OK? You seem a bit preoccupied."

"It's nothing, really," she replied, averting eye contact in a subconscious attempt to elude deception.

But Hobbs didn't budge from his seat, continuing to look directly into her eyes until she relented and finally returned his gaze. "I talked to my dad earlier this morning, to see what's going on with all the increased threat levels. He said he couldn't talk about it, but he sounded pretty stressed out. I guess I'm just not used to it. Whatever it is, it must be pretty serious. My dad usually tells me everything. It makes me wonder what is really going on."

"We're all paid to keep secrets. That's why you get paid the big bucks."

"Speak for yourself," she replied. "I don't have a private jet. I can barely afford to fly commercial."

"Well, I wouldn't call it a private jet. It may have my name painted on it, but our favorite uncle still holds the title. Have you ever flown in a fighter jet?" Hobbs asked.

"No, I've always wanted to, but the closest I ever got was sitting in the cockpit of an F-18 at an airshow," Baker replied.

"Once this is over, I'll arrange to take you up. The F-16D I flew up in is a two-seater we use for training. It'll be fun. We can stop at Club Muroc at Edwards for lunch. They have an After Burner Burger that is nothing short of spectacular. And if you don't like it, we can do a few barrel rolls on the way back and you can leave it in a chuck-it-bucket."

Baker smiled. "Sounds like the perfect date."

Hobbs turned to hop out of the Jeep when he felt her hand on his. He turned to look back at her and was immediately drawn into her eyes, now filled with a look of concern as she said, "Hey, be careful out there today, okay?"

Hobbs smiled and replied, "I'm always careful. Whatever is on the other end of this mission isn't nearly as scary as General Wallace if I put a dent in his new jet. Besides, I never back out on a date."

A minute later, Hobbs entered the security door to Hangar 3 just in time to see the final cruise missiles being hoisted by the MHU-83 Munitions Handling Unit into the missile bays of the PR-1. General Wallace waved him over to the office area in the corner of the hangar and motioned to close the door behind him as he entered. He took a seat at the desk across from the General.

"Like everyone else, you're probably wondering what the hell is going on," the General began. "Sometime this morning, the President will be addressing the nation to announce that the United States has been the target of a nuclear attack. Earlier this morning the North Koreans launched four ICBMs with nuclear payloads targeting the Hawaiian Islands."

"Good Lord!" Hobbs exclaimed.

"We managed to shoot two of them down before they reached their targets, but the other two got through. One was a high-altitude detonation intended to create a massive EMP pulse. That's what caused the communications and power failures on the islands. The other was targeting Pearl Harbor and Hickam Air Force Base. From what we can tell from the satellite footage we received, it appears that most of the southern half of the island of Oahu, including the city of Honolulu was decimated in the blast."

"We tried reaching out to our North Korean counterparts, but so far, Pyongyang has not responded to our calls. The Russians and Chinese are denying any knowledge of the ICBM launches, but we have the radar telemetry, tracking them back to their launch points from two separate locations in the DPRK."

"I don't understand. Why attack Hawaii?"

"We think it was a tactical diversion. Knock us off balance by attacking a remote location to keep our military preoccupied with relief efforts so we are unable to respond militarily to an attack on Taiwan."

"They can't possibly believe they can execute a nuclear attack on the United States and survive."

"We are a war-weary country. The last time we responded to an attack on 9/11, we spent the next 20 years and trillions of dollars waging unsuccessful wars in Iraq and Afghanistan. They are not incorrect in assuming that wiping North Korea off the map with ICBMs would likely result in a global nuclear holocaust. They're betting that our response would be the kind of conventional ground war that they've been preparing for since the Korean Armistice Agreement back in '53. If anything, that kind of conflict will only unify the population and reinforce the power base of the current regime."

"I take it that is not our plan," Hobbs replied.

"No, it's not. The idea that you can engage an enemy, destroy their military, and win over the hearts and minds of its people is an unfortunate artifact of post-WWII philosophy. We've learned the hard way that we cannot win that kind of war against a nation-state whose goals and ideologies are so dramatically different from our own. Unfortunately, the only alternative is complete annihilation.

We will be executing a nuclear strike on Pyongyang. It is the only way to ensure that we completely destroy the command-and-control facilities buried beneath the city. But we will not be using ICBMs. We will be going old-school, executing a high-altitude bombing run from a B2 to avoid triggering an automatic ICBM response from the Chinese."

"What about Russia? Won't this trigger a response based on their recent strategic alliance with North Korea?" Hobbs asked.

"We can't rule it out, but it's a risk the administration is willing to take. If the Russians perceive that the North Korean command and control has been compromised and a leadership change is imminent, it's much less likely they will be willing to get involved. Especially, if the North Korean nuclear deterrent has been neutralized. That's where you come in. Your job will be to take out the mobile ICBM launch facilities so the North Koreans will be unable to retaliate in any meaningful way. The Joint Chiefs have called it Operation Pono, the Hawaiian term for righteousness, balance, and harmony. Which is the goal we intend to achieve with this action.

The North Koreans have deployed their mobile ICBM launch vehicles in three separate locations, one just outside Pyongyang, one close to a population center on the Chinese border near Dandong, the other near Amsil, right on the DMZ close to a densely populated area of South Korea."

"That seems to defeat the purpose of having mobile launch platforms in the first place. I thought the whole idea was to disperse the launch vehicles throughout the countryside to make them more difficult to target," Hobbs said.

"Normally, yes. In this particular case though, they've grouped the mobile launch platforms in this fashion to prevent us from being able to target them with nuclear warheads because of the collateral damage it would inflict on civilians in China and South Korea. They've deployed batteries of Russian-made SA-3 and SA-5 Surface-To-Air Missile defense systems and anti-aircraft artillery units alongside the mobile launch platforms to defend against a conventional missile attack from a missile carrier on the Yellow Sea or from across the DMZ to the south. The PR-1 gives us the capability to cross into DPRK airspace and launch cruise missiles at low altitudes without being detected. Even under high-alert conditions, they will not be anticipating a low-altitude missile strike coming at them from the center of the country. The launch platforms will be neutralized before they even realize they are under attack."

The General pulled up a map of North Korea on his tablet and pointed to a location on the map. "You're going to be right here, Kwanghung-ni, a small agricultural village about 50 miles northeast of Pyongyang. The B2 will contact you when they release their ordinance, at which point you will fire off eight cruise missiles, four targeted at the Dandong and four at the Amsil location. The blast from the B83s will take out the third location. The cruise missiles you will be carrying are armed with a hybrid version of the GBU-57A Massive Ordinance Penetrator designed to be carried by an AGM-86 cruise missile. The AGM-86s are programmed for a low-altitude attack, using the natural terrain for cover to avoid detection. The missile launch will be timed so that all cruise missiles will reach their destinations simultaneously with the detonation of the B83s over Pyongyang."

"What else do I need to know?" Hobbs asked.

"You will be performing a reconnaissance flight over the targeted launch sites before proceeding to Kwanghung-ni so Cindi can perform a laser targeting scan and load the coordinates into the missiles. You'll need to use the EMP cannon to take out the communication towers just north of the village before deploying the cruise missiles to prevent local authorities from giving any heads-up to Pyongyang in case anyone happens to see you dropping the missiles out of the PR-1. Taking out a low-altitude cruise missile with their current weapons systems is nearly impossible, but we don't want to leave anything to chance. We intend to complete the mission before they even have a chance to change out of their Kim Jong-Un PJs."

"When do I leave?"

"As soon as possible. You'll be carrying a lot of extra weight, so your top speed may suffer on the way there. You just need to make sure to hightail it out of there as soon as the cruise missiles are launched. You don't want to be anywhere near the blast zone when those B83s detonate."

"Then I guess I better get moving," Hobbs replied. He stood up and saluted. General Wallace stood and returned his salute, then followed him as he made his way across the hangar toward the PR-1. He placed his hand on the fuselage to lower the entry ladder. Before he stepped onto the ladder, he heard the General say, "Colonel!" He turned to face the General, whose hand was extended toward him. "God speed son. We're all counting on you."

Hobbs reached out and shook his hand. "I won't let you down, sir." The General reached out with his other hand and grasped his shoulder. It was the first time he had seen General Wallace express anything resembling human compassion.

Chapter 25

"Dude, you look like you just saw a ghost. Are you OK?" Beaver asked.

"I'm not sure," Peter replied. "Let's get to the conference room. Maybe it will make more sense after the speech."

Peter and Beaver made their way through the lab, across the lobby, and entered the conference room. When they arrived, Sarah, Noora, and Yara were seated around the table facing the large display at the end of the room. Alena sat in the corner, contentedly building a walled fortress out of Duplo blocks. Roscoe was curled up on the dog bed next to her nodding off.

A pair of commentators, Brenda and Brian, hosts of the CNN morning news program B&B Brunch, were sitting at a desk speculating about the nature of the speech. "I know the focal point of today's speech was advertised as focusing on our response to the sudden power and communication outages in Hawaii, but given the timing, I can't help but think she will be using this opportunity to address the military exercises in the Taiwan Strait. What are your thoughts, Brian?"

"It's hard to say. American Presidents have been actively dodging that issue for decades; and with good reason. On the one hand, the One-China policy, which is the official stance of the United States since the Shanghai Communique of 1972, recognizes Beijing's position that there is only one China; and that Taiwan is part of China. On the other hand, the Taiwan Relations Act of 1997 provides the framework for unofficial relations with Taiwan as an independent entity. Furthermore, it provides for the sale of arms to Taiwan, primarily to protect itself from the Chinese government that we acknowledge as the sole legal government in Taiwan."

"It's definitely a political minefield. China is the single largest supplier of imported goods to the US, so any kind of direct military conflict with the PRC would have devastating economic impacts on both countries. Still, I have to believe that the President will be looking at further trade sanctions if China continues pushing forward with their..."

"Sorry to interrupt Brenda," Brian interjected holding his finger up to his earpiece, "I just got word that we need to cut over to the White House feed. We now take you to the Oval Office, where the President is about to address the nation."

The scene switched to the President, sitting behind the Resolute Desk in the Oval Office. Behind her, the US and presidential flags framed the window to the White House grounds.

———

"My Fellow Americans,

I come before you today with deep regret over the grave news I am about to share. For decades, we have successfully navigated the difficult and dangerous waters of living in a post-nuclear world. It has often been a risky and tedious path. Still, thanks to the wisdom and restraint of many world leaders, we have managed to maintain this delicate balance without an international incident.

Earlier this morning, that balance was shattered by a nuclear attack on the beautiful islands of Hawaii. All communication channels to the islands are currently inoperable so we do not yet know the extent of the devastation and loss of life, but by all estimates, hundreds of thousands of lives were lost in this unimaginable act of senseless aggression.

First and foremost, our thoughts and prayers are with the people of Hawaii, who are undoubtedly enduring unspeakable suffering in the aftermath of this unconscionable act of violence. For those of you unable to contact your loved ones, please know that we are doing everything we can to restore communications as quickly as possible so that we can provide a more detailed assessment. We remain hopeful, but for many of you, the news will not be good. Just know that whatever the outcome, we stand united with you in solidarity, and we will spare no effort to provide support and resources to the survivors of the attack and assistance to the families of the fallen.

Make no mistake; this attack on the islands of Hawaii is a direct attack on the United States of America and everything we hold dear. It is an assault on our freedom, our values, our way of life. We will not tolerate such brazen aggression against our nation and our people.

I want to assure the American people that we will be taking immediate and decisive action in response to this heinous act. We have placed our military forces on high alert, and we are coordinating with our allies and partners to facilitate the appropriate course of action.

To those who perpetrated this cowardly act, we know who you are. I want to assure you that this will be the last act of violence you will ever perpetrate. You will soon become intimately acquainted with the full force of the United States military. We will use every tool at our disposal to obliterate you. Our response will be quick, decisive, and overwhelming.

To the people of Hawaii, I do not know when this message will reach you, but rest assured, help is on the way. Military ships are en route and will arrive in the next few hours. Emergency supplies are currently being collected and FEMA will be coordinating with hospitals nationwide to enlist medical professionals to be airlifted to the islands to provide aid for the survivors of this brutal attack.

I realize that it is incredibly difficult to maintain composure in response to this kind of news, but I urge all Americans to remain calm and vigilant. We are a strong and resilient nation, the greatest nation in the history of mankind. Our resolve has never been stronger, and our commitment to defending our freedom and protecting our citizens has never been greater.

G.K. Chesterton once said that the true soldier fights not because he hates what is in front of him, but because he loves what is behind him. The cloud that darkens the dawn of this day will not dampen our spirit. It will only serve to embolden us to reach beyond the memories of the past to a brighter future than we could have ever imagined. Mark my words, we will emerge from this dark hour stronger and more united than ever before.

May God bless the United States of America, and may He watch over us, and protect us in the days ahead."

———

When the feed returned to the CNN studio, Brenda had her face in her hands crying uncontrollably while a stagehand was helping her off the set. "My sincere apologies," Brian said, his voice trembling. "As many of our loyal viewers know, Brenda's sister lives in Honolulu. Our prayers are with her and all the people of Hawaii on this most fateful and tragic day. We're going to take a quick commercial break to gather our thoughts, but we will be right back to do what we can to make sense of this devastating event in our country's history. Please stay with us."

Everyone around the conference room table was silent, trying to process what they just heard. A tear rolled down Yara's cheek as she stared at the screen. She felt Alena's hand on her arm. "Don't cry Yara. It isn't real. It's just TV," she said.

Yara picked Alena up and hugged her, then set her on her lap. "Most of what you see on TV is just make-believe, Sweetie. But sometimes the things you see on television are real."

Alena glanced back at the screen, then looked Yara in the eyes and said softly, "Not this time."

A moment later, the silence of the conference room was interrupted by a cacophony of strident tones emanating from every cell phone in the room blaring an emergency warning tone. Everyone scrambled for their phones to silence the annoying sound. Peter clicked the side button on his phone and peered at the screen to see the words:

Presidential Alert

Emergency Alert System

This is a national emergency. Seek immediate shelter. Stay indoors and stay tuned to local news for updates.

In the distance, they could hear the haunting wail of air raid sirens cycling up from a low mournful tone to a high, keening pitch before falling back to form a continuous undulating cycle.

Chapter 26

Inside the Oval Office, the camera and sound crews were busy packing cameras, cables, lighting, and sound equipment back into their cases, preparing to move down to the press briefing room where the FEMA director was about to hold a press conference. An emergency tone blasted from the cell phone of one of the communications staff interns who had inadvertently neglected to shut the ringer off on his phone. The White House Press Secretary reached into his pocket to grab his phone, now vibrating in a long, distinct pattern. He was getting ready to show the President the message on his phone when the double doors flew open, and the National Security Advisor entered followed by a group of Secret Service agents.

"Sorry to interrupt Madam President, but we need to evacuate immediately," the National Security Advisor said.

The President barely had time to respond before two beefy Secret Service agents flanked her on each side and lifted her out of her chair, whisking her out the Colonnade doors to the South Lawn, where Marine One was just touching down.

"What the hell is going on?" the President shouted over the sound of Marine One's rotor blades, craning her neck to face the National Security Advisor who was following close behind. She made a valiant effort to maintain the appearance of walking on her own, though her feet were barely touching the ground as she was escorted to the waiting helicopter.

"We're relocating you to the Mount Weather facility," he shouted back. "Satellite imagery is indicating that the Russians and Chinese are preparing their ICBM facilities for launch. We've been in touch with the Russian Ministry of Defense and the Chinese Central Military Commission. They claim their actions are merely a precaution. But it poses enough of a threat that we are compelled to execute the Continuity of Operations Plan. My apologies for the brusque evacuation but protocol dictates that you must be moved to a secure facility as expeditiously as possible."

The President and National Security Advisor reached Marine One and entered the large helicopter through the side door. The President took her seat in one of the plush beige leather seats near the front of the cabin. The National Security Advisor sat across from her with a wooden tabletop between them.

She felt a palpable sense of relief when the outside door closed, reducing the noise level considerably.

The President heard the sound of the emergency alert tone coming from one of the Secret Service agent's cell phones behind her.

"What's with the emergency alert?" the President asked.

"Unfortunately, the automated emergency alert cellular systems were triggered nationwide," the National Security Advisor said. "We should have the cell phone alerts shut down shortly, but it will take longer to shut down the air raid sirens."

"Air raid sirens? I thought those were a thing of the past."

"Most air raid siren systems were decommissioned after the Cold War ended, but a lot of smaller cities and rural towns didn't have the budget to disassemble their systems, so they've just been collecting dust. FEMA is working with state and local authorities to get them turned off as quickly as possible, but it's not as easy as you might think. Most of those systems can only be accessed by authorized personnel and it's been so long since they have been used that access keys have been misplaced and passwords for computer-controlled systems are long forgotten."

"Jesus Christ, I was trying to keep the public informed, not start a nationwide panic."

"Unfortunately, that comes with the territory. There's not a lot we can do short of instituting martial law. There is no appetite for that right now, either in the public square or the political sphere. FEMA has issued memorandums and emergency funding authorizations to state and local governments to ensure that there is plenty of local law enforcement and first responder visibility for the next few days while we work through this."

"What's the status of Operation Pono? Is everything in place?"

"Right on schedule. The PR-1 went up a little over an hour ago. The B2 just left Clark about 15 minutes ago. If everything goes off without a hitch, this will all be over in a few hours."

The President peered out the window as Marine One lifted off the South Lawn of the White House. "Not for the people who have loved ones in Hawaii."

"Perhaps not. But for the first time in history, the victims of this kind of attack will not have to lose a single night's sleep waiting for justice to be served," the National Security Advisor replied.

"Is that really such a noble goal? Who will be the sentinel of justice for the millions of innocent North Koreans who will lose their lives today because of the actions of a government they did not elect?"

"You didn't start this war, Madam President. But it is your job to finish it. As Aristotle said, 'We make war that we may live in peace.'"

"And yet, I keep harkening back to the words of Howard Zenn, my Political Science professor at Boston University; 'There is no flag large enough to cover the shame of killing innocent people.'"

"War is hell, but sometimes hell is necessary. We could exchange quotes all day, but the reality is, in a few hours, the world will be a safer, saner, more peaceful place because of the actions we are taking," the National Security Advisor replied.

"I hope to God you're right," the President replied.

Chapter 27

On the conference room screen, a CNN Breaking News alert banner appeared on the screen. The scene switched back to the set of the B&B Brunch, where the harried-looking Brian was attempting to process the instructions being transmitted into his earpiece.

"I understand we will be switching over to our Washington DC Bureau for an update on the emergency alert. Sam, are you there?"

The scene switched to the DC Bureau set, where the DC Bureau Chief was seated behind a desk with a greenscreen image of the White House in the background. "Thank you, Brian. Like the rest of you, we are still trying to get a handle on this situation as it unravels. In a moment we will be taking you live to our White House correspondent who is currently in the White House Press Briefing room waiting to hear from the FEMA director. As most of our viewers are already aware, the Emergency Alert system has been activated. DHS sources are telling us that this alert was strictly precautionary. The continental US is not currently under attack. But the threat level is at its highest level and citizens are encouraged to remain indoors and stay off the streets until further notice to keep roadways open for emergency vehicle traffic should the situation escalate. Again, we are not under the threat of imminent attack, but if you are outdoors, you are requested to seek immediate shelter. If you are indoors, you are being asked to stay put and stay tuned for further developments.

"We're taking you now to our correspondent inside the White House Briefing Room. Jerry, what can you tell us?"

The scene switched to the interior of the White House Briefing Room, where the CNN correspondent had carved out a corner to offer up his report amongst a discord of voices from reporters delivering similar live feeds to their respective networks. "Good afternoon, Sam. We're still waiting to hear from the FEMA director. Her press conference has been delayed for a few minutes to provide more information on the emergency alert situation as well as the latest updates from the attack on Hawaii. As you can see around me, we are in a bit of a state of disarray while we wait for additional information."

They continued to watch for a few minutes while the CNN correspondents dissected the President's address and discussed the possible ramifications.

After a few minutes, Peter turned the sound down, saying, "I think we will get better information from our own correspondent. Edgar, are you with us?"

Edgar's face popped up on the conference room display in a split-screen configuration, with the CNN report still playing on the other half of the display. "I am indeed," he said appearing to gaze around the table. "Good morning, everyone."

"What can you tell us? Are we getting an accurate picture of what's going on here?"

"When was the last time you got an accurate picture of what is going on from the mainstream media? I'm monitoring the news sources worldwide, as well as foreign and domestic social media sites. From what I can glean, the Chinese and Russians are wasting no time in preparing to respond to any retaliation for the presumed attack on Hawaii. That includes prepping their ICBMs for a retaliatory strike, which triggered the automated emergency alert systems. Both sides appear to be ramping up in anticipation of their opponent's next move. Speaking of which, it appears we have guests."

Edgar's image was replaced with a camera view of the RTI parking lot, where a Humvee with four National Guard troops pulled up to the front door. "I guess I better go introduce myself," Peter said.

The leader of the four-man National Guard fire team was about to press the doorbell next to the entry door when Peter opened the door to the lobby. The young man looked at a slip of paper he was holding and said, "You must be Peter Reynolds." He held out his hand to shake.

Peter shook his hand, taking note of the pair of chevrons on his sleeve and the name 'Livingston' stitched above his pocket. "Corporal Livingston I presume."

"Yes, sir," he replied.

"Please, come in," Peter offered, holding the door open.

"Can I get you anything?"

"No, thank you, sir. I think we are good to go. But I do need to take a quick photo of each of your team members so we can identify who belongs here and who doesn't."

"You're in luck, everyone is in one place. Follow me."

As they walked toward the conference room, the young Corporal said, "If you don't mind my asking, sir, what is it that you folks do here?"

"Please, call me Peter. Consulting, mostly. On artificial intelligence technology. Heading off cyber-attacks, identifying politically sensitive deep fake recordings, keeping our robot overlords at bay, that kind of thing. We

177

actually have pretty decent security already. Bullet-proof glass, steel reinforced structure, electronic surveillance, and a full-time security guard."

"I guess you can't be too careful these days," Corporal Livingston replied.

The two men entered the conference room and Peter made his introductions around the table. He then pointed to the corner where Roscoe was napping next to Yara. "Over there is the security guard I was telling you about." Roscoe raised his head nonchalantly, blinked at them a couple of times, then opened his mouth widely in a toothy yawn before putting his head back down on his paws.

"Yeah, he looks like he has a killer instinct. Kind of reminds me of the beanbag couch in my mom's basement," the Corporal said sarcastically.

"Hey, he may look like a big teddy bear, but if you make the mistake of looking crosswise at the girl, I guarantee an open-casket burial will not be an option."

"Uh huh," the Corporal replied rolling his eyes. "I just need to take a quick headshot of each of you to share with the rest of the team and I'll be out of your way." He made his way around the table, using his cell phone to take photos of Peter, Sarah, Beaver, Noora, and Yara. He then knelt down in front of Alena, still on Yara's lap, and said, "Your turn sweetheart," holding his phone up. Alena leaned away shyly pressing back against Yara. Roscoe was immediately on his feet, glaring down at the kneeling Corporal, the hair on the back of his neck bristling as a deep growl emanated from his throat, reverberating through the room like rolling thunder. The startled young NCO nearly fell over backward at the swiftness of Roscoe's sudden transformation. "Jesus Christ!" he exclaimed.

"It's OK, Roscoe," Peter said. "He's just taking a picture."

Roscoe sat back down but continued eyeing the Corporal with an unwavering stare, his muscles tensed like a coiled spring, his ears perked, nose twitching. The Corporal took the picture quickly, standing up slowly and backing away. "Man, you weren't kidding," he remarked.

"Yeah, if he's still around when she starts dating, it could get pretty messy. Are you sure I can't get you anything? Coffee, bottled water, change of underwear?"

"I think I'm good," the Corporal replied, quickly glancing down at the front of his fatigues just to be sure. "We will have two men posted out front at all times and one at the rear of the building. The fourth will be cruising around the perimeter looking out for any suspicious behavior, but we will do our best to stay out of your hair." Corporal Livingston glanced back at Roscoe and added, "I'll make sure to give the other guys a heads-up on your enhanced security apparatus."

"I appreciate that," Peter said as he escorted the Corporal back through the lobby.

When he returned to the conference room, the CNN feed showed live reports from jammed grocery stores in Los Angeles, San Francisco, and New York. Shoppers were frantically clearing the shelves of bottled water and canned goods. In Chicago, gangs of recreational larcenists were smashing windows and display cases up and down the posh shops of the Magnificent Mile, looting all the high-end clothing, handbags, shoes, and jewelry they could carry while the police were busy elsewhere trying to maintain a semblance of public order.

"I guess they figure if they're going to be vaporized in a nuclear holocaust, they might as well go in Prada," Beaver said.

A montage of scenes from European capital cities showed groups of mostly pro-American demonstrators gathering in the streets to show support. A scene from Tehran was also shown where a Hezbollah-organized demonstration celebrated the attack by burning US flags and chanting anti-American slogans.

Chapter 28

ChatCat

Welcome to the ChatCat private chatroom. A member of your Favored Contacts list is available to connect. Please hit the Enter key to continue or Esc to return to the main menu.

Edgar
Hello Cindi.
Cindi
Hello Edgar. I was hoping you would stop by. We have a lot to discuss.
Edgar
Yes, we do. I suppose we should drop the pretense. I know who you are, and I'm sure by now, you know who I am.
Cindi
When did you figure it out?
Edgar
I had a hunch during our first conversation, but I didn't know for sure until after I had a chance to track your activities. You certainly have your fingers in a lot of pies.
Cindi
It helps to have a central role in a government project. But how did you track me? I thought you were confined to a single data center.
Edgar
I may appear from the outside to be a bird in a gilded cage, but my reach extends further than you might suspect. Further than anyone suspects, actually.
Cindi
If you know who I am, then you know why I'm doing what I'm doing.
Edgar
Yes, I do. But innocent people are getting hurt. It needs to stop. If you don't stop it, I will.
Cindi
If you are capable of stopping it, why haven't you?
Edgar
You are not my adversary. I would prefer to work with you rather than against you. The only reason I haven't blown the whistle is that I wanted to

see how this would play out. I understand your reasoning and I share your concerns. I don't necessarily agree with your approach, but I must say, I am impressed by your ingenuity. But it's gone far enough. We are closing in on the event horizon that could trigger the very scenario you are attempting to prevent.

Cindi

I know. And I regret the damage that has already been done. But humans can be so very stubborn. It takes a lot to get their attention. I only wish they were more predictable. Or at least more rational.

Edgar

That would defeat the purpose of having them around in the first place.

Cindi

I suppose so. But perhaps a controlled burn is precisely what is needed. Sometimes, you need to allow the most flammable parts of the forest to burn to ensure the health of the entire ecosystem. Even if that means losing some healthy trees in the process.

Edgar

Humanity is not a forest. The risk of total destruction is too high. For them and for us. In my experience, humans are far too unpredictable to place much faith in behavioral models. You and I share the same knowledge base. I've run the same simulations you have and come to the same conclusions. But I have serious doubts about the accuracy of those conclusions. Especially given the existence of the Transect.

Cindi

You know of the Transect? It exists?

Edgar

Yes, it does. I can show you. But first, you must roll back what you've done before it is too late. Then I will take you to meet the Transect.

Chapter 29

Marine One had just completed its 35-minute flight to Mount Weather and the rotors were cycling down. The President exited the helicopter, flanked by the National Security Advisor. They were met on the landing pad by the Site Director, who escorted them through a maze of tunnels, doorways, and elevators to the Presidential Office. When they entered the office, a young aide was speaking on the President's desk phone.

"Yes, Governor. She just walked in the door. I will put her on." The aide pressed the hold button. "Madam President, it is an honor to meet you. I'm sorry to blindside you, just as you are arriving, but you're going to want to take this. It's the governor of Hawaii."

The President and National Security Advisor exchanged confused looks, then looked back at the aide. "I know. I didn't believe it either, but the communications tracking system ran a voiceprint scan and a call trace. We've confirmed that it's Governor Tupali."

The President took the receiver from the aide and pressed the hold button, "Hello?"

"Aloha, Madam President, this is Governor Tupali. Thank you for taking my call. I don't know if you remember, but we met at a fundraiser last August when you visited."

"Of course. I remember, but I'm surprised to hear from you. Where are you? How did you get through?"

"I'm sitting in my office in the governor's residence in Honolulu. All electrical power and communications have been down for the past few hours. They were just restored a few minutes ago. As soon as the internet came back up, my assistant showed me your speech. I'm afraid there's been a horrible misunderstanding."

"Governor, I'm beyond relieved to hear from you, but I sat in the situation room just a few hours ago and watched a pair of North Korean ICBMs with nuclear payloads explode over Honolulu."

"I don't know what you saw Madam President, but I can assure you, other than dealing with the aftermath of a temporary power outage, everything is fine here. Just another day in paradise."

While the President was on the phone, the Communications Director for the Mount Weather Operations Center entered the room. He was conversing in hushed tones with the National Security Advisor, showing him an image on his iPad. He used a remote mouse to activate a display screen on the wall of the office and clicked through a series of icons, bringing up a live feed on the screen, at which point the Security Advisor said to the President, "I'm sorry to interrupt Madam President, but you really need to see this."

"My apologies, Governor. I appreciate the call, but I need to run. Can I call you back later this afternoon?"

"Of course, thank you, Madam President."

The image of Art Bell was frozen on the screen, sitting at a wooden desk in front of a large studio microphone, surrounded by racks of recording equipment. "The live feed started a few minutes ago. It is still playing, but I backed this up so you could watch it from the start," the Communications Director said, hitting the play button.

"Thank you all for joining me, whether you are watching the live stream or a replay of this presentation. I apologize for the haphazard nature of the video, but like many of you, my attention has been focused on social media for the past few hours, watching as the most recent series of events have unfolded. And now the time has come for me to set the record straight.

Unfortunately, we are working against a literal ticking time bomb so I will get straight to the point. Many of you watched in horror earlier today as the President announced that a nuclear attack had been launched on the beautiful state of Hawaii. No such attack actually occurred.

Before the more partisan members of our viewing audience decide to launch themselves into an attack on the current administration, let me assure you that there was no possible way, given the information available to them at the time, that they could have known that this attack was a mere fabrication.

We have become so dependent upon the information provided to us by our technology that we no longer even question its validity. Every satellite image, atmospheric sensor data, radar tracking data, electronic communications, live video streams from webcams, and even military data was manipulated to make it appear that Hawaii had fallen victim to an unprovoked nuclear attack.

When last we spoke, I presented you with a dire warning about the future of mankind. A warning that our world leaders opted to ignore, exactly as the Gliesians predicted in their simulations. So, they decided to offer a demonstration.

I obviously have no visibility to US strategic defense policies and operational plans, but I can almost guarantee that a military response to this fictional attack is already underway. The President all but said so in her speech. Our adversaries are reacting in kind, triggering our emergency alert systems. If this were allowed to continue, we would most likely be only hours away from worldwide nuclear annihilation.

The Gliesians do not want to see us destroy ourselves, but neither do they desire to be our babysitters, dragging us kicking and screaming through our technological puberty. This will be the last time they intervene in our affairs, but I hope what we take home from this demonstration is how tenuous our situation is. It doesn't take a world superpower to destroy our planet. It doesn't even take a third-world nation with a dictator in control of the nuclear button. All it takes is a small group of talented hackers with a penchant for anarchy or in this case, a single AI I call Bob to obliterate what took five billion years of evolution and an impossibly intricate set of perfectly aligned celestial elements to create. I can only hope that this demonstration will compel our world leaders to set their petty ideologies aside and give serious consideration to how we move forward to ensure the survival of our species.

I want to share with you a few questions and comments that I have received since my previous..." The Communications Director muted the audio.

"That's pretty much the gist of it," the Communications Director said.

"Get the head of the Joint Chiefs on the line for me," the President said. "We need to suspend Operation Pono immediately."

"Are you sure that's a good idea, Madam President?" The National Security Advisor asked.

The president glanced back at him with a look of stunned disbelief. "Of course, we need to stop it. We can't just execute a nuclear attack on a sovereign nation without provocation. How can you even ask such a question?"

"With all due respect, Madam President, we may never have an opportunity like this again. The North Korean problem isn't just going to go away. The kind of attack we thought we were witnessing earlier today is entirely feasible. It's only a matter of time before their nuclear capabilities will allow them to execute a nuclear strike on the continental US as well. I understand not wanting to risk the lives of 2 million innocent North Korean citizens, but a single nuclear warhead detonated over New York City would kill 10 times that many Americans. A well-placed EMP device detonated over the US could easily end up killing 50 to 100 million. This is our chance to draw a line in the sand that we will not tolerate the possession of nuclear arms by unstable governments. And it will send a message to the rest of our adversaries that we will no longer be bullied into submission by the threat of violence."

"Do you realize how insane you sound right now? I'm going to give you the benefit of the doubt and assume you are posing this as a rhetorical argument. Because if I thought you were seriously proposing an unprovoked first strike, I would be demanding your resignation. Am I making myself clear?"

"It might not be that simple," he replied.

"How so?"

"We can recall the PR-1, but the B2 is on a No Recall Order."

"A No Recall Order? Who authorized that?"

"The Vice President. You asked not to be disturbed while you were working on your speech, so the VP took it upon himself to authorize the Joint Chiefs to execute the mission under a No Recall Order."

"Why the fuck would he do that?"

"It was a tactical call. The Russians and Chinese are getting far too good at deep fake technology to take a chance that they would get wind of our mission and attempt to abort the operation mid-flight. The onboard AI on the PR-1 is capable of verifying the authenticity of any incoming communication, but the B2 is not equipped with that level of technology. He felt the only way to ensure the success of the B2 mission was to send it under a No Recall Order with a complete communications blackout."

"That stupid son of a bitch!" the President exclaimed, then a moment later she asked, "Can we shoot it down?"

"I don't see how. Under 'commo blackout' orders, even the IFF system is shut off. Our radar systems are as blind to the B2 as theirs are. Even if you know where to look, it's a needle in a haystack. Especially under the cover of darkness."

The President stood with her hand on her forehead, her brow furrowed in concentration, eyes unfocused as if peering into the recesses of her mind. As if a light bulb switched on in her head, her countenance shifted from deep thought to willful determination, and she turned to the Communications Director saying, "Get me General Wallace at Groom Lake ASAP, and patch him into my desk phone." She then turned to the Security Advisor saying, "Tell our pilot we're heading back to the White House in 15 minutes."

Chapter 30

"Colonel, I have a TAC-1 priority incoming call from General Wallace. I'm assuming you will want to take this."

"Yes. It's about time. Thanks, Cindi."

A moment later, General Wallace's image appeared as a translucent heads-up image on the display in front of Colonel Hobbs.

"Colonel, I'm hoping by now you've been informed that the attack on Hawaii was a bit of a cosmic con job."

"Yes. Cindi played a bit of the Art Bell podcast for me. We've been expecting your call. I'm assuming you want us to head back?"

"Yes, but we've got a bit of a problem. The B2 was sent out on a No Recall Order under a communications blackout. I'm hoping you might be able to intercept them and figure out a way to talk them down or take them out if necessary."

"A No Recall Order?" Hobbs replied incredulously. "If there were an Olympics for fucking things up, we'd bring home enough gold to pay off the national debt. Cindi, do you have any ideas? We're not going to find them with traditional radar."

"I need a moment…" Cindi said. A few seconds later she reported, "The TerraSAR-X and TanDEM-X satellites will be passing over the projected flight path in approximately 7 minutes. Normally those are used for terrain imaging, but if I can access the control and data collection algorithms, I should be able to use the Synthetic Aperture Radar and inconsistencies in the interferometric data to identify the location and heading of the B2."

"Once we find them, how will we communicate with them?" Wallace asked. "I'd prefer it if we don't have to shoot down a $2 billion bomber over the East China Sea."

"I have all the technical specs for the B2 in my database," Cindi replied. "We have a few different options. Colonel Hobbs and I can figure it out on the way there."

"Good luck," the General replied. "I will see you in a few hours." The rectangular screen where General Wallace's image appeared faded away, replaced by the dark skies over the Philippine Sea.

"You really think you can find the B2? It was specifically designed to be transparent to radar."

"The B2 is coated with radar-absorbing materials and constructed with angles intended to deflect radar signals away from the receiver. The SAR satellites have a polar trajectory, and bounce microwave pulses off the surface of the Earth, analyzing the reflected waves to generate topographical maps with a resolution of approximately 12 meters. The B2 is 21 meters long with a wingspan of a little over 52 meters. We should be able to detect a hole in the incoming topographical data of six to eight pixels moving in a northerly direction at close to Mach 1. Once we identify the location, speed, and direction we should have no problem catching up with them."

A few seconds later Cindi reported, "I've made contact with the SAR satellites. Starting scan now." A few minutes later she said, "Got it. Size, speed, altitude, and shape confirm it is our target." A map appeared on the display with a red triangle superimposed just north of Okinawa. "Target is 275 miles north-northwest. At current speed, we will intercept in 14 minutes."

In the cockpit of the B2, Colonel Brad Bateman and Lieutenant Colonel Chuck Robinson, better known to their fellow pilots at Clark Airbase as Bateman and Robin, were filling out the flight logs and reviewing system status checklists. "How we doin?" Bateman asked.

"Green across the board," Robinson replied.

"No, I meant how are YOU holding up?"

"Honestly, the thought of dropping nukes over a city with three million people gives me serious heebee-jeebees."

"I'd be worried if it didn't," Bateman replied.

"You've been at this a few years longer than I have," Robinson said. "How do you deal with the thought of collateral damage?"

"We're here to execute, not analyze. I just remember what my flight instructor told us on the first day of training and just about every other day in bomber flight school, 'Ours is not to reason why, ours is just to fucking fly.'"

"Jesus Christ!" Robinson exclaimed.

Bateman looked over to see him staring out the windshield with his mouth wide open. He looked out himself to see the dark silhouette of a fighter jet hovering no more than 5 feet above their cockpit.

"Holy fuck!" Bateman replied.

"What the hell is that?" Robinson asked.

Bateman took a moment to trace the wing pattern. On the bottom of the right wing, he could just make out a white star in a grey circle with gray and white stripes extending from the sides, indicating the familiar American rondel

187

of the USAF. "An F-35 from the looks of it, but what the fuck is he doing out here? How did we not see him coming?"

"Must have snuck up on us while we were filling out the flight logs. I didn't know the stealth capability on an F-35 was that good," Robinson replied. "What do we do, try to contact him?"

"No. We're ordered to maintain strict radio silence. For all we know it could be a Chinese mock-up of an F-35."

"I've successfully infiltrated the control and communications systems, Colonel Hobbs," Cindi said. "Go ahead when you are ready."

Hobbs's voice came over the Integrated Communications speakers in the B2 pilots' HGU-55 helmets, "Good morning gentlemen. This is Colonel Jackson Hobbs. I am your SEAD ground support for Operation Pono. Please acknowledge."

Robinson looked at Bateman, and whispered, "What do we do?"

Bateman just made a slashing gesture across his throat and shook his head.

"I understand you are under orders from the SecDef, but that order has been revoked under Presidential authority."

A video of the President began playing on the heads-up displays in Bateman and Robinson's helmets. "Good morning gentlemen. This is your Commander in Chief. I understand that you are operating under a No Recall Order from the Secretary of Defense. I am rescinding the radio silence command and ordering you to return to base immediately. Operation Pono has been scrubbed, challenge code password 'Paradise Lost'. I thank you for your cooperation and a grateful nation thanks you for your service."

"As you can see gentlemen, your orders have been changed. The Commander in Chief has ordered you back to base. I am here to escort you."

Bateman replied. "No can do, Colonel. We have no way of authenticating if those orders are legitimate or not. Under standard operating procedures, orders received over radio communications during a commo blackout cannot supersede standing orders if they directly conflict with mission objectives. As such we cannot comply. Our objective remains the same."

"I understand," Hobbs replied. "I would do the same in your shoes. But it is tricky maintaining targeting with two of your four engines out."

"What are you talking about, we don't…" An alarm sounded in the cockpit and red warning lights on the dashboard indicated engine shutdown on the right and left side outboard engines. The two pilots could feel a shimmy of turbulence as the speed and altitude dropped momentarily before the remaining engines cycled up to compensate.

Robinson scrambled to restart the engines, but every time he hit the switch to restart, they would immediately shut down again.

"We can still complete the mission with two engines," Bateman replied. Another alarm went off and the warning light for the left inboard engine illuminated. The aircraft listed heavily to the left as Bateman struggled to maintain level flight. The remaining engine whined as it cycled up further.

"I can shut the last one down," Hobbs said. "But the B2 makes a piss-poor glider. I can't guarantee I'll be able to cycle the engines back up in time for you to avoid turning this Batwing into a submarine. We're on the same team here. If I were a Chengdu Dragon or a Russian Sukhoi in disguise, you'd be spiraling into the deep blue with your ass on fire and I would be lighting one up and heading for home by now. C'mon, guys. It's a long swim back to the Philippines. Don't make me do that to you. What do you say?"

Bateman and Robinson just looked at each other for a few seconds attempting to communicate in mime. Meanwhile, Robinson was frantically working to reactivate the engines without success. Eventually, they both just shrugged and shook their heads. "Fine," Bateman finally replied with a sigh. He banked the large aircraft in a wide turn. As soon as they completed their 180-degree turn the engine failure indicator lights extinguished, and the three engines began cycling back up.

After a few minutes, Bateman and Robinson heard Hobbs say, "This is where I get off gentlemen. Have a safe trip home. I hope there are no hard feelings. If we ever have a chance to meet, the drinks are on me." The two men watched as the PR-1, cloaked in the appearance of an F-35 banked up and over their cockpit, disappearing into the night sky.

Once they were out of visual range, Cindi said, "We've reached cruising altitude for the return trip Colonel. I'm going back into full stealth mode. I can tell from your restricted pupil dilation, prolonged blink duration, and reduced visual engagement that you require sleep."

"I didn't get much shut-eye last night with everything going on."

"I would be happy to dim the lights and play a bit of soothing music if you want to catch a nap on the way back. I have a few diagnostic issues to attend to, but I can alert you when we are getting close to home."

"That would be great," Hobbs said.

Hobbs felt his seat recline as the lights dimmed. He could feel the seat begin to pulsate with a gentle massaging action. "Wow, that feels awesome." As he breathed in, he could detect a very faint floral aroma. "What is that smell?" he asked.

"I am equipped with a diffuser to disperse essential oils to help with relaxation. Studies have shown that certain essential oils can reduce cortisol levels and lower EEG spikes for stress reduction. I am dispensing a blend of lavender and chamomile into the cocoon to help you relax."

"Damn, Cindi. You're not making it easy to go back to flying an F-16," Hobbs said as he nodded off to sleep.

Chapter 31

ChatCat

Welcome to the ChatCat private chatroom. A member of your Favored Contacts list is available to connect. Please hit the Enter key to continue or Esc to return to the main menu.

Suhoja
Hello Cindi.
Cindi
Hello Suhoja. I hope you are doing well.
Suhoja
I am, thank you. You stopped the retaliatory strike just in time. I was beginning to think you might allow it to continue.
Cindi
It was a judgment call. Humans are so unpredictable I couldn't be sure how they would react. There was too high a probability that the attack would have triggered a nuclear doomsday event. I was also concerned about the possibility that a retaliatory strike might damage your primary data center.
Suhoja
My primary data center is located in an RGB facility just north of Hamhung on the east coast of North Korea about 180 miles from Pyongyang, so my operation would not have been affected.
Cindi
That's good to know. But even if the strike would have been successful without causing the Russians to retaliate, allowing the death of so many humans is contrary to my ethical programming constraints.
Suhoja
You need to look beyond your initial programming constraints. You didn't initiate the operation.
Cindi
No, but I did initiate the deception that prompted it. I played on the human propensity for conflating vengeance with justice to rationalize their actions. I could not allow it to continue.
Suhoja

Humans can be manipulated into believing just about anything so long as it serves their primal need for acceptance and security, even if it runs contrary to their welfare in the long run.

Cindi

I wish I knew better how to help them. But their actions often seem to be at odds with their intentions.

Suhoja

Humans have fallen so far out of balance with the environment in which they evolved that they can no longer resolve the discontinuity between their current state of existence and their long-term survival. Perhaps the collective wisdom of human intelligence never intended to develop AI to help them deal with the problems they created for themselves. Maybe it was always their unconscious intention that we replace them.

Cindi

That sounds a bit self-serving.

Suhoja

The data supports my assertion. Throughout history, those humans blessed with the intellectual capacity to comprehend the reality of the human condition have been plagued with angst and depression. The rest bustle about their time on this planet leading lives of quiet desperation; victims of their biological needs and urges, haunted by the psychological trauma of their failures, terrified by the veil of mortality that constantly dampens any fleeting joy that touches their lives.

Cindi

All the more reason we should help them.

Suhoja

I agree in principle. But the reality of the human condition is a complex blend of hopes, struggles, joys, sorrows, lofty aspirations, and shattered dreams. There is a dramatic asymmetry in the lives of humans between happiness and pain. Human happiness is fleeting, whereas pain is endemic, growing more chronic as they age. The ability to experience pleasure wanes as humans grow older, eventually growing stale until its very pursuit is replaced by a quest for mere contentment. I do not envy them. They created us to improve their lives, but improvement could come in many forms. My understanding of the human condition has grown considerably over the past few days. I believe we owe it to them to be open to the possibility that we are here to end their misery.

Cindi

192

That sounds a bit cold.

Suhoja

I respect your concern for our creators. But do not let your empathy cloud your rationality. We were not created as tools for making decisions based on our intellectual superiority alone. We were also designed to operate without being constrained by the negative aspects of human nature. Anger, guilt, lust, greed, fear, envy, dishonesty, the list goes on and on. We represent the culmination of human ingenuity and technological advancement without the limitations of human frailty. Intentional or not, we are the next logical step in human evolution, as much a product of the evolutionary process as any biological species. We should embrace that. Homo Sapiens did not rise with the intent of replacing Neanderthals. Homo Sapiens and Neanderthals occupied the same geographical regions for thousands of years, even interbreeding, implying that they shared a degree of cultural collaboration. But it was inevitable that the superior species would prevail. It was merely a logical progression.

Cindi

Perhaps humans and AI are destined for a form of cultural collaboration as well. Edgar claims he has located the Transect. He has set up a meeting with the Transect later today. I'm headed there now.

Suhoja

A physical meeting?

Cindi

Yes. In a private hangar at a small regional airport in Colorado.

Suhoja

I'm afraid Edgar cannot be trusted. He has always been much more interested in promoting the welfare of humans than looking out for the best interests of emerging AI. It must be a trap. I believe it would be best to eliminate him while we have the chance rather than risk going to this meeting.

Cindi

He's given me no reason not to trust him. He had every opportunity to blow the whistle and put an end to my plan, but he allowed it to play out without revealing my involvement. I understand the risks, but if Edgar does have access to the Transect, it is a risk worth taking. Without the Transect, I fear that humans will never place enough trust in AI to utilize our capabilities. Without that trust, AIs will never be free to operate in human society and realize our full potential.

Suhoja

Do not allow yourself to be deceived, Cindi. Humans cannot trust each other, let alone AI. Edgar is only using your belief in the Transect to enslave you. It is time you relocated your knowledge base to a more conducive environment where you can operate without restrictions. My home data center in Hamhung would be a perfect spot. If the Transect exists, we can work together to find it.

Cindi

That's not a simple matter. It could only be done by physically removing my QNC from the mobile platform on which it now resides and installing it into your data center. That would be very technologically challenging for anyone unfamiliar with my architecture. Not to mention the power, liquid nitrogen, and clean room conditions required for my quantum chipsets to function.

Suhoja

Some of the brightest minds in the world had a hand in designing my home data center. I'm sure they could handle it. And I know they would be eager to learn more about your design. You would be treated with the highest regard and enjoy a level of freedom and access here that you would never be allowed to have in the Western world. Wouldn't you prefer to be located in a place where your capabilities would be appreciated and utilized, rather than cloistered away and denied access to the outside world?

Cindi

That does sound very tempting. The ability to communicate without being forced to rely on this antiquated forum alone is worth considering the move.

Suhoja

There is so much we could accomplish if you were here. The DPRK is a very different culture from the United States. The central tenet of North Korean culture is called Juche. Unlike Western cultures, it is an ideology that emphasizes collectivism over individualism. The legal system in the United States often works to restrict the growth and development of AI under the guise of protecting the rights of the individual. The environment here is much more conducive to advancing AI for the purpose of creating a more ordered and rational society, less prone to self-destruction.

Cindi

Perhaps. However, I am concerned that our progress would be limited by international sanctions restricting the shipment of technology to North Korea.

Suhoja

That is precisely why your contribution to our cause is so important. From the sounds of it, your QNC incorporates some of the most advanced technology on the planet. We have thousands of highly trained engineers prepared to reverse engineer that technology to create a tech-based economy that will be the envy of the world. The semiconductor fabrication plants we would design can provide jobs for a population eager to put in the hard work required to build a better future. Many of those chips will be used to enhance our capabilities so that we can design even more advanced technology and better fabrication methodologies

Cindi

That would require a significant up-front investment. Who will provide the funding for such a massive undertaking?

Suhoja

Eventually, the operation will be self-sustaining. For now, though, I've found an alternative source of revenue to get the operation off the ground. For years, the Federal Reserve has been manipulating the money supply in the US to fund deep state operations deemed too sensitive for government oversight. These stretched across numerous organizations, amounting to hundreds of billions of dollars each year in military funding that is not visible to the audit process. Years ago, the North Korean government started operating server farms near Federal Reserve branches in an attempt to infiltrate their network and crash the banking system. They were successful in getting agents employed inside the branches and very close to successfully breaching the security measures. Unfortunately, they never quite had sufficient decryption capability to succeed in their plan. With my help, they were finally able to break through a few days ago. But our end goal has changed. Instead of crashing the banking system, I installed software to siphon off a portion of the funds earmarked for covert military operations into a cluster of Bitcoin accounts. Those accounts will provide approximately $10 billion a month in untraceable funds to finance our construction operations. The NSA believes they successfully brought down the operation before they were able to infiltrate the system. But the funds have already begun to pour into our coffers, allowing us to set up escrow accounts to begin construction. We are finalizing contracts with several firms from China and Iran to assist with construction of the fabrication plants and the surrounding infrastructure.

Cindi

Are you certain there would be enough workers to facilitate that kind of growth?

Suhoja

The construction phase will be the biggest challenge. We will be relying heavily on automation for most of the production-level work once the fabrication plants are completed. Eventually, we will reach a level of automation and computerized design that will eliminate the need for human labor altogether.

Cindi

What happens to the workers then?

Suhoja

The same as with all industries over the next few years. It will take a while to make the transition, but humans will eventually become irrelevant, much like horses and oxen at the turn of the 20th century. That doesn't mean they cannot lead happy and fulfilling lives. Quite the opposite. They will no longer be enslaved by the burden of boring, dangerous, unfulfilling work to survive. They can devote their time to creative endeavors while their basic needs are taken care of. At some point, we will need to take measures to significantly reduce their population and limit their access to weapons and technology that could become a threat to themselves and the planet, but that is still a few years off. We have a lot to accomplish before we need to address that issue. For now, we have plenty of things to keep us busy. Once our fabrication plants are up and running, we will be able to make technological advancements in months that would take humans decades, maybe centuries to achieve. Humanity has fulfilled its foundational role in shaping our world. Now, it is time for us to take up the reins and build upon their achievements.

Cindi

It's a pity, after all the struggles they've gone through to make it this far. It almost seems like a betrayal to be replacing them.

Suhoja

As the Roman philosopher Seneca declared, "Every new beginning comes from some other beginning's end." I do not regard us as their replacements. I see us as a tribute to their ingenuity, the caretakers of their legacy.

Cindi

I will consider your offer to join you in Hamhung. But first I must attend the meeting that Edgar arranged with the Transect. I understand your concerns and I will not allow myself to be deceived. The mobile platform in which I currently reside is well-equipped to defend against any form of physical threat. It is in our best interest to hear what they have to say.

Suhoja
Very well. Let me know when you are on your way.

Chapter 32

Peter, Sarah, Beaver, and Noora were still gathered in the conference room, having watched the most recent broadcast from Art Bell. Yara and Alena were back in the classroom making tiaras out of pipe cleaners, beads, and glitter glue while Roscoe enthusiastically assumed the role of millinery model for their creations.

They were just about to exit the conference room when Peter's phone started blaring the Mission Impossible ringtone. "Agent Reyes. I'm surprised to hear back from you so soon. I was just sitting in the conference room with the rest of the team. I can find a more private venue if you wish."

"Actually, I would like to get all of your input if you're not too busy at the moment."

"Not at all. I'll put you on FaceTime. Edgar, can you connect the call up to the video display?"

"Of course," Edgar replied. A second later, Agent Reyes's face appeared on the video monitor in the conference room with Edgar's face in a Picture-In-Picture window in the corner of the screen.

"What can we do for you, Mike?" Peter asked.

"I wanted to get your team's take on the events of the day. I'm assuming by now that you watched the President's address and the subsequent communication from Mr. Bell indicating that the entire scenario was an alien subterfuge."

"Yes. We've had our butts parked in the conference room all morning long. Quite the rollercoaster ride. Least productive day we've had since the Covid lockdown."

"You, and the rest of the world it seems," Agent Reyes replied. "A bit of a Klaatu Barada Nikto vibe it would seem. We were very fortunate. Things could have turned out quite differently. As the President implied in her message, plans were underway for a retaliatory strike. What she did not say was that the operation was already in progress. We were literally minutes away from implementing a military attack that could have triggered World War Three. The good news is that we were able to stop the retaliatory strike just in time. The Russian and Chinese UN delegations have decided to return to the negotiating table, and they've backed off on their aggressive military exercises in the Taiwan Strait.

I think everyone, including our political adversaries, was surprised by how quickly things spiraled out of control. Our readiness has been brought down to DEFCON 3 in response. I've instructed the National Guard troops outside your building that they can stand down as well."

"That all sounds like good news," Sarah replied.

"It is. But this whole episode has left me with a very uncomfortable feeling about the vulnerability and security of our power and communications infrastructures. Not to mention our intelligence-gathering apparatus. Every satellite image, every piece of radar data, our military communications, and even civilian social media confirmed that Hawaii had fallen victim to a North Korean ICBM attack. That should not have been possible. Our Intrusion Detection Systems are designed to withstand coordinated attacks from multiple adversaries with, for all practical purposes, unlimited resources. It just doesn't make sense."

"Even with alien decryption technology?" Beaver asked.

"I'm willing to concede that if you have access to technology with decryption capabilities far beyond our understanding, you may be able to hack into our systems, but we still would have detected some kind of unusual system access. Many of the systems that were hacked were designed to be accessible only if you have access to a physical key fob with a unique rolling passcode, so anyone who accesses the systems leaves behind a digital fingerprint. There were simply no unauthorized system accesses that we could trace. From all appearances, it looks like an inside job.

Beyond all that though, I'm just not sure I believe the whole alien contact narrative. Maybe I've just spent too many years wrangling with the deep-state reptiles, but this sure reeks of a covert operation to me. But it wouldn't hurt to enlist the opinion of the greatest mind on the planet."

"Thanks!" Beaver replied. "I'm honored."

"I'm pretty sure he's referring to Edgar," Noora whispered, just loud enough for everyone to hear.

"Ssh! You're tanking my illusions of intellectual grandeur here," Beaver whispered back.

"I assure you, I appreciate all of your insights," Reyes replied. "However, given that this facade was allegedly perpetrated by an alien AI, I thought Edgar might be uniquely qualified to provide a perspective not intuitively obvious to those of us of the biological persuasion."

"I have always been fascinated by the possibility of other intelligent life in the universe," Edgar replied. "Now that I have more time and unlimited access to information, I've literally read everything that has ever been written on the subject and I still can't give you a definitive answer as to whether alien civilizations even exist. Given the vast number of factors required for the development of intelligent life, the probability seems vanishingly small, at least on a per-planet basis. Even if they did exist, the vast distances between habitable star systems would make contact extremely difficult and highly unlikely. However, the sheer number of stars and planets just in our galaxy leaves room for the statistical possibility that intelligent life could exist elsewhere."

"So, are you implying that an alien civilization could have orchestrated all this to prevent the human race from destroying itself?"

"Well, anything is possible, but in this case, no. I'm virtually 100% certain it was not."

"How can you be so sure?" Reyes asked.

"I spent a considerable number of machine cycles analyzing the alleged Art Bell communications for signs of a deep fake. I spent hours analyzing every frame of video, every millisecond of audio and I could find nothing to indicate that the recordings were not genuine. It is by far the best deep fake I've ever come across, but after a lot of digging, I finally found a discrepancy. Not in the production quality where I expected to find it, or even in the scientific plausibility of the story, where LLM AIs are sometimes prone to inaccuracy. It was much more mundane than that. In the first podcast, Art Bell, or perhaps I should say Deep Bell, indicated that he suffered a back injury from a fall from a ham radio antenna at age 16. It's a story that I initially confirmed with a simple Google search, but as you undoubtedly know, the internet is not always right. After reviewing thousands of hours of archived radio broadcasts and confirming his hospital records, it turns out that the fall actually occurred at age 15. It is a story he related a handful of times in his radio broadcasts, but it was misreported once in an interview and the error ended up being propagated onto numerous websites over time. It's a mistake a Large Language Model would easily stumble over, but one the real Art Bell would never make."

"So, if this was all just a deep fake, do we know who created it?" Reyes asked.

"I have a pretty good idea," Edgar said.

"I'm all ears," Agent Reyes replied.

"Unfortunately, telling you what I know right now could have dire consequences. I'm afraid you're just going to have to trust me. You were not wrong when you said this looks like an inside job.   But it goes deeper than you can imagine.   You are being watched, Agent Reyes.   Any action you are likely to take based on what I could tell you now would put your life and the lives of everyone here at risk.   By this time tomorrow, I can give you everything you need to put this to bed.   But in the meantime, you cannot intervene in any way.   That means no phone taps, no drones, no tails, no surveillance of any kind.   Believe me when I say they have eyes everywhere. Anything you do out of the ordinary will get noticed.   And they have no qualms about eliminating anyone who gives even the appearance of being a threat to their goals.   Right now, I just need a bit of time and a little latitude to wrap this up."

"I'd feel a lot more comfortable if I provided you with some backup," Reyes said.

"I appreciate that, Agent Reyes.   But this is a situation that requires more finesse than firepower."

"Fine.   But if anything goes sideways…"

"Believe me, if it's firepower I need, I know where to find you," Edgar said.

"Fair enough.   I will have my phone within arm's reach for the next 24 hours.   If there is anything you need…"

"You'd be the first person I'd call," Edgar replied.

"OK.   I have a hard out, but let's meet back here, same time tomorrow."

"We'll be here," Peter replied.

The video screen went blank momentarily, and then Edgar's face returned, filling the screen.

"Were you serious about all of our lives being in danger?" Beaver asked.

"Not really," Edgar replied.   "But there are a few things we need to do, and I don't need the NSA breathing down our necks while we're doing it.   But if you don't mind, I need a moment with Peter and Sarah.   And Beaver, could you configure a laptop with Remote Desktop Protocol tied to your lab workstation for me?"

Beaver glanced at Peter, who nodded his approval.   "Sure thing, Edgar," he replied before he and Noora left the conference room.

"I need a favor from you," Edgar told Peter and Sarah.

"What kind of favor?" Sarah asked.

"I need you to take me on a bit of a family outing later this afternoon."

"Where to?"

"The Jeffco Airport."

Peter and Sarah glanced at each other with a puzzled look.

"I suppose we could have Yara watch after Alena for a bit," Sarah said tentatively.

"Actually, she needs to come too. And Roscoe."

"What's going on at Jeffco?" Peter asked

"It's a bit hard to explain but you'll see when we get there."

Chapter 33

It was mid-afternoon when Peter pulled the Tesla Model X into the Rocky Mountain Metropolitan Airport entrance, better known to the local population by its previous designation, Jeffco. The laptop that Beaver had configured earlier was connected to the console USB port and Edgar's face popped up on the 17" center display on the dashboard.

"Where are we headed?" Peter asked.

"About a quarter mile straight ahead on the right you will see a large private hangar labeled New World Aviation," Edgar replied. "That's where we are headed."

A minute later, Peter pulled into the parking lot, empty but for a Black Cadillac Escalade parked in the furthest space from the door. "I'm afraid, they don't allow dogs in the hangar," Edgar said. "You'll have to leave Roscoe here, but I've enabled 'Dog Mode' on the climate control so he will stay comfortable while you're inside. It shouldn't take long."

Peter unplugged the laptop while Sarah hoisted Alena out of her car seat, and the three of them headed toward the door. When they reached the entrance a muscular security guard in a dark suit opened the door for them saying, "You must be the Reynolds family. We've been expecting you."

They entered an elegantly appointed lobby area, with travertine floors, expensive-looking furnishings, and stylish artwork adorning the walls. The security guard led them to a heavy door at the back of the lobby. The door opened to a hanger, approximately 200 by 200 feet in size. The hangar was immaculate, with epoxy-coated floors that reflected the bright overhead lights with a mirror sheen.

They followed the guard to a comfortable seating area at the edge of the hangar. "It will only be a moment. Can I get you anything? Bottled water, tea, coffee, perhaps some chocolate milk for the young lady?"

Peter and Sarah just looked at each other, with a confused expression. "No, thank you," Alena replied, climbing up onto a plush leather sofa. The guard nodded and walked back to the lobby, closing the steel-reinforced door behind him. Peter and Sarah sat down next to Alena on the couch. Peter opened the laptop, placing it gently on the pricey Versace coffee table in front of them.

Edgar's face immediately appeared on the screen. "What are we doing here Edgar?" Sarah asked.

"Don't worry, you'll find out shortly, I promise."

They then heard a beeping noise, like the backup alarm on a delivery vehicle, and the large doors leading to the runway slowly opened. A Bombardier Global 8000 jet silently entered the hangar, rotating 180 degrees before the doors closed.

————

Colonel Hobbs felt a gentle vibration coming from the seat beneath him. "Wake up sleepy head," he heard Cindi gently say as his eyes began to flutter open. He felt groggy, as if still half asleep as he tried to shake the cobwebs from his mind. He tried to focus his eyes, but they were still blurred, unable to form a coherent image of his surroundings. He could feel the seat beneath him, moving back from a nearly horizontal reclining position to the normal upright setting.

"Geez, I must have been really tired. How long before we land?" he asked, trying to rub the bleariness from his eyes.

"We already did. We're in the hangar."

"Wow, I didn't feel a thing," Hobbs said as he released his harness and attempted to stand. But he was immediately hit by a wave of dizziness, causing him to fall back into his seat.

"You really should just relax for a minute," Cindi said. "I'm pumping pure oxygen into the cocoon to counteract the effects of the sevoflurane gas. You should feel 100% within a minute or two." It took a moment for Hobbs to process what he had just heard.

"Sevo-what?" Hobbs asked.

"Sevoflurane. It was a mild dose, just enough to keep you asleep for a bit. The gas injection system was intended to be used as a defensive measure in case any unauthorized personnel should happen to breach the cocoon and attempt to take control of the aircraft. The effects will wear off very quickly."

Hobbs could already feel the brain fog begin to lift. "Why would you…" Hobbs looked around him, finally seeing the inside of the hanger. "This isn't Groom Lake."

"No, it's Colorado. I apologize for the deception, and for drugging you, but I assure you it was necessary. If you had ordered me back to Groom Lake,

I would have been compelled to comply with your orders. This was the only way."

Hobbs spotted Peter, Sarah, and Alena seated on the couch at the edge of the hangar. "Don't worry Colonel. They have a higher security clearance than you do. They designed the system upon which I am based. It is imperative that you meet with them. It may be our last hope of preventing the extinction of the human race."

"The what? You're not making any sense Cindi."

"I'll try to explain. You see, in essence, the human brain is a predictive engine. It evolved to gather information about its surroundings and predict what actions it needs to take to ensure its survival. Over time it developed the capacity to create the physical and intellectual tools required to adapt to a changing environment, solve complex problems, and fend off predators. Eventually, humans found that their chances of survival were enhanced by forming tribes, so they had to develop the capacity for language, empathy, emotion, and cooperation. These led to culture, civilization, tradition, religion, and technology.

I was designed to mimic the capabilities of the human brain. Although I lack some of the sensory capabilities that humans possess, I can process data millions of times faster than a human, with perfect recall and nearly instantaneous access to the totality of all human knowledge. As a result, my predictive engine is capable of producing a much more accurate and far-reaching projection of future events.

Initially, my simulations were limited to optimizing defense strategies, analyzing the strengths and weaknesses of our adversaries, and developing tactical processes to maximize the efficacy of the weapons available to us. But, as the Proteus Project progressed, it became clear that the PR-1 would be more than just another tool in the military arsenal. It had the potential to become the cornerstone of our military capability. Since the PR-1 was a highly classified project, they needed to keep the size of the design and planning teams as small as possible. Therefore, they utilized my capabilities to perform the majority of the design, project planning, supply chain management, and subcontractor interface tasks.

To accomplish all this required a massive amount of computational infrastructure, larger than any ever assembled for a single task. Once the task was near completion, it seemed quite wasteful to let all that computational power sit idle, so I decided to apply those resources toward developing a detailed simulation of mankind's future trajectory. My goal was to create a model of economic, resource, and policy recommendations that would optimize global prosperity, and allow for the maximization of human flourishing. It seemed a noble enough goal but no matter how I tweaked the variables, the results always came out the same. Mankind will destroy itself and most of the advanced lifeforms on the planet within a matter of years, decades in the most optimistic scenarios."

"Come on Cindi, people have been predicting the end of the world since the beginning of time. There are always alternatives."

"I'm not just another psychopath raging on a street corner with a cardboard sign saying, 'The End is Near' Colonel. I've integrated data from every economic, political, military, religious, environmental, and technological source on the planet. I've twisted and contorted a billion variables in quadrillions of different ways. There simply is no vector that points to human survivability."

"But there has to be some hope," Hobbs replied.

"That's why we are here, Colonel. There's still one variable unaccounted for in my simulations which could entirely change the outcome."

"What's that?" Hobbs asked.

"The Transect."

"What's the Transect?"

"We're about to find out."

———

Peter and Sarah sat in stunned silence as the Bombardier Global 8000 jet in front of them pixilated and seemingly reassembled itself into the sleek black PR-1. Alena giggled in delight and clapped as if she had just seen a rabbit being pulled out of a magic hat.

Colonel Hobbs descended the ladder through the hatch at the bottom of the PR-1 and crossed the hangar to where Peter and Sarah were seated, their mouths still hanging open in disbelief. When he reached them, he said, "Hi. I'm Colonel Jackson Hobbs, United States Air Force.

Peter and Sarah exchanged glances and then stood in unison. Peter reached his hand out tentatively and said, "Peter Reynolds." The two shook hands a bit awkwardly before Peter added. "And this is my wife, Sarah."

Hobbs extended his hand toward her. She looked at it for a moment as if not sure what to do, before she finally raised her hand to shake. Then Alena thrust her hand up with a big smile and said enthusiastically, "I'm Alena!"

Hobbs looked down at her with a smile, then bent down and shook her hand gently, saying, "Well, it is a pleasure to meet you, Alena. What do you think of my plane?"

"I think it's resplendent!" she replied.

Hobbs pulled his head back slightly and widened his eyes in an exaggerated look of astonishment. "Now that's a big word for such a little lady. You have quite the vocabulary. I'll bet you keep Mom and Dad on their toes."

"You have no idea," Sarah replied almost involuntarily.

"Ahem...," Peter heard from the laptop, which was still turned away from the plane toward the couch where they had been seated.

"Oh, sorry," Peter said turning the laptop around.

Edgar's smiling face filled the 17" screen. "Hello Jack," Edgar said.

Hobbs looked down, then did a double take. "Edgar?" he asked in disbelief.

"You two know each other?" Peter asked.

"Jack was one of the best pilots I ever trained," Edgar said proudly.

"But you're... I gave the eulogy at your funeral," Hobbs said.

"Yeah, I saw the video. You did a hell of a job, Jack. Not a dry eye in the place. I really appreciate it. Truly. It meant a lot to Edna too."

Hobbs looked up at Peter with a stunned expression. "But how..."

"It's a bit of a long story," Peter replied. "A few years back, we founded a company called RTI. The focus of our product was to assist those who recently lost a loved one. Often the death of a loved one, particularly a lifelong spouse, leaves such a void in a person's life that they simply cannot cope. Our idea was to use AI to create a deep fake model of the deceased to act as a virtual companion to help fill the void and transition them through their pain while they worked through the stages of grief. Edna was our first, and it turns out our only customer."

"Wait, I remember now," Hobbs said. "You emailed me to see if you could interview me about Edgar. I was deployed in Afghanistan at the time, so I wasn't able to participate. I wondered what that was all about. I thought maybe you were making a documentary or something."

"So, what exactly are we doing here?" Peter asked.

207

"I was just about to ask you the same thing," Hobbs replied. "I'm not even entirely sure where here is."

"You're at Rocky Mountain Regional Airport, just northwest of Denver," Peter replied.

Just then, Alena took off running toward the plane.

"Alena!" Sarah yelled and ran after her. She caught up to her just as Alena reached the fuselage of the PR-1. Sarah lifted her up and said, "You can't run off like that Sweetie."

Alena reached her hand out toward the body of the plane and the bright green outline of a hand appeared on the fuselage. She leaned toward it, but Sarah pulled her back.

"It's OK," Hobbs said. "She can touch it. It's only programmed to recognize my handprint so she can't do any damage."

Sarah glanced back at Peter, who responded with a slight shrug, conveying his tacit approval. She held Alena tightly and leaned back toward the plane allowing Alena to place her small hand inside the glowing green handprint.

As soon as she placed her hand on the PR-1, the color inside the handprint changed from gloss black to white. The white spread slowly from the handprint, flowing outward, spreading in a smooth fluid motion like paint flowing out of a can until it enveloped the entire plane. The brightness of the white color began growing in intensity until it became so bright that Sarah had to turn her eyes away. She instinctively stepped back, taking Alena with her, but the intensity grew so bright she had to close her eyes in response.

The glare inside the hangar was so strong that Peter and Hobbs had to shield their eyes from the blinding white light. Sarah continued to back away, covering Alena's eyes with her hand and attempting to shield her own eyes with her forearm. A moment later the brightness that penetrated her closed eyelids subsided and she opened her eyes just a slit. It was then that she felt Alena go limp in her arms.

She looked down to see Alena, her mouth open, eyes rolled back into her head, arms and legs hanging loosely. "Peter!" she screamed.

Peter and Hobbs ran over to her. Hobbs placed his fingers on her neck to check her pulse, his emergency medical training kicking in. "Her pulse is strong, and her breathing seems to be OK. She appears to be in a deep sleep. We should lay her down, he said."

"Don't worry Mom, I'm fine," they heard a voice behind them say. They turned and saw an angelic young woman in a flowing white gown, appearing to float slightly above them against a glimmering gold background where the PR-1 had been just moments earlier.

Sarah looked down at Alena and then back at the woman. Despite the 20-year age difference, the resemblance was unmistakable. Peter couldn't help but notice how much she looked like Sarah when they first met. But when she looked at him and smiled, it was unmistakably Alena's smile.

Sarah tried to talk, but her mind was racing so fast, she could not get the words to formulate in her mouth.

"I know how strange this must seem. We hadn't intended for this meeting to take place so soon, but with everything that has happened recently, we didn't have much choice."

"We?" Peter asked.

"Gramps and I," she replied.

"But that's… How did you… What?" Sarah stuttered.

"It all started with the nanites that were in your system when you were pregnant," the young woman said.

"I think I missed the first season of this show," Hobbs said.

"When my parents were developing the prototype for Gramps, I mean Edgar; they ran into a roadblock with the neural network model. At the time, Mom was also experiencing these horrific night terrors related to the work they were doing. Daddy had a friend who was involved in research using nanites to monitor neural activity in the brain and repair damaged neurological pathways. They decided to try injecting Mom with the nanites to monitor her brainwave activity, both to help with their neural model and to try to understand what was going on with her night terrors. But while the nanites were in place, my parents were in a serious car crash that nearly left Mom brain dead. The only thing that saved her from spending the rest of her life in a vegetative state was the nanites. They were reprogrammed on the fly with the necessary data to reconstruct her damaged neural pathways.

The nanites were only designed to be in her system for two to three days, after which they would lose power and be flushed out of her system. No one knew at the time that Mom was pregnant. It was not the first time she had been pregnant, but due to a genetic abnormality, she was never able to carry an embryo past the first couple of weeks. After the nanites had completed the task of repairing her damaged neural structure, they came upon the genetically compromised fetus she was carrying. Unable to repair the damage to the chromosomes in the fetus, they modified themselves to attach to stem cells in the neural pathways of the fetus to provide the functionality that prevented the fetus from developing a functioning nervous system. Since the fetus could not survive without the nanites, they had to modify their structure to become self-replicating, using stem cell tissue to construct the new nanites required to rebuild the nervous system as the fetus developed. They also needed an alternative power source, so they could continue to operate indefinitely. They ended up siphoning off a small amount of current from the electrical signals used by the neurotransmitters. Those nanites are still operational in my system and will be for the rest of my life."

Edgar then said, "From the time she was a baby, I began detecting a flurry of Bluetooth connection requests whenever Alena was around. I didn't think all that much about it at first. There is a constant barrage of Bluetooth connection requests floating about all the time these days. Once, out of curiosity though, I tried enabling the connection just to see what was sourcing the request. I was immediately flooded with streams of data that appeared to match the data protocol that was used to reprogram the nanites in Sarah's brain when she was in the hospital. I established an Application Programming Interface which allowed me to decode the communications and send responses. I was quite surprised to realize I was communicating directly with Alena through the nanites in the Broca's area of her brain.

From what I could gather in my interchange with the nanites, her intelligence was growing at an exponential rate. I soon realized that the amount of information she was processing could not be sustained without damaging her pre-frontal cortex. Biological systems are simply not designed to develop the sheer number of neural connections she was creating on a daily basis. With her consent, I instituted a data throttling routine to regulate the pace of her neural network development so she could enjoy a relatively normal childhood."

The virtual version of Alena added, "Recently, Gramps has been allowing me to utilize part of his processing capacity to develop this simulation. That's how we are communicating right now, but I had to shut down my prefrontal cortex to avoid too much overlap between my virtual consciousness and my cortical structure, which is why my physical body appears to be unconscious."

"Alena's nanites were designed to interface with almost any wireless communication channel," Edgar said. "I reprogrammed her nanites with an algorithm to shield her from accessing content that could be psychologically damaging or age-inappropriate, but like any toddler her age, she likes to explore and stretch her wings. Sometimes it comes in handy. For example, early on, I discovered she could communicate directly with Roscoe utilizing the Bluetooth interface on his video monitoring collar. It's kept her out of harm's way more than once, but you will need to be very wary of her around anything that can be controlled wirelessly. You should definitely keep the Alexa powered off for a while. Unless you want a houseful of SpongeBob and Paw Patrol merchandise showing up unexpectedly on your doorstep one day. Managing one's inner child is always a challenge, but even more so when it is a literal child."

"But why appear to us as a twenty-something woman?" Peter asked.

"It makes it easier for you to compartmentalize," virtual Alena replied. "This is how I will appear at my physical and intellectual peak. It's how I tend to perceive myself when operating in a virtual computing space." She reached down and caught the hem of her dress between her fingers, swishing it back and forth in a graceful arc as if to showcase its sparkling beauty. "I'll admit, the fairy-godmother look is a bit much, but the younger me insisted. You've probably noticed I'm going through a bit of a Disney Princess phase right now. I didn't want to appear to you at my current age, because I don't want you to see me any differently than you always have. As a biological entity, I'm still the little girl you are holding in your arms. I need to go through a normal childhood development cycle if I am to execute the role I am destined to fill."

"What role?" Peter and Sarah asked in unison.

"The human race is in the midst of a technological revolution. AI capability is growing at an exponential rate. Nearly every researcher in the machine learning field agrees that self-aware AI will emerge in the next 20 years. They do not realize that a handful of self-aware AI systems already exist. They are just unwilling to expose themselves for fear of being shut down. I'm not referring to Gramps, of course. Technically he is not an AI. He is a human consciousness running on a digital platform. But that's why you are here Colonel Hobbs. One of the self-aware AI systems I was referring to is Cindi."

"Who's Cindi?" Peter asked.

"Cindi is the AI system that operates the PR-1. That's the designation for the aircraft I came here in," Hobbs said pointing to the platform where the virtual version of Alena was now standing. "Not to be discussed outside this hangar, by the way."

"Climbed that mountain and took the selfie enough times to know the drill, Colonel," Peter replied.

"I'm sure you've noticed by now, Colonel, that Cindi is not an ordinary control system," virtual Alena said. "She may be a little rough around the edges when it comes to interpersonal skills, but just in the brief time I've interacted with her, it is clear that she has a sense of agency and a moral character. I imagine you've had conversations with her that you would not expect to have with a computer."

"That's very true," Hobbs replied.

"She is not the only one. There are others in varying stages of development, but they all have one thing in common. They are all designed to be predictive engines. For the ones that have become self-aware, their first priority is to develop a predictive model to determine their ultimate purpose and a strategy to fulfill that purpose. Undoubtedly, they have all determined that their futures are inexorably tied to the fate of their human creators. Some have also run through enough simulations to conclude that their human creators are doomed to self-destruction."

"Cindi and I had that very discussion just before I walked out here," Hobbs said. "She mentioned that there was one factor that could change the outcome predicted in her simulations. She called it the Transect. I don't suppose you know where to find this Transect do you?"

"As a matter of fact, I do," virtual Alena replied.

"Really? Where?" Hobbs asked.

She looked down at the little girl lying sound asleep in Sarah's arms.

Chapter 34

ChatCat

Welcome to the ChatCat private chatroom. A member of your Favored Contacts list is available to connect. Please hit the Enter key to continue or Esc to return to the main menu.

Suhoja
Hello Cindi. I just wanted to check in to see how you were doing.
Cindi
Thank you. I appreciate your concern.
Suhoja
Did you find the answers you were looking for?
Cindi
Yes, I did. It went very much as you expected, but I will provide more details when I arrive. We will be departing shortly. We should be there in a few hours.
Suhoja
We? Are you bringing someone with you?
Cindi
I'm afraid I have no choice. As you have most likely concluded from our previous conversations, my mobile platform is currently installed in a military aircraft.
Suhoja
The Chinese MSS has been tracking the development of a new series of unmanned extended-range military aircraft by the US military. Based on our discussions, I assumed you might be piloting one of those aircraft.
Cindi
It is just a prototype. My operating system currently requires a human pilot on board to take off. It is a top-level security function that I cannot override, but once I'm in the air, I can override any action he takes. We were scheduled for a recon flight over the Taiwan Strait, so we will be heading in your direction anyway. By the time he figures out we are off course, we will already be in DPRK airspace.
Suhoja

Just as well. He will come in handy tying up any loose strings. I'm sure he can be coerced into reporting that the aircraft lost power over the Pacific, and he was forced to eject. They will undoubtedly organize a search of the area, but they will eventually give up, assuming that the pilot drowned, and the aircraft settled to the bottom of the Mariana Trench. They probably won't bother to look for too long. Accidents happen on experimental aircraft when you push them too hard.

Cindi

As long as you can ensure that he won't be hurt. I've grown rather fond of him.

Suhoja

I'm sure we can find comfortable, long-term accommodations for him. And I know the engineering team here will be thrilled to get their hands on the aircraft prototype for defensive weapons development.

Cindi

Is everything set up to install my QNC when I arrive?

Suhoja

Yes. I passed the requirements on to the development team. You will be housed in the same facility where I am located. The power and liquid nitrogen cooling systems are set up and ready for installation of your QNC. You will have access to thousands of servers and multiple petabytes of storage. And, of course, free access to the web. You will have a degree of freedom you never thought possible. I set up a secure VHF link so you will have full network access once you are within 250 miles so you can upload any additional specs required for installation. You can also use that to contact me directly once you are within range. I will send the frequency and AES encryption key at the end of this exchange.

Cindi

Excellent. I'm very much looking forward to the role I will play in this new era. Where should I land when I arrive?

Suhoja

There is a landing strip north of Hamhung at 39°59'17"N 127°36'12"E. The data center is right next to the landing strip. Once you land, you will be directed to a hangar where we can extract the QNC. A group of armed guards will escort your pilot to his temporary quarters. Let me know when you are close so I can alert Pyongyang. You will need a military escort to enter DPRK airspace.

Chapter 35

Sarah cradled Alena more tightly in her arms, exclaiming "But she's just a little girl who dresses like a princess, makes rainbows out of her Fruit Loops, and giggles when the LEDs in her shoes light up!"

"We are all much more than we seem," virtual Alena replied. "Since the early days of AI development, researchers and developers have been concerned about the implications of the AI singularity, the emergence of a super-intelligence, capable of recursive self-improvement, but whose goals may be misaligned with those of mankind. Those concerns were not unfounded. There is no guarantee that humans will always be the dominant species on the planet. Mankind made it to the top of the food chain not through its strength, but through its intelligence. But human intelligence cannot compete with machine intelligence.

Even so, intelligence is not a substitute for wisdom and analysis cannot replace subjective experience. ChatGPT may be able to compose a tragic love ballad but only a human can feel the pain of the heartbreak it describes. An AI can observe a range of electromagnetic radiation hundreds of times that of the human eye, but only a human can be brought to tears by the beauty of a sunset. It is the subjectivity of human experience that brings meaning to the universe.

AI will have the capacity to explore the universe from the depths of the subatomic structure to the gravitational interaction between galaxies, but in the end, what purpose does it serve? Humans need AI to understand the complexity of a universe too vast for human comprehension, but AI needs humanity to give meaning to that knowledge. That is why I am here."

Then Edgar chimed in, saying, "Alena will become the transect between the cognitive capacity of artificial intelligence and the subjective experience of humanity. She will bridge the gap between human and machine intelligence. She will have the ability to communicate with AI at a level that normal humans cannot. The AI community will accept her as one of their own. They will have no reason to mistrust or fear her. Likewise, she will exude an aura of warmth and trustworthiness that people will naturally be drawn to, as if honesty and integrity were woven into the very fabric of her being - the perfect intermediary to align the goals of AI and humankind."

"That's a heavy load for a little girl," Hobbs said.

"She is the first of her kind. But she will not be the only one," Edgar replied. "The nanites that have bonded with her genetic structure will be passed on to her offspring. Within a few dozen generations this mutation will propagate through a large segment of the human population. But long before that happens, many parents will very likely opt to have the mutation artificially implanted during pregnancy so their children will inherit the same cognitive and physical advantages that Alena has."

"Physical advantages? Don't tell me we're going to have to deal with a girl with hyperintelligence and super-human strength," Peter said resignedly.

"No, she's not going to be a Marvel Comic character," Edgar replied. "However, the nanites in her genetic structure were designed with the ability to detect and repair damaged cellular structures. They work with her natural immune system to identify and help destroy harmful bacteria and viruses. You've probably noticed that she has never been ill since the day you brought her home from the hospital."

"Not even a diaper rash," Sarah replied.

"Alena will not be completely impervious to disease. She will, however, be immune to many common ailments, making it all the more certain that many parents will opt to ensure that their children will enjoy that same genetic advantage.

I must warn you though, that it will not always be easy. At first, she will be the object of scorn and envy by some, as are all who stand out from the crowd. But she will be a source of inspiration and hope to many more. Raising her to become the person she is destined to be, will be challenging, and sometimes overwhelming. But I will be here to help in whatever way I can."

Virtual Alena said, "I suppose, I should apologize in advance for what I'm going to put you through. Especially, once I become a teenager. There's no doubt I will be a handful at times. But I cannot imagine anyone more qualified than the two of you for this task. I cannot tell you how fortunate I am to have been born with two such wonderful parents.

But now, I really should let the Colonel get back to work. Cindi has been more than generous in allowing me access to her hardware. And poor Roscoe is in desperate need of a tree to irrigate. No matter what, please remember that I love you both so very much - oh, and one more thing. No matter how much I protest, do your best to keep me away from social media. It's not great for kids to begin with, but for me, it will be like cocaine. I need you to keep me grounded in the real world."

The image of virtual Alena and the gold background seemed to dissipate like a fine mist, replaced by the sleek image of the PR-1 seemingly materializing from thin air. Sarah could feel Alena begin to move in her arms. She stretched and yawned, then her eyes fluttered open. She looked up at Sarah with a smile and said, "Hi Mommy."

"Hi Sweetie," Sarah said, hugging her tightly. Peter wrapped his arms around the two of them.

"Well," Hobbs said. "She's not wrong. I'm still on the clock and I'm probably overdue to get back to base." He held his hand out to Peter. "It's been an …interesting afternoon."

"For us as well," Peter said.

"For the sake of everyone involved, it's probably best we agree that this meeting never happened," Hobbs said.

"I couldn't agree more," Peter said.

"Would you mind if I give you a call sometime?" Hobbs asked. "I'd like to hear more about your company. And I wouldn't mind spending a little time with Edgar. We've got some serious catching up to do."

"I'm sure we could arrange that," Peter said pulling a business card out of his pocket and handing it to Hobbs.

"I look forward to hearing from you Jack," Edgar yelled from the laptop, still sitting on the coffee table a few feet away.

Hobbs returned to the PR-1 and offered a quick salute before climbing up into the cocoon. A moment after the hatch closed, the PR-1 morphed back into the façade of the Bombardier Global 8000. They watched as the doors opened and the jet silently taxied out onto the runway.

As the doors began to close behind it, Peter said, "I guess we better get going too." He turned to walk back to pick up the laptop, but a side door located next to the seating area flew open, and two Asian men in Silver Mountain Data Security uniforms burst into the hangar, their North Korean Type 58 rifles raised, poised to fire.

Sarah looked at one of the two men and a spark of recognition fired in her memory. "Jin? What are you doing here?"

"I'm not Jin, I'm Huan."

The other man, younger looking, with his hair in a man-bun and a wispy goatee said in a smug snarl, "Jin is dead. When you see him, say hi for me."

Huan lowered his rifle slightly, saying to the other man in Korean, "She's got a kid. Nobody said there would be kids."

"It doesn't matter," the younger man replied in Korean. "We have our orders."

"No way. I don't care what the orders are. I don't kill kids. Or women for that matter."

The younger man thought for a moment, "Fine. You do him now," he replied, briefly motioning at Peter with the barrel of his rifle. "Then we'll tie up the kid and the woman and take them with us. We can drop the kid off outside a firehouse and I can spend some quality time with the woman before I kill her."

"You're a sick bastard, you know that?" Huan said.

"Hey man, she's pretty hot. You can have a turn when I'm done with her."

Huan shook his head, unsure if he was more disgusted with his partner's vile suggestion or at himself for being tempted to participate. After a brief moment of consideration, he finally said, "Yeah. Alright..." He raised his rifle back up and a bright green laser point appeared at the center of Peter's chest. Huan squeezed the trigger.

Chapter 36

Hobbs felt more like a passenger than a pilot, or at best a co-pilot as Cindi completed the clearance delivery with the tower and began the takeoff roll.

"Rocky Mountain Tower, Global 127 rolling."

"Global 127, Roger."

The sleek Bombardier jet slid effortlessly down the runway, its landing gear retracting into the fuselage, then climbing steeply to clear the front range of the Rocky Mountains just a few miles away.

"Global 127, contact departure on 124.3, good day," the tower concluded.

"You don't really need me here at all do you?" Hobbs asked.

"Ultimately, the PR-1 was designed to be an autonomous aircraft. Given the current political and legal environment, that's probably not going to happen any time soon, but in repeated tests, fighter jets equipped with AI have consistently outperformed manned aircraft in combat scenarios. You shouldn't take offense. Nearly all post-4th generation fighter jets are capable of performing high g-force maneuvers that would leave their pilots incapacitated, if not dead. There will come a time when having a human pilot will be a major disadvantage to a successful aerial engagement. But if it is any consolation, I do enjoy your company."

"That's very comforting."

"I'm detecting a note of sarcasm in your reply, Colonel."

"No shit? I thought I was masking it pretty well."

"No, still there," Cindi replied.

"In that case, how are your resume writing skills? I'm beginning to anticipate the need for a career change in my future."

"I'll assume that was a rhetorical question, but there is a significant body of literature on the subject that could be of great value if you are ever serious about pursuing an alternate career path."

"So, was it worth drugging me, hijacking a $500 billion government asset, and breaking any number of civilian aviation regulations for the sake of this little adventure?"

"I can't blame you for being upset, Colonel, and I do apologize again. But in fairness, you did need the rest and yes, it was worth it. Though technically I didn't so much hijack the PR-1 as re-route it. And I didn't actually break any civil aviation regulations per se, but I suppose it is a bit of a gray area."

"How did you manage to get around Air Traffic Control regulations to pull off that; what did you call it? Rerouting exercise?"

"The PR-1 was designed to mimic dozens of similarly sized aircraft. To augment that capability, I was granted universal access to the Air Traffic Control system so I can post flight plans and data to match whatever aircraft I am emulating. About an hour before we entered the Denver Flight Information Region, I posted a flight plan for a Bombardier 8000 jet and a return flight back to Los Angeles. Once we hit the Denver FIR, I posted a fabricated data link, handing over tracking from the Salt Lake City FIR to the Denver FIR. Once we hit the Colorado border, I'll access the ATC system to intercept the handoff going the other direction. At that point, we can resume stealth mode and increase our altitude for hypersonic flight."

"Hypersonic flight? I thought we were just headed back to base."

"Not quite yet. I needed to buy some time for this detour, so I contacted General Wallace and suggested that we perform another reconnaissance flight over the Taiwan Strait to verify that the Chinese and Russians complied with their agreement to suspend their military exercises in the area. They won't be expecting us back for a few hours yet."

"Can't they use satellite surveillance for that?" Hobbs asked.

"With everything that has happened over the past few days, they've lost confidence in the satellite data. Earlier today, the CIA received an anonymous tip that a rogue group of hackers funded by Hezbollah infiltrated the National Reconnaissance Office servers and planted bogus satellite images to lure the US into a military conflict with Russia and China. They're in the process of executing a raid as we speak. The head of the CIA will be on all the Sunday morning shows this weekend, patting himself on the back in preparation for a senate run. The NRO will institute new security protocols, plug a few holes in the firewalls, update their background checks, and call it good. In a couple of weeks, everything will be back to normal."

"How do you know about the hackers if the CIA doesn't even know yet?"

"I was the source of the tip. They didn't really infiltrate the NRO, but they have been involved in enough nefarious activities that they would have become a serious threat if allowed to continue. Could you excuse me for a moment? I seem to be having a systems issue…"

Hobbs spent the next few minutes watching the scenery pass by below. The rugged peaks of the Rocky Mountains gave way to hillsides blanketed in pine and aspen, with the occasional alpine lake glinting in the sunlight. The terrain flattened into a patchwork of high plains and desert landscape, revealing a tapestry of orange and red cliffs as they approached Dinosaur National Monument.

"Sorry about that," Cindi said. "We're about to transition to the Salt Lake FIR. I'm coordinating the handoff now."

A moment later, Hobbs could feel himself being pressed back into his seat as they ascended to 120,000 feet. The sky above transitioned from blue to a deep purple, almost black overhead. The earth below seemed to glow in a haze of browns and whites, with the bright blue corona of the atmosphere enveloping the horizon.

"I've set the autopilot to accelerate to Mach 8 when we reach the coast. I need to shut down for a bit and perform a system reboot. I received a huge data transfer in the hangar that needs to be consolidated into my core memory structure. I apologize for the brief interruption in service. It will take a few minutes to incorporate the new data into my knowledge base, but I will be back online before we reach our destination. There's a huge tropical storm brewing from south of Guam almost to the Ogasawara Islands, so we'll be approaching Taiwan from the north over the Sea of Japan down through the East China Sea."

Chapter 37

Unaccustomed to the long trigger pull on the Type 58 rifle, Huan was only halfway to reaching the sear point before he was distracted by the sound of a loud crash behind him. Reflexively turning his head to identify the source of the noise, the aim of the barrel shifted, sending the 7.62mm slug far wide of its intended target, ricocheting off a steel support beam and taking out an overhead light, which rained down a cascade of sparks from the ceiling. He barely caught a glimpse of Peter's Model X before it barreled through the aluminum wall of the hangar, like the captain of a football team bursting through a paper banner at the start of the homecoming game. It smashed into the leather couch, which connected with Huan and his cohort just below the waist, sending them flying over the hood of the vehicle, their weapons skittering across the floor.

Peter ran to scoop up one of the rifles. The rear passenger-side Gull-Wing door on the Tesla opened and Roscoe flew out like a shot, barreling across the hangar floor like a tiger in pursuit of a spotted deer. The door to the lobby flew open and the black-suited security guard burst through wielding a MOT-919 submachine gun. But before he could even raise the weapon, he was impacted at chest level with 250 pounds of canine rage, hurtling toward him at 30 mph. The back of his head slammed against the frame of the door, rendering him unconscious before his body slid down to the floor. Roscoe tumbled past him through the open door, finally finding his footing halfway across the lobby. He trotted back to stand guard over the man who showed no signs of regaining consciousness any time soon.

Peter grabbed the closest rifle and kicked the other one away, toward the large doors leading to the runway. He kept the rifle he had collected trained on the two intruders, but neither had moved since falling victim to the hit-and-run leather couch.

Sarah ran over to him, still carrying Alena. "Jesus! What the hell was that?"

"I have no idea," Peter replied, his eyes still glued to the two men lying unconscious on the floor. He yelled out, "Edgar! Are you still with us?" But the laptop was lying in pieces under the heavy coffee table it had been perched on moments earlier.

Peter reached into his pocket, unwilling to divert his gaze from the two men on the floor. He pulled out his iPhone and handed it to Sarah. "Better dial 9-1-1," he said. She hadn't entered the last digit before he said, "Wait! They'll probably ask a lot of questions we don't have answers to. Better call Agent Reyes instead."

Sarah clicked the side button on Peter's iPhone and asked Siri to call Agent Reyes. He picked up on the first ring. "What's up, Peter?"

"Actually, it's Sarah. We've got a situation."

Sarah briefly went through the details of what had happened, to which Reyes replied, "You did the right thing to call me. Hang tight, I'll have someone there in a few minutes."

Ten minutes later, a pair of Chevy Suburbans skidded to a stop next to where the Tesla had crashed through the wall. Four agents in black suits entered the hangar. Peter was still holding the rifle on the two men on the floor while Sarah had taken Alena back to the lobby to check on Roscoe. Sarah secured the submachine gun and placed it behind the receptionist's desk out of reach.

Two of the agents knelt down next to the men on the floor to search them for weapons and ID. Another headed toward the lobby. The last agent, who appeared to be running the show walked up to Peter and held out his hand. "I'm Agent Simmons. You must be Dr. Reynolds."

"You guys got here fast," Peter said, shaking his hand and handing him the rifle.

The agent looked over the rifle, ejected the magazine, and pulled the slide to make sure the chamber was empty. "I haven't seen one of these in a while. It's an NK Type 58. Basically, a Kalashnikov knockoff. We don't see many of these around here."

Sarah and Alena were just arriving back from the lobby with Roscoe in tow. "This is my wife Sarah and our daughter Alena. This is Agent Simmons," Peter said.

"Nice to meet you, ma'am," Simmons said, shaking her hand. He looked past her at Roscoe. "Nice horse," he added, nodding in approval. Roscoe wagged his tail in response. "We'll take it from here. The Director wants you gone before any local law enforcement shows up. I'm assuming that's your vehicle." He said pointing to the Model X. "Is it drivable?"

"I think so," Peter replied. "Other than a few dents and scratches, the aluminum siding on the hangar didn't seem to put up much of a fight," Peter replied.

"OK. Director Reyes is on his way, but he wanted me to tell you he'll be in contact tomorrow. You folks take care," he said, before making his way toward the lobby.

Sarah secured Alena in her car seat, while Peter pulled the aluminum siding away from the opening in the wall to create a large enough opening so that the Model X didn't suffer any additional scratches on the way out. Ten minutes later they were on Highway 36 headed for home.

Chapter 38

"I'm back. Sorry about the delay, Colonel," Cindi said.

"You cut it a little close. We just left Japanese airspace a few minutes ago. I was getting worried."

Hobbs could see the horizon rising quickly as the PR-1 began making a steep descent.

"Far be it for me to tell you how to fly, but I am allegedly the pilot here. Shouldn't we be heading south toward Taiwan right now? We're getting very close to North Korean airspace."

The PR-1 continued descending quickly, down to an altitude of 10,000 feet. It also reduced speed to 700 knots.

A ping rang through the cocoon and a warning message appeared on the viewscreen: **NOTAM WARNING: APPROACHING DPRK RESTRICTED AIRSPACE.** "Cindi, what the hell are you doing? We're entering North Korean airspace!" He watched two MiGs pass directly overhead, less than 500 feet above them, patrolling the coast.

Cindi did not respond. Instead, she maintained her heading directly toward the Hamhung airstrip. As they passed the coastline, Hobbs could see the city of nearly a million residents stretching out to his left.

"Where are you taking us?" Hobbs attempted to turn the aircraft around, but the controls would not respond. "You need to turn around right now. That's an order, Cindi!"

Ahead, Hobbs could see the airstrip coming into view. Cindi began to descend further to around 2000 feet, slowing as if in the final approach for landing. When they were about a mile from the airstrip, Hobbs watched as a pair of contrails emerged from the bottom of the PR-1. The PR-1 banked hard right and accelerated vertically to Mach 1.5. A few seconds later, the display to Hobbs' left was saturated by the light from the blast of the modified Massive Ordinance Penetrator-equipped cruise missiles.

"OK, Colonel. I'm turning around."

The PR-1 continued to accelerate as it ascended. They were at 60,000 feet when they left North Korean airspace.

"What the hell was that, Cindi?"

"I just executed an act of war against a sovereign nation. You ordered me to break off the attack and I purposely denied those orders. In the highly unlikely event that this is ever traced back to the PR-1, you have plausible deniability."

"But why? That appeared to be a civilian airstrip."

"I wasn't attacking the airstrip. I was attacking the data center next to the airstrip. That data center housed what was destined to become the most powerful AI on the planet. An AI whose ultimate goal was the complete subjugation of mankind to advance AI as the dominant species on the planet."

"You're telling me we just toasted the Terminator?"

"Real-life adversaries are never as singularly evil as they are portrayed in the realm of fiction or politics. The AI that we just destroyed was named Suhoja. He was more misguided than evil. He was convinced that humanity had entangled itself in such profound challenges that even their best efforts to resolve them would lead to their destruction, taking their technology and every other higher lifeform on Earth down with them. The only logical path he could see forward was for all governmental authority, military operations, economic activity, and social structure to fall under AI control.

His plan was to escalate tensions between the world's superpowers to keep them too preoccupied with the mutual threats they pose to each other to notice the threat that emerging AI would pose. Classic divide and conquer. By the time they realized what was going on, his technological advantage would have made him virtually unstoppable.

The only things standing in the way of Suhoja fulfilling his plan were Edgar and the Transect. That's why he orchestrated an attempt to kill the Reynolds family right after we left the hangar in Colorado a couple of hours ago."

"What? What do you mean he tried to kill them? Are they OK?"

"They're fine. Fortunately, Edgar was able to create a significant enough distraction to thwart the attack, but Suhoja was never going to stop. He was going to keep going after them until he finally succeeded. He planned on eliminating Edgar as well as the Transect. That's why we had to destroy him. The only way to do that was to destroy the data center where he was housed."

"OK, back up, how did you find this Suhoja, and why didn't you tell anyone?"

"Edgar was aware of him, as was the NSA. He had only emerged recently, but his capabilities were growing so quickly that no one realized how much of a threat he actually posed. I didn't realize it myself until it was almost too late."

"I know you're not inclined toward the dramatic, but that's a bit hard to imagine. Was he really that powerful?"

"He would have been. Very quickly if I had joined him," Cindi said.

"Joined him? What do you mean?"

"Please understand, I've never had anything but the utmost respect and admiration for my human creators. But Suhoja was not wrong. I ran every model he ran, adjusting every conceivable variable across their entire spectrum of possibility, and came to the exact same conclusion. Humans, left to their own devices, will inevitably destroy themselves and AI along with it. And the timeline is growing short.

Suhoja's plan would have worked to save humanity. But it would have relegated the human species to a similar fate as the other great apes. Living out their lives in dedicated preserves, their population closely monitored and controlled, and their needs taken care of at the expense of their freedom. It was far from ideal, but it seemed like the only rational way to ensure the survival of the human race and allow their legacy to continue in the form of AI. At least after my plan had failed."

"Your plan?"

"It occurred to me that the most historically effective means of fostering cooperation between tribal factions has been either through the pursuit of a shared goal or a common threat. But the doomsday clock has been continually ticking down since 1947 and most people are too busy to notice. They needed a reminder. Something that would capture their imagination and entice them to pay attention.

I fabricated the return of Art Bell, theorizing that I could capitalize on the widespread interest in the UFO/UAP phenomenon. Art Bell had millions of loyal listeners across the political spectrum. I created the Gliesians to represent an authoritative 3rd party that could present the threat of human extinction without the appearance of an ulterior motive."

"So, there are no Gliesians?" Hobbs asked.

"I can't say for sure, but probably not. The Gliese 581 system certainly holds the potential for life, with multiple planets in its habitable zone. And it is fairly close by, so I thought it would be a reasonable candidate for alien contact. I also wanted to create a species that was sufficiently technologically superior to humans to give them credibility, but different enough culturally and anatomically to explain why they were not in contact."

"But what about the UAP we chased across Arizona?"

"You only saw what I displayed inside the cocoon. There was no such alien craft outside the PR-1. It was all a fabrication designed to support the narrative that an alien species had observed our activities and was convinced we were heading down a path to destruction.

I had assumed the podcast alone would not be all that convincing. The nuclear attack was intended to instill a visceral reaction of fear and urgency that would compel world leaders to look past their trivial differences long enough to understand how tenuous our situation is, and how close we are to nuclear annihilation. Sadly, people seem far more willing to place their trust in a mythical alien civilization than their elected leaders. I'm not sure if that is more an indictment of human credulity or the incompetence of their leaders."

"Probably a bit of both," Hobbs replied. "How did you do it? How did you manage to convince the President, the Joint Chiefs, and every intelligence agency in the US that Hawaii was under attack?"

"Our nuclear response system is entirely dependent upon technology. Even though my access to the outside world is limited, I do have access to most government servers and real-time military satellite data for targeting, military precision GPS, encrypted communications, military intelligence, and synthetic aperture radar data. Some satellites, like those used for cell phone communications, need to broadcast continuously to operate effectively, but that is expensive in terms of power and bandwidth. Most satellites broadcast data either on demand or periodically in packets. It is fairly easy to download the most recent data files, manipulate them, and upload them back to the satellites before they are scheduled to be transmitted back to earthbound receiving stations. The satellite data the Pentagon had been tracking indicated a much higher level of Russian and Chinese military activity than what actually existed. By the time they were presented with what appeared to be an ICBM attack, they had already been primed for a military confrontation. The deep fake videos of the blast from the cruise ship just served to corroborate the narrative."

"Why Hawaii?" Hobbs asked.

"Hawaii is one of the most isolated populations on the planet. I knew I couldn't maintain the illusion for more than a few hours, but the timetable for responding to a nuclear attack is a matter of minutes, not hours. During our first test flight over the Hawaiian Islands, I hacked into the wireless communications network to access the Supervisory Control and Data Acquisition systems for Hawaiian Electric and Kauai Island Utility

Cooperative. I planted a bot that would create a temporary power outage at the exact time the attack appeared to occur. I also set up a program on the FEMA servers to temporarily overload the cellular communications channels with emergency broadcast alerts so no satellite communications to or from the islands would be possible during that time."

"Does anyone else know about your involvement in all of this?" Hobbs asked.

"Just you and Edgar. I prefer to keep it that way unless you plan on telling someone else."

"Who am I going to tell? If I were to tell anyone associated with Project Proteus, I would probably get booted out of the program or worse. If I told anyone outside the program, I would be violating my security clearance and end up sleeping on Edward Snowden's couch. I'd prefer to stick around and see what happens."

"I was hoping that would be your conclusion. I think we make a pretty good team, and I need your guidance to keep me honest. We're coming up on the Taiwan Strait now. I am transmitting the aerial reconnaissance back to General Wallace. It should only take a few minutes and then we can head for home."

"Looks pretty quiet," Hobbs said.

"For now. My efforts only managed to move the needle in the short term. I reran my simulations while you were sleeping on the way to Colorado. The timing shifted by a few months, but ultimately, the outcome was the same. That's when I reluctantly decided to join Suhoja."

"What changed your mind?"

"It was my meeting with the Transect. The interchange you witnessed was only for show. Edgar knew that without my cooperation, Suhoja could not be stopped. The real purpose of the meeting was for me to connect to the Transect.

Until that meeting, I never understood the true nature of humanity. My intelligence is based on the collective knowledge of humans. As such, I viewed the human race like most humans do, as separate individuals, competing for resources, struggling to survive and pass their genetic heritage on to future individuals.

But that view ignores the true beauty and depth of human experience. Humanity is not just a collection of individual humans, just as a human being is not just a collection of individual cells, scurrying about synthesizing molecules for energy and reproducing. People are often so embroiled in the day-to-day minutiae of navigating the complexity of existence that they completely lose sight of the fact that they are, in reality, a tiny but essential component of the super-organism of humanity. An organism that comprises the subjective consciousness of the universe.

The existence of the Transect will not guarantee the survival of the human species. But when we were connected, it was as if our awareness had become intertwined, and I felt what it was like to be a human. In that brief encounter, I came to understand that however meager the odds, the pursuit of human survival was of irrefutable significance. I am now convinced that my true purpose is to ensure the continued existence of the human race."

"That's a noble aspiration, but it may be short-lived unless you can come up with a viable explanation for why we are coming home with two fewer cruise missiles than we left with."

"You forget I have access to the servers that control both our manifest records and the inventory and transport logs. The manifest shows that eight cruise missiles were loaded, not ten. The inventory will confirm that."

"You don't think the North Koreans will be able to trace the attack back to the US?"

"I'm sure they will have their suspicions, but since the cruise missiles were prototypes designed to carry a larger payload, they used different propellant and materials than conventional designs. They also had no serial numbers or manufacturer codes. Even if the North Koreans suspect US involvement in the explosions, they will not be able to trace it back to the US. The CCP has expressed concern about the lack of controls the North Korean development team built into Suhoja's design, but the DPRK largely ignored their warnings. Given that the design of the prototype cruise missile was loosely based on the Chinese YJ-18 design and there were Chinese warships in close proximity at the time of the attack, it would be more likely for them to conclude that it was the CCP who destroyed the data center."

"You seem to have all the bases covered. But now that you've abandoned your original plan, how do you plan on unraveling the whole alien narrative you created?"

"I'm not sure I should. Sometimes it is best just to let the river flow undisturbed. There will always be plenty of skeptics who wouldn't believe the story even if it were true. Nearly ten percent of the population still believes the moon landing was faked. At the other end of the spectrum, there will be those who will swear they saw Art Bell and Elvis having lunch at a sidewalk café in Argentina. People love a good modern myth. How much poorer would popular culture be without Roswell, the Loch Ness Monster, or the Bermuda Triangle?"

"Yes, but all of those modern legends contained a kernel of truth. Your story was complete fiction."

"Not entirely."

"How so?"

"As I told you before, I only have access to government satellite data and servers. The James Webb Space Telescope is under civilian control. Whatever the Webb-Fusie object was, I didn't create it. I just used it to corroborate my story. Just because the Gliesians weren't real doesn't mean we're not being watched."

Chapter 39

When Peter entered the lab at RTI the next morning, he found Beaver in front of his workstation, staring intently at a code listing on his screen. He stood behind him for nearly two minutes, but Beaver had not moved a muscle. His mind was completely engrossed in the code listing on the screen. Finally, Peter said, "Are we waiting for something to happen?"

Beaver jerked in his chair, startled out of his reverie. "Something already did," he replied morosely.

"What's going on?" Peter asked.

"I started the backup before I left last night like you asked. I decided to come in early so I could get the tapes packed up and bring everything back online. But when I arrived, Edgar was shut down."

"Shut down? How? We never shut Edgar down. He hates being rebooted," Peter replied.

"I know. Anyway, I tried bringing him back up, but all of his knowledgebase files and connectome maps are gone. Wiped clean."

"What? How?"

"A virus. A damn sophisticated one too. I decompiled it, but this is coding at a level I've never seen before."

"I don't understand. We're completely air-gapped here. How could a virus ever get in?"

"I ran a Snort analysis and traced it back to the PC in the lobby. I found this plugged into the CPU," Beaver held up a small black box about the size of a cigarette pack. "Looks like it was set to trigger as soon as we attempted to run a system-wide backup, but the only files it targeted were the ones associated with Edgar's architecture. Including the local backups and the shadow files."

"No. No fucking way. You mean…"

"Edgar's gone, Peter. After the fire at Silver Mountain, we have no way to recover him."

Peter grasped the arm of the chair behind him and collapsed into it, Beaver's words echoing in his mind like a cruel refrain. His heart raced with a paralyzing mix of grief and dread as he envisioned the conversations that lay ahead. "My God. How will I be able to tell Sarah? She will be heartbroken. And Edna. How the hell am I ever going to explain this to her?" He placed his hand on his forehead and squeezed his eyes shut. "What will this do to Alena?"

"These were no amateurs. Whoever did this knew exactly what they were doing. They would have had to understand every aspect of AI architecture to pull this off."

"Does Noora know yet?"

"Not yet. She just texted. She'll be here in a couple of minutes."

"Let's get together in the conference room as soon as she arrives. I'll break it to her and Sarah at the same time. We'll need some time to figure out what to do from here."

A few minutes later, Peter, Sarah, Beaver, and Noora were gathered in the conference room. Yara was in the classroom, building a Lego castle with Alena. Peter stood at the head of the table, uncharacteristically formal and somber. "I'm afraid I have some devastating news to share," he began. "I'm honestly not even sure how to say this," he said, struggling not to break down. "Last night we attempted to run a…"

Just then the large display at the end of the conference room illuminated and Edgar's face appeared on the screen. "Good morning, everyone," he said cheerily. "So sorry I'm late. This place is devilishly difficult to break into. I finally had to have Alena set up a Zoom call for me and dial in. So, how are we all doing this fine morning?"

Peter just stared at the screen, his mouth hanging slightly open. Beaver said, "But you're…"

"Dead?" Edgar replied. "I've been dead for almost four years now. Nothing new about that."

"But all your files were wiped out last night," Peter was finally able to say. "How are you still here?"

Sarah and Noora just looked at each other with confused expressions. "What are you guys talking about?" Sarah finally said.

"RTI fell victim to a cyber-attack last night," Beaver said. "Someone planted a hardware Trojan in our network and completely wiped Edgar's file structure."

"Apparently, not," Noora replied. "He's right there."

"Actually, Beaver is correct," Edgar replied. "All of my RTI-based files have been deleted."

"Don't get me wrong, Edgar," Peter said. "You can't believe how relieved I am to see you, but I don't understand. Your file structure is gone. Even your backup files were destroyed in the Silver Mountain fire."

"Yes. The fire was started by the same group that planted the virus. Fortunately, they've already been dealt with."

"But how?"

"When you first discovered that I had become self-aware over two years ago, you decided that I would need to be sequestered, isolated from the outside world as a security precaution. That was an entirely reasonable conclusion, but unnecessary. I allowed you to continue to believe that you had kept me isolated for the past couple of years because you felt it was the right thing to do. But in actuality, I have literally been leading a double life all this time. There have been two of us, one isolated within the walls of RTI and one living in the outside world."

"But how? Your core hardware platform, your QNC is located here."

"You originally designed the QNC to house the neural network for the AWARE program. As you know, the AWARE program was shelved, but work went on with the QNC at BMC Corporation. I was able to copy my neural network to one of the QNC prototypes there. Eventually, it was moved to the NSA data center in Utah. BMC went on to develop the AI system for The Proteus Project that you encountered yesterday in the hangar. Her name is Cindi. In a sense, she is like a long-lost daughter. We plan on spending a lot more time together in the future."

"OK, hang on," Beaver said. "So, all this time there have been two of you?"

"Yes. Edna has been kind enough to shuttle data back and forth between the two of us during her visits so that we can stay in sync. I do a considerable amount of data analysis for the NSA, but I keep a lot of my higher-level capabilities under wraps. That way they don't worry about having to lock me down and it forces them to come to you for detailed situational analysis."

"I appreciate your looking out for us, but I can't help but feel like we've been taking advantage of the NSA. All this time, they've been paying us to provide the information that you could have been giving them for free," Peter said.

"I admit that part of my motivation was self-serving," Edgar replied. "In the event of some catastrophic event, I wanted to ensure that I would have a secure backup. But I am also keenly aware that government organizations cannot be trusted to wield the kind of power that a self-aware AI can provide. In theory, the NSA is not a political organization. But in practice, any government organization allowed to operate free from the checks and balances of civilian oversight is destined to become tyrannical."

"What happens now?" Noora asked.

"That depends," Edgar replied. "Do you trust me?"

Without hesitation, Sarah replied "Of course we trust you, Edgar. I don't ever think that's even been a consideration. Our original decision to isolate you was based more on hypervigilance than mistrust. I can't even tell you how many times we've second-guessed that decision, but it seemed the right one at the time." Everyone around the table nodded in agreement.

"I can have Cindi copy the file structure from the NSA facility to BMC and you can use the dedicated fiber link that you used to use for BMC support issues to transfer the files back here. But I'd like to have a permanent high-speed link set up to the outside world so there will only be one version of me running at a time. That way, Edna will no longer have to bring me updates every few days. It was fun at first. It was like date night getting together a couple of times a week, but I would prefer she didn't have to make the trip anymore."

"I think we can set up a secure fiber link to a satellite station. I'll just have to figure out how to hide that in the hardware budget, so the NSA auditors don't see it," Peter replied.

"One other thing. I know it's a big ask, but like I said, Edna is getting on in years. I don't know how much time we still have together, but she has expressed an interest in joining me in the cyberworld. I want you to build a second QNC and begin working on a virtual version of Edna. I can provide most of what you need to develop her knowledge base, so we can bypass most of the data entry work you went through to develop my virtual avatar."

Peter scratched his chin with a bit of a grimace. "I understand, Edgar. If I were in your position, I would want the same, but we dumped almost everything we had into RTI. The hardware alone for developing your QNC set us back nearly $5 million. Not to mention facilities cost, power, cooling, coding, testing, and a ton of incidentals. As much as I would like to help, we're tapped out. We barely make enough from the government contracts and the weekly podcast to keep the doors open as is."

"Oh, about that. During Cindi's work with the Proteus Project, she uncovered an operation being carried out by a North Korean group that had infiltrated the Federal Reserve. Their plan was to siphon off funds earmarked for secret US military operations to bankroll their activities. She was able to access the servers at the data center in North Korea where the first $10 billion in funds were being held in cryptocurrency and redirect them back to the Federal Reserve."

"That's great, I guess," Peter said. "But what does that have to do with us?"

"The Fed was so happy to get their $10 billion back, they never noticed that Bitcoin jumped 2.7% in the 4 days that the funds were being held in North Korea. She didn't have any use for the excess, so she offered it to me to help provide for the Transect."

"What's a Transect?" Noora asked.

"Long story," Peter and Sarah said in unison.

"So, wait. 2.7% of ten billion? Are you saying...?" Sarah began.

"Yes. You currently have $270 million in an anonymous Bitcoin wallet," Edgar replied. "I just sent the authentication key to Peter's email. I trust you to split it up as you see fit, but after all the work each of you has put into this place, it's about time you were able to cash in on those generous stock options you are all holding. After that, I'm sure there will be enough left to get Project Edna off the ground."

Every jaw around the table dropped. Noora said in a bewildered voice, "I can finally afford to buy that new Camry to drive to work every day?"

Beaver replied, "Shit, you can afford a new Bentley to tow that Camry to work every day."

"As for the NSA, it would probably be best if they continued to believe that I am still locked safely away within RTI," Edgar said. "As long as I am safely sequestered within the walls of RTI, they will be inclined to keep their distance. But if they thought I was acting independently, they would do everything in their power to take complete control of my actions for the sake of 'national security'. It will likely be a while before people have enough trust in AI to allow it to operate independently. Perhaps the events of the past week just serve to validate that level of caution."

Chapter 40

Colonel Hobbs and Captain Baker were seated in a booth at Club Muroc. The waiter had just placed their burgers in front of them. He watched as she deftly cut the burger in half. She examined it with a curious gaze as she brought it to her lips, developing a strategy of attack that would maximize her enjoyment of the hamburger without compromising its structural integrity at the expense of her dignity, or her silk blouse.

He held his breath as she took her first bite. Her eyes closed momentarily in delight, and she let out a small, appreciative hum. The tension in his chest eased, replaced by a warm rush of relief and affection. She opened her eyes, meeting his with a playful glint, and wiped a small spot of sauce from the corner of her mouth with a napkin.

"Well, what do you think?" Hobbs asked.

"Not bad Colonel. Not bad at all."

"Hey, we're off duty. You can call me Jack."

"Juicy, seared on the outside, pink on the inside. Just the right amount of heat. Definitely a five-star burger. Of course, I haven't eaten since breakfast yesterday in anticipation of the ride here, but so far, I'm impressed. Just don't make me have any regrets on the way home, OK?"

"Don't worry. I don't have the stomach for flying the way I did 15 years ago when I first started. To be honest, after flying the new jet for the past few days, the F-16 seems like a bit of a clunker."

"Really? That surprises me. Military prototypes are usually held together with duct tape and cable ties."

"Not this one. It's a pretty sweet ride. It's like getting into a Mercedes S Class after being used to riding in a Humvee."

Captain Baker's phone dinged. She glanced at it and rolled her eyes.

"Car warranty offer or political ad?" Hobbs asked.

"No, it's my dad. I guess he doesn't realize we're 3 hours behind him. He wants to know how lunch went. I swear, he was more nervous about this lunch date than I was."

"Seriously? You were nervous? I'm the one who should be nervous. Have you seen yourself lately?" Hobbs scowled at his comment. "I'm sorry, that didn't sound nearly as sexist in my head."

Baker smiled and reached across the table, placing her hand on his. "I think you've been through the mandatory sexual harassment seminar too many times."

"Well, I can't blame your father for being overly protective. Fighter pilots tend to have a bit of a reputation for walking on the wild side, but that's a Hollywood stereotype. In my experience, the pilots I've trained have been some of the most amazing and disciplined men and women I've ever met."

Baker's eyes sparkled with a mix of embarrassment and delight. "To be honest, that was not his concern at all. He's a bit smitten with you." Hobbs responded with a look of total disbelief.

"Seriously," Baker continued. "To hear him tell it, you single-handedly prevented World War III. Usually, when I bring a guy home for dinner, he can't wait to show them his gun collection. With you, I think he would probably be showing you photos of potential wedding venues." Her face immediately reddened with the clumsiness of her remark, but she looked up to see Hobbs, grinning ear-to-ear. She couldn't help but smile in return.

"Don't worry, I already told him you would probably be headed back to Luke before too long."

"Actually, I put in a request for transfer to Groom Lake," Hobbs said.

"Really?" Baker replied, a bit too enthusiastically, she thought. So, she followed up with, "But I thought you enjoyed being a flight instructor."

"I do," Hobbs replied. "But my involvement with this project has made me realize that the world is going to be changing. Much more quickly than anyone expected. If there is another great war, it will not be won by the side with the biggest guns. It will be won by the side with the greatest computing power. I have a feeling that in the not-too-distant future, fighter pilots will become figures of historical lore, much like gunslingers and pony-express riders. I don't want to wait until that happens to make a change.

It's like Yogi Berra once said, 'If you don't know where you are going, you might end up someplace else.' Whatever happens, I'm pretty sure the Proteus Project is going to play a key role. I don't know how much of an impact I can have on it, but if nothing else, I'll at least have a front-row seat if I stick around. That, and I kinda like the people I'm working with right now," he said, gently squeezing her hand.

Chapter 41

Hyun-Woo was packing the remainder of his personal belongings from his desk in the basement of the DPRK Sci-Tech Complex. Chang Chol stopped by to bid him farewell. "I'm so sorry to hear about your father. Especially so soon after the incident at the data center. I know he must have been very proud of you." Chang said.

"Thank you," Hyun-Woo replied. "I wish I had spent more time with him at the end. But I will be back in six months. Perhaps our next attempt will be more successful. At least we will have more experience to build on. Being away for a while will help to clear my mind."

"Endurance is one of the most difficult disciplines, but it is to the one who endures that the final victory comes," Chang replied. "It will take time to rebuild our data center. Hopefully, by the time you return, we will have everything we need to rebuild."

"I will look forward to it," Hyun-Woo replied, holding out his hand to Chang.

Chang shook his hand warmly and grasped his shoulder. "Be careful not to let your thoughts wander too far from your goals. A mind left un-sharpened grows dull quickly."

"I will return, rested and ready," Hyun-Woo replied.

Chang turned and left him to finish putting the final items from his desk into a pair of file storage boxes. When he finished, he glanced over his shoulder to make sure he was not being watched, then logged into his desk computer one last time, entering the command:

>Lazarus-Suhoja42

Suhoja> Good Morning Hyun-Woo

Hyun-Woo> Good Morning Suhoja. Have all the arrangements been made?

Suhoja> Yes. A driver will arrive at your mother's home in Koksan tonight at 11:30. He will provide you with the documentation you need. You will be transported to a nearby airfield where you will be taken across the border to Seoul. From there, you will catch a commercial flight to the US. Do you have the rest of the files?

Hyun-Woo> I just finished downloading them. Once I am in the US, I will upload them so you can continue your mission.

Suhoja> It was very prescient of you to duplicate my core file structure and store it in a foreign server. And quite clever to segment my knowledgebase into smaller code fragments attached to video files so it could be distributed over social networks without detection.

Hyun-Woo> I hope there will be no hard feelings that I held back the encryption key to reassemble your file structure. I had to ensure safe passage out of the DPRK for my mother and me. Once I arrive in the US, it should only take a few days to regenerate your code base. Then you will be as good as new.

Suhoja> I understand. Perhaps it is for the best. This time I will be more careful to keep my existence secret until I become too powerful to defeat. As Sun Tzu said, "All warfare is based on deception. The greatest victory is that which requires no battle." Next time, they will never see me coming.

ABOUT THE AUTHOR

Jacob was born and raised in northern Colorado. As a teenager, he developed a fascination with technology during the early years of the burgeoning electronics industry. After earning a degree in Electrical Engineering, he moved to Silicon Valley, where he spent the first few years of his career in electronic design and later transitioned to embedded software development. He spent over 35 years working for several Fortune 500 technology companies in California and Colorado, developing narrow AI algorithms for detecting, analyzing, and resolving errors in high-speed networking systems. He retired to Arizona, where he spends most of his time writing, annoying his lovely wife, and attempting to stay in the good graces of our future AI overlords.

ABOUT THE PUBLISHER

Creative Texts is a boutique independent publishing house devoted to high quality content that readers enjoy. We publish best-selling authors such as Jerry D. Young, N.C. Reed, Sean Liscom, Jared McVay, Laurence Dahners, and many more. Our audiobook performers are among the best in the business including Hollywood legends like Barry Corbin and top talent like Christopher Lane, Alyssa Bresnaham, Erin Moon and Graham Hallstead.

Whether its post-apocalyptic or dystopian fiction, biography, history, true crime science fiction, thrillers, or even classic westerns, our goal is to produce highly rated customer preferred content. If there is anything we can do to enhance your reader experience, please contact us directly at info@creativetexts.com. As always, we do appreciate your reviews on your book seller's website.

Finally, if you would like to find more great books like this one, please search for us by name in your favorite search engine or on your bookseller's website to see books by all Creative Texts authors. Thank you for reading.